Nothing But You

NOTHING BUT YOU

—

LOVE STORIES

FROM

THE NEW YORKER

EDITED BY ROGER ANGELL

RANDOM HOUSE

NEW YORK

Library of Congress Cataloging-in-Publication Data

Nothing but you/Love stories from *The New Yorker*/edited by Roger Angell.
p.   cm.
ISBN 0-679-45701-1
1. Love stories, American.   2. Short stories, American.
3. American fiction—20th century.   I. Angell, Roger.
II. *The New Yorker* (New York, N.Y.: 1925)
PS648.L6L685   1997
813' .08508—dc20   96-43079

Random House website address: http:/www.randomhouse.com/

Printed in the United States of America on acid-free paper
Book design by J. K. Lambert
24689753
First Edition

"All this time I have been thinking of nothing but you. I live only in the thought of you. I wanted to forget, to forget you; but why, oh, why have you come?"

—Chekhov, "The Lady with the Lap Dog"

CONTENTS

INTRODUCTION

Reading the stories in this book will make many of us wish to fall in love again, but just as often, I think, it will be quite the other way: My God, spare me, just this once. Save me from this unexpected woman, this unlikely man—from this sudden happiness and then the crushing loss. Don't let me wait for her phone call or for another one of her ill-spelled, beautiful letters. Enough of plans and heartfelt talks and wearying complication, enough with tears. But then, as we go on reading, we may change our minds. I don't care—I want it all, no matter what. Bring it back, let me be in love again.

What we can envy these lovers, either way, is their energy. Give them a whisper of romance, the barest twitch of intrigue, one heated breath from the open ovens of sex, and they are changed beyond all recognition. Eagerly they wander into the garden, scratch out an eye, fall into the river, throw over a wife or a husband or a devoted partner, and leap headlong into postures of entranced pleasure and humiliation, hopeless attachment or sensual ennui—all for the sake of the red-haired woman from 6 Krochmalna Street; for the old gentleman with the umbrella; for the seamstress who appears at her doorway with a towel in her hand; for the young woman seen weeping on the street; for the attention of a careless, long-departed family of neighbors or of a childhood friend, who, like as not, has barely noticed the connection or kept a moment's memory of whatever it was that meant the world to this lonely girl or to that impoverished professor. Nothing will stop these lovers. A ring on the phone, the glimpse of an estranged spouse or remembered sweetheart, a chance for an entanglement or a shot at escape, and they are out the door and out of sight. Away they go—dashing through traffic and off to San Francisco, to Uzbekistan, to Brisbane, to the Rue Saint-Didier, to Barcelona, to the King's Inn in Dublin, to Nashville and Yonville, overnight to many distant cities. That electric title for Donald Barthelme's story, which closes this collection, was spotted by him on the side of a passing mover's van. Love drives us onward—or keeps us at home, noticing and longing, or grasping after what was here all along. What a mess! What a situation! What a subject for a writer!

When the idea for this collection first came to me—an anthology of *New Yorker* fiction, the first one in thirty years, but this time assembled around a single theme—I was enticed by a dozen-odd particular stories that had stayed clear in my mind for years (many of them are in this book), and also by the delusion that others would be easy to find, because we all know what makes a love story, after all. But the definition wouldn't stay put. The more stories I read (and set aside and read again), the more kinds of love and lovers began to move in around me and demand attention. I quickly saw that I would have to make room for a mother's love for her dying son, and for the baby-sitter called in to allow her married friend to keep a tawdry rendezvous, and for a neighborhood of young mothers caught in an addictive happiness over their babies, and so on, but I was disconcerted by the number of stories that were about despair and separation and death, as well as love—the opposites together, interlocked. I had wanted a book stuffed with *l'amour*, with plenty of sex and excitement, some sweetness and some getting it on, with matching portions of heavy breathing and twerpy longings— yes, fans of romance, there is a first kiss in the book—but along with this, of course, came much more: marriages and their consequences and endings, missed chances, changes of heart, wild jokes, glooms, the inexplicable, and enduring silences. I make no apology, then, for the sloppy latitude of this book, or for some stories that may seem to be only glancingly about love, or for others that are flighty in their intentions. Love becomes life, as we ought to know by now, and there is no accounting for it.

By limiting this selection to stories that have appeared in the magazine since 1965 (a rule that I broke to admit a gemlike John Cheever story from the summer of '64), I passed up a chance to reprint several *New Yorker* classics—celebrated love stories like Cheever's "The Country Husband," Jean Stafford's "Children Are Bored on Sunday," Jerome

Salinger's "A Perfect Day for Bananafish" or "For Esmé, with Love and Squalor," Harold Brodkey's "Sentimental Education," and others. But these tales, I felt, were so familiar to us all—almost as strong in memory as "The Lady with the Lap Dog," "Death in Venice," or "The Dead"—that we could honor their authors this time by asking them to make room for others in our crowded gallery. (I can find no way to appease the ten or twenty *New Yorker* writers—they know who they are—whose stories absolutely deserve to be in here but were, for one reason or another, passed over. Length was the most common problem—the only stricture that could have done in Edith Templeton's sensual masterpiece "The Darts of Cupid," for example.) No author is represented more than once, but a few newcomers have made the cut, sometimes with a first-ever story. Young writers belong in a book like this.

Because I was so aware of those famous earlier love stories, I formed the notion that most of the entries in this roundup would come from the late sixties, the seventies, and the early eighties, but it didn't work out that way. Like their predecessors, modern-day story writers can't get love out of their heads, it would seem, and their characters, while more free in its practices, can't stop talking about it at the same time. This was a big surprise to me. It was also my view that this collection, taken as a thirty-year cross section, might provide a vivid geological chart of the changing critical strata and preoccupations of contemporary fiction, but that didn't happen either. While reading these stories, we can find a thrilling pleasure in the confident flourishes of Nabokov; in the frantic rush of sex and and worry in Isaac Bashevis Singer; in Woody Allen's acrobatic twists of plot; in the way O'Hara's people talk (by chance, his "How Young, How Old" was the very last of his two hundred and forty-one stories to run in the magazine); in the measured unravellings of family and loss by William Maxwell; in the mysterious itinerants of Alice Munro; in the different shades of darkness in Raymond Carver and William Trevor, and so forth. But it is the lovers here whom we recognize first of all, and to whom we then give our riveted attention, while the writers happily—I *think* happily—stand aside. Love has carried the day, sweeping our authors and characters downstream in a swirl of passions and literary sediments, mixing together postmodernists and regionalists, true-tale-tellers and ironists, childhood ruminators and bold students of adultery, and spilling their work out across a broad delta of feelings, which we can traverse here at our own pace, two or three stories at a time, and, while gazing around, perhaps begin to think about ourselves more lightly and forgivingly than has been our recent custom.

AFFECTION, NOT PUNCTILIOUSNESS, requires me to name my colleagues in *The New Yorker*'s fiction department who, taken together, had a hand in the first excited manuscript readings and in the last, closing-day proofreadings of the stories that now come together in this anthology. The list begins with the august handful already on staff when I came to work in 1956 and ends with the cheerful, overworked incumbents just down the hall from me now: William Maxwell, Robert Henderson, Carroll Newman, Elizabeth Cullinan, Rachel MacKenzie, Robert Hemenway, Derek Morgan, Frances Kiernan, Jane Anderson, Charles McGrath, Daniel Menaker, Jane Mankiewicz, Veronica Geng, Trish Deitch, Linda Asher, Gwyneth Cravens, Alice Quinn, Julia Just, Pat Strachan, Deborah Garrison, David McCormick, Betsy Schmidt, Hal Espen, Jay Fielden, Cressida Leyshon, and Bill Buford. And the magazine's editors: William Shawn, Robert Gottlieb, and Tina Brown. My co-editor and discerning Cupid's helper in the selection and preparation of this anthology was Mary D. Kierstead, who also shines forth amidst this constellation of distinguished colleagues and friends.

—*Roger Angell*

Nothing But You

THE DIVER

V. S. PRITCHETT

In a side street on the Right Bank of the Seine where the river divides at the Île de la Cité there is a yellow-and-red brick building occupied by a firm of leather merchants. When I was twenty, I worked there. The hours were long, the pay was low, and the place smelled of cigarettes and boots. I hated it. I had come to Paris to be a writer but my money had run out, and in this office I had to stick. How often I looked across the river, envying the free lives of the artists and writers on the other bank. Being English, I was the joke of the office. The sight of my fat, pink, innocent face and my fair hair made everyone laugh; my accent was bad, for I could not pronounce a full "O." Worst of all, like a fool, I not only admitted I didn't have a mistress but boasted about it. To the office boys, this news was extravagant. It doubled them up. It was a favorite trick of theirs, and even of the salesman—a man called Claudel, with whom I had to work—to call me to the street door at lunchtime and then, if any girl or woman passed, give me a punch and shout, "How much to sleep with this one? Twenty francs? Forty? A hundred?"

I put on a grin, but, to tell the truth, a sheet of glass seemed to come down between me and any female I saw.

About one woman the lads did not play this game. She was a woman between thirty and forty, I suppose—Mme. Chamson, who kept the mender's and cleaner's down the street. You could hear her heels as she came, half running, to see Claudel, with jackets and trousers of his on her arm. He had some arrangement with her for getting his suits cleaned and repaired on the cheap. In return—well, there was a lot of talk. She had sinfully tinted hair, as hard as varnish, built up high over arching, exclaiming eyebrows, and when she got near our door there was always a joke coming out of the side of her mouth. She would bounce into the office in her tight navy-blue skirt, call the boys and Claudel together, shake hands with them all, and tell them some tale which always ended with a dirty glance around and in whispering. Then she stood back and shouted with laughter. I was never in this secret circle, and if I happened to grin she gave me a severe and offended look and marched out scowling. One day, when one of her tales was over, she called back from the door, "Standing all day in that gallery with all those naked women, he comes home done for, finished."

The office boys squeezed each other with pleasure. She was talking about her husband, who was an attendant at the Louvre—a small, moist-looking fellow whom we sometimes saw with her, a man fond of fishing, whose breath smelled of white wine. Because of her arrangement with Claudel and her stories, she was a very respected woman.

I did not like Mme. Chamson; she looked to me like some predatory bird, but I could not take my eyes off her pushing bosom and her crooked mouth. I was afraid of her tongue. She caught on quickly to the fact that I was the office joke, but when they told her that on top of this I wanted to be a writer, any curiosity she had about me was finished. "I could tell him a tale," she said. For her I didn't exist. She didn't even bother to shake hands with me.

Streets and avenues in Paris are named after writers. There are statues of poets, novelists, and dramatists making gestures to the birds, nursemaids, and children in the gardens. How was it these men had become famous? How had they begun? For myself, it was impossible to begin. I walked about packed with stories, but when I sat in cafés or in my room with a pen in my hand and a bare sheet of paper before me, I could not touch it. I seemed to swell in the head, the chest, the arms and legs, as if I were trying to heave an enormous load onto the page and could not move. The portentous moment had not yet come. And there was another reason. The longer I worked in the leather trade and talked to the office boys, the typists there, and Claudel, the more I acquired a double personality; when I left the office and walked to the Métro, I practiced French to myself. In this bizarre language, the stories inside me flared up; I was acting and speaking them as I walked, often in the subjunctive, but when I sat before my paper the English language closed its sullen mouth.

And what were these stories? Impossible to say. I would set off in the morning and see the gray, ill-painted buildings of the older quarters leaning together like people, their shutters thrown back, so that the open windows looked like black and empty eyes. In the mornings, the bedding was thrown over the sills to air, and hung out, wagging like tongues about what goes on in the night between men and women. The houses looked sunken-shouldered and exhausted by what they told, and crowning the city was the church of Sacré-Cœur, very white, standing, to my mind, like some dry Byzantine bird, hollow-eyed and without conscience, presiding over the habits of the flesh and—to judge by what I read in newspapers—its murders, rapes, and shootings for jealousy and robbery. As my French improved, the secrets of Paris grew worse. It amazed me that the crowds I saw on the street had survived the night, and many indeed looked as sleepless as the houses.

After I had been a little more than a year in Paris—fourteen months, in fact—a drama broke the monotonous life of our office. A consignment of dressed skins had been sent to us from Rouen. It had been sent by barge—not the usual method in our business. The barge was an old one and was carrying a mixed cargo, and, within a few hundred yards of our warehouse, it was rammed and sunk one misty morning by a Dutch boat taking the wrong channel. The whole office—but especially

Claudel, who saw his commission gone to the bottom—was outraged. Fortunately, the barge had gone down slowly and near the bank, close to us; the water was not too deep. A crane was brought down on another barge to the water's edge, and soon, in an exciting week, a diver was let down to salvage what he could. Claudel and I had to go to the quay, and whenever a bale of our stuff came up we had to get it into the warehouse and see what the damage was.

Anything to get out of the office. For me the diver was the hero of the week. He stood in his round helmet and suit on a wide tray of wood hanging from four chains; then the motor spat, the chains rattled, and down he went with great dignity under the water. While the diver was underwater, Claudel would be reckoning his commission over again— would it be calculated on the sale price or only on what was saved? "Five bales so far," he would mutter fanatically. "One and a half per cent." His teeth and his eyes were agitated with changing figures. I, in imagination, was groping in the gloom of the riverbed with the hero. Then we would step forward; the diver was coming up. Claudel would hold my arm as the man appeared with a tray of sodden bales, the brown water streaming off them. The diver, looking like a swollen frog, would step off the plank onto the barge, where the crane was installed. A workman unscrewed his helmet, the visor was raised, and then we saw the young man's rosy, cheerful face. A workman lit a cigarette and gave it to him, and out of the helmet came a long, surprising jet of smoke. There was always a crowd watching from the quay wall, and when he did this they all smiled and many laughed. "See that?" they would say. "He's having a puff," and the diver grinned and waved to the crowd.

Our job was to grab our stuff. Claudel would check the numbers of the bales on his list, and have them loaded onto barrows. Then we saw them wheeled to our warehouse, dripping all the way, and there I had to hang up the skins on poles. It was like hanging up drowned animals or even, I thought, human beings.

On the Friday afternoon of that week, when everyone was tired and the crowd looking down from the street wall had thinned to next to nothing, Claudel and I were still down on the quay. The diver had come up, and the crane was just hoisting the last dripping bale clear of the water. We were seeing him for the last time before the weekend. I was waiting to watch what I had not yet seen: how he got out of his suit. I walked down nearer to the quay's edge to get a good view. Claudel shouted to me to get on with the job, and as he shouted I heard a whizzing noise above my head and then felt a large, heavy, slopping lump hit me on the shoulders. Even as I turned round I was flying in the air, arms outspread with wonder. Paris turned upside down. A second later, I crashed into cold darkness and water was running up my legs, swallowing me. I had fallen into the river.

The wall of the quay was not high. I came up spitting mud and in a couple of strokes caught an iron ring on the wall. Two men pulled my hands. Everyone was laughing as I climbed out.

I stood there drenched and mud-smeared, with straw in my hair, and water pouring off me into a puddle that got larger and larger.

"Didn't you hear me shout?" said Claudel.

Laughing and arguing, two or three men led me to the shelter of the wall, where I began to wring out my jacket and shirt and squeeze the water out of my trousers. It was a warm day, and I stood in the sun and saw my trousers steam and heard my shoes squelch.

"Give him a hot rum," someone said.

Claudel was torn between looking after our few bales left on the quay and taking me across the street to a bar. But after checking the numbers and muttering a few more figures to himself, he decided to enjoy the drama and go with me. He called out that we'd be back in a minute.

We got to the bar, and Claudel saw to it that my arrival was a sensation. Always nagging at me in the office, he was now proud of me. "He fell into the river," he announced. "He nearly drowned. I warned him. I shouted. Didn't I?"

The one or two customers admired me. The barman brought me the rum. I could not get my hand into my pocket, because it was wet.

"You pay me tomorrow," said Claudel, putting a coin on the counter.

"Drink it quickly," said the barman.

I was laughing and explaining now, but Claudel kept interrupting. "One moment he was on dry land, the next he was flying in the air, then plonk in the water. Three elements," he said.

"Only fire is missing," said the barman.

They argued about how many elements there were. A whole history of swimming feats, drowning stories, bodies found, murders in the

Seine sprang up. Someone said the morgue used to be full of drowned corpses. And then an argument started, as it sometimes did in this part of Paris, about the exact date at which the morgue had been moved from the island. I joined in, but my teeth had begun to chatter.

"Another rum," the barman said.

And then I felt a hand fingering my jacket and my trousers. It was the hand of Mme. Chamson. She had been down at the quay once or twice during the week to have a word with Claudel. She had seen what had happened.

"He ought to go home and change into dry things at once," she said in a firm voice. "You ought to take him home."

"I can't do that. We've left five bales on the quay," said Claudel.

"He can't go back," said Mme. Chamson. "He's shivering."

I sneezed.

"You'll catch pneumonia," she said. And to Claudel, "You ought to have kept an eye on him. He might have drowned." She was very stern with him.

"Where do you live?" she said to me.

I told her.

"It will take you an hour to get there," she said.

Everyone was silent before the decisive voice of Mme. Chamson.

"Come with me to the shop," she ordered, and pulled me brusquely by the arm.

She led me out of the bar and said as we walked away, my boots squeaking and squelching, "That man thinks of nothing but money. Who'd pay for your funeral? Not he!"

Twice, as she led me, her prisoner, past the shops, she called out to people at their doors, "They nearly let him drown!"

Three girls used to sit mending in the window of her shop, and behind them there was usually a man pressing clothes. But it was half past six now and the shop was closed. Everyone was gone. I was relieved. This place had disturbed me. When I first went to work for our firm, Claudel had told me he could fix me up with one of the mending girls; sharing a room would halve our expenses and she could cook and look after my clothes. That was what started the office joke about my not having a mistress.

Now, when we got to the shop, Mme. Chamson led me down a passage inside, which was muggy with the smell of dozens of dresses and
suits hanging there, and into a dim parlor beyond. It looked out on the
smeared gray wall of the courtyard.

"Stay here," said Mme. Chamson, planting me by a sofa. "Don't sit
on it in those wet things. Take them off."

I took off my jacket.

"No. Don't wring it. Give it to me. I'll get a towel."

I started drying my hair.

"All of them," she said.

Mme. Chamson looked shorter in her room, her hair looked duller,
her eyebrows less dramatic. I had never really seen her close up. She had
become a plain, domestic woman; her mouth had straightened. There
was not a joke in her. Her bosom swelled with management. The rumor
that she was Claudel's mistress was obviously an office tale.

"I'll see what I can find for you. You can't wear these."

I waited for her to leave the room, and then I took off my shirt and
dried my chest, picking off the bits of straw from the river that had
stuck to my skin.

She came back. "Off with your trousers, I said. Give them to me.
What size are they?"

My head went into the towel. I pretended not to hear. I could not
bring myself to undress before Mme. Chamson. But while I hesitated
she bent down and her sharp fingernails were at my belt.

"I'll do it," I said anxiously.

Our hands touched and our fingers mixed as I unhitched my belt.
Impatiently she began on my buttons, but I pushed her hands away.
She stood back, blank-faced and peremptory in her stare. It was the
blankness of her face, her indifference to me, her ordinary womanli-
ness, and the touch of her practical fingers that left me without defense.
She was not the ribald, coquettish, dangerous woman who came wagging her hips to our office, not one of my Paris fantasies of sex and danger. She was simply a woman. The realization of this was disastrous to
me. An unbelievable change was throbbing in my body. It was uncon-
trollable. My eyes angrily, helplessly, asked her to go away. She stood
there implacably. I half-turned, bending to conceal my enormity as I

lowered my trousers, but as I lowered them inch by inch so the throbbing manifestation increased. I got my foot out of one leg but my shoe caught in the other. On one leg I tried to dance my other trouser leg off. The towel slipped and I glanced at her in red-faced angry appeal. My trouble was only too clear. I was stiff with terror. I was almost in tears.

The change in Mme. Chamson was quick. From busy indifference, she went to anger. "Young man," she said. "Cover yourself. How dare you? What indecency! How dare you insult me!"

"I'm sorry. I couldn't help . . ." I said.

Mme. Chamson's bosom became a bellows puffing outrage. "What manners," she said. "I am not one of your tarts. I am a respectable woman. This is what I get for helping you. What would your parents say? If my husband were here!"

She had got my trousers in her hand. The shoe that had betrayed me fell now out of the leg to the floor. She bent down coolly and picked it up.

"In any case," she said—and now I saw for the first time this afternoon the strange twist of her mouth return to her, as she nodded at my now concealing towel—"that is nothing to boast about."

My blush had gone. I was nearly fainting. I felt the curious, brainless stupidity that goes with the state nature had put me in. A miracle saved me. I sneezed and then sneezed again; the second time with force.

"What did I tell you!" said Mme. Chamson, passing now to angry self-congratulation. She flounced out to the passage that led to the shop, and coming back with a pair of trousers, she threw them at me and, red in the face, said, "Try those. I'll get a shirt." She went past me to the door of the room beyond, saying, "You can thank your stars my husband has gone fishing." I heard her muttering as she opened drawers. She did not return. There was silence.

IN THE AIRLESS little salon that looked out (as if it were a cell in which I was caught) on the stained, smeared gray wall of the courtyard, the silence lengthened. It began to seem that Mme. Chamson had shut herself away in her disgust and was going to have no more to do with me. I saw a chance of getting out, but she had taken away my wet clothes. I pulled on the pair of trousers she had thrown; they were too long, but

I could roll them up. I should look an even bigger fool if I went out in the street dressed only in these. What was Mme. Chamson doing? Was she torturing me? I stood listening. I studied the mantelpiece, where I saw what I supposed was a photograph of Mme. Chamson as a girl in the veil of her First Communion. Presently I heard her voice.

"Young man," she called harshly, "do you expect me to wait on you? Come and fetch your things!"

Putting on a polite and apologetic look, I went to the inner door, which led into a short passage. She was not there.

"In here," she said curtly.

I pushed the next door open. This room was dim also, and I saw the end of a bed, and in the corner a chair with a dark skirt on it and a stocking hanging from the arm, and on the floor a pair of shoes, one of them on its side. Then, suddenly, I saw at the end of the bed a pair of bare feet. I looked at the toes. How had they got there? And then I saw: Without a stitch of clothing on her, Mme. Chamson—but could this naked body be she?—was lying on the bed, her chin propped on her hand, her lips parted as they always were when she came in, on the point of laughing, to the office, but now with no sound coming from them. Her eyes, generally wide open, were half closed, watching me with the stillness of some large white cat. I looked away and then I saw two other large brown eyes gazing at me, two other faces—her breasts. It was the first time in my life I had ever seen a naked woman, and it astonished me to see the rise of a haunch, the slope of her belly, and the black hair like a mustache beneath it. Mme. Chamson's face was always strongly made up with some almost orange color, and I was surprised to see how white her body was from the neck down; it was not the white of statues but some sallow color of white and shadow, marked at the waist by the tightness of the clothes she had taken off. I had thought of her as old, but she was not; her body was young and idle.

The sight of her transfixed me. It did not stir me. I simply stood there gaping. My heart seemed to have stopped. I wanted to rush from the room, but I could not. She was so very near. My horror must have been on my face, but she seemed not to notice that, but simply stared at me. There was a small movement of her lips, and I dreaded that she was going to laugh. She did not, but slowly she closed her lips and said at last between her teeth, in a voice low and mocking, "Is this the first time you have seen a woman?" And after she said this, a sad look came into her face.

I could not answer.

She lay on her back and put out her hand and smiled fully. "Well?" she said. And she moved her hips.

"I—" I began, but I could not go on. All the fantasies of my walks about Paris as I practiced French rushed into my head. This was the secret of all those open windows of Paris, of the vulturelike head of Sacré-Cœur looking down on it. In a room like this, with a wardrobe in the corner and with clothes thrown on a chair, was enacted—what? Everything—but, above all, to my panicking mind, the crimes I read about in the newspapers. I was desperate as her hand went out.

"You have never seen a woman before?" she said again.

I moved a little, and, out of reach of her hand, I said, fiercely, "Yes, I have." I was amazed at myself.

"Ah!" she said, and when I did not answer she laughed. "Where was that? Who was she?"

It was her laughter, so dreaded by me, that released something in me. I said something terrible. The talk of the morgue, at the bar, jumped into my head. I said coldly, "She was dead. In London."

"Oh, my God," said Mme. Chamson, sitting up and pulling at the coverlet. But it was caught, and she could only cover her feet.

It was her turn to be frightened. Across my brain, newspaper headlines were tapping out. "She was murdered," I said. I hesitated. I was playing for time. Then it came out. "She was strangled."

"Oh, no!" she said, and she pulled the coverlet violently up with both hands, until she had got some of it to her breast.

"I saw her," I said. "On her bed."

"You *saw* her? How did you see her?" she said. "Where was this?"

Suddenly the story sprang out of me; it unrolled as I spoke. It was in London, I said. In our street. The woman was a neighbor of ours; we knew her very well. She used to pass our window every morning on her way up from the bank.

"She was robbed!" said Mme. Chamson. Her mouth buckled with horror.

I saw I had caught her. "Yes," I said. "She kept a shop."

"Oh, my God, my God!" said Mme. Chamson, looking at the door behind me, then anxiously round the room.

It was a sweetshop, I said, where we bought our papers, too.

"Killed in her shop," groaned Mme. Chamson. "Where was her husband?"

"No," I said. "In her bedroom at the back. Her husband was out at work all day, and this man must have been watching for him to go. He was the laundryman. He used to go there twice a week. She'd been carrying on with him. She was lying there with her head on one side, and a scarf twisted round her neck."

Mme. Chamson dropped the coverlet and hid her face in her hands. Then she lowered them and said suspiciously, "But how did *you* see her like this?"

"Well," I said, "it happened like this. My little sister had been whining after breakfast and wouldn't eat anything, and Mother said, 'That kid will drive me out of my mind. Go up to Mrs. Blake's'—that was her name—'and get her a bar of chocolate, milk chocolate, no nuts, she only spits them out.' And Mother said, 'You may as well tell her we don't want any papers after Friday, because we're going to Brighton. Wait, I haven't finished yet—here, take this money and pay the bill. Don't forget that; you forgot last year, and the papers were littering up my hall. We owe for a month.'"

Mme. Chamson nodded at this detail. She had forgotten she was naked. She was the shopkeeper, and she glanced again at the door as if listening for some customer to come in.

"I went up to the shop, and there was no one there when I got in—"

"A woman alone!" said Mme. Chamson.

"So I called, 'Mrs. Blake!,' but there was no answer. I went to the inner door and called up a small flight of stairs, 'Mrs. Blake!'—Mother had been on at me, as I said, about paying the bill. So I went up."

"You went up?" said Mme. Chamson, shocked.

"I'd been up there with Mother, once when Mrs. Blake was ill. We knew the family. Well—there she was. As I said, lying on the bed, naked, strangled, dead."

Mme. Chamson gazed at me. She looked me slowly up and down from my hair, then studied my face, and then down my body to my feet. I had come barefoot into the room. And then she looked at my bare arms, until she came to my hands. She gazed at these as if she had never seen hands before. I rubbed them on my trousers, for she confused me.

"Is this true?" she accused.

"Yes," I said, "I opened the door and there—"

"How old were you?"

I hadn't thought of that but I quickly decided. "Twelve," I said.

Mme. Chamson gave a deep sigh. She had been sitting taut, holding her breath. It was a sigh in which I could detect just a twinge of disappointment. I felt my story had lost its hold.

"I ran home," I said quickly, "and said to my mother, 'Someone has killed Mrs. Blake.' Mother did not believe me. She couldn't realize it. I had to tell her again and again. 'Go and see for yourself,' I said."

"Naturally," said Mme. Chamson. "You were only a child."

"We rang up the police," I said.

At the word "police," Mme. Chamson groaned peacefully. "There is a woman at the laundry," she said, "who was in the hospital with eight stitches in her head. She had been struck with an iron. But that was her husband. The police did nothing. But what does my husband do? He stands in the Louvre all day. Then he goes fishing, like this evening. Anyone could break in here."

She said this vehemently, looking through me into some imagined scene, and it was a long time before she came out of it. Then she saw her own bare shoulder and pouting she said slowly, "Is it true you were only twelve?"

"Yes."

She studied me for a long time. "You poor boy," she said. "Your poor mother." And she put her hand to my arm and let her hand slide down it gently to my wrist. Then she put out her other hand to my other arm and took that hand, too, as the coverlet slipped a little from her. She looked at my hands and lowered her head. Then she looked up at me slyly. "*You* didn't do it, did you?" she said.

"No!" I said indignantly, pulling back my hands, but she held on to them. My story vanished from my head.

"It is a bad memory," she said.

To me, she looked once more as she had looked when, soaking wet, I had first come with her into her salon—a soft, ordinary, decent woman. My blood began to throb.

"You must forget about it," she said. And then, after a long pause, she pulled me to her. I was done for, lying on the bed.

"Ah," she laughed, pulling at my trousers. "Forget. Forget."

And then there was no more laughter. Once, in the height of our struggle, I caught sight of her eyes; the pupils had disappeared and there were only the blind whites, and she cried out, "Kill me! Kill me!" from her twisted mouth.

AFTERWARD, WE LAY talking. She asked if it was true I was going to be a writer, and when I said yes she said, "You want talent for that. Stay where you are. It's a good firm. Claudel has been there for twelve years. And now, get up. My little husband will be back."

She got off the bed. Quickly, she gave me a complete suit belonging to one of her customers—a gray one, the jacket rather tight.

"It suits you," she said. "Get a gray one next time."

I was looking at myself in a mirror when her husband came in, carrying his fishing rod and basket. He did not seem surprised. She picked up my sodden clothes and rushed angrily at him. "Look at these! Soaked. That fool Claudel let this boy fall in the river. He brought him here."

Her husband simply stared.

"And where have you been?" she went on. "Leaving me alone like this. Anyone could break in. This boy saw a woman strangled in her bed in London. She had a shop. A man came in and murdered her. What d'you say to that?"

Her husband stepped back and looked with appeal at me.

"Did you catch anything?" she said to him, still accusing.

"No," said her husband.

"Well, not like me," she said, mocking me. "I caught this one."

"Will you have a drop of something?" said her husband.

"No, he won't," said Mme. Chamson. "He'd better go straight home to bed."

We shook hands. M. Chamson let me out through the shop door while Mme. Chamson called down the passage to me, "Bring the suit back tomorrow. It belongs to a customer."

· · ·

EVERYTHING WAS CHANGED for me after that. At the office I was a hero.

"Is it true that you saw a murder?" the office boys said.

And when Mme. Chamson came along and I gave her back the suit she said, "Ah, here he is—my fish." And then boldly, "When are you coming to collect your things?" And then she went over to whisper to Claudel and ran out.

"You know what she said just now?" said Claudel to me, looking very shrewdly. "She said, 'I am afraid of that young Englishman. Have you seen his hands?' "

(1970)

A Country Wedding

Laurie Colwin

On a cool, misty morning in early June, Freddie Delielle and her husband, Grey, drove into the country, toward the town of New Brecon, where Freddie's oldest friend, Penny Stern, was going to be married in her grandmother's country house. A band of fog hung over the Hudson River. Freddie, who was beginning to feel damp under her hair, could see a red smudge in the hazy sky: when the sun broke through, it was going to be hot.

Grey drove, his cuffs carefully folded back. His suit jacket was hung from a hook in the back of the car; it was the suit he had worn to his own wedding eight years ago. Next to him, Freddie sat poised as if encased in eggshells. She was not much of a dresser, and her lack of interest in personal adornment was well documented among her friends. She would have been happy to spend her life wearing her old bluejeans and the frayed shirts of her younger brother, but you could not go to a wedding looking like a laundry basket. The bride-to-be had taken Freddie in hand, and the result was the blue-and-white striped linen dress in which Freddie felt imprisoned. She was afraid to move or blink or sweat, and she feared that the mere act of sitting in the car was wrinkling her in the back. She felt like a child trapped in a party dress, a feeling she could remember exactly. She slipped off her shoes and propped her feet on the dashboard, as she was sure a seat belt would ruin the front of her dress.

Grey was more used to being dressed up than Freddie, but he did not like it any more than she did. He was a Wall Street lawyer, with a closet half full of pin-striped suits. The other half was full of walking shorts, hiking boots, old bluejeans, and waders for the trout season. He had been Freddie's guide to the outdoors, which she had experienced mostly through books. As a child, she had read endlessly about bats, birds, frogs, and the life of swamps, but her parents were entirely urban, and no one had taken her into the natural world until she met Grey. Together they had hiked, trekked, climbed, explored swamps, gone for owl walks, and kept life lists of birds. When the trout season opened, Freddie was perfectly happy to sit on a bank swatting midges and reading while Grey stood up to his hips in cold water. On their honeymoon they had gone to Dorset to search for fossils.

Freddie, Grey, and Penny Stern had all grown up together in London, the children of American parents who had sent them to a slightly progressive, coeducational day school in Westminster. Freddie had known Grey most of her life. He was three years her senior, and she could remember herself as a rather messy ten-year-old girl watching the thirteen-year-old Grey on the football field, his round knees muddy above his high socks, playing soccer with a fierce air of concentration. When she looked at him now, she could see the boy he had been, and she could not remember a time when she had not loved him.

They had all been sent to America for college, but Freddie and Grey had not re-met until Freddie was in graduate school studying economics and Grey was working for a law firm. They were married within six months. It never made sense to either of them that people who barely knew each other got married; it would have been unthinkable for Freddie or Grey to marry someone they had not known all their lives.

FREDDIE KNEW THE road to Penny's grandmother's house by heart. She had stayed there as a child, and visited frequently as an adult. In fact, Grey had proposed to her near a swamp off the Old Wall Lane, less than a mile from Mrs. Stern's house. Freddie remembered that day clearly: not only had she been proposed to but she had seen the great blue heron for the first time.

They turned off the highway and onto the county road. The sun had not yet dried off the dew, and the fat green leaves looked moist and velvety. The air smelled mild and sweet, of newly cut grass and chamomile. Freddie leaned back carefully. To be in a car with your husband, going to the wedding of your oldest friend, to visit a house you knew every corner of made life seem as correct, upright, and proper as a Quaker meetinghouse. The fact that her lawful-wedded husband had not, for example, been the first man to set eyes on her new dress was the thorn on the rose, the termite lurking under the wooden porch steps.

Freddie had—or, rather, she had recently had—a lover. To say this sentence to herself made her quiver, as if she had been stung by a hornet. The man in question was an older, beautifully dressed, prematurely retired banker named James Clemens. Like Freddie, he was an occasional journalist; they had met at a cocktail party given by the *Journal of American Finance*. He was married to a very stylish woman named Vera, an interior designer; he had two grown sons, he amused himself by dealing in first editions, and he was writing a book about the relationship of economics to architectural style.

Three months ago Penny had taken Freddie shopping, dragging her through a number of overheated, very expensive shops and department stores and sending her home with a beautiful blue-and-white striped linen dress in a fancy box. Once at home alone, Freddie, who had worn a nice suit for the occasion, climbed back into her worn old turtleneck and a pair of corduroy trousers that once had been olive green. No sooner had she thrown her suit over a chair when the doorbell rang, and James Clemens appeared. He looked at her, shook his head, and remarked, "As always, a vision of radiant loveliness." His coat was spattered with rain.

He closed the door behind him and took her into his arms. He was thirsty for her, but he found her reluctant. Instead of kissing him back, she led him to the kitchen for a cup of tea.

James and Freddie had been hungering and thirsting for each other for two years, although they had unsuccessfully resolved to part any number of times. Their usual pattern was tea, and then a trip up the stairs to the ratty couch in Freddie's bare little study. But something final was in the air, and they did not go upstairs. Instead, at Freddie's suggestion, they sat in the living room and drank their tea.

On the coffee table was the dress box. James, who knew one fancy shop from another, recognized it at once. "Did someone leave it here by mistake?" he said.

"It's mine," Freddie said. "It contains an expensive dress."

"Really?" James said. "But that means you intend to wear it somewhere, and we know what you think of social life."

"It is a poisoned well," Freddie said. "This is for my friend Penny's wedding in June. I told you about her."

"The one with the formidable grandmother."

"The very one," Freddie said. Penny's grandmother was the only person in the world who called Freddie by her given name of Fredrica.

"Well," said James, stretching his legs, "it certainly would be nice to see you in it."

Freddie sat on the edge of the sofa. The idea of trying on this dress, which she would wear to the wedding of her oldest friend, who was one of Grey's oldest friends, struck her as very wrong. It was a violation of something. She attempted to explain this to James.

"A woman absolves herself of guilt by brushing her teeth in the morning," James said.

Freddie had never seen him angry before. "Is that a quote?"

"It's a quote from some misogynist Spaniard whose name escapes me at the moment," said James. "I must say, I've never suspected you of being quite so sentimental. After all, we've been to bed together countless times and suddenly you get proprietary about a dress because you're going to wear it on some sacred occasion."

Freddie opened the box and pulled out the dress. She shook it out and held it up in front of her.

James surveyed her without expression. "Quite a departure from your usual garb," he said.

"You'll have to help me fold it back up," said Freddie. "If I do it myself, I'll crease it."

"If you don't mind my saying so," James said, "I think you'll want to hang it up. And you might think of putting it in a dress bag, so your other garments won't smudge it."

"Very funny," said Freddie. She draped the dress carefully over the box and put it on the dining-room table. Then she came back and sat down on the sofa. James sat down next to her.

"This has to stop," Freddie said.

"A nuptial rears its ugly head, and suddenly you want to break up."

"I always want to break up."

"Is that really true?" James said.

"Yes," said Freddie. "Isn't it true for you?"

"That's a terrible thing to say," he said.

"Truth is not always lovely," Freddie said.

James regarded her. "Sometimes I'd really like to pop you one," he said. He took her warm hand, and they sat on the sofa without speaking.

James did not like long periods of silence. To lighten the gloom, he said, in a voice not devoid of cheer, "You're quite right. I knew this was coming. A little parting is probably in order. It's always done us good in the past."

"I think this shouldn't be a little parting," said Freddie, whose command over her voice was far from total. Their previous separations had never lasted longer than a month.

"It's probably for the best," James finally said. "I guess this couldn't go on indefinitely." He did not say it with conviction.

The raw weather had turned to sleet. James and Freddie sat on the sofa side by side in the dim light. Love made strange bedfellows, Freddie thought, and then did absolutely nothing to help them out.

FIVE MILES DOWN the county blacktop was a dirt road called Old Wall Lane. It began in the state forest and ended on the border of old Mrs. Stern's property. Grey felt there were two ways to take this road: to whip around its bends at high speed, raising a cloud of dust, or to slide down it in second, since it was downhill all the way. Grey took the gentle course.

Halfway down, he stopped the car. "Head out and up," he said. "Quick!"

They rolled down their windows and stuck their heads out. Sailing toward them was a red-tailed hawk. It floated over the car, low enough to see its speckled breast. The sight of a hawk up close always made Freddie's heart pound. She and Grey each autumn climbed Mirage Mountain, in western Connecticut, to watch the annual hawk migration. It was a childhood longing of Grey's to own and train a kestrel, and for their first wedding anniversary Freddie had got him a first edition of "The Goshawk," by T. H. White.

At the bottom of the road was Wall Swamp, where Grey had proposed. Since then, they had explored the swamp by canoe, and had actually swum in it one blazing-hot afternoon. Grey stopped the car and got out to stretch his legs. Freddie got out, too. She stood close to her husband, who smelled sweet and fresh as bread. "Don't crush me," she said as Grey put his arm around her. They embraced as from a distance, so as not to mess up Freddie's dress.

"This is a pretty fancy business," Grey said. "Not like *our* wedding." Freddie and Grey had got married in London, with their parents and siblings as witnesses, in a registry office, and, after lunch, taken off in a rented car and driven to Dorset to explore the coast and search for ammonites and other fossils. "I like ours better," Grey said, pulling Freddie close.

"I actually don't care if this dress gets creased," said Freddie.

They stood in the middle of the road, closed their eyes, and kissed like teen-agers.

Parting had been the sensible thing to do. A love affair could be compared to a cellar hole. Old Mrs. Stern's property had several such holes, remnants of eighteenth-century households. After a long while, without a map of the property, it was impossible to tell where they were. Standing on a road kissing your husband, taking the car to be serviced, letters, meals, telephone calls, arrangements, and errands could fill up the hole of a love affair so well that after a while it would be possible to stand comfortably on top of it.

· · ·

A STRIPED TENT had been pitched next to the house. As they drove up the long driveway, Freddie could see waiters with baskets of flowers dressing the tables. Penny's mother, in a lilac dress, stood in the center of the tent, directing waiters and maids.

On the steps of the house stood the ferocious old Mrs. Stern. She had declared that this would be the last wedding she would live to see, but she looked far from frail. She was a stout old lady, with white hair and stark, piercing blue eyes. She wore a yellow dress and leaned on a cane that looked more like a bishop's crosier, an effect of which she was not unaware.

"Fredrica, my dear one," she said, clutching Freddie's hand. "And Grey. How lovely to see you so nice and early. Have you had breakfast? No? Well, Grey, do go sit with David. He's all alone and lonely in the sun room. No one pays any attention to the groom at all. As for you, my dearest, go instantly up to Penny, who is having some sort of nervous crisis. She sent her father down to the pharmacy to buy her some emery boards, and she knows perfectly well that we have hundreds of them in the supply cupboard. Oh, well. And she hasn't eaten a thing. Do make her eat."

Upstairs in her childhood bedroom, Penny sat in her long, white wedding dress smoking a cigarette and staring into the dressing-table mirror. A wreath of flowers hung over the back of the chair. Penny was tall and pale, and wore her pale hair pulled back in a chignon. She and Freddie had been friends since they were ten. In the summers, both families came home to America for a holiday, and Freddie and Penny always spent a month together at old Mrs. Stern's. In this room they had snuck cigarettes, drunk purloined beer, read love comics, plotted revenge on their school enemies, and read under the covers with flashlights after they had been told to go to sleep.

"Is David still alive?" she said to Freddie by way of greeting.

"I'm afraid he's dead," said Freddie. "The wedding is off."

"God, this is hell," Penny said. "This would never have happened if we had been allowed to run off to City Hall, like you guys."

"Oh, come on," Freddie said. "You wanted to get married here. Besides, your gran says it's her last wedding."

"She's been saying that for thirty years," said Penny. "She'll be saying that when my as yet unborn children get married." She blew a smoke ring and watched it float toward the ceiling and disperse. She sighed. "The end of my girlhood. The end of all good things. Why am I doing this?"

"It's not so bad."

Penny looked up. She was suddenly in a very dark mood. "*You're* a fine one to talk," she said.

"That's over," said Freddie.

"Really?" Penny said. "You didn't tell me. Did it just happen?"

"It happened the day we went shopping, as a matter of fact."

"What made you do it?"

"You mean other than the fact that I was a nervous wreck and felt horrible all the time?" said Freddie. "I just did it. It feels very strange. Just because something is the right thing to do doesn't mean that you feel wonderful."

"You poor little duck," Penny said. "Hand me another of them smokes. Whether it's over or not is not the point. The point, of course, is that it existed at all. It proves *my* point: marriage is unlivable."

"He's a fine young laddie you're marrying."

"Really?" Penny said. "I can't seem to stand the thought of him at the moment."

A sweet breeze blew in through the window. Freddie lit two cigarettes and watched the air bat the smoke around. She and Penny never smoked except when they were together. It was a childhood tradition. Neither of them inhaled but both blew very beautiful smoke rings, a skill they had been perfecting for years.

"Did you feel sick on your wedding day?" asked Penny.

"I can't remember," said Freddie. "But I don't think so. After all, I didn't have to go through all this."

"I wasn't at your wedding," Penny said gloomily.

"I noticed that."

"I'll never forgive myself," Penny said.

"If you remember correctly," Freddie said, "you were taking exams."

"I will never forgive myself for not seeing your sickly, ashy face on the morning of your wedding. God, this dress is uncomfortable. I now see why you hate clothes. By the way, they won't let me wear a watch in this getup. What's the time?"

"You have forty minutes," said Freddie. "Do you require a last meal?"

"I'm starving, now that you mention it," Penny said. "Bring me something. Toast. Coffee. Anything."

WHEN FREDDIE RETURNED with a tray of coffee, buttered toast, and bacon, along with two oversized linen napkins provided by Penny's mother, lest the bride get crumbs or butter on her dress, she found Penny exactly where she'd left her.

"What's going on down there?" Penny said.

"People keep showing up. Grey and David are planning a fishing trip. Your father forgot the emery boards and says they're not necessary anyway. Hawks and Ricardo are here chatting up your gran."

Dr. Hawks was the local Congregational minister, and Dr. Ricardo was the rabbi of Mrs. Stern's New York congregation. They would jointly perform the ceremony.

"I could eat fifteen times this much toast," said Penny, making herself a bacon sandwich. "I don't suppose you'd hop downstairs and get more."

"I have strict instructions not to bring you anything else."

Penny sighed and sipped her coffee. "I'll be very happy once this is all over. I have to keep remembering that it only lasts a couple of hours."

"It lasts a lifetime," Freddie said.

"There's always divorce," said Penny. "Is your entanglement really over?"

"It better be," Freddie said. "When I look back over the last two years, I can't believe the person who lived that life is me. I never had interesting romances like you. *That* was my interesting romance. I thought if I gave it up I would be my same old self, but I seem to be some other old self."

In Penny's room it didn't seem so hard at all. James did not know anything about her real life, her past, her childhood. They were each other's exception, and had nothing to do with the other at all.

"You'll get over it," said Penny.

"Actually, I don't think I will," Freddie said.

AFTER THE CEREMONY, the party sat down to lunch. Waiters hovered with trays of champagne. Plates were filled, emptied, refilled, and taken away. The three-tiered cake was cut amid cheers and toasts. Between courses, the bride and groom table-hopped, making sure they talked to everyone.

Right before the ceremony, Freddie and Grey had switched the place cards so they could sit together. This did not go unnoticed by old Mrs. Stern, but they grinned at her so happily that she was forced to forgive them. Freddie took Grey's hand under the table. The ceremony, so unlike their own spare vows, had affected them both. At lunch they sat close together, their knees touching. Freddie felt as if she had been on a long journey and had come back with a grateful heart to everything she belonged to.

When the waiters appeared with coffee, Penny left her place and came to fetch Freddie. "Let's go for a ride," she said.

Arm in arm they ran down the hill through the apple orchard, through a gate in the low stone wall, and past the rock garden to a little pond. Lying upside down on the bank, looking like a giant turtle in the sun, was the Old Town canoe Penny and Freddie had played Indian scouts in as children.

Freddie flipped it over and pushed it into the water. "I've splattered my dress," she said.

"It's only water," Penny said. "It won't stain."

They hiked up their skirts and slipped off their shoes, and Penny hopped in. Freddie gave the canoe a shove, and jumped in, too.

"I filched a couple of cigs," said Freddie, taking one from behind each ear. She had stuck a book of matches into her bra.

They paddled across the pond. Beside a willow, they stopped and lit their cigarettes.

"Do you think they think we've bolted?" Penny said.

"They think we're going for a spin. Your grandmother waved to us," Freddie said.

"Then they probably think this is some charming part of the day's events," Penny said.

"It is, isn't it?"

"This is the end of my girlhood," Penny said again glumly.

"We haven't been girls for years," said Freddie.

They sat smoking and watching the water spiders jump from ripple to ripple. There was an occasional flutter on the surface as a brown trout rose to snap at a mayfly.

Across the pond, the house sat securely on its rise, a big white-and-yellow clapboard house with six chimneys. From a distance it looked secure, remote. If she squinted, Freddie could see Grey talking to Penny's father. It made her heart beat faster to see him.

The sun came through the willow branches, speckling the water with light. Freddie could conjure up James in a flash; you might part, but you could not forget. She could imagine him sitting on the bank waiting for her to float back to him.

"I guess we've had it," Penny said. "I mean we ought to paddle home." She sighed. "Doesn't everything feel *unknown* to you?"

"It's as plain as the nose on your face," Freddie said.

"I feel as if life is all spread out in front of me but I don't know what's there," said Penny.

"That's what life is like," Freddie said.

They flicked their cigarettes into the water, and, sitting up straight as Indian scouts, with their wedding clothes billowing behind them, they paddled back, shooting across the water in that swift, determined way of long ago.

(1984)

BLACKBIRD PIE

RAYMOND CARVER

I was in my room one night when I heard something in the corridor. I looked up from my work and saw an envelope slide under the door. It was a thick envelope, but not so thick it couldn't be pushed under the door. My name was written on the envelope, and what was inside purported to be a letter from my wife. I say "purported" because even though the grievances could only have come from someone who'd spent twenty-three years observing me on an intimate, day-to-day basis, the charges were outrageous and completely out of keeping with my wife's character. Most important, however, the handwriting was not my wife's handwriting. But if it wasn't her handwriting, then whose was it?

I wish now I'd kept the letter, so I could reproduce it down to the last comma, the last uncharitable exclamation point. The tone is what I'm talking about now, not just the content. But I didn't keep it, I'm sorry to say. I lost it, or else misplaced it. Later, after the sorry business I'm about to relate, I was cleaning out my desk and may have accidentally thrown it away—which is uncharacteristic of *me,* since I usually don't throw anything away.

In any case, I have a good memory. I can recall every word of what I read. My memory is such that I used to win prizes in school because of my ability to remember names and dates, inventions, battles, treaties, alliances, and the like. I always scored highest on factual tests, and in later years, in the "real world," as it's called, my memory stood me in good stead. For instance, if I were asked right now to give the details of the Council of Trent or the Treaty of Utrecht, or to talk about Carthage, that city razed by the Romans after Hannibal's defeat (the Roman soldiers plowed salt into the ground so that Carthage could never be called Carthage again), I could do so. If called upon to talk about the Seven Years' War, the Thirty Years', or the Hundred Years' War, or simply the First Silesian War, I could hold forth with the greatest enthusiasm and confidence. Ask me anything about the Tartars, the Renaissance popes, or the rise and fall of the Ottoman Empire. Thermopylae, Shiloh, or the Maxim gun. Easy. Tannenberg? Simple as blackbird pie. The famous four and twenty that were set before the king. At Agincourt, English longbows carried the day. And here's something else. Everyone has heard of the Battle of Lepanto, the last great sea battle fought in ships powered by galley slaves. This fracas took place in 1571 in the eastern Mediterranean, when the combined naval forces of the Christian nations of Europe turned back the Arab hordes under the infamous Ali Muezzin Zade, a man who was fond of personally cutting off the noses of his prisoners before calling in the executioners. But does anyone remember that Cervantes was involved in this affair and had his left hand lopped off in the battle? Something else. The combined French and Russian losses in one day at Borodino were seventy-five thousand men—the equivalent in fatalities of a fully loaded jumbo jet crashing every three minutes from breakfast to sundown. Kutuzov pulled his forces back toward Moscow. Napoleon drew breath, marshalled his troops, and continued his advance. He entered the downtown area of Moscow, where he stayed for a month waiting for Kutuzov, who never showed his face again: The Russian generalissimo was waiting for snow and ice, for Napoleon to begin his retreat to France.

Things stick in my head. I remember. So when I say I can re-create the letter—the portion that I read, which catalogues the charges against me—I mean what I say.

In part, the letter went as follows:

Dear,

Things are not good. Things, in fact, are bad. Things have gone from bad to worse. And you know what I'm talking about. We've come to the end of the line. It's over with us. Still, I find myself wishing we could have talked about it.

It's been such a long time now since we've talked. I mean really *talked*. Even after we were married we used to talk and talk, exchanging news and ideas. When the children were little, or even after they were more grown-up, we still found time to talk. It was more difficult then, naturally, but we managed, we found time. We *made* time. We'd have to wait until after they were asleep, or else when they were playing outside, or with a sitter. But we managed. Sometimes we'd engage a sitter just so we *could* talk. On occasion we talked the night away, talked until the sun came up. Well. Things happen, I know. Things change. Jack had that trouble with the police, and Linda found herself pregnant, etc. Our quiet time together flew out the window. And gradually your responsibilities backed up on you. Your work became more important, and our time together was squeezed out. Then, once the children left home, our time for talking was back. We had each other again, only we had less and less to talk about. "It happens," I can hear some wise man saying. And he's right. *It happens*. But it happened to us. In any case, no blame. *No blame*. That's not what this letter is about. *I want to talk about us*. I want to talk about *now*. The time has come, you see, to admit that *the impossible* has happened. To cry *Uncle*. To beg off. To—

I read this far and stopped. Something was wrong. Something was fishy in Denmark. The sentiments expressed in the letter may have belonged to my wife. (Maybe they did. Say they did, grant that the sentiments expressed *were* hers.) But the handwriting *was not her handwriting*. And I ought to know. I consider myself an expert in this matter of her handwriting. And yet if it wasn't her handwriting, who on earth *had* written these lines?

I should say a little something about ourselves and our life here. During the time I'm writing about we were living in a house we'd taken for the summer. I'd just recovered from an illness that had set me back in most things I'd hoped to accomplish that spring. We were surrounded on three sides by meadows, birch woods, and some low, rolling hills—a "territorial view," as the realtor had called it when he described it to us over the phone. In front of the house was a lawn that had grown shaggy, owing to lack of interest on my part, and a long gravelled drive that led to the road. Behind the road we could see the distant peaks of mountains. Thus the phrase "territorial view"—having to do with a vista appreciated only at a distance.

My wife had no friends here in the country, and no one came to visit. Frankly, I was glad for the solitude. But she was a woman who was used to having friends, used to dealing with shopkeepers and tradesmen. Out here, it was just the two of us, thrown back on our resources. Once upon a time a house in the country would have been our ideal—we would have *coveted* such an arrangement. Now I can see it wasn't such a good idea. No, it wasn't.

Both our children had left home long ago. Now and then a letter came from one of them. And once in a blue moon, on a holiday, say, one of them might telephone—a collect call, naturally, my wife being only too happy to accept the charges. This seeming indifference on their part was, I believe, a major cause of my wife's sadness and general discontent—a discontent, I have to admit, I'd been vaguely aware of before our move to the country. In any case, to find herself in the country after so many years of living close to a shopping mall and bus service, with a taxi no farther away than the telephone in the hall—it must have been hard on her, very hard. I think her *decline*, as a historian might put it, was accelerated by our move to the country. I think she slipped a cog after that. I'm speaking from hindsight, of course, which always tends to confirm the obvious.

I don't know what else to say in regard to this matter of the handwriting. How much more can I say and still retain credibility? We were alone in the house. No one else—to my knowledge, anyway—was in the house and could have penned the letter. Yet I remain convinced to this day that it was not her handwriting that covered the pages of the letter. After all, I'd been reading my wife's handwriting since before she was my wife. As far back as what might be called our pre-history days—the time she went away to school as a girl, wearing a gray-and-white school uniform. She wrote letters to me every day that she was away, and she was away for two years, not counting holidays and summer vacations. Altogether, in the course of our relationship, I would estimate (a conservative estimate, too), counting our separations and the short periods of time I was away on business or in the hospital, etc.—I would estimate, as I say, that I received seventeen hundred or possibly eighteen hundred and fifty handwritten letters from her, not to mention hundreds, maybe thousands, more informal notes ("On your way home, please pick up dry cleaning, and some spinach pasta from Corti Bros"). I could recognize her handwriting anywhere in the world. Give me a few words. I'm confident that if I were in Jaffa, or Marrakech, and picked up a note in the marketplace, I would recognize it if it was my wife's handwriting. A word, even. Take this word "*talked*," for instance. That simply isn't the way she'd write "talked"! Yet I'm the first to admit I don't know *whose* handwriting it is if it isn't hers.

Secondly, my wife *never* underlined her words for emphasis. Never. I don't recall a single instance of her doing this—not once in our entire married life, not to mention the letters I received from her before we were married. It would be reasonable enough, I suppose, to point out that it could happen to anyone. That is, anyone could find himself in a situation that is completely atypical and, *given the pressure of the moment*, do something totally out of character and draw a line, the merest *line*, under a word, or maybe under an entire sentence.

I would go so far as to say that every word of this entire letter, so-called (though I haven't read it through in its entirety, and won't, since I can't find it now), is utterly false. I don't mean false in the sense of "untrue," necessarily. There is some truth, perhaps, to the charges. I don't want to quibble. I don't want to appear small in this matter; things are bad enough already in this department. No. What I want to say, all I want to say, is that while the sentiments expressed in the letter may be my wife's, may even hold *some* truth—be legitimate, so to speak—the force of the accusations levelled against me is diminished, if not entirely undermined, even discredited, because she *did not* in fact write the letter. Or, if she *did* write it, then discredited by the fact that she didn't write it in her own handwriting! Such evasion is what makes men hunger for facts. As always, there are some.

ON THE EVENING in question, we ate dinner rather silently but not unpleasantly, as was our custom. From time to time I looked up and smiled across the table as a way of showing my gratitude for the delicious meal—poached salmon, fresh asparagus, rice pilaf with almonds. The radio played softly in the other room; it was a little suite by Poulenc that I'd first heard on a digital recording five years before in an apartment on Van Ness, in San Francisco, during a thunderstorm.

When we'd finished eating, and after we'd had our coffee and dessert, my wife said something that startled me. "Are you planning to be in your room this evening?" she said.

"I am," I said. "What did you have in mind?"

"I simply wanted to know." She picked up her cup and drank some coffee. But she avoided looking at me, even though I tried to catch her eye.

Are you planning to be in your room this evening? Such a question was altogether out of character for her. I wonder now why on earth I didn't pursue this at the time. She knows my habits, if anyone does. But I think her mind was made up even then. I think she was concealing something even as she spoke.

"Of course I'll be in my room this evening," I repeated, perhaps a trifle impatiently. She didn't say anything else, and neither did I. I drank the last of my coffee and cleared my throat.

She glanced up and held my eyes a moment. Then she nodded, as if we had agreed on something. (But we hadn't, of course.) She got up and began to clear the table.

I felt as if dinner had somehow ended on an unsatisfactory note. Something else—a few words maybe—was needed to round things off and put the situation right again.

"There's a fog coming in," I said.

"Is there? I hadn't noticed," she said.

She wiped away a place on the window over the sink with a dish towel and looked out. For a minute she didn't say anything. Then she said—again mysteriously, or so it seems to me now—"There is. Yes, it's very foggy. It's a heavy fog, isn't it?" That's all she said. Then she lowered her eyes and began to wash the dishes.

I sat at the table a while longer before I said, "I think I'll go to my room now."

She took her hands out of the water and rested them against the counter. I thought she might proffer a word or two of encouragement for the work I was engaged in, but she didn't. Not a peep. It was as if she were waiting for me to leave the kitchen so she could enjoy her privacy.

Remember, I was at work in my room at the time the letter was slipped under the door. I read enough to question the handwriting and to wonder how it was that my wife had presumably been busy somewhere in the house and writing me a letter at the same time. Before reading further in the letter, I got up and went over to the door, unlocked it, and checked the corridor.

It was dark at this end of the house. But when I cautiously put my head out I could see light from the living room at the end of the hallway. The radio was playing quietly, as usual. Why did I hesitate? Except for the fog, it was a night very much like any other we had spent together in the house. But there was *something else afoot* tonight. At that moment I found myself afraid—afraid, if you can believe it, in my own house!—to walk down the hall and satisfy myself that all was well. Or if something was wrong, if my wife was experiencing—how should I put it?—difficulties of any sort, hadn't I best confront the situation before letting it go any further, before losing any more time on this stupid business of reading her words in somebody else's handwriting!

But I didn't investigate. Perhaps I wanted to avoid a frontal attack. In any case, I drew back and shut and locked the door before returning to the letter. But I was angry now as I saw the evening sliding away in this foolish and incomprehensible business. I was beginning to feel *uneasy*. (No other word will do.) I could feel my gorge rising as I picked up the letter purporting to be from my wife and once more began to read.

The time has come and gone for us—us, you and me—to put all our cards on the table. Thee and me. Lancelot and Guinevere. Abélard and Héloïse. Troilus and Cressida. Pyramus and Thisbe. JAJ and Nora Barnacle, etc. You know what I'm saying, honey. We've been together a long

time—thick and thin, illness and health, stomach distress, eye-ear-nose-
and-throat trouble, high times and low. Now? Well, I don't know what I
can say now except the truth: I can't go it another step.

At this point, I threw down the letter and went to the door again,
deciding to settle this once and for all. I wanted an accounting, and I
wanted it now. I was, I think, *in a rage*. But at this point, just as I
opened the door, I heard a low murmuring from the living room. It
was as if somebody were trying to say something over the phone and
this somebody were taking pains not to be overheard. Then I heard the
receiver being replaced. Just this. Then everything was *as before*—the
radio playing softly, the house otherwise quiet. But I had heard a
voice.

In place of anger, I began to feel panic. I grew afraid as I looked
down the corridor. Things were the same as before—the light was on in
the living room, the radio played softly. I took a few steps and listened.
I hoped I might hear the comforting, rhythmic clicking of her knitting
needles, or the sound of a page being turned, but there was nothing of
the sort. I took a few steps toward the living room and then—what
should I say?—I lost my nerve, or maybe my curiosity. It was at that
moment I heard *the muted sound of a doorknob being turned*, and afterward the unmistakable sound of a door opening and closing quietly.

My impulse was to walk rapidly down the corridor and into the living room and get to the bottom of this thing once and for all. But I
didn't want to act impulsively and possibly discredit myself. I'm not impulsive, so I waited. But there *was* activity of some sort in the house—
something was afoot, I was sure of it—and of course it was my duty, for
my own peace of mind, not to mention the possible safety and well-
being of my wife, to act. But I didn't. I couldn't. The moment was there,
but I hesitated. Suddenly it was too late for any decisive action. The
moment had come and gone, and could not be called back. Just so did
Darius hesitate and then fail to act at the Battle of Granicus, and the
day was lost, Alexander the Great rolling him up on every side and giving him a real walloping.

I went back to my room and closed the door. But *my heart was racing*. I sat in my chair and, trembling, picked up the pages of the letter
once more.

But now here's the curious thing. Instead of beginning to read the letter through, from start to finish, or even starting at the point where I'd stopped earlier, I took pages at random and held them under the table lamp, picking out a line here and a line there. This allowed me to juxtapose the charges made against me until the entire indictment (for that's what it was) took on quite another character—one more acceptable, since it had lost its chronology and, with it, a little of its punch.

So. Well. In this manner, going from page to page, here a line, there a line, I read in snatches the following—which might under different circumstances serve as a kind of abstract:

> . . . withdrawing farther into . . . a small enough thing, but . . . talcum powder sprayed over the bathroom, including walls and baseboards . . . a shell . . . not to mention the insane asylum . . . until finally . . . a balanced view . . . the grave. Your "work" . . . Please! Give me a break . . . No one, not even . . . Not another word on the subject! . . . The children . . . but the real issue . . . not to mention the loneliness . . . Jesus H. Christ! Really! I mean . . .

At this point I distinctly heard the front door close. I dropped the pages of the letter onto the desk and hurried to the living room. It didn't take long to see that my wife wasn't in the house. (The house is small—two bedrooms, one of which we refer to as my room or, on occasion, as my study.) But let the record show: *every light in the house was burning.*

A HEAVY FOG lay outside the windows, a fog so dense I could scarcely see the driveway. The porch light was on and a suitcase stood outside on the porch. It was my wife's suitcase, the one she'd brought packed full of her things when we moved here. What on earth was going on? I opened the door. Suddenly—I don't know how to say this other than how it was—a horse stepped out of the fog, and then, an instant later, as I watched, dumbfounded, another horse. These horses were grazing in our front yard. I saw my wife alongside one of the horses, and I called her name.

"Come on out here," she said. "Look at this. Doesn't this beat anything?"

She was standing beside this big horse, patting its flank. She was dressed in her best clothes and had on heels and was wearing a hat. (I hadn't seen her in a hat since her mother's funeral, three years before.) Then she moved forward and put her face against the horse's mane.

"Where did you come from, you big baby?" she said. "Where did you come from, sweetheart?" Then, as I watched, she began to cry into the horse's mane.

"There, there," I said and started down the steps. I went over and patted the horse, and then I touched my wife's shoulder. She drew back. The horse snorted, raised its head a moment, and then went to cropping the grass once more. "What is it?" I said to my wife. "For God's sake, what's happening here, anyway?"

She didn't answer. The horse moved a few steps but continued pulling and eating the grass. The other horse was munching grass as well. My wife moved with the horse, hanging on to its mane. I put my hand against the horse's neck and felt a surge of power run up my arm to the shoulder. I shivered. My wife was still crying. I felt helpless, but I was scared, too.

"Can you tell me what's going on?" I said. "Why are you dressed like this? What's that suitcase doing on the front porch? Where did these horses come from? For God's sake, can you tell me what's happening?"

My wife began to croon to the horse. Croon! Then she stopped and said, "You didn't read my letter, did you? You might have skimmed it, but you didn't read it. Admit it!"

"I did read it," I said. I was lying, yes, but it was a white lie. A partial untruth. But he who is blameless, let him throw out the first stone. "But tell me what is going on anyway," I said.

My wife turned her head from side to side. She pushed her face into the horse's dark wet mane. I could hear the horse *chomp, chomp, chomp.* Then it snorted as it took in air through its nostrils.

She said, "There was this girl, you see. Are you listening? And this girl loved this boy so much. She loved him even more than herself. But the boy—well, he grew up. I don't know what happened to him. Something, anyway. He got cruel without meaning to be cruel and he—"

I didn't catch the rest, because just then a car appeared out of the fog, in the drive, with its headlights on and a flashing blue light on its roof. It was followed, a minute later, by a pickup truck pulling what looked like a horse trailer, though with the fog it was hard to tell. It could have been anything—a big portable oven, say. The car pulled right up onto the lawn and stopped. Then the pickup drove alongside the car and stopped, too. Both vehicles kept their headlights on and their engines running, which contributed to the eerie, bizarre aspect of things. A man wearing a cowboy hat—a rancher, I supposed—stepped down from the pickup. He raised the collar of his sheepskin coat and whistled to the horses. Then a big man in a raincoat got out of the car. He was a much bigger man than the rancher, and he, too, was wearing a cowboy hat. But his raincoat was open, and I could see a pistol strapped to his waist. He had to be a deputy sheriff. Despite everything that was going on, and the anxiety I felt, I found it *worth noting* that both men were wearing hats. I ran my hand through my hair, and was sorry I wasn't wearing a hat of my own.

"I called the sheriff's department a while ago," my wife said. "When I first saw the horses." She waited a minute and then she said something else. "Now you won't need to give me a ride into town after all. I mentioned that in my letter, the letter you read. I said I'd need a ride into town. I can get a ride—at least, I think I can—with one of these gentlemen. And I'm not changing my mind about anything, either. I'm saying this decision is irrevocable. Look at me!" she said.

I'd been watching them round up the horses. The deputy was holding his flashlight while the rancher walked a horse up a little ramp into the trailer. I turned to look at this woman I didn't know any longer.

"I'm leaving you," she said. "That's what's happening. I'm heading for town tonight. I'm striking out on my own. It's all in the letter you read." Whereas, as I said earlier, my wife never underlined words in her letters for emphasis, she was now speaking (having dried her tears) as if virtually every other word out of her mouth ought to be underlined.

"What's gotten *into* you?" I heard myself say. It was almost as if I couldn't help adding pressure to some of my own words. "Why are you *doing* this?"

She shook her head. The rancher was loading the second horse into the trailer now, whistling sharply, clapping his hands and shouting an occasional "Whoa! Whoa, damn you! Back up now. Back up!"

The deputy came over to us with a clipboard under his arm. He was holding a big flashlight. "Who called?" he said.

"I did," my wife said.

The deputy looked her over for a minute. He flashed the light onto her high heels and then up to her hat. "You're all dressed up," he said.

"I'm leaving my husband," she said.

The deputy nodded, as if he understood. (But he didn't, he couldn't!) "He's not going to give you any trouble, is he?" the deputy said, shining his light into my face and moving the light up and down rapidly. "You're not, are you?"

"No," I said. "No trouble. But I resent—"

"Good," the deputy said. "Enough said, then."

The rancher closed and latched the door to his trailer. Then he walked toward us through the wet grass, which, I noticed, reached to the tops of his boots.

"I want to thank you folks for calling," he said. "Much obliged. That's one heavy fog. If they'd wandered onto the main road, they could have raised hob out there."

"The lady placed the call," the deputy said. "Frank, she needs a ride into town. She's leaving home. I don't know who the injured party is here, but she's the one leaving." He turned then to my wife. "You sure about this, are you?" he said to her.

She nodded. "I'm sure."

"O.K.," the deputy said. "That's settled, anyway. Frank, you listening? I can't drive her to town. I've got another stop to make. So can you help her out and take her into town? She probably wants to go to the bus station or else to the hotel. That's where they usually go. Is that where you want to go to?" the deputy said to my wife. "Frank needs to know."

"He can drop me off at the bus station," my wife said. "That's my suitcase on the porch."

"What about it, Frank?" the deputy said.

"I guess I can, sure," Frank said, taking off his hat and putting it back on again. "I'd be glad to, I guess. But I don't want to interfere in anything."

"Not in the least," my wife said. "I don't want to be any trouble, but I'm—well, I'm distressed just now. Yes, I'm distressed. But it'll be all right once I'm away from here. Away from this awful place. I'll just check and make doubly sure I haven't left anything behind. Anything *important*," she added. She hesitated and then she said, "This isn't as sudden as it looks. It's been coming for a long, long time. We've been married for a good many years. Good times and bad, up times and down. We've had them all. But it's time I was on my own. Yes, it's time. Do you know what I'm saying, gentlemen?"

Frank took off his hat again and turned it around in his hands as if examining the brim. Then he put it back on his head.

The deputy said, "These things happen. Lord knows none of us is perfect. We weren't made perfect. The only angels is to be found in Heaven."

My wife moved toward the house, picking her way through the wet, shaggy grass in her high heels. She opened the front door and went inside. I could see her moving behind the lighted windows, and something came to me then. *I might never see her again.* That's what crossed my mind, and it staggered me.

The rancher, the deputy, and I stood around waiting, not saying anything. The damp fog drifted between us and the lights from their vehicles. I could hear the horses shifting in the trailer. We were all uncomfortable, I think. But I'm speaking only for myself, of course. I don't know what they felt. Maybe they saw things like this happen every night—saw people's lives flying apart. The deputy did, maybe. But Frank, the rancher, he kept his eyes lowered. He put his hands in his front pockets and then took them out again. He kicked at something in the grass. I folded my arms and went on standing there, not knowing what was going to happen next. The deputy kept turning off his flashlight and then turning it on again. Every so often he'd reach out and swat the fog with it. One of the horses whinnied from the trailer, and then the other horse whinnied, too.

"A fellow can't see anything in this fog," Frank said.

I knew he was saying it to make conversation.

"It's as bad as I've ever seen it," the deputy said. Then he looked over at me. He didn't shine the light in my eyes this time, but he said something. He said, "Why's she leaving you? You hit her or something? Give her a smack, did you?"

"I've never hit her," I said. "Not in all the time we've been married. There was reason enough a few times, but I didn't. She hit me once," I said.

"Now, don't get started," the deputy said. "I don't want to hear any crap tonight. Don't say anything, and there won't be anything. No rough stuff. Don't even think it. There isn't going to be any trouble here tonight, is there?"

The deputy and Frank were watching me. I could tell Frank was embarrassed. He took out his makings and began to roll a cigarette.

"No," I said. "No trouble."

My wife came onto the porch and picked up her suitcase. I had the feeling that not only had she taken a last look around but she'd used the opportunity to freshen herself up, put on new lipstick, etc. The deputy held his flashlight for her as she came down the steps. "Right this way, Ma'am," he said. "Watch your step, now—it's slippery."

"I'm ready to go," she said.

"Right," Frank said. "Well, just to make sure we got this all straight now." He took off his hat once more and held it. "I'll carry you into town and I'll drop you off at the bus station. But, you understand, I don't want to be in the middle of something. You know what I mean." He looked at my wife, and then he looked at me.

"That's right," the deputy said. "You said a mouthful. Statistics show that your domestic dispute is, time and again, potentially the most dangerous situation a person, especially a law-enforcement officer, can get himself involved in. But I think this situation is going to be the shining exception. Right, folks?"

My wife looked at me and said, "I don't think I'll kiss you. No, I won't kiss you goodbye. I'll just say so long. Take care of yourself."

"That's right," the deputy said. "Kissing—who knows what that'll lead to, right?" He laughed.

I had the feeling they were all waiting for me to say something. But for the first time in my life I felt at a loss for words. Then *I took heart* and said to my wife, "The last time you wore that hat, you wore a veil with it and I held your arm. You were in mourning for your mother. And you wore a dark dress, not the dress you're wearing tonight. But those are the same high heels, I remember. Don't leave me like this," I said. "I don't know what I'll do."

"I have to," she said. "It's all in the letter—everything's spelled out in the letter. The rest is in the area of—I don't know. Mystery or speculation, I guess. In any case, there's nothing in the letter you don't already know." Then she turned to Frank and said, "Let's go, Frank. I can call you Frank, can't I?"

"Call him anything you want," the deputy said, "long as you call him in time for supper." He laughed again—a big, hearty laugh.

"Right," Frank said. "Sure you can. Well, O.K. Let's go, then." He took the suitcase from my wife and went over to his pickup and put the suitcase into the cab. Then he stood by the door on the passenger's side, holding it open.

"I'll write after I'm settled," my wife said. "I think I will, anyway. But first things first. We'll have to see."

"Now you're talking," the deputy said. "Keep all lines of communication open. Good luck, pardee," the deputy said to me. Then he went over to his car and got in.

The pickup made a wide, slow turn with the trailer across the lawn. One of the horses whinnied. The last image I have of my wife was when a match flared in the cab of the pickup, and I saw her lean over with a cigarette to accept the light the rancher was offering. Her hands were cupped around the hand that held the match. The deputy waited until the pickup and trailer had gone past him and then he swung his car around, slipping in the wet grass until he found purchase on the driveway, throwing gravel from under his tires. As he headed for the road, he tooted his horn. *Tooted.* Historians should use more words like "tooted" or "beeped" or "blasted"—especially at serious moments such as after a massacre or when an awful occurrence has cast a pall on the future of an entire nation. That's when a word like "tooted" is necessary, is gold in a brass age.

I'D LIKE TO say it was at this moment, as I stood in the fog watching her drive off, that I remembered a black-and-white photograph of my wife holding her wedding bouquet. She was eighteen years old—*a mere girl,* her mother had shouted at me only a month before the wedding. A few minutes before the photo, she'd got married. She's smiling. She's just finished, or is just about to begin, laughing. In either case, her mouth is open in amazed happiness as she looks into the camera. She is three months pregnant, though the camera doesn't show that, of course. But what if she *is* pregnant? So what? Wasn't everybody pregnant in those days? She's happy, in any case. I was happy, too—I know I was. We were both happy. I'm not in that particular picture, but I was close—only a few steps away, as I remember, shaking hands with someone offering me good wishes. My wife knew Latin and German and chemistry and physics and history and Shakespeare and all those other things they teach you in private school. She knew how to properly hold a teacup. She also knew how to cook and to make love. She was a prize.

But I found this photograph, along with several others, a few days after the horse business, when I was going through my wife's belongings, trying to see what I could throw out and what I should keep. I was packing to move, and I looked at the photograph for a minute and then I threw it away. I was ruthless. I told myself I didn't care. Why should I care?

If I know anything—and I do—if I know the slightest thing about human nature, I know she won't be able to live without me. She'll come back to me. And soon. Let it be soon.

No, I don't know anything about anything, and I never did. She's gone for good. She is. I can feel it. Gone and never coming back. Period. Not ever. I won't see her again, unless we run into each other on the street somewhere.

There's still the question of the handwriting. That's a bewilderment. But the handwriting business isn't the important thing, of course. How could it be after the consequences of the letter? Not the letter itself but the things I can't forget that were *in* the letter. No, the letter is not paramount at all—there's far more to this than somebody's handwriting. The "far more" has to do with subtle things. It could be said, for instance, that to take a wife is to take a history. And if that's so, then I understand that I'm outside history now—like horses and fog. Or you could say that my history has left me. Or that I'm having to go on *without history*. Or that history will now have to do without me—unless my wife writes more letters, or tells a friend who keeps a diary, say. Then, years later, someone can look back on this time, interpret it according to the record, its scraps and tirades, its silences and innuendos. That's when it dawns on me that autobiography is the poor man's history. And that I am saying goodbye to history. Goodbye, my darling.

(1986)

THE NICE RESTAURANT

MARY GAITSKILL

It's so cool about you," said Evan. "You're thirty-four years old and you're a pedophile's dream. Even with your big juicy ass."

"Maybe," said Laurel. "But you're the tender young thing here."

"I am *not* the tender young thing! You are! You are!" In delighted outrage, Evan squirmed and bucked in his chair.

Laurel smiled and stretched. Evan was, in fact, nine years younger than she.

They were seated at a table in the outdoor section of an expensive restaurant on the outskirts of L.A., surrounded by sibilant foliage and flowers. White umbrellas mounted on the glass-topped tables held the light in wide cups of flat perfection, under which the diners preened and basked. Faces were matte and cool in the beautifying flatness. Daylight waned intensely, delineating everything with maddening exactitude. Evan leaned across the table toward Laurel, and the tip of his long nose seemed about to whip from side to side with ardor. A waiter set down a glass of water; in its gently stirring reflection a tiny, fluid image of Evan trembled against the curve of the glass. Laurel felt wiggly with beauty, nearly sick with it. She felt as if every pretty detail contrived by the restaurant people was a manifestation of her and Evan's personal delight. Which was, of course, exactly how you were supposed to feel.

"Your face was wildly expressive just now," Evan said.

"I was feeling seduced and repelled at once."

"Oh?" Evan sat up expectantly.

"By the restaurant, you goose. I was getting drawn in by the whole nice-restaurant thing—the little flowers on the table, the smiling waiters, the whole ambience of 'Aren't we special people to be here in this wonderful restaurant where everything is nice.' Then I got disgusted by it."

"Don't be disgusted. It's us that's making it nice, not the restaurant."

"Yeah, but you know what I mean. There's something just so frail and embarrassing about the whole 'date' thing anyway, and then on top of that there's the God-damned restaurant where everything is perfect."

"I'm out with Mrs. Hell. Come on, soon we'll be back in our lives, and once again there'll be grit and grime and little hairs sprouting on things. Can't we just have this moment of softness and flowers?"

JUST TWO YEARS before, after conducting an exhaustive series of almost comically wretched sex affairs, Laurel had grimly embarked on a course of celibacy, sincerely, albeit drunkenly, declaring that she would never Do It again. ("It's a modern idea that you're supposed to have sex. Women used to be old maids. They *never* had sex, and it didn't kill them.") She had let Evan get near her because he was so young, because he had a girlfriend, and because he flattered her.

Evan wrote for a fancy trend journal, and Laurel ran a sputtering graphics-design business. They had met through a mutual acquaintance. He had gambolled harmlessly about her for two years, calling her for light conversation and occasionally inviting her to some garish magazine-related event. Slowly, they progressed from the infrequent coffee date to dinner at her apartment. Although Evan had long since lost the girl-friend, Laurel thought nothing of it when, after the second dinner, he earnestly remarked that he had always wanted to cuddle her. Familiarity, drunkenness, and a desire to be touched made her forget that, although he was her young admirer, Evan was also a large, energetic adult male, and soon they were tussling on the couch as she remarked, "Evan, this *isn't* cuddling." His aggression was first amusing, then annoying, then frightening, with eroticism flashing between the annoyance and fright. Pressing forward, he stuck his knee between her legs and opened her thighs; the maneuver was so blunt, so fresh in its young carnality that she was disarmed. Disarmament could have become pleasure, but she barked at Evan to sit up, and after a lot of groping and struggling, they did.

"Look," she said. "I took you seriously when you said you wanted to cuddle. You're obviously really attractive, and I like you a lot, but I don't want to fuck you. I'm too screwed up to have sex, and I don't want to ruin the friendship."

"I always knew you were pretty screwed up," he said.

"Yeah, well," she muttered. "So are a lot of people."

"The same membrane that stretched once will always stretch again."

"How seductive."

"I was speaking metaphorically." His voice was playful, but aggression glittered in his eyes. She considered Evan as a potential assailant and sobered quickly. He moved forward. She placed her fist firmly against his Adam's apple.

"Evan," she said. "I don't want this to get ugly, do you?"

His eyes changed. He sat back. He left minutes later, rather morosely squeezing her ass on the way out.

She went to bed relieved but woke the next day obsessed with the memory of that carnal leg. She invited him to dinner the next week. Vigorously, they dispensed with her celibacy on the bed, on the couch, on the floor. A month later they sat in the nice restaurant, feeling full of themselves.

"I didn't start out wanting to make fun of them," Evan was saying. "Because it's too easy and because everybody else already has. But how can I not, after that bogus ritual with Loki the love god?"

Evan was working on an article about the men's movement; he had just participated in a three-day workshop on male sexuality, and his open-mindedness had been severely taxed.

"Well, you know, sometimes people express the most important things in silly ways," Laurel said.

"I was prepared for silliness. I was even prepared for rituals. But I wasn't prepared for the shallowness. I mean, they were having us do these chants and they didn't even know what they meant or where they came from. And that love-god thing! Where we were supposed to go and offer a gift to this shoddily constructed statue? I don't even think that qualifies as a ritual."

Laurel half-listened, delighting in the movement of his long, graceful hands, his buoyant voice, the changeability of his sensitive gray irises. Whenever he came to visit her and knocked on her door, she'd see his face in the half-moon-shaped window at the top of the door, and then, as she came closer, he would move off to the side, out of her range of vision. So that when she opened the door, she was slightly startled to see him standing there, huge and healthy and bristling with joy at the sight of her.

"Evan," she said abruptly. "How come, when you knock on my door, you always step off to the side so I can't see you in the window?"

Evan stuck out his chest and wiggled like a puppy massaging itself on a nubbly rug. "I love it that you notice that!" he yelled. He lunged across the table, his forehead crazily raised, lips pulled in as if to keep ridiculous sounds from bursting out. "Nobody else would. I do it because I have the kind of conflicted feelings you had about the restaurant—I see you coming to answer, and it's too much, this rising moment of anticipation and wonderfulness. We're looking at each other through the window, and it's all so open and sweet—it reaches a certain pitch and then I start to feel like a geek. So I step off to the side. Which not only relieves the geek thing, but it creates a kind of double-tiered effect to the greeting."

Laurel leaned forward and brushed her lips against his, enjoying the light, fleshy dryness. An agreeable landscape of need and satiety, arranged in endless, alternating layers, expanded before her.

"Of course, there's also the element of bewilderment on your face. For just a split second when you come out the door? You look confused because I'm not directly in front of you, and you have to look for me for a second. It makes you look really vulnerable. It's delicious."

Gently, Laurel bit Evan's lower lip and then withdrew into her chair. She said, "It's slightly monstrous, what you just said, but I love the subtlety of it. I've never been involved with a guy who could express anything quite that way."

"Honey, no offense, but I think you've known some idiots."

One of their shared myths, fully developed within weeks, was that Evan had rescued Laurel from her series of terrible boyfriends. Although the idea had been propelled into full-blown myth by its undeniable basis in reality, Laurel had noted that they both nurtured the vivid status of the myth a little too fondly. While Evan seemed genuinely pained at her stories, it was also clear to her that he enjoyed hearing them. Just that afternoon, they had rehashed the story of Vaughan: She had been sitting in Vaughan's car with him when, in response to a question she had asked, he took her face in his hand and turned it toward him, answering her with the imperial limpidity of his gaze. He let go of her face and said, "It's as simple as this. If a woman lets me do that, I not only know she'll sleep with me; it sets the emotional tone for the whole thing."

"That's so disgusting!" Evan had howled. "I can just picture him, the smug, shallow, handsome fool! How could you let him perform that stupid gesture on you?"

"I *enjoyed* the corniness of it. It was like I was a fourteen-year-old on a date with Davy Jones, and we were both wearing lacy blouses and pink lipstick. It was a very appealing role to play. And then he took it further by pointing out the phonyness. Sort of like creating a sense of camaraderie."

"Camaraderie! Camaraderie! It's the height of arrogance to do something like that and then point it out." He paused. "Did you suck his cock?"

"What do you think? Evan, you're getting hysterical."

"I know. I can't help it. It's sort of a masochistic thrill. So what happened with old Vaughan?"

The story of Vaughan became sillier and ultimately more painful, yet for some reason it was the hand-face gesture that Evan held on to, wringing it for shameful nuance. "The subtler things are always the grossest," he said.

. . .

A WAITER WITH a chest like a busy pigeon brought them hot breads and herbed oil and glasses of wine. He solicited their order; they needed a minute.

IF THE OLD boyfriends often stalked the stage as villains, they sometimes donned clown outfits and threw pies. Chief among the clowns was Geoffrey, a diminutive sadist whom Laurel had described as "Elmer Fudd as high-school principal." Evan loved picturing the real Geoffrey's outrage at such a characterization. Surrounded by gagged and bound adolescent slave girls, he furiously paced Evan's imagination, ranting at an invisible audience: "Elmer Fudd! Elmer Fudd! Just ask *them* if *they* think it's about Elmer Fudd! Here, just take that gag out of her mouth! She'll tell you!" And for days all Laurel had to do was say, "Just take that gag out of her mouth!" and Evan would crack up.

Evan had old girlfriends, of course, but in comparison with the old boyfriends, enlivened as they were by Evan's dramatic projections, the pouting girls simply slouched against the walls. Evan gallantly presented them as mere pale prototypes for Laurel, but every now and then one of their little nymph faces would veer from the shadows into sultry relief, exposing fraught contours of cheekbone and eyelash, hinting the subtle heat of breath, the quick gleam of vital eyes.

"The last time I felt this way about anybody was with that girl Chloe," Evan had once remarked as they lay together. "It was the kinkiest relationship I'd had—until now, of course—even though we didn't do anything dramatic. It was all really understated and undiscussed, and that's what made it stronger. I would just fuck her really hard and say stuff to her that she thought was dirty. And I would feel her having this conflicted reaction of repulsion and excitement, even stronger repulsion and more desperate excitement, both of them held down really tight and boiling up against the lid. It was incredibly violative, even though it was just normal sex."

THE WAITER CAME back. They ordered salads and oysters, pork chops and bluefish, and more wine. Dusk seeped in and bled off the perfect delineation that had been so present moments earlier. Laurel was suddenly aware of two things: one, that she was in love with Evan, and, two, that their affair would be, by her choice, a short one. The emotional intensity and cerebral distance attached to these thoughts rubbed together strangely.

"But then there was the special work-shop in which we were supposed to discuss our sexual fantasies," Evan was saying.

Laurel's prurience reared its head. "Were they, um, candid?" she asked.

"They were unbelievably insipid. It was stuff like doing it in a row-boat on a moonlit lake, or somebody's wife giving him a blow job in a field of daisies."

"They were probably just describing the bare outlines. They probably didn't want to get into the nasty parts."

"I think they were just wimps."

"How did they react to your fantasies?"

"Well, I didn't really talk about my fantasies."

"Evan! You jerk! Why not?"

"Are you kidding? In the midst of all that sweet romantic stuff I'm going to talk about my— It would've been a slap in the face of everyone there."

"If they were wimps, you were, too."

"I was not a wimp," Evan said with dignity. "I was sparing the feelings of middle-aged guys."

"Oh, please. You were embarrassed, like they were."

"My fantasies aren't any of their business. I was there to research an article, not to bond."

Laurel shrugged, conceding.

"There was an interesting moment, though. One of the guys—he brought up a fantasy about sex with black women. He didn't elaborate, but just that little bit alone—I could feel discomfort move through the room."

"I'm surprised that interracial stuff would still have that kind of charge."

"If he was thinking about a particular black woman, it wouldn't have. But for it to be about black women generally was what made it uncool. I mean, that fairly reeked." He paused. "I should've told him about the time I fucked the black maid."

"Evan, that's ridiculous. It's too corny."

"Well, I was seventeen." He selected a little piece of bread, dipped it in oil, and ate it with a pretty trill of his Adam's apple.

The waiter brought the oysters, and salads glistening and garnished with little pieces of toasted bread and the heads of sacrificed flowers. Laurel stared at the blossoms; they were pansies, and their rich purple and yellow hues were helplessly beautiful in the oily mass of lettuces.

"So what happened with you and the maid?" she asked. "Did you have an affair?"

"No. It was a one-time thing. We had flirted with each other for a long while and then one day when we were alone I asked her into my room to hear some music. We smoked some dope and started making out. She was only a year or so older than me and she was, like, too beautiful."

"What did you talk about with her?"

"Music, Jamaica—where she was from. Things you talk about when you know you're going to have sex."

"Did you get off on the idea that it was, you know, the maid?"

"It's funny, I didn't. I was really young, and I wasn't thinking about anything except that she was gorgeous and that I wanted to fuck her. But then my mom came home right after it happened, when we were coming out of my bedroom. I guess she knew what had gone on because she shook her head and said, 'Oh, Evvie!' in this sad, disapproving way. And that gave the whole thing a nice illicit charge. Like, afterward, when I'd see Lucille around the house."

In silence, they ravaged the dainty leaves and flowers, Evan exuberantly tucking escaping fronds back into his chewing lips. Laurel looked into the bright windows of the restaurant, at the mincing gestures of the other eaters. She looked at the narrow, jealously in-turned shoulders of a middle-aged woman in a natty pink jacket, which yelled out with a vibrancy that was cruelly smothered in knit. Her body language spoke of timidity, disappointment, and parsimony. All at once, everybody in the restaurant looked as though they were straining to have, through their absurdly expensive, unattractive clothing, an engagement with life that had so far eluded them.

"Race stuff is always complicated," she said. "When my car was in the shop and I had to take the city bus a few weeks ago? I had to wait a long time at this one bus stop where I was the only white person, and I was definitely the most flamboyantly dressed person there. And I was really self-conscious about being white."

"You were scared?"

"I was afraid that somebody would make fun of me. Mostly because there were a lot of teen-agers there, and teen-agers like to make fun of people, and I seemed to be a good target. I was just horribly self-conscious."

"The last time I was in New York, I had a funny mass-transit experience," Evan said. "I was running to make the I.R.T., and it shut in my face, and I was mad, so I punched the door. The train sat there long enough for me to see these two young black guys inside mocking me for not getting the train. So I give 'em the finger. And the older one stands up, and—I don't know how to describe it—he didn't really grab his dick, but he put both hands on either side of it and sort of shook it at me, like a 'suck my dick' kind of thing. So I grab *my* dick and shake it and mouth the words 'suck my dick.' Naturally, at that moment the subway doors slowly rattle open."

"Really!"

"And they lunge at the door! Which closes in their faces! As the train pulls away, they're dissing me furiously through the window and I maintain the 'suck my dick' posture until they disappear into the tunnel."

"Gosh! That sounds like fun, in a way. Girls don't ever get to do that kind of thing. What could a woman say? 'Suck my tit!' You could grab your boob and shake it."

"I don't think that would have the desired effect."

"When I was in Venice once, this fat crazy guy ran up in my face and started yelling dirty stuff. He said, 'You fat-ass whore, spreading your pussy all over town.' And so on."

Evan dropped his oyster fork with almost feminine distaste. "If I'd been there when that happened? He'd be dead, and the world would be better."

"Well, I wonder what he would've done if I'd grabbed my breast and—"

"Bad idea, hon."

"I'm not serious, I just like the ludicrousness. But if I'd yelled at him the same way he was yelling at me, he might've secretly liked it. *I* might've. We could've bellowed all up and down the street, insulting everybody."

"It's really cute that you'd have that idea," he said. "You'd never do it, thank God. But I can imagine you telling him off in front of the mirror at home. I can see you stamping your little feet."

"Evan," she said. "Why do you always say things like that?"

"What?"

"My cute idea, my stamping feet. I've never told the mirror off in my life. And I *have* yelled at people on the street. Just without the tit grab. Why are you always giving me this 'cute little' crap?"

"Because you are," he said seriously. "Because what I mean is—"

"I'm nine years older than you. I left home when I was sixteen, and I've worked for a living since then, in really crummy jobs until my business finally took off. You've never had a grunt job in your life. Your mama was still making the bed for you just two years ago. What are you talking about?"

His forehead tensely stood still, then slowly dropped into a painfully gentle expression. "Because I don't—I know you've had a lot of experiences. But it's like it hasn't affected you, at least not in the way you'd expect. Like table dancing, and that old guy who supported you. . . . People would think that kind of thing would mean you were really compromised or something. But you're—you're the purest person I've ever known. I know it sounds maudlin. But you are."

Somewhat incongruously, Laurel suddenly remembered a story he had told her about his ex-girlfriend Chloe. He had gone to spend a weekend in Arizona with her and her disapproving Catholic parents, during which he'd snuck into her bedroom while the family was at Mass and, in the spirit of rebellion and iconoclasm, taken a nap in Chloe's pink, canopied, elaborately dust-ruffled bed. Although he had never been a bed wetter as a child, he woke a scant twenty minutes later in urine-soaked pink sheets and was forced to spend the next half hour in the laundry room, manically pacing as the machine moaned. Chloe had never said anything about the mattress, which had not responded well to his efforts with a little purple blow-dryer.

"Honey?" he said. "What is it? You look like—"

"Nothing." She reached for a glass of water. "I just—Nobody ever said that to me before."

"I know. And I don't understand why not. It's so obvious. I mean, there you are."

The waiter presented their dishes of food, meat and fish symmetrically striped from the grill, with bountiful color-coördinated vegetables. Laurel stared at the food, feeling funny. She had spent years hoping some crummy old boyfriend or other would say something like this to her. And now here it was, right in front of her, in a fancy restaurant no less.

Evan's expression as he ate was humble, even slightly chastened.

IT GREW DARK and cold. She and Evan were the only diners left on the patio. The restaurant's paper lanterns bobbed in the private darkness. Laurel brooded. Evan talked some more about the men.

"I'm really worried about this article," he said. "Because I don't want to be facile. But these guys were pathetic. Even the older, sort of erudite ones."

"I'm a little disappointed," said Laurel. "I was hoping there'd be some guy upon whose huge, hairy chest you could lay your head. I mean, in a cathartic, dad kind of way."

"It's an interesting idea, but it didn't happen. One of the facilitators was an older guy who was a tiny bit fatherly, but he was bisexual and no way was I going to lay my head on *his* hairy chest. The main guy was really too bratty to be a dad figure. At times it seemed like the whole point of the retreat was for him to brag about his sexuality while these frustrated guys admired him."

"They couldn't have been totally frustrated. Didn't you say most of them were married?"

"Yeah, but even so. Like at one point we were supposed to reveal our insecurity with women? Even the married ones had all this worry and fear either about pleasing their wives or about whether or not they were really missing the action by being married and square. Meanwhile, our surfer-dude leader is prancing around talking about all his women."

"And did you reveal your insecurity? Or did you at least make something up?"

"I said I was insecure about you."

"Oh!"

Once again, Evan had redeemed his arrogance, at least as far as she was concerned; his acculturated self-love included an enthusiastic eagerness to love her. If he saw something about her that was unlovable, he embraced it with the greed of a child fascinated by a flawed toy, valued more for its idiosyncrasy than a new and perfect one would be. It wasn't just her, either. He joked and jollied grumpy grocers, deliverymen, and counter persons; he juiced exhausted old people and supported the shy. Really, he could be so nice it was ridiculous.

She remembered something else about the violated Chloe. "Before she met me, she was a wreck," he had said. "I was the one who got her focussed, who got her to major in journalism."

A waiter, muffled in darkness, approached them with wine. They accepted. Laurel took long drinks that made her throat feel sweet and fuzzy.

"When you had sex with the maid?"

"Yes?"

"Well, I was wondering, did you talk about it with her afterward? Were there any looks exchanged?"

"No. I saw her once outside the building with some black guy. I think he might've been her boyfriend."

Laurel waited. Evan picked at his pork-chop bone. He downed his glass of wine.

"And?" she said.

"And what?"

"What happened when you saw her outside?"

"We said hi."

"Wasn't it weird?"

"No. She was cool."

Laurel shifted in her chair. "Evan, did this woman have a green card?"

"I sense this conversation just took a turn for the worse. I don't think so, because I remember my mother helped her get one, and then she was pissed because Lucille quit immediately after that. I hate where I think you're going with this."

"Do you have some reason to hate it?"

"Oh, come *on*."

"Well, I was just wondering. Because when girls are attracted to you, they want to, like, go on a date, or at least hang out and talk. And she knew that wasn't going to happen with you. You were sort of the boss, except you couldn't even give her a goddam raise."

"No," he said. "No, no, no. It wasn't a boss thing, it wasn't a victimized-underclass thing. I basically acted with her like I acted with every other pretty girl I met when I was seventeen. We did hang out and talk! We listened to music! I would've done the same thing if she were white, if she were the neighbor's daughter!"

"But would she?"

"Why not?" He paused, a momentary uncertainty crossing his face. "Although at one point she did go for the door."

"She *ran* for the door?"

"No, she didn't run for the door. She suddenly changed her mind and got up to leave. She was saying something about her religion and birth control—"

"I can't stand it! Damn it Evan, you raped the maid."

"If you want to pick a fight with me, surely you can do better."

"Yeah, I could lecture you about your condescending attitudes toward those 'pathetic' men, most of whom work their butts off to support families. But at least you kept your mitts off them."

"This is so unfair!"

"Girls don't talk about religion and birth control when they want to do it with you."

"Are you kidding? That's a practical matter; of course they talk about it. As soon as I said I'd pull out, she was O.K. with it."

Laurel imagined the Jamaican girl trying to get out the door, which was suddenly body-blocked by a large, strong blond boy, the son of her employer. "God, you probably did rape her," she said, wondering. "And you don't even know it."

"I did not rape anyone!" Evan bawled. "If I did I would certainly know it!"

A waiter presented himself with a feline tact that was almost obnoxious. Laurel demanded the check; Evan cried out for Scotch.

"I should get outraged and storm out," Laurel said.

"No!" Evan lunged forward and grabbed her hand.

"Scotch for the gentleman." The waiter made his dry announcement in mid-retreat.

"She probably didn't want to have sex with me, totally. But neither do a lot of girls who wind up doing it with you. Maybe I did do something a tiny bit bad, but not that bad. You have to understand, I treated women horribly at that age. I was interested in sex, not relationships."

"But this was different. She wasn't a peer. For all she knew, if she said no, you would make up some shit and tell your mom and get her fired, maybe deported. And I can't believe you were so naïve you didn't know that."

"Laurel, that was not what was going on."

"Why was she trying to get out the door?"

"She was probably worried that *doing* it with me would get her in trouble, not the other way around. She kept saying my mother might come home."

The waiter brought the Scotch, and Evan sipped from it without speaking. He sat on one hip, his body turned sideways, one long leg crossing the other at a slightly persnickety angle. Grudgingly, Laurel admired his nervous grace. She crossed her own legs and sniffed. It had become uncomfortably cold on the patio.

"I almost wish I *had* raped her," said Evan. "Then this conversation would be tragedy instead of farce."

"You're such a little snot."

"You're so sanctimonious."

They sat in stiffly individuated silence. Laurel crossed her legs more tightly, winding her calves together and tucking the toes of one foot tautly behind the opposite ankle.

"Let me try again," she said. "Your fantasies are all about raping secretaries and victimizing teen-age girls. You want to pretend I'm a thirteen-year-old incest victim even though I'm older than you."

"Oh, is this what we're really arguing about?"

"Look, your fantasies are on a par with mine, and that's cool with me. But I can't believe you weren't into a big power trip with that girl who just happened to be a black maid. And it seems like you don't understand the difference between fantasy and reality about half the time. Like when I told you I'd done assembly-line work and you asked if I did it for the experience? Like you didn't understand that some people actually have to do that kind of work for money, because you never had to do it."

"I said that because I don't think you should've had to do that kind of work."

They sat quietly. She could no longer see his face, but in the darkness his form was austere and upright. He was very present in his indignation, fully occupying his solid haunches and his broad, open chest. Even in his foolish self-certainty, Evan had a strength that moved her, and, at that moment, she had an intimation of how his strength would mature as he grew. Evan was a big, good-looking boy; was it so surprising if the maid had wanted to imbibe a little of this exuberant animal with his cruelty and kindness and heat all rolled together in a confused bundle of young maleness?

"What goes on between you and me is complicated," he was saying. "I show you things I don't show other people. What happened with me and Lucille when I was seventeen was not complicated. It was of the moment, and we were both participating."

Laurel imagined the maid sitting on the side of the bed, reapplying her lipstick. Laurel's indignation and empathy hovered about the imaginary Lucille, trying to attach itself to her. But the maid, annoyed, shrugged it off; it fell on the floor, and Lucille stepped over it as she left the room, with Evan cheerfully bringing up the rear. Mom tsk-tsked. Life continued apace.

"It's actually pretty funny," she said. "You come back from the male-sexuality workshop and get in a fight with your earnest girlfriend about raping the maid."

"Which I didn't even do." Evan laughed, heartily and with relief.

Once again, Laurel felt the abrasion of thought and feeling, close together but running in opposite directions. She took his cold hand and held it. They gave each other shy, tiny squeezes and rubbed each other's palms with absurdly small and sensitive finger movements.

"So you never told me what you gave Loki the love god."

"A cube of sugar. From the snack table."

"Aww."

"You should've seen the other guys. They went out and gathered bunches of clover, they cut valentines out of red handkerchiefs, somebody took off his pinkie ring. It was heartrending—and I don't mean pathetic. I mean, it was emotionally agonizing to see all that hope and want."

She absolutely loved him. She also doubted she would be involved with him for longer than a year or two. Instead of sadness, she experienced a pleasing visceral agitation that made her feel greedy. She inhaled with her mouth open and savored the cold intake on her palate.

"Come on, you big meatball," she said. "Let's get out of here. It's fucking freezing."

Inside, the restaurant was a triumph of controlled light and warmth. Most of its spacious rooms were newly vacant; there were half-eaten desserts on white plates, cups of cold, creamy coffee, and crushed napkins faintly marked with lipstick. In the central room, an enormous bunch of flowers rose up out of an enormous vase; beneath it, a handsomely dressed old couple lingered over bevelled glasses of liqueur, and a handsome waiter cleared a table with desultory grace. Laurel saw Lucille reach for the door, the knob slipping in her sweating hand before her grasp was obstructed; she rode home on a rattling subway train, eating a candy bar. The subway roared in the dark tunnel, the lights flickered off and on. A sharp pain shot up Laurel's calf and she grunted in surprise as she sat down hard, right over her twisted ankle.

"Oh, honey!" Evan exclaimed tenderly as he bent toward her.

The old people watched with subtle approval as Evan easily bore Laurel up in his arms. She embraced his neck and leaned into him. As he carried her out the door she looked over his shoulder; the bright beauty of the massive flower arrangement fairly hit her in the eye.

(1995)

GOODBYE MARCUS
GOODBYE ROSE

JEAN RHYS

"When first I wore my old shako," sang Captain
Cardew, "Ten, twenty, thirty, forty, fifty years ago,"
and Phoebe thought what a wonderful bass voice he
had. This was the second time he had called to take
her for a walk, and again he had brought her a large
box of chocolates.

Captain Cardew and his wife were spending the
winter of 1898 in Jamaica, when they visited the
small island of Dominica where she lived and found
it so attractive and unspoilt that they decided to stay.
They even talked of buying a house and settling
there for good.

He was not only a very handsome old man but a
hero who had fought bravely in some long-ago war
which she thought you only read about in history
books. He'd been wounded and had a serious opera-

tion without an anesthetic. Anesthetics weren't much used in those days. (Better not think too much about that.)

It had been impressed on her how kind it was of him to bother with a little girl like herself. Anyway, she liked him; he was always so carefully polite to her, treating her as though she were a grownup girl. A calm unruffled man, he grew annoyed only if people called him "Captain" too often. Sometimes he lost his temper and would say loudly things like: "What d'you think I'm Captain of now—a penny-a-liner?" What was a penny-a-liner? She never found out.

It was a lovely afternoon and they set out. She was wearing a white blouse with a sailor collar, a long full white skirt, black stockings, black buttoned boots, and a large wide-brimmed white hat anchored firmly under her chin with elastic.

When they reached the Botanical Gardens, she offered to take him to a shady bench and they walked slowly to the secluded part of the Gardens that she'd spoken of and sat under a large tree. Beyond its shadow they could see the yellow dancing patches of sunlight.

"Do you mind if I take off my hat? The elastic is hurting me," Phoebe said.

"Then take it off, take it off," said the Captain.

Phoebe took off her hat and began to talk in what she hoped was a grownup way about the curator, Mr. Harcourt-Smith, who'd really made the Gardens as beautiful as they were. He'd come from a place in England called the Kew. Had he ever heard of it?

Yes he had heard of it. He said, "How old are you, Phoebe?"

"I'm twelve," said Phoebe, "—and a bit."

"Ho!" said the Captain. "Then soon you'll be old enough to have a lover!" His hand, which had been lying quietly by his side, darted toward her, dived inside her blouse, and clamped itself around one very small breast. "Quite old enough," he remarked.

Phoebe remained perfectly still. He's making a great mistake, a great mistake, she thought. If I don't move he'll take his hand away without really noticing what he's done.

However the Captain showed no sign of that at all. He was breathing rather heavily when a couple came strolling round the corner. Calmly, without hurry, he withdrew his hand and after a while said, "Perhaps we ought to be going home now."

Phoebe, who was in a ferment, said nothing. They walked out of the shade into the sun, and as they walked she looked up at him as though at some aged but ageless god. He talked of usual things in a usual voice, and she made up her mind that she would tell nobody of what had happened. Nobody. It was not a thing you could possibly talk about. Also, no one would believe exactly how it had happened, and whether they believed her or not she would be blamed.

If he was as absentminded as all that—for surely it could be nothing but absentmindedness—perhaps there oughtn't to be any more walks. She could excuse herself by saying that she had a headache. But that would only do for once. The walks continued. They'd go into the Gardens or up the Morne, a hill overlooking the town. There were benches and seats there but few houses and hardly anybody about.

He never touched her again, but all through the long bright afternoons Captain Cardew talked of love and Phoebe listened, shocked and fascinated. Sometimes she doubted what he said: surely it was impossible, horrifyingly impossible. Sometimes she was on the point of saying not "You oughtn't to talk to me like this" but, babyishly, "I want to go home." He always knew when she felt this and would at once change the subject and tell her amusing stories of his life when he was a young man and a subaltern in India.

"Hot?" he'd say. "This isn't hot. India's hot. Sometimes the only thing to do is take off your clothes and see that the punkah's going."

Or he'd talk about London long ago. Someone—was it Byron?—had said that women were never so unattractive as when they were eating, and it was still most unfashionable for them to eat heartily. He'd watch in wonder as the ethereal creatures pecked daintily, then sent away almost untouched plates. One day he had seen a maid taking a tray laden with food up to the bedrooms, and the mystery was explained.

But these stories were only intervals in the ceaseless talk of love, various ways of making love, various sorts of love. He'd explain that love was not kind and gentle, as she had imagined, but violent. Violence, even cruelty, was an essential part of it. He would expand on this; it seemed to be his favorite subject.

The walks had gone on for some time when the Captain's wife, Edith, who was a good deal younger than her husband, became suspicious and began making very sarcastic remarks. Early one evening, when the entire party had gone up the Morne to watch the sunset, she'd said to her husband, after a long look at Phoebe, "Do you really find the game worth the candle?" Captain Cardew said nothing. He watched the sun going down without expression, then remarked that it was quite true that the only way to get rid of a temptation was to yield to it.

Phoebe had never liked Mrs. Cardew very much. Now she began to dislike her. One afternoon they were in a room together and Mrs. Cardew said, "Do you see how white my hair's becoming? It's all because of you." And when Phoebe answered truthfully that she didn't notice any white hairs: "What a really dreadful little liar you are!"

After this she must have spoken to Phoebe's mother, a silent, reserved woman, who said nothing to her daughter but began to watch her in a puzzled, incredulous, even faintly suspicious way. Phoebe knew that very soon she would be questioned; she'd have to explain.

So she was more than half relieved when Edith Cardew announced that they'd quite given up their first idea of spending the rest of the winter on the island and were going back to England by the next boat. When Captain Cardew said "Goodbye" formally the evening before they left, she had smiled and shaken hands, not quite realizing that she was very unlikely ever to see him again.

THERE WAS A flat roof outside her bedroom window. On hot fine nights she'd often lie there in her nightgown, looking up at the huge brilliant stars. She'd once tried to write a poem about them but not got beyond the first line: "My stars. Familiar jewels." But that night she knew that she would never finish it. They were not jewels. They were not familiar. They were cold, infinitely far away, quite indifferent.

The roof looked onto the yard and she could hear Victoria and Joseph talking and laughing outside the pantry; then they must have gone away and it was quite silent. She was alone in the house, for she'd not gone with the others to see the Cardews off. She was sure that now they had gone her mother would be very unlikely to question her, and then began to wonder how he had been so sure not only that she'd never tell anybody but that she'd make no effort at all to stop him talking. That could only mean that he'd seen at once that she was not a good girl—who would object—but a wicked one—who would listen. He must know. He knew. It was so.

It was so, and she felt not so much unhappy about this as uncomfortable, even dismayed. It was like wearing a dress that was much too big for her, a dress that swallowed her up.

Wasn't it quite difficult being a wicked girl? Even more difficult than being a good one? Besides, didn't the nuns say that Chastity in Thought, Word, and Deed was your most precious possession? She remembered Mother Sacred Heart, her second favorite, reciting in her lovely English voice: "So dear to Heaven is saintly chastity . . ." How did it go on? Something about "a thousand liveried angels lackey her. . . ."

"A thousand liveried angels" now no more. The thought of some vague irreparable loss saddened her. Then she told herself that anyway she needn't bother any longer about whether she'd get married or not. The older girls that she knew talked a great deal about marriage; some of them talked about very little else. And they seemed so sure. No sooner had they put their hair up and begun going to dances than they'd marry someone handsome (and rich). Then the fun of being grownup and important, of doing what you wanted instead of what you were told to do, would start. And go on for a long long time.

But she'd always doubted if this would happen to her. Even if numbers of rich and handsome young men suddenly appeared, would she be one of the chosen?

> If no one ever marries me—
> And I don't see why they should—
> For nurse says I'm not pretty
> And I'm seldom very good. . . .

Well there was one thing. Now she felt very wise, very grownup, and she could forget these childish worries. She could hardly believe that only a few weeks ago she, like all the others, had secretly made lists of her trousseau, decided on the names of her three children: Jack. Marcus. And Rose.

Now goodbye Marcus. Goodbye Rose. The prospect before her might be difficult and uncertain, but it was far more exciting.

(1976)

HOW TO GIVE THE WRONG IMPRESSION

KATHERINE HEINY

You never refer to Boris as your roommate, although of course that's exactly what he is. You're actually apartment mates and you only moved in together the way any two friends move in together for the school year, nothing romantic. Probably Boris would be horrified if he knew how you felt. You're a Psych major, you know this is unhealthy, but when you speak of him you always say Boris, or, better yet, This guy I live with. He may be just your roommate but not everyone has to know.

You buy change-of-address cards with a picture on the front, of a bear packing a trunk. You send them to your friends and your parents. After some hesitation, you write "Boris and Gwen" on the back, above the address. After all, he does live here.

You help Boris buy a bed. This is a great activity for you, it's almost like being engaged. You lie on display beds with him in furniture stores. Toward the end of the day, you are tired and spend longer and longer just resting on the beds.

Boris lies next to you, telling you about the time his sister peed in a display toilet at Sears when she was three. You glance at him sideways. He looks tired, too, although the whites of his eyes are still bright—the kind of eyes you thought only blue-eyed people had, but his eyes are brown.

A salesman approaches, sees you, smiles. He knocks on the frame of the bed with his knuckles. "Well, what do you folks think?" he asks.

Boris turns to you. You ask the salesman about interest rates, delivery fees, assembly charges. You never say, Well, it's your bed, Boris, in front of the salesman.

WHEN YOUR PARENTS come through town and offer to take you and Boris out to dinner, you accept. But this is risky, this all depends on whether you've implied anything to your parents beyond what was on the change-of-address card. You think about it and decide it's pretty safe, but you spend a great deal of time hoping your father will not ask Boris what his intentions are.

Boris, love of your life, goes to the salad bar three times and doesn't stick a black olive on each of his fingers, a thing he often does at home. On the way out, he holds your hand. You are the picture of young love. Boris may make the folks' annual Christmas letter.

You always have boyfriends. You try to get them taller than Boris, but it's not easy. Sometimes after they pick you up, they roll their shoulders uncomfortably in the elevator and say, Gwen, I think Boris is going to slash my tires or something, he's so jealous.

Snort. Oh, please, you say. Later, in a lull in the conversation, you ask casually, Why do you think Boris is so jealous of you? One of your boyfriends says it's because Boris found six hundred excuses to come into the living room while you two were drinking wine. Another one says it's the way Boris shook hands with him. This is interesting. You were still in your bedroom when that happened. Whatever they answer, you file it away and replay it later in your mind.

· · ·

YOU ALWAYS ENCOURAGE him to ask Dahlia Kosinski out.

When he comes back from his Ethics study group and says, Oh, my God, Dahlia looked so incredibly gorgeous tonight, you do not say, I heard she almost got kicked out of the Ethics class for sleeping with the professor. You say, I think you should ask her out.

Noooo, Boris says, drawing circles on the kitchen table with his pencil.

Sure, you say, Just pick up the phone. In fact, you do pick up the phone. You call information and get Dahlia's number. Say, Want me to dial?

Boris shakes his head. Let's go get something to eat, he says. He puts his arms around you and dances you away from the phone. You think that Dahlia Kosinski is probably too tall for Boris's chin to rest on her head like this.

You didn't write Dahlia's phone number down on the scratch pad by the phone when you called information, because you don't need Boris looking at it and mulling it over when you're not around. This whole procedure is nerve-racking, but not to worry—he'll never ask her out, and it's always, always better to know than to wonder.

IN PIGEON LAB, you name your pigeon after him because the two other girls name their pigeons after their husbands. You spend a lot of time making fun of Boris when these two other girls make fun of their husbands. This, as a matter of fact, is not hard to do.

You tell them about how he keeps a flare gun in the trunk of his car. Ask them how many times they think his car is going to break down in the middle of the Mojave Desert or at sea.

You tell them that he has this thing for notebooks. He keeps one in the glove compartment of his car and records all this information in it whenever he fills the gas tank. You say, I mean, there can be four hundred cars behind us at the gas station, honking, and there's Boris, frantically scribbling down the number of gallons and the price and everything.

They are so amused by this that you tell them he has another notebook where he records all the cash he spends. You say, If he leaves a waitress two dollars, he runs home and writes it down. You add, I'm surprised he doesn't also record the serial numbers.

Because this last part isn't even about Boris, it's about your father, worry that you are becoming a pathological liar.

YOU NEVER ACT jealous in front of Linette, his best friend from undergrad. She spends the day at your apartment on her way to a game she's going to be in. She plays basketball for some college in California.

She is as tall and slender as you feared and not as coarse and brawny as you wanted. You had hoped she would lope around the apartment, pick you up and chuck you to Boris, saying, Well, Bo, I guess we could toss a little thing like her right through the hoop.

Actually, Boris and Linette do go play some basketball, and when they come back, you all sit on the couch and drink beer. Linette puts her hand on Boris's thigh, which is lightly sweating, and you hope it's just from basketball. You resist the urge to put your hand on his other thigh. You imagine yourself and Linette frantically claiming Boris's body parts, slapping your hands on his legs, then his arms, then his chest. Only knowing how much pleasure he would get out of this keeps you from doing it.

Instead, you finish your beer in one long swig, anxious to show that you can drink right along with any basketball player, and you rise. You say, It's been nice to meet you, Linette, but I have to go, I have a date. You don't have boyfriends anymore, just dates.

Yes, you say again, I have to go get ready. You say this so Linette will believe that you are looking the way you normally look around the house, that you are actually about to go make yourself better-looking. She does not need to know that you're already wearing a lot of makeup, that this is about as good as it gets.

YOU PRETEND YOU don't want to kiss him. He calls from a bar on Halloween, too drunk to drive, when you are home studying. You drive to pick him up, wearing sweats and your glasses. You only wear your glasses on nights when you don't plan to see him.

He sings on the ride home, pulling on your braid. Wonder why he's in such a good mood. Was Dahlia Kosinski at this bar?

In the kitchen, he drinks your orange juice out of the carton. You say, Put that back.

Boris says, Too late, and holds the carton upside down to demonstrate. Three drops of orangey water fall on the floor.

Damn, you say and throw the sponge on the floor. This is a good indication of how irritable you are, because the floor was already sticky enough to rip your socks off.

I'm sorry, Gwen, Boris says, I'll go get more tomorrow, I promise.

Forget it, you say, rubbing the sponge around with your toe.

If you forgive me, I'll kiss you, Boris says.

Now you don't even have to pretend you don't want to kiss him, because, you have to face it, that was pretty obnoxious.

Oh, spare me, you say, and cross your arms over your chest. Boris leans over and kisses you on the eyebrow. Don't in any way change your posture, but you can close your eyes.

He touches your lips with his tongue. Wonder why you have to suffer this mutant behavior on top of everything else. He must look like someone trying to be the Human Mosquito. Does this even count as a kiss? This is a very good question, and you will spend no small amount of time pondering it.

BORIS CUTS HIMSELF shaving and leaves big drops of blood on the sink. You approach cautiously; it looks as if a small animal had been murdered.

You consider your options. You could point silently but dramatically at the sink when Boris returns. You could leave him an amused but firm note, "Dear Boris, I don't even want to know what happened in here. . . ." Or you can do nothing and assume that he'll eventually do something about it. That is probably your best option. But what if he thinks you left it there? What if he thinks you shave your legs in the sink or something? Best to clean it up and not mention it. This you do, pushing a paper towel around the sink with a spoon.

YOU TAKE BORIS home for Thanksgiving dinner. All goes smoothly except for your grandmother glaring at him after the turkey is carved and announcing, The one thing I will not tolerate is this living together, and I say that aloud for all the young people to hear.

Boris looks up from his turkey drumstick like a startled wolf cub, a spot of grease smeared on his cheek.

Later, when you are walking back toward the train station, he says, What did your grandmother mean by that?

Hoot. You say, I don't know, but the way she said "all the young people" made it sound like there were a whole group of young people, drinking beer or something.

Boris is not to be distracted. The thing is, he says, we aren't living together in *that* way.

You try not to wince. You do shiver. You take Boris's hand as he bounds along on his long legs, your signal that he either has to slow down or pull you along. He tucks both your hand and his hand into the pocket of his jacket. You look up at his face out of the corner of your eye. In the cold, you watch him breathe perfect plumes of white that match the sheepskin lining of his jacket. You think how happy you would be if Boris thought you were half as beautiful as you think he is at this moment.

You walk this way for a few minutes. Then he tells you that your hand is sweating, making a lake in his pocket, and gives you his gloves to wear.

YOU TAKE TO going out with Boris for frozen yogurt almost every night at about midnight. You are always the last people in the yogurt place, and the guy who works there closes up around you. Tonight Boris says, Gwen, you have hot fudge in the corner of your mouth, and wipes it away, hard, with the ball of his thumb. Wonder if you feel too comfortable with him to truly be in love.

But then he licks the fudge off his thumb and smiles at you, his hair still ruffled from the wind outside. He is the love of your life, no question about it.

For Christmas, you buy Boris a key chain. This is what you had always imagined you would give a boyfriend someday, a key chain with a key to your apartment. Only it's not exactly a parallel situation with Boris, of course, in that he's not your boyfriend and he already has a key to your apartment, because he lives there. O.K., you admit it, there are no parallels other than that you are giving him a key chain.

Still, you can tell the guy in the jewelry store anything you like. Go ahead, say it: This is for my boyfriend, do you think he'll like it?

For Christmas, Boris gives you a framed poster of the four major food groups. You amuse yourself by trying to think of one single more unromantic gift he could have given you. You amuse yourself by wondering if you can make this into an anecdote for the girls in Pigeon Lab.

When people ask you what Boris gave you for Christmas, you smile shyly and insinuate that you were both too broke to afford much.

THE GIRLS IN Pigeon Lab have a Valentine's Day party and invite you and Boris. Probably you shouldn't show him the invitation, since his name is on it and he might wonder why you and he are invited as a couple. Just say, Look, I have a party to go to, want to come?

Sure, Boris says, and the best part of the whole thing is that this way you know without asking that he doesn't have plans with someone else.

You don't have boyfriends anymore, and these days you don't even have dates. You tell Boris this is because you have too much work to do, and often on Saturday nights you make a big production of hauling your Psychology of Women textbook out to the sofa and propping it on your lap, even though it hurts your thighs and you never read it.

Instead, you talk to Boris, who is similarly positioned on the other end of the sofa, his feet touching yours. Sometimes he lies with his head in your lap and falls asleep that way. You never get up and leave him; you stay, touching his hair, idly clicking through the channels, watching late-night rodeo.

One night Boris wakes up during the calf roping. Oh, my God, he says, watching a calf do a four-legged split, its heavy head wobbling, This is breaking my heart.

THIS THING WITH Dahlia Kosinski reminds you of a book you read as a child, "Good News, Bad News."

The good news is the Ethics study group has a party and Boris invites you to go. The bad news is that Dahlia Kosinski is there and she's beautiful in a careless, sloppy way you know you never will be: shaggy black hair, too much black eyeliner, a leopard-print dress with a stain on the shoulder. You know that her nylons have a big run somewhere and she doesn't even care. The good news is that Dahlia has heard of you. Hello, she says, Are you Gwen? The bad news is that she makes some joke about a book she read once called "Gwendolyn the Miracle Hen," and Boris laughs. The good news is that Dahlia has what appears to be a very serious boyfriend. The bad news is that they have a fight in the bathroom, so maybe they're not really in love. The worse news is that in the car on the way home Boris says, I don't think Dahlia will ever leave that boyfriend of hers. Everyone I've talked to says they're very serious—which means that he's looked into Dahlia's love life, he's made inquiries. Wonder how there can be a bad news followed by a worse news. Does that ever happen in the book? Bad news: you're pushed out of an airplane. Worse news: you don't have a parachute?

BORIS TELLS YOU that one night he stopped by the frozen-yogurt place without you and the guy behind the counter made some sort of pass at him and wanted to know if you were Boris's girlfriend.

Ask, What did you tell him?

What choice did I have? Boris says in a tone that crushes you like a grape.

Linette stops by again. This time she spends the night, disappearing into Boris's room with a six-pack. You hear them laughing in there. Whatever else you do, call someone and go out that night.

When you are in the kitchen the next morning, Boris wanders out. You ask him how he feels. Tired, he says. Linette kept me up all night talking about whether she should go to grad school or not.

Wonder if he's telling the truth. Say, Should she?

God, no, Boris says, She's such a birdbrain.

Oh, you say loudly, over the banging of your heart.

YOU CLEAN THE bathroom late one night after Boris has gone to bed. You wear a T-shirt and a pair of Boris's boxer shorts that you stole out of a bag of stuff he's been planning to take to the Salvation Army. It gives you immense pleasure to wear these boxer shorts, but you only wear them after he's gone to bed, and you never sleep in them. You do have some pride.

Your cleaning is ambitious: you wipe the tops of the doors, the inside of the shower curtain; you even unscrew the drain and pull out a hair ball the size of a rat terrier. It is so amazing that you consider taking a picture with your smiling face next to it for size reference, but in the end you just throw it out.

You are standing on the edge of the tub, balancing a bowl of hot, soapy water on your hip and swiping at the shower-curtain rod with a sponge when Boris walks in and says, Well, hello, Mrs. Clean.

You smile. He yawns. Do you need some help? he says.

You let him hold the bowl of water while you turn your back to him and reach up and run the sponge along the shower-curtain rod.

I never knew you had to clean those, Boris says. I can't believe it's one in the morning. I feel like we're married and this is our first apartment or something.

Your throat closes. Until this moment you had not thought about the fact that this *was* your and Boris's first apartment, that once the lease is up there might not be a second apartment, and you might not see him every day.

Hey, says Boris, You're wearing my boxer shorts. He puts the bowl of water on the sink and turns the waistband inside out so he can read the tag. They are! he says, delighted.

You freeze. Clear your throat. Yeah, well, you say.

Even standing on the edge of the tub, you are only a few inches taller than Boris, and he slides an arm around your waist. He brushes your hair forward over your shoulders and traces a V on your back for a long moment, as though you were a mannequin and he were a fashion de-signer contemplating some new creation.

Then you feel him kiss the back of your neck above your T-shirt. You remember Halloween and think about saying, Boris, are those your lips? but you don't. You don't do anything. You still haven't moved, your arms are over your head, hands braced against the rod.

You're so funny, Gwen, Boris whispers against your skin.

Really, you say. A drop of soapy water lands on your eyelid, soft as cotton, warm as wax. Me?

(1990)

Marito in Città

John Cheever

Some years ago there was a popular song in Italy called "Mariti in Città." The air was as simple and catching as a street song. The words went: "*La moglie se ne va, il marito resta qua, il povero marito, solo in città,*" and dealt with the plight of a married man alone, in the lighthearted and farcical manner that seems traditional, as if to be alone were an essentially comic situation such as getting tangled up in a trout line. Mr. Estabrook had heard the song while travelling in Europe with his wife (fourteen days, ten cities), and some capricious tissue of his memory had taken an indelible impression of the words and the music. He had not forgotten it; indeed, it seemed that he could not forget it, although it was in conflict with his regard for the possibilities of aloneness.

The scene, the moment when his wife and four children left for the mountains, had the charm, the air of ordination, and the deceptive simplicity of an old-fashioned magazine cover. One could have guessed at it all—the summer morning, the station wagon, the bags, the clear-eyed children, the filled coin rack for toll stations, some ceremonious observation of a change in the season, another ring in the planet's age. He shook hands with his sons and kissed his wife and his daughters and watched the car move along the driveway with a feeling that this instant was momentous, that had he been given the ability to scrutinize the forces that were involved he would have arrived at something like a revelation. The women and children of Rome, Paris, London, and New York were, he knew, on their way to the highlands or the sea. It was a weekday, and so he locked Scamper, the dog, in the kitchen and drove to the station singing, "*Marito in città, la moglie se ne va,*" et cetera, et cetera.

One knows how it will go, of course—it will never quite transcend the farcical strictures of a street song—but Mr. Estabrook's aspirations were earnest, fresh, and worth observing. He was familiar with the vast and evangelical literature of solitude, and he intended to exploit the weeks of his aloneness. He could clean his telescope and study the stars. He could read. He could practice the Bach two-part inventions on the piano. He could—so like an expatriate who claims that the limpidity and sometimes the anguish of his estrangement promise a high degree of self-discovery—learn more about himself. He would observe the migratory habits of birds, the changes in the garden, the clouds in the sky. He had a distinct image of himself, his powers of observation greatly heightened by the adventure of aloneness.

When he got home on his first night, he found that Scamper had got out of the kitchen and slept on a sofa in the living room, which he had covered with mud and hair. Scamper was a mongrel, the children's pet. Mr. Estabrook spoke reproachfully to the dog and turned up the sofa cushions. The next problem that he faced was one that is seldom touched on in the literature of solitude—the problem of his rudimentary appetites. This was to sound, in spite of himself, the note of low comedy. *O marito in città!* He could imagine himself in clean chinos, setting up his telescope in the garden at dusk, but he could not imagine who was going to feed this self-possessed figure.

He fried himself some eggs, but he found that he couldn't eat them. He made an Old-Fashioned cocktail with particular care and drank it. Then he returned to the eggs, but he still found them revolting. He drank another cocktail and approached the eggs from a different direction, but they were still repulsive. He gave the eggs to Scamper and drove out to the state highway, where there was a restaurant. The music, when he entered the place, seemed as loud as parade music, and a waitress was standing on a chair, stringing curtains onto a rod. "I'll be with you in a minute," she said. "Sit down anywheres." He chose a place at one of the empty tables. He was not actually disappointed in his situation; he had by design surrounded himself with a large number of men, women, and children, and it was only natural that he should feel then, as he did, not alone but lonely. Considering the physical and spiritual repercussions of this condition, it seemed strange to him that there was only one word for it. He was lonely, and he was in pain. The food was not just bad; it seemed incredible. Here was that total absence of recollection that is the essence of tastelessness. He could eat nothing. He stirred up his stringy pepper steak and ordered some ice cream, to spare the feelings of the waitress. The food reminded him of all those who through clumsiness or bad luck must make their lives alone and eat this fare each night. It was frightening, and he went to a drive-in movie.

The long summer dusk still filled the air with a soft light. The wishing star hung above the enormous screen, canted a little toward the audience with a certain air of doom. Faded in the fading light, the figures and animals of a cartoon chased one another across the screen, exploded, danced, sang, pratfell. The fanfare and the credits for the feature, for what he had come to see, went on through the last of the twilight, and then, as night fell, a screenplay of incredible asininity began to unfold. His moral indignation at this confluence of hunger, boredom, and loneliness was violent, and he thought sadly of the men who had been obliged to write the movie, and of the hard-working actors who were paid to repeat these crude lines. He could see them at the end of the day, getting out of their convertibles in Beverly Hills, utterly discouraged. Fifteen minutes was all he could stand, and he went home.

Scamper had shifted from the dismantled sofa to a chair, whose light silk covering he had dirtied with hair and mud. "Bad Scamper," Mr. Estabrook said, and then he took those precautions to save the furniture that he was to repeat each night. He upended a footstool on the sofa, upended the silk chairs, put a wastebasket on the love seat in the hallway, and put the upholstered dining-room chairs upside down on the table, as they do in restaurants when the floor is being mopped. With the lights off and everything upside down, the permanence of his house was challenged, and he felt for a moment like a ghost who has come back to see time's ruin.

Lying in bed, he thought, quite naturally, of his wife. He had learned, from experience, that it was sensible to make their separations ardent, and on the night but one before she left he had declared himself; but Mrs. Estabrook had responded with an exasperated sigh. She was tired. On the next night, he declared himself again. Mrs. Estabrook seemed acquiescent, but what she then did was to go down to the kitchen, put four heavy blankets into the washing machine, blow a fuse, and flood the floor. Standing in the kitchen doorway, utterly unaccommodated, he wondered why she did this. She had merely meant to be elusive! Watching her, a dignified but rather heavy woman, mopping up the kitchen floor, he thought that she had wanted, like any nymph, to run through the bosky wood—dappled her back, the water flashing at her feet—and, being short-winded these days, and there being no bosky wood, she had been reduced to putting blankets into a washing machine. It had never crossed his mind before that the passion to be elusive was as strong in her sex as the passion to pursue was in his. This glimpse of things moved him; contented him, in a way; but was, as it so happened, the only contentment he had that night.

THE IMAGE OF a cleanly, self-possessed man exploiting his solitude was not easy to come by, but then he had not expected that it would be. On the next night, he practiced the two-part inventions until eleven. On the night after that, he got out his telescope. He had been unable to solve the problem of feeding himself, and in the space of a week had lost more than fifteen pounds. His trousers, when he belted them in around his middle, gathered in folds like a skirt. He took three pairs of trousers down to the dry cleaner's in the village. It was past closing time, but the proprietor was still there, a man crushed by life. He had torn Mrs.

Hazelton's lace pillowcases and lost Mr. Fitch's silk shirts. His equipment was in hock, the union wanted health insurance, and everything that he ate—even yoghurt—seemed to turn to fire in his esophagus. He spoke despairingly to Mr. Estabrook. "We don't keep a tailor on the premises no more, but there's a woman up on Maple Avenue who does alterations. Mrs. Zagreb. It's at the corner of Maple Avenue and Clinton Street. There's a sign in the window."

It was a dark night and that time of year when there are many fireflies. Maple Avenue was what it claimed to be, and the dense foliage doubled the darkness on the street. The house on the corner was frame, with a porch. The maples were so thick there that no grass grew on the lawn. There was a sign—"Alterations"—in the window. He rang a bell. "Just a minute," someone called. The voice was strong and gay. A woman opened the door with one hand, rubbing a towel in her dark hair with the other. She seemed surprised to see him. "Come in," she said, "come in. I've just washed my hair." There was a small hall, and he followed her through this into a small living room. "I have some trousers that I want taken in," he said. "Do you do that kind of thing?"

"I do everything." She laughed. "But why are you losing weight? Are you on a diet?"

She had put down her towel, but she continued to shake her hair and rough it with her fingers. She moved around the room while she talked, and seemed to fill the room with restlessness—a characteristic that might have annoyed him in someone else but that in her seemed graceful, fascinating, the prompting of some inner urgency.

"I'm not dieting," he said.

"You're not ill?" Her concern was swift and genuine; he might have been her oldest friend.

"Oh, no. It's just that I've been trying to cook for myself."

"Oh, you poor boy," she said. "Do you know your measurements?"

"No."

"Well, we'll have to take them."

Moving, stirring the air and shaking her hair, she crossed the room and got a yellow tape measure from a drawer. In order to measure his waist she had to put her hands under his jacket—a gesture that seemed amorous. When the measure was around his waist, he put his arms around her waist and thrust himself against her. She merely laughed and shook her hair. Then she pushed him away lightly—much more like a promise than a rebuff. "Oh, no," she said, "not tonight, not tonight, my dear." She crossed the room and faced him from there. Her face was tender, and darkened with indecision, but when he came toward her she hung her head, shook it vigorously. "No, no, no," she said. "Not tonight. Please."

"But I can see you again?"

"Of course, but not tonight." She crossed the room and laid her hand against his cheek. "Now, you go," she said, "and I'll call you. You're very nice, but now you go."

He stumbled out of the door, stunned but feeling wonderfully important. He had been in the room three minutes—four at the most—and what had there been between them, this instantaneous recognition of their fitness as lovers? He had been excited when he first saw her—had been excited by her strong, gay voice. Why had they been able to move so effortlessly, so directly toward one another? And where was his sense of good and evil, his passionate desire to be worthy, manly, and, within his vows, chaste? He was a member of the Church of Christ, he was a member of the vestry, a devout and habitual communicant, sincerely sworn to defend the articles of faith. He had already committed a mortal sin. But driving under the maples and through the summer night, he could not, under the most intense examination, find anything in his instincts but goodness and magnanimity and a much enlarged sense of the world. He struggled with some scrambled eggs, practiced the inventions, and tried to sleep. *O marito in città!*

It was the memory of Mrs. Zagreb's front that tormented him. Its softness and fragrance seemed to hang in the air while he waited for sleep, it followed into his dreams, and when he woke his face seemed buried in Mrs. Zagreb's front, glistening like marble and tasting to his thirsty lips as various and soft as the airs of a summer night.

IN THE MORNING, he took a cold shower, but Mrs. Zagreb's front seemed merely to wait outside the shower curtain. It rested against his cheek as he drove to the train, read over his shoulder as he rode the eight-thirty-three, jiggled along with him through the shuttle and the downtown train, and haunted him through the business day. He thought he was going mad.

As soon as he got home, he looked up her number in the *Social Register* that his wife kept by the telephone. This was a mistake, of course, but he found her number in the local directory and called her. "Your trousers are ready," she said. "You can come and get them whenever you want. Now, if you'd like."

She called for him to come in. He found her in the living room, and she handed him his trousers. Then he was shy and wondered if he hadn't invented the night before. Here, with his shyness, was the truth, and all the rest had been imagining. Here was a widowed seamstress handing some trousers to a lonely man, no longer young, in a frame house that needed paint, on Maple Avenue. The world was ruled by common sense, legitimate passions, and articles of faith. She shook her head. This then was a mannerism and had nothing to do with washing her hair. She pushed it off her forehead; ran her fingers through the dark curls. "If you have time for a drink," she said, "there's everything in the kitchen."

"I'd love a drink," he said. "Will you have one with me?"

"I'll have a whiskey-and-soda," she said.

Feeling sad, heavyhearted, important, caught up on those streams of feeling that never surface, he went into the kitchen and made their drinks. When he came back into the room, she was sitting on a sofa, and he joined her there; seemed immersed in her mouth, as if it was a maelstrom; spun around thrice and sped down the length of some stupendous timelessness. The dialogue of sudden love doesn't seem to change much from country to country. We say across the pillow, in any language, "Hullo, hullo, hullo, hullo, hullo," as if we were involved in some interminable and tender transoceanic telephone conversation, and the adulteress, taking the adulterer into her arms, will cry, "Oh, my love, why are you so bitter?" She praised his hair, his neck, the declivity in his back. She smelled faintly of soap—no perfume—and when he said so, she said softly, "But I never wear perfume when I'm going to make love."

They went side by side up the narrow stairs to her bedroom—the largest room in a small house, but small at that, and sparsely furnished, like a room in a summer cottage, with old furniture that had been painted white and with a worn white rug. Her suppleness, her wiles, seemed to him like a staggering source of purity. He thought he had never known so pure, gallant, courageous, and easy a spirit. So they kept saying "Hullo, hullo, hullo, hullo" until three, when she made him leave.

He walked in his garden at half past three or four. There was a quarter moon, the air was soft and the light vaporous, the clouds formed like a beach and the stars strewn among them like shells and moraines. Some flower that blooms in July—phlox or nicotiana—had scented the air, and the meaning of the vaporous light had not much changed since he was an adolescent; it now, as it had then, seemed to hold out the opportunities of romantic love. But what about the strictures of his faith? He had broken a sacred commandment, broken it repeatedly, joyously, and would break it at every opportunity he was given; therefore, he had committed a mortal sin and must be denied the sacraments of his church. But he could not alter the feeling that Mrs. Zagreb, in her knowledgeableness, represented uncommon purity and virtue and that his wife represented something less. But if these were his genuine feelings, then he must resign from the vestry, the church, improvise his own schemes of good and evil, and look for a life beyond the articles of faith. Had he known other adulterers to take Communion? He had. Was his church a social convenience, a form of hypocrisy, a means of getting ahead? Were the stirring words said at weddings and funerals no more than customs and no more religious than the custom of taking off one's hat in the elevator at Brooks Brothers when a woman enters the car? Christened, reared, and drilled in church dogma, the thought of giving up his faith was unimaginable. It was his best sense of the miraculousness of life, the receipt of a vigorous and omniscient love, widespread and incandescent as the light of day. Should he ask the suffragan bishop to reassess the Ten Commandments, to include in their prayers some special reference to the feelings of magnanimity and love that follow sexual engorgements?

He walked in the garden, conscious of the fact that she had at least given him the illusion of playing an important romantic role, a lead—a thrilling improvement over the sundry messengers, porters, and clowns of monogamy—and there was no doubt about the fact that her praise had turned his head. Was her excitement over the declivity in his back cunning, sly, a pitiless exploitation of the enormous and deep-buried vanity in men? The sky had begun to lighten, and, undressing for bed, he looked at himself in the mirror. Yes, her praise had all been lies. His abdomen had a dismal sag. Or had it? He held it in, distended it, examined it full face and profile, and went to bed.

THE NEXT DAY was Saturday, and he made a schedule for himself. Cut the lawn, clip the hedges, split some firewood, and paint the storm windows. He worked contentedly until five, when he took a shower and made a drink. His plan was to scramble some eggs and, since the sky was clear, set up his telescope, but when he had finished his drink he went humbly to the telephone and called Mrs. Zagreb. He called her at intervals of fifteen minutes until after dark, and then he got into his car and drove over to Maple Avenue. A light was burning in her bedroom. The rest of the house was dark. A large car with a state seal beside the license plate was parked under the maples, and the chauffeur was asleep in the front seat.

He had been asked to take the collection at Holy Communion, and so the next morning he did, but when he got to his knees to make his general confession he could not admit that what he had done was an offense to divine majesty. The burden of his sins was not intolerable; the memory of them was anything but grievous. He improvised a heretical thanksgiving for the constancy and intelligence of his wife, the clear eyes of his children, and the suppleness of his mistress. He did not take Communion, and when the priest fired a questioning look in his direction he was tempted to say clearly, "I am unashamedly involved in an adultery." He read the papers until three, when he called Mrs. Zagreb, and she said he could come whenever he wanted. He was there in ten minutes, and made her bones crack as soon as he entered the house. "I came by last night," he said.

"I thought you might," she said. "I know a lot of men. Do you mind?"

"Not at all," he said.

"I know a lot of men," she said. "Someday I'm going to write everything I know about men on a piece of paper and burn it in the fireplace."

"You don't have a fireplace," he said.

"That's so," she said, but they said nothing much else for the rest of the afternoon and half the night but "Hullo, hullo, hullo, hullo."

. . .

WHEN HE CAME home the next evening, there was a letter from his wife on the hall table. He seemed to see directly through the envelope into its contents. In it she would explain intelligently and dispassionately that her old lover, Olney Pratt, had returned from Saudi Arabia and asked her to marry him. She wanted her freedom, and she hoped he would understand. She and Olney had never ceased loving one another, and they would be dishonest to their innermost selves if they denied this love another day. She was sure they could reach an agreement on the custody of the children. He had been a good provider and a patient man, but she did not wish ever to see him again.

He held the letter in his hand, thinking that his wife's handwriting expressed her femininity, her intelligence, her depth; it was the hand of a woman asking for freedom. He tore the letter open, fully prepared to read about Olney Pratt, but he read instead: "Dear Lover-bear, the nights are *terribly* cold, and I *miss* . . ." On and on it went for two pages. He was still reading when the doorbell rang. It was Doris Hamilton, a neighbor. "I know you don't answer the telephone, and I know you don't like to dine out," she said, "but I'm determined that you should have at least one good dinner this month, and I've come to shanghai you."

"Well," he said.

"Now, you march upstairs and take a shower, and I'll make myself a drink," she said. "We're going to have hot boiled lobster. Aunt Molly sent down a bushel this morning, and you'll have to help us eat them. Eddie has to go to the doctor after dinner, and you can go home whenever you like."

He went upstairs and did as he was told. When he had changed and come down, she was in the living room with a drink, and they drove over to her house in separate cars. They dined by candlelight off a table in the garden, and, washed and in a clean duck suit, he found himself contented with the role he had so recently and so passionately abdicated. It was not a romantic lead, but it had some subtle prominence. After dinner, Eddie excused himself and went off to see his psychiatrist, as he did three nights each week. "I don't suppose you've seen anyone," Doris said. "I don't suppose you know the gossip."

"I really haven't seen anyone."

"I know. I've heard you practicing the piano. Well, Lois Spinner is suing Frank, and suing the buttons off him."

"Why?"

"Well, he's been carrying on with this disgusting slut, a perfectly disgusting woman. His older son, Ralph—he's a marvellous boy—saw them together in a restaurant. They were *feeding* one another. None of the children ever want to see him again."

"Men have had mistresses before," he said tentatively.

"Adultery is a mortal sin," she said gaily, "and was punished in many societies with death."

"Do you feel this strongly about divorce?"

"Oh, he had no intention of marrying the pig. He simply thought he could play his dirty games, humiliate, disgrace, and wound his family, and return to their affections when he got bored. The divorce was not his idea. He's begged Lois not to divorce him. I believe he's threatened to kill himself."

"I've known men," he said, "to divide their attentions between a mistress and a wife."

"I daresay you've never known it to be done successfully," she said.

The fell truth in this had never quite appeared to him. "Adultery is a commonplace," he said. "It is the subject of most of our literature, most of our plays, our movies. Popular songs are written about it."

"You wouldn't want to confuse your life with a French farce, would you?"

The authority with which she spoke astonished him. Here was the irresistibility of the lawful world, the varsity team, the best club. Suddenly the image of Mrs. Zagreb's bedroom, whose bleakness had seemed to him so poignant, returned to him in an unsavory light. He remembered that the window curtains were torn and that those hands that had so praised him were coarse and stubby. The promiscuity that he had thought to be the wellspring of her pureness now seemed to be an incurable illness. The kindnesses she had shown him seemed perverse and disgusting. She had grovelled before his nakedness. Sitting in the summer night, in his clean clothes, he thought of Mrs. Estabrook, serene and refreshed, leading her four intelligent and handsome children across some gallery in his head. Adultery was the raw material of farce, popular music, madness, and self-destruction.

"It was terribly nice of you to have had me," he said. "And now I think I'll run along. I'll practice the piano before I go to bed."

"I'll listen," said Doris. "I can hear it quite clearly across the garden."

The telephone was ringing when he came in. "I'm alone," said Mrs. Zagreb, "and I thought you might like a drink." He was there in a few minutes, went once more to the bottom of the sea, into that stupendous timelessness, secured against the pain of living. But when it was time to go, he said that he could not see her again. "That's perfectly all right," she said. And then, "Did anyone ever fall in love with you?"

"Yes," he said, "once. It was a couple of years ago. I had to go out to Indianapolis to set up a training schedule, and I had to stay with these people—it was part of the job—and there was this terribly nice woman, and every time she saw me she'd start crying. She cried at breakfast. She cried all through cocktails and dinner. It was awful. I had to move to a hotel, and naturally I couldn't ever tell anyone."

"Good night," she said. "Good night and goodbye."

"Good night, my love," he said. "Good night and goodbye."

His wife called on Thursday night while he was setting up the telescope. Oh, what excitement! They were driving down the next day. His daughter was going to announce her engagement to Frank Emmet. They wanted to be married before Christmas. Photographs had to be taken, announcements sent to the papers, a tent must be rented, wine ordered, et cetera. And his son had won the sailboat races on Monday, Tuesday, and Wednesday. "Good night, my darling," his wife said, and he fell into a chair, profoundly gratified at this requital of so many of his aspirations. He loved his daughter, he liked Frank Emmet, he even liked Frank Emmet's parents, who were rich, and the thought of his beloved son at the tiller, bringing his boat first down the last tack toward the committee launch, filled him with great cheer. And Mrs. Zagreb? She wouldn't know how to sail. She would get tangled up in the mainsheet, vomit to windward, and pass out in the cabin once they were past the point. She wouldn't know how to play tennis. Why, she wouldn't even know how to ski! Then, watched by Scamper, he dismantled the living room. In the hallway, he put a wastebasket on the love seat. In the dining room, he up-ended the chairs on the table and turned out the lights. Walking through the dismantled house, he felt again the chill and bewilderment of some-one who has come back to see time's ruin. Then he went up to bed, singing, "*Marito in città, la moglie se ne va, il povero marito!*"

(1964)

The Jack Randa Hotel

***

Alice Munro

On the runway, in Honolulu, the plane loses speed, loses heart, falters, and veers onto the grass and bumps to a stop. A few yards, it seems, from the ocean. Inside, everybody laughs. First a hush, then the laugh. Gail laughed herself. Then there was a flurry of introductions all around.

Beside Gail are Larry and Phyllis, from Spokane.

Larry and Phyllis are going to a tournament of Left-handed Golfers, in Fiji, as are many other couples on this plane. It is Larry who is the Left-handed Golfer—Phyllis is the wife going along to watch and cheer and have fun.

They sit on the plane—Gail and the Left-handed Golfers—and lunch is served in picnic boxes. No drinks. Dreadful heat. Jokey and confusing announcements are made from the cockpit. *Sorry about the prob-*

lem. Nothing serious, but it looks like it will keep us stewing here a while longer. Phyllis has a terrible headache, which Larry tries to cure by applying finger pressure to points on her wrist and palm.

"It's not working," Phyllis says. "I could have been in New Orleans by now with Suzy."

Larry says, "Poor lamb."

Gail catches the fierce glitter of diamond rings as Phyllis pulls her hand away.

Wives have diamond rings and headaches, Gail thinks. They still do. The truly successful ones do. They have chubby husbands, left-handed golfers, bent on a lifelong course of appeasement.

Eventually the passengers who are not going to Fiji but on to Sydney are taken off the plane. They are led into the terminal and there are deserted by their airline guide. They wander about, retrieving their baggage and going through Customs, trying to locate the airline that is supposed to honor their tickets. At one point, they are accosted by a welcoming committee from one of the island's hotels, who will not stop singing Hawaiian songs and flinging garlands around their necks. But they find themselves on another plane at last, and they eat and drink and sleep, and the lines to the toilets lengthen and the aisles fill up with debris and the flight attendants hide in their cubbyholes chatting about children and boyfriends. Then comes the unsettling bright morning and the yellow-sanded coast of Australia far below, and the wrong time of day, and even the best-dressed, best-looking passengers are haggard and unwilling, torpid, as from a long trip in steerage. And before they can leave the plane there is one more assault. Hairy men in shorts swarm aboard and spray everything with insecticide.

"So maybe this is the way it will be getting into Heaven," Gail imagines herself saying to Will. "People will fling flowers on you that you don't want, and everybody will have headaches and be constipated and then you will have to be sprayed for Earth germs."

This is her old habit—trying to think of clever and lighthearted things to say to Will.

AFTER WILL WENT away, it seemed to Gail that her shop was filling up with women. Not necessarily buying clothes. She didn't mind this. It was like the long-ago days, before Will. Women were sitting around in the ancient armchairs beside Gail's ironing board and cutting table, behind the faded batik curtains, drinking coffee. Gail started grinding the coffee beans herself, as she used to do. The dressmaker's dummy was soon draped with beads and had a scattering of scandalous graffiti. Stories were told about men, usually about men who had left. Lies and injustices and confrontations. Betrayals so horrific—yet so trite—that you could only rock with laughter when you heard about them. Men made fatuous speeches (*I am sorry, but I no longer feel committed to this marriage*), they offered to sell back to the wives cars and furniture that the wives themselves had paid for. They capered about in self-satisfaction because they had managed to impregnate some dewy dollop of womanhood younger than their own children. They were fiendish and childish. What could you do but give up on them? In all honor, in pride, and for your own protection?

Gail's enjoyment of all this palled rather quickly. Too much coffee could make your skin look livery. An underground quarrel developed among the women when it turned out that one of them had placed an ad in the Personal Column. Gail shifted from coffee with friends to drinks with Cleata, Will's mother. As she did this, oddly enough, her spirits grew more sober. Some giddiness still showed in the notes she pinned to her door so she could get away early on summer afternoons. (Her clerk Donalda was on her holiday, and it was too much trouble to hire anybody else.)

Gone to the Opera.

Gone to the Funny Farm.

Gone to stock up on Sackcloth and Ashes.

Actually, these were not her own inventions but things Will used to write out and tape on her door in the early days, when they wanted to go upstairs.

She heard that such flippancy was not appreciated by people who had driven some distance to buy a dress for a wedding, or girls on an expedition to buy clothes for college. She did not care.

On Cleata's veranda Gail was soothed. She became vaguely hopeful. Like most serious drinkers, Cleata stuck to one drink—hers was Scotch—and seemed amused by variations. But she would make Gail a gin-and-tonic, a white-rum-and-soda. She introduced her to tequila.

"This is heaven," Gail sometimes said, meaning not just the drink but the screened veranda and hedged back yard, the old house behind them with its shuttered windows, varnished floors, inconveniently high kitchen cupboards, and out-of-date flowered curtains. (Cleata despised decorating.) This was the house where Will, and Cleata, too, had been born, and when Will first brought Gail into it she had thought, This is how really civilized people live. The carelessness and propriety combined, the respect for old books and old dishes. The absurd things that Will and Cleata thought it natural to talk about. And the things they didn't talk about. In Cleata's house, even now, Gail knows that she is not supposed to mention Will's present defection, or the illness that has made Cleata's arms and legs look like varnished twigs within their deep tan, and has hollowed the cheeks framed by her looped-back white hair. She and Will have the same slightly monkeyish face, with dreamy, mocking dark eyes.

WHEN SHE MET Will and Cleata, Gail thought they were like characters in a book. A son living with his mother, apparently contentedly, into middle age. Gail saw a life that was ceremonious and enviable, with at least the appearance of celibate grace and safety. She still sees some of that, though the truth is complicated. Will had not always lived at home, and he is neither celibate nor discreetly homosexual. He had been gone for years, into his own life—working for the National Film Board in Montreal and the Canadian Broadcasting Corporation in Toronto—and had given that up only recently when Gail met him, to come back to Walley and be a teacher. What made him give it up? This and that, he had said. Machiavellis here and there. Empire building. Exhaustion.

Gail came to Walley one summer in the seventies. The boyfriend she was with then was a boatbuilder, and she sold clothes that she had made—capes with appliqués, shirts with billowing sleeves, long, bright skirts. She got space in the back of the craft shop, when winter came on. She learned about importing ponchos and thick socks from Bolivia and Guatemala. She found local women to knit sweaters. One day Will stopped her on the street and asked her to help him with the costumes for the play he was putting on—"The Skin of Our Teeth." Her boyfriend had moved to Vancouver.

She told Will some things about herself early on, in case he should think that with her capable build and pink skin and wide gentle forehead she was exactly the kind of woman to start a family on. She told him that she had had a baby, and that when she and her boyfriend were moving some furniture in a borrowed van, from Thunder Bay to Toronto, carbon-monoxide fumes had leaked in, just enough to make them feel sick but enough to kill the baby, who was seven weeks old. After that Gail got an infection. She decided she did not want to have another child, and it would have been difficult anyway, so she had a hysterectomy.

Will admired her. He said so. He did not feel obliged to say, What a tragedy! He did not even obliquely suggest that the death was the result of choices Gail had made. He was entranced with her then. He thought her brave and generous and resourceful and gifted. The costumes she designed and made for him were perfect, miraculous. Gail thought that his view of her, of her life, showed a touching innocence. It seemed to her that far from being a free and generous spirit she had often been anxious and desperate and had spent most of the time doing laundry and worrying about money and feeling she owed a lot to any man who took up with her. She did not think she was in love with Will then, but she liked his looks—his energetic body, so upright it seemed taller than it was, his flung-back head, shiny high forehead, springy ruff of graying hair. She liked to watch him at rehearsals, or just talking to his students. How skilled and intrepid he seemed as a director, how potent a person-ality as he walked the high-school halls or the streets of Walley. And then the slightly quaint, admiring feelings he had for her, his courtesy as a lover, the foreign pleasantness of his house and his life with Cleata—all this made Gail feel like somebody getting a unique wel-come in a place where perhaps she did not truly have a right to be. That did not matter then—she had the upper hand.

So, when did she stop having it? When he got used to sleeping with her, when they moved in together, when they did so much work on the cottage by the river and it turned out that she was better at that kind of work than he was?

Was she a person who believed that somebody had to have the upper hand?

There came a time when just the tone of his voice, saying "Your shoelace is undone" as she went ahead of him on a walk—just that—

could fill her with despair, warning her that they had crossed over into a bleak country where his disappointment in her was boundless, his contempt impossible to challenge. She would lose control eventually, break out in a rage—they would have days and nights of fierce hopelessness. Then the breakthrough, the sweet reunion, the jokes, and bewildered relief. So it went on in their life, she couldn't really understand it or tell if it was like anybody else's. But the peaceful periods seemed to be getting longer, the dangers retreating, and she had no inkling that he was waiting to meet somebody like this new person, Sandy, who could seem to him as alien and delightful as Gail herself had once been.

Will probably had no inkling of that, either. He had never had much to say about Sandy—*Sandra*—who had come to Walley from Australia last year on an exchange program, to see how drama was being taught in Canadian schools. He had said she was a Young Turk. Then he had said she mightn't even have heard of that expression. Very soon, there had developed some sort of electricity, or danger, around her name. Gail got some information from other sources. She heard that Sandy had challenged Will, in front of his class. Sandy had said that the plays he wanted to do were not relevant. Or maybe she said that they were not revolutionary.

"But he likes her," one of his students said. "Oh, yeah, he *really likes* her."

Sandy didn't stay around long. She went on to observe the teaching of drama in other schools. But she wrote to Will, and presumably he wrote back. For it turned out that they had fallen in love. Will and Sandy had fallen seriously in love, and at the end of the school year, when Sandy had to go home, Will went with her.

He and Gail agreed not to correspond. Perhaps later, Will said. Gail said, "Suit yourself."

But one day at Cleata's house Gail saw his writing on an envelope that must have been left out, on purpose, where she could see it. Cleata must have left it there—Cleata who never spoke one word about the fugitives. Gail wrote down the return address—16 Eyre Rd., Toowong, Brisbane, Queensland, Australia.

It was when she saw Will's writing that she understood how useless everything had become to her. This bare-fronted pre-Victorian house in Walley, and the veranda, and the drinks, and the catalpa tree that she was always looking at, in Cleata's back yard. All the trees and streets in Walley, all the liberating views of the lake, and the comfort of the shop. Useless, cutouts, fakes, and props. The real scene was hidden from her, in Australia.

That was why she found herself sitting on the plane, beside the woman with the diamond rings. Her own hands have no rings on them, no polish on the nails. The skin is dry from all the work she does with cloth. She used to call the clothes she made "handcrafted" until Will made her embarrassed about that description. She still doesn't quite see what was wrong.

She has sold the shop, she has sold it to Donalda, who has been wanting to buy it for a long time. Gail has taken the money, and she has got herself onto a flight to Australia and has not told anyone where she is going. She has lied, talking about a long holiday that would start off in England. Then somewhere in Greece for the winter, then who knows?

Last night she did a transformation on herself. She cut off her heavy, reddish-gray hair and put a dark-brown rinse on what was left of it. The color that resulted was strange—a deep maroon, obviously artificial but rather too sombre for any attempt at glamour. She picked out from her shop—even though the contents no longer belonged to her—a dress of a kind she would never usually wear, a jacket-dress of dark-blue linen-look polyester with lightning stripes of red and yellow. She is tall, and broad in the hips, and she usually wears things that are loose and graceful. This outfit gives her chunky shoulders and cuts her legs at an unflattering spot above the knees. What sort of woman did she think she was making herself into? The sort that a woman like Phyllis would play bridge with? If so, she has got it wrong. She has come out looking like somebody who has spent most of her life in uniform, at some worthy poorly paid job (perhaps in a hospital cafeteria?) and now has spent too much money for a dashing dress that will turn out to be inappropriate and uncomfortable, on the holiday of her life.

That doesn't matter. It is a disguise.

In the airport washroom, on a new continent, she sees that the dark hair coloring, insufficiently rinsed out the night before, has mixed with her sweat and is trickling down her neck.

. . .

GAIL HAS LANDED in Brisbane, still not used to what time of day it is, and persecuted by so hot a sun. She is wearing her horrid dress but she has scrubbed her neck, so the stain no longer shows.

She has taken a taxi. Tired as she is, she cannot settle, cannot rest until she has seen where they live. She has already bought a map and found Eyre Road. A short, curving street. She asks to be let out at the corner, where there is a little grocery store. This is the place where they buy their milk, most likely, or other things that they may have run out of. Detergent, aspirin, tampons.

The fact that Gail never met Sandy was of course an ominous thing. It must have meant that Will knew, very quickly, how the tide would turn. Later attempts to ferret out a description did not yield much. Tall rather than short. Thin rather than fat. Fair rather than dark. Gail had a mental picture of one of those long-legged, short-haired, energetic, and boyishly attractive girls. *Women.* But she wouldn't know Sandy if she ran into her.

Would anybody know Gail? With her dark glasses and her unlikely hair, she feels so altered as to be invisible. It's also being in a strange country which has transformed her. She's not tuned into it yet. Once she gets tuned in, she may not be able to do the bold things she can do now. She has to walk this street, look at the house right away, or she may not be able to do it at all.

The road that the taxi climbed was steep, up from the brown river. Eyre Road runs along a ridge. There is no sidewalk, just a dusty path. No one walking, no cars passing, no shade. Fences of boards or a kind of basket weaving—wattles?—or in some cases high hedges covered with flowers. No, the flowers are really leaves, purplish-pink or crimson in color. Trees unfamiliar to Gail are showing over the fences. They have tough-looking, dusty foliage, scaly or stringy bark, a shabby, ornamental air. An indifference or vague ill will about them, which she associates with the tropics.

Walking on the path ahead of her are a pair of guinea hens, stately and preposterous.

The house where Will and Sandy live is hidden by a board fence, painted a pale green. Gail's heart shrinks, her heart is in a cruel clutch, to see that fence, that green.

The road is a dead end, so she has to turn around. She walks past the house again. In the fence there are gates to let a car in and out. There is also a mail slot. She noticed one of these before, in a fence in front of another house, and the reason she noticed it was that there was a magazine sticking out. So the mailbox is not very deep, and a hand, slipping in, might be able to find an envelope resting on its edge. If the mail has not been taken out yet, by a person in the house. Gail does slip a hand in, and finds a letter there, just as she had thought she might. She puts the letter into her purse. Why does she do this? Just to find out anything about them. Even if it's only what they owe on their phone bill. Anything at all.

She calls a taxi from the shop at the corner of the street. "What part of the States are you from?" the man in the shop asks her.

"Texas," she says. She has an idea that they would like you to be from Texas, and indeed the man lifts his eyebrows, whistles.

"I thought so," he says.

It is Will's own writing, on the envelope. Not a letter to Will, then, but a letter from him. A letter he has sent to Ms. Catherine Thornaby, 491 Hawtre Street. Also in Brisbane. Another hand has scrawled across it, "Return to Sender, Died Sept. 13." For a moment, in her disordered state of mind, Gail thinks that this means Will has died.

She has got to calm down and collect herself, stay out of the sun for a bit.

Nevertheless, as soon as she has read the letter in her hotel room, and has tidied herself up, she takes another taxi, this time to Hawtre Street, and finds, as she expected, a sign in the window. "Flat to Let."

But what is in the letter that Will has written to Ms. Catherine Thornaby, on Hawtre Street?

Dear Ms. Thornaby,

You do not know me, but I hope that once I have explained myself, we may meet and talk. I believe that I may be a Canadian cousin of yours, my grandfather having come to Canada from Northumberland sometime in the 1870's, about the same time as a brother of his went to Australia. My grandfather's name was William, like my own, his brother's name was Thomas. Of course I have no proof that you are descended from this Thomas. I simply looked in the Brisbane phone book and was delighted to find there a Thornaby spelled in the same way. I used to think this family-tracing business was the silliest, most boring thing imaginable but now that I find myself doing it, I discover there is a strange excitement about it. Perhaps it is my age—I am 56—that urges me to find connections. And I have more time on my hands than I am used to. My wife is working with a theatre here which keeps her busy till all hours. She is a very bright and energetic young woman (she scolds me if I refer to any female over 18 as a girl and she is all of 28!). I taught drama in a Canadian high school but I have not yet found any work in Australia.

Wife. He is trying to be respectable in the eyes of the possible cousin.

Dear Mr. Thornaby,

The name we share may be a more common one than you suppose, though I am at present its only representative in the Brisbane phone book. You may not know that the name comes from Thorn Abbey, the ruins of which are still to be seen in Northumberland. The spelling varies—Thornaby, Thornby, Thornabbey, Thornabby. In the Middle Ages the name of the Lord of the Manor would be taken as a surname by all the people working on the estate, including laborers, blacksmiths, carpenters, etc. As a result there are many people scattered around the world bearing a name that in the strict sense they have no right to. Only those who can trace their descent from the family in the twelfth century are the true, armigerous Thornabys. That is, they have the right to display the family coat of arms. I am one of these Thornabys and since you do not mention anything about the coat of arms and do not trace your ancestry back beyond this William I assume that you are not. My grandfather's name was Jonathan.

Gail writes this on an old portable typewriter that she has bought from the secondhand shop down the street. By this time she is living at 491 Hawtre Street, in an apartment building called the Miramar. It is a two-story building covered with dingy cream stucco, with twisted pillars on either side of a grilled entryway. It has a perfunctory Moorish or Spanish or Californian air, like that of an old movie theatre. The manager told her that the flat was very modern.

"An elderly lady had it, but she had to go to the hospital. Then somebody came when she died and got her effects out, but it still has the basic furniture that goes with the flat. What part of the States are you from?"

Oklahoma, Gail said. Mrs. Massie, from Oklahoma.

The manager looks to be about seventy years old. He wears glasses that magnify his eyes, and walks quickly, but rather unsteadily, tilting forward. He speaks of difficulties—the increase of the foreign element in the population, which makes it hard to find good repairmen, the carelessness of certain tenants, malicious acts of passersby who continually litter the grass. Gail asks if he has put in a notice, yet, to the post office. He says he has been intending to, but the lady received hardly any mail. Except one letter came. It was a strange thing that it came right the day after she died. He sent it back.

"I'll do it," Gail says. "I'll tell the post office."

"I'll have to sign it, though. Get me one of those forms they have, and I'll sign it, and you can give it in. I'd be obliged."

The walls of the apartment are painted white—this must be what is modern about it. It has bamboo blinds, a tiny kitchen, a green sofa bed, a table, a dresser, and two chairs. On the wall one picture, which might have been a painting or a tinted photograph. A yellowish-green desert landscape, with rocks and bunches of sage, and dim, distant mountains. Gail is sure that she has seen this before.

She paid the rent in cash. She had to be busy for a while, buying sheets and towels and groceries, a few pots and dishes, the typewriter. She had to open a bank account, become a person living in the country, not a traveller. There are shops hardly a block away. A grocery store, the secondhand store, a drugstore, a tea shop. They are all humble establishments with strips of colored paper hanging in the doorways, wooden awnings over the sidewalk in front. Their offerings are limited. The tea shop has only two tables, the secondhand store contains scarcely more than the tumbled-out accumulation of one ordinary house. The cereal boxes in the grocery store, the bottles of cough syrup and packets of pills in the drugstore, are set out singly on the shelves, as if they were of special value or significance.

But she has found what she needs. In the secondhand store she found some loose flowered-cotton dresses, a straw bag for her groceries. Now she looks like the other women she sees on the street. Housewives, middle-aged, with bare but pale arms and legs, shopping in the early morning or late afternoon. She bought a floppy straw hat, too, to shade her face, as they do. Dim, soft, freckly, blinking faces.

Night comes suddenly around six o'clock, and she must find occupation for the evenings. There is no television in the apartment. But a little beyond the shops there is a lending library, run by an old woman out of the front room of her house. This woman wears a hairnet, and gray lisle stockings—in spite of the heat. (Where, nowadays, can you find gray lisle stockings?) She has an undernourished body and colorless, tight, unsmiling lips. She is the person Gail calls to mind when she writes the letter from Catherine Thornaby. She thinks of this library woman by that name whenever she sees her—which is almost every day, because you are allowed only one book at a time and Gail usually reads a book a night. She thinks, There is Catherine Thornaby, dead and moved into a new existence a few blocks away.

All the business about armigerous and nonarmigerous Thornabys came out of a book. Not one of the books that Gail is reading now but one she read in her youth. The hero was the nonarmigerous but deserving heir to a great property. She cannot remember the title. She lived with people then who were always reading "Steppenwolf" or "Dune" or something by Krishnamurti, and she read historical romances apologetically. She did not think Will would have read such a book or picked up this sort of information.

And she is sure that he will have to reply, to tell Catherine off.

She waits, and reads the books from the lending library, which seem to come from an even earlier time than those romances she read twenty years ago. Some of them she took out of the public library in Winnipeg, before she left home, and they seemed old-fashioned even then. "The Girl of the Limberlost." "The Blue Castle." "Maria Chapdelaine." Such books remind her, naturally, of her life before Will. There was such a life, and she could still salvage something from it, if she wanted to. She has a sister living in Winnipeg. She has an aunt there, in a nursing home, who still reads books in Russian. Gail's grandparents came from Russia, her parents could still speak Russian, her real name is not Gail but Galya. She cut herself off from her family—or they cut her off— when she left home at eighteen to wander about the country, as you did in those days. First with friends, then with a boyfriend, then with another boyfriend. She strung beads and tie-dyed scarves and sold them on the street.

Dear Ms. Thornaby,

I must thank you for enlightening me as to the important distinction between the armigerous and the nonarmigerous Thornabys. I gather that you have a strong suspicion that I may turn out to be one of the latter. I beg your pardon—I had no intention of treading on such sacred ground or of wearing the Thornaby coat of arms on my T-shirt. We do not take much account of such things in my country and I did not think you did so in Australia, but I see that I am mistaken. Perhaps you are too far on in years to have noticed the change in values. It is quite different with me, since I have been in the teaching profession and am constantly brought up, as well, against the energetic arguments of a young wife.

My innocent intention was simply to get in touch with somebody in this country outside the theatrical-academic circle that my wife and I seem to be absorbed in. I have a mother in Canada, whom I miss. In fact your letter reminded me of her a little. She would be capable of writing such a letter for a joke but I doubt whether you are joking. It sounds like a case of Exalted Ancestry to me.

When he is offended and disturbed in a certain way—a way that is hard to predict and hard for most people to recognize—Will becomes heavily sarcastic. Irony deserts him. He flails about, and the effect is to make people embarrassed—not for themselves, as he intends, but for him. This happens seldom, and usually when it happens it means that he feels deeply unappreciated. It means that he has even stopped appreciating himself.

So that is what happened. Gail thinks so. Sandy and her young friends, with their stormy confidence, their crude righteousness, might be making him miserable. His wit not taken notice of, his enthusiasm dismissed as out-of-date. No way of making himself felt among them. His pride in being attached to Sandy going gradually sour.

She thinks so. He is shaky and unhappy and casting about to know somebody else. He has thought of family ties, here in this country of non-stop blooming and impudent bird life and searing days and suddenly clamped-down nights.

Dear Mr. Thornaby,

Did you really expect me, just because I have the same surname as you, to fling open my door and put out the "welcome mat"—as I think you say in America, and that inevitably includes Canada? You may be looking for another mother here, but that hardly obliges me to be one. By the way you are quite wrong about my age—I am younger than you by several years, so do not picture me as an elderly spinster in a hairnet with gray lisle stockings. I know the world probably as well as you do. I travel a good deal, being a fashion buyer for a large store. So my ideas are not so out-of-date as you suppose.

You do not say whether your busy energetic young wife was to be a part of this familial friendship. I am surprised you feel the need for other contacts. It seems I am always reading or hearing on the media about these "May-December" relationships and how invigorating they are and how happily the men are settling down to domesticity and parenthood. (No mention of the 'trial runs' with women closer to their own age or mention of how those women are settling down to their lives of loneliness!) So perhaps you need to become a papa to give you a "sense of family"!

Gail is surprised at how fluently she writes. She has always found it hard to write letters, and the results have been dull and sketchy, with many dashes and incomplete sentences and pleas of insufficient time. Where has she got this fine, nasty style—out of some book, like the armigerous nonsense? She goes out in the dark to post her letter, feeling bold and satisfied. But she wakes up early the next morning, thinking that she has certainly gone too far. He will never answer that, she will never hear from him again.

She gets up and leaves the building, goes for a morning walk. The shops are still shut up, the broken venetian blinds are closed, as well as they can be, in the windows of the front-room library. She walks as far as the river, where there is a strip of park beside a hotel. Later in the day she could not walk or sit there, because the verandas of the hotel were always crowded with uproarious beer drinkers, and the park was within their verbal or even bottle-throwing range. Now the verandas are empty, the doors are closed, and she walks in under the trees. The brown water of the river spreads sluggishly among the mangrove stumps. Birds are flying over the water, lighting on the hotel roof. They are not seagulls, as she thought at first. They are smaller than gulls, their throats and breasts are pink, and their bright gray wings are touched with pink, too.

In the park two men are sitting—one on a bench, one beside the bench in a wheelchair. She recognizes them—they live in her building, and go for walks every day. Once, she held the grille open for them to pass through. She has seen them at the shops, and sitting at the table in the tearoom window. The man in the wheelchair looks quite old and ill. His face is puckered like blistered paint. He wears dark glasses and a coal-black toupee and a black beret over that. He is all wrapped up in a blanket. Even later in the day, when the sun is hot—every time she has seen them—he has been wrapped in this plaid blanket. The man who pushes the wheelchair and who now sits on the bench is young enough to look like an overgrown boy. He is tall and large-limbed but not manly. A young giant, bewildered by his own extent. Strong but not athletic, with a stiffness, maybe of timidity, in his thick arms and legs and neck. Red hair not just on his head but on his bare arms and above the buttons of his shirt.

Gail halts in her walk past them. She says good morning. The young man answers almost inaudibly. It seems to be his habit to look out at the world with majestic indifference, but she thinks her greeting has given him a twitch of embarrassment or apprehension. Nevertheless, she speaks again. She says, "What are those birds I see everywhere?"

"Galah birds," the young man says, making the first word sound something like her childhood name. She is going to ask him to repeat it, when the old man bursts out in what seems like a string of curses. The words are knotted and incomprehensible to her, because of the Australian accent on top of some European accent, but the concentrated viciousness is beyond any doubt. And these words are meant for her—he is leaning forward, in fact struggling to free himself from the straps that hold him in. He wants to leap at her, lunge at her, chase her out of sight. The young man makes no apology and does not take any notice of Gail but leans toward the old man and gently pushes him back, saying things to him which she cannot hear. She sees that there will be no explanation. She walks away.

FOR TEN DAYS, no letter. No word. She cannot think what to do. She walks every day. That is mostly what she does. The Miramar is only a mile or so away from Will's street. She never walks in that street again or goes into the shop where she told the man that she was from Texas. She cannot imagine how she could have been so bold, the first day. She does walk in the streets nearby. Those streets all go along ridges. In between the ridges, which the houses cling to, there are steep-sided gullies full of birds and trees. Even as the sun grows hot, those birds are not quiet. Magpies keep up their disturbing conversation and sometimes emerge to make menacing flights at her light-colored hat. The birds with the name like her own cry out foolishly, as they rise and whirl about and subside into the leaves. She walks till she is dazed and sweaty and afraid of sunstroke. She shivers in the heat—most fearful, most desirous, of seeing Will's utterly familiar figure, that one rather small and jaunty, free-striding package of all that could pain or appease her in the world.

> Dear Mr. Thornaby,
> This is just a short note to beg your pardon, if I was impolite and hasty in my replies to you, as I am sure I was. I have been under some stress lately, and have taken a leave of absence to recuperate. Under these circumstances one does not always behave as well as one would hope, or see things as rationally. . . .

One day she walks past the hotel and the park. The verandas are clamorous with the afternoon drinking. All the trees in the park have come out in bloom. The flowers are a color that she has seen and could not have imagined on trees before—a shade of silvery-blue, or silvery-purple, so delicate and beautiful that you would think it would shock everything into quietness, into contemplation, but apparently it has not.

When she gets back to the Miramar she finds the young man with red hair standing in the downstairs hall, outside the door of the apartment where he lives with the old man. From behind the closed apartment door come the sounds of a tirade.

The young man smiles at her this time. She stops, and they stand together, listening.

Gail says, "If you would ever like a place to sit down while you're waiting, you know you're welcome to come upstairs."

He shakes his head, still smiling, as if this were a joke between them. She thinks she should say something else before she leaves him there, so she asks him about the trees in the park.

"Those trees beside the hotel?" she says. "Where I saw you the other morning? They are all out in bloom now. What are they called?"

He says a word she cannot catch. She asks him to repeat it. "Jack Randa," he says. "That's the Jack Randa Hotel."

Dear Ms. Thornaby,

I have been away, and when I came back I found both your letters waiting for me. I opened them in the wrong order, though that really doesn't matter.

My mother has died. I have been "home" to Canada for her funeral. It is cold there, autumn. Many things have changed. Why I should want to tell you this I simply do not know. We have certainly got off on the wrong track with each other. Even if I had not got your note of explanation after the first letter you wrote, I think I would have been glad in a peculiar way to get the first letter. I wrote you a very snippy and unpleasant letter and you wrote me back one of the same. The snippiness and unpleasantness and readiness to take offense seems somehow familiar to me. Ought I to risk your armigerous wrath by suggesting that we may be related after all?

I feel adrift here. I admire my wife and her friends so much. I admire their zeal and directness and commitment, their hope of using their talents to create a better world. (I must say though that it often seems to me that the hope and zeal exceed the talents.) I cannot be one of them. I must say that they saw this before I did. It must be because I am woozy with jet lag after that horrendous flight that I can face up to this fact and that I write it down in a letter to someone like you who has her own troubles and quite correctly has indicated she doesn't want to be bothered with mine. I had better close, in fact, before I burden you with further claptrap from my psyche. I wouldn't blame you if you had stopped reading before you got this far. . . .

Gail lies on the sofa pressing this letter with both hands against her stomach. Many things are changed. He has been in Walley, then—he has been told how she sold the shop and started out on her great world trip.

But wouldn't he have heard that anyway, from Cleata? Maybe not. Cleata was closemouthed. And when she went into the hospital, just before Gail left, she said, "I don't want to see or hear from anybody for a while. These treatments are bound to be a bit bizarre."

Cleata is dead.

Gail knew that Cleata would die, but somehow thought that everything would hold still, nothing could really happen there, while she, Gail, remained here.

Cleata is dead and Will is alone except for Sandy, and Sandy perhaps has stopped being of much use to him.

There is a knock on the door. Gail jumps up in a great disturbance, looking for a scarf to cover her hair.

It is the manager, calling her false name.

"I just wanted to tell you I had somebody here asking questions. He asked me about Miss Thornaby and I said, Oh, she's dead. She's been dead for some time now. He said, Oh, has she? I said, Yes, she has, and he said, Well, that's strange."

"Did he say why?" Gail says, "Did he say why it was strange?"

"No. I said, She died in the hospital and I've got an American lady in the flat now. I forgot where you told me you came from. He sounded like an American himself, so it might've meant something to him. I said there was a letter come for her after she was dead, did you write that letter? I told him I sent it back. Yes, he said, I wrote it, but I never got it back. There must be some kind of mistake, he said."

Gail says there must be. "Like a mistaken identity," she says.

"Yes. Like that."

Dear Ms. Thornaby,

It has come to my attention that you are dead. I know that life is strange, but I have never found it quite this strange before. Who are you and what is going on? It seems this rigmarole about the Thornabys must have been just that—a rigmarole. You must certainly be a person with time on your hands and a fantasizing turn of mind. I resent being taken in, but I suppose I understand the temptation. I do think you owe me an explanation now as to whether or not *my* explanation is true and this is some joke. Or am I dealing with some "fashion buyer" from beyond the grave? (Where did you get that touch or is it the truth?)

WHEN GAIL GOES out to buy food, she uses the back door of the building, she takes a roundabout route to the shops.

On her return by the same back-door route she comes upon the young red-haired man standing between the dustbins. If he had not been so tall you might have said that he was hidden there. She speaks to him but he doesn't answer. He looks at her through tears, as if the tears were nothing but a wavy glass, something usual.

"Is your father sick?" Gail says to him. She has decided that this must be the relationship, though the age gap seems greater than usual between father and son and the two of them are quite unalike in looks, and the young man's patience and fidelity are so far beyond—nowadays they seem even contrary to—anything a son customarily shows. But they go beyond anything a hired attendant might show, as well.

"No," the young man says, and though his expression stays calm a drowning flush spreads over his face, under the delicate redhead's skin.

Lovers, Gail thinks. She is suddenly sure of it. She feels a desperate pity.

Lovers.

She goes down to her mailbox after dark and finds there another letter.

> I might have thought that you were out of town on one of your fashion-buying jaunts, but the manager tells me you have not been away since taking the flat, so I must suppose your "leave of absence" continues. He tells me also that you are a brunette. I suppose we might exchange descriptions—and then, with trepidation, photographs—in the brutal manner of people meeting through newspaper ads. It seems that in my attempt to get to know you I am willing to make quite a fool of myself. Nothing new of course in that. . . .

Gail does not leave the apartment for two days. She does without milk, drinks her coffee black. What will she do when she runs out of coffee? She eats odd meals—tuna fish spread on crackers when she has no bread to make a sandwich, a dry end of cheese, a couple of mangoes. She goes out into the upstairs hall of the Miramar—first opening the door a crack, testing the air for an occupant—and walks to the arched window that overlooks the street. And from long ago a feeling comes back to her—the feeling of watching a street, the visible bit of a street, where a car is expected to appear, or may appear, or may not appear. She even remembers now the cars themselves—a blue Austin mini, a maroon Chevrolet, a family station wagon. Cars in which she travelled short distances, in a bold daze of consent. Long before Will.

She doesn't know what clothes Will will be wearing, or how his hair is cut, or if he will have some change in his walk or expression, some change appropriate to his life here.

He cannot have changed more than she has. She has no mirror in the apartment except the little one on the bathroom cupboard, but even that can tell her how much thinner she has got and how the skin of her face has toughened. Instead of fading and wrinkling as fair skin often does, hers has got a look of dull canvas. It could be fixed up—she sees that. With the right kind of makeup a look of exotic sullenness could be managed. Her hair is more of a problem—the red that shows at the roots, with tinsel-strands of gray, gives an effect of isolated gaudiness. Nearly all the time she keeps it hidden by a scarf.

When the manager knocks on her door again, she has only a second or two of crazy expectation. He begins to call her name.

"Mrs. Massie, Mrs. Massie! Oh. I hoped you'd be in. I wondered if you could just come down and help me. It's the old bloke downstairs, he's fallen off the bed."

He goes ahead of her down the stairs, holding to the railing, and dropping each foot shakily, precipitately, onto the step below.

"His friend isn't there. I wondered. I didn't see him yesterday. I try to keep track of people, but I don't like to interfere. I thought he probably would've come back in the night. I was sweeping out the foyer and I heard a thump and I went in there. I wondered what was going on. Old bloke all by himself, on the floor."

The apartment is no larger than Gail's and laid out in the same way. It has curtains drawn over the bamboo blinds, which make it very dark. It smells of cigarettes and old cooking and some kind of pine-scented air freshener. The sofa bed has been pulled out, made into a double bed, and the old man is lying on the floor beside it, having dragged some of the bedclothes with him. His head without the toupee is smooth and gray as a dirty piece of soap. His eyes are half shut and a noise is coming from deep inside him like the noise of an engine hopelessly trying to turn over.

"Have you phoned the ambulance?" Gail says.

"If you could just pick up the one end of him," the manager says. "I have a bad back and I dread putting it out again."

"Where is the phone?" says Gail. "He may have had a stroke. He may have broken his hip. He'll have to go to the hospital."

"Do you think so? His friend could lift him back and forth so easy. He had the strength. And now he's disappeared."

Gail says, "I'll phone."

"Oh, no. Oh, no. I have the number written down over the phone in my office. I don't let any other person go in there."

Left alone with the old man, who probably cannot hear her, Gail says, "It's all right. It's all right. We're getting help for you." Her voice sounds foolishly sociable. She leans down to pull the blanket up over his shoulders, and to her great surprise a hand flutters out and searches for and grabs her own. His hand is slight and bony, but warm enough, and dreadfully strong. "I'm here, I'm here," she says, and wonders if she is impersonating the red-haired young man, or some other young man, or a woman, or even his mother.

The ambulance comes quickly, with its harrowing pulsing cry, and the ambulance men with the stretcher cart are soon in the room, with the manager stumping after them, saying, ". . . couldn't be moved. Here is Mrs. Massie come down to help in the emergency."

While they are getting the old man onto the stretcher Gail has to pull her hand away, and he begins to complain, or she thinks he does— that steady involuntary-sounding noise he is making acquires an extra *ah-unh-anh.* So she takes his hand again as soon as she can, and trots beside him as he is wheeled out. He has such a grip on her that she feels as if he were pulling her along.

"He was the owner of the Jacaranda Hotel," the manager says. "Years ago. He was."

A few people are in the street, but nobody stops, nobody wants to be caught gawking. They want to see, they don't want to see.

"Shall I ride with him?" Gail says. "He doesn't seem to want to let go of me."

"It's up to you," one of the ambulance men says, and she climbs in. (She is dragged in, really, by that clutching hand.) The ambulance man puts down a little seat for her, the doors are closed, the siren starts as they pull away.

Through the window in the back door, then, she sees Will. He is about a block away from the Miramar and walking toward it. He is wearing a light-colored short-sleeved jacket and matching pants—probably called a safari suit—and his hair has grown whiter or been bleached by the sun, but she knows him at once, she will always know him, and will always have to call out to him when she sees him, as she does now, even trying to jump up from the seat, trying to pull her hand out of the old man's grasp.

"It's Will," she says to the ambulance man. "Oh, I'm sorry. It's my husband."

"Better not see you jumping out of a speeding ambulance, had he?" the man says. Then he says, "Oh-oh. What's happened here?"

For the next minute or so he pays professional attention to the old man. Soon he straightens up and says, "Gone."

"He's still holding on to me," says Gail. But she realizes as she says this that it isn't true. A moment ago he was holding on, with great force, it seemed—even enough force to pull her back, when she would have sprung toward Will—but now it is she who is holding on to him. His fingers are still quite warm.

When she gets back from the hospital she finds the note that will be the last.

Gail. I know it's you.

Her rent is paid. She has left a note for the manager. She has taken her money out of the bank, got herself to the airport, found a flight. Her last library book remains in the apartment, accumulating fines.

She sees it lying beside the green couch. She sees the desert picture. She hears Will's voice at the door.

Gail. Gayla.

I know you're there.

I know you're still there.

Let me in. Answer me.

Talk to me. Answer me.

I know you're there. I can smell you through the keyhole. I can hear you, I can hear your heart, and your stomach rumbling and your brain jumping up and down.

Gail! Gayla!

Or perhaps the manager has told him, has shown him the note, which says nothing but *I have to leave.*

Or he hasn't come back, he never will come back, he will take himself and Sandy off to some other place.

IN THE AIRPORT shop she sees a number of tiny boxes, made of clay by Australian aborigines. They are round, and light as pennies. She chooses one that has a pattern of yellow dots, irregularly spaced, on a dark-red ground. Against that, a swollen black figure with short splayed limbs— a turtle, maybe, helpless on its back.

She actually thinks, A present for Cleata. Then she remembers.

She might send it to Will. She might take it all the way back to Canada, then send it to Will. The yellow dots flung out that way remind her of a walk that she and Will went on, last fall. They walked from their house by the river up the wooded bank, and there they came upon something they had heard about but never seen before.

Hundreds, maybe thousands of butterflies were hanging in the trees, resting before their long flight down the shore of Lake Huron, across Lake Erie, and on south to Mexico. They hung like gaudy leaves, like flakes of gold tossed up in the trees.

"Like the shower of gold in the Bible," Gail said, and Will told her that she was confusing Jove with Jehovah.

On that day, Cleata had already begun to die. Will had already met Sandy.

What would you put in a box like that? A bead, a feather, a potent pill? Gail would put a note, folded up nearly to the size of a spitball.

Now it's up to you to follow me.

(1995)

Hey, Joe

Ben Neihart

Joe was newly sixteen. He had the rosy aspect, and the swagger, and the skinny arms, and the bad reputation. He was a brooder, a magazine reader, a swaying dancer at mellow, jazzy rap parties. He kept his hair cut short like the other smoked-out newbies at Metairie Park Country Day, and the only shoes he wore were black suede Pumas.

School had just let out for the Labor Day weekend, so Joe was home, changing clothes, in a hurry to be gone before his mother returned from work. He hated to leave her alone on a Friday night, with her books and the cell phone. He hated the actual leavetaking most of all—her quick kiss, the sound of the front door's bolt lock when he closed it behind him. He wished she didn't spend so much time by herself. Why didn't she hang with her old friends? She was always working—at Tulane Medical Center, in the fund-raising office, asking doctors and scientists and presidents of Corporation Whatever for money. "It's gonna suck the life right out of me," she sometimes joked. Joe hated her saying that, because he could see that it was true; in the past year, it seemed, skin and muscle hung more loosely on her frame, and on her face, even though she did exercises in the high-ceilinged ballroom of the New Orleans Athletic Center, downtown.

He wandered about the living room, looking for his glasses, which he wore only at home. They were hidden somewhere beneath the spoils of his mom's latest shopping spree. On the floor were neat piles of new compact disks, hard-cover novels by European women with killer black hairdos, and shoeboxes. Slung over the furniture were silk blouses, palazzo pants in four shades of cream, and bras and panties, all of them with price tags still attached.

"And the value of this showcase is . . ." Joe said, and then he hurried down the hall to the bathroom.

In his underwear, he crouched over the bathroom sink. It was his pond, shell-shaped, with separate faucets for hot and cold water. The mirror was steamproof, and flattering; it put your face at a remove, so you weren't right on top of yourself as you did your routine. He squirted some Dial onto a washcloth and worked up a lather to freshen his underarms. He rubbed on some deodorant next, then washed his face and brushed his teeth.

He went into his mom's bedroom. As always, it was neatly set up for when she would come home this evening. The king-size bed was made; a pair of jeans and an immaculate white T-shirt and fresh panties lay on the pillow; the blinds were closed to keep the room cool in the late-summer sunlight. Joe liked the feel of the wood floor under his bare feet. He hopped onto the doctor's-office scale beside the dresser. One hundred twenty pounds. Good, he told himself, lean and portable.

He pulled his mom's door shut on his way to his own bedroom, the smallest room of the house—even smaller than the bathroom. He liked the fact that when he lay down to sleep he could touch the walls on either side of his bed. On weekend mornings, his mom would come into the room to wake him up early so they could spend the morning together in the back yard, sitting on the stone benches in her little rock garden. Between them, they'd drink a pitcher of orange juice, and then

Joe would go inside to fix enormous tumblers of iced tea, to clear the thickness from their throats. It was as if they hadn't missed each other in the comings and goings of the week. Long, contented silences; bare feet stretching in the dewy grass; the sun pumping higher into the sky.

Now Joe pulled the front off one of his waist-high Sony speakers, which had been hollowed out to hold his business, the top-shelf weed he imported from Gainesville and sold to his friends. He unrolled a zip-lock freezer bag and took a deep breath of the sweet, fearsome herb. He took a pinch to roll a quick joint. Time to give fashion, he thought. He lit up and collapsed onto his bed. He didn't have to turn on his stereo; music presented itself, as if it had lain dormant in the joint: "Nickel bag, a nickel bag . . ."

As he got stoned, he looked at his hands, which were covered with scars. His legs and feet were, too. Each scar was the proof of a mountain-bike tumble, or, in one case, a skid across the coral beach on Fitzroy Island in the Great Barrier Reef, where they had gone last Christmas—Joe, his mom, and his dad, just before he died. They had pushed Daddy's wheelchair to the edge of the Coral Sea. "A sea like green milk," Daddy had said. Joe and his mom hurtled past the breaking waves and dove head on, grasping handfuls of water, racing, floating. When they were finished, they stood beside Daddy, dripping onto his sunburned legs and shoulders. "Oh," he said. "Oh, does that feel good."

NOW JOE HEARD the mail truck stop outside. Friday was a magazine day. He drew himself out of bed, sprayed some Lysol around. He locked up the house and galloped down the driveway. The mailbox was rooted in a pile of pink, round stones. Joe kicked them with his toe. He left the bills and letters in the box and pulled out the new *Vogue*. He sat down on the slope of curb where his driveway met the street. He'd wait here, he decided, for his ride to the Quarter, where it was his habit to spend Friday nights.

He set the magazine on his bare legs and took stock of the cover. The model was the angel of Joe's life. Her name was Linda, and the cattish regard of her eyes could pull you out of a funk. Joe had been following her career for five years now. In interviews, Linda said that all she had ever wanted to be was a model; she didn't want to be an actress or a singer or a politician, and she didn't want to talk about her charities or whatever, and she talked to her mom every day, and they talked about modelling, because that was Linda's job.

On this cover, Linda sat in the grass; she wore a grape velvet dress that was tight in the bodice. The lightest strands of her hair—the color of Coke in a glass full of melting ice—caught the sun, reminding Joe of the old Dutch society paintings that he had admired in his "World of Art: The Netherlands" class. In those paintings the background was usually dark—an inky, enamel cloud—to set off the lighter wires of the subject's hair and her lucent, honeycomb ruff and her knot of blue pearls.

He looked into Linda's eyes and tried to imitate her smile. He pressed his knees together and palmed the hair on his legs as if smoothing a skirt. Then he noticed the small type near the bottom of the cover: "LINDA EVANGELISTA IN LOVE." He turned to the table of contents. He felt as if the boundary between his fingers and the page were disintegrating. There! He paged through the dark-hued Steven Meisel photographs, and then he stopped. A two-page spread of Linda, wearing a gray cropped sweater. She lay beneath her boyfriend, Kyle, the actor from "Twin Peaks," on a blanket that was suffused with morning sunlight. They were kissing, openmouthed. Her hand—with polished, short nails—gently held the side of his neck.

"Work it, Linda," Joe said happily, and then he lay back on the driveway, holding the magazine to his chest. Music billowed from the house next door, where a former friend of his, Al Theim, lived—a Michael Bolton number, sung as if the singer had taken an Uplift enema. Joe howled along in a fake, sour-bellied voice: "Nothing cures a broken heart like time, love, and tenderness."

IT WAS JUST like Al Theim to broadcast that kind of shit. Joe couldn't believe he'd once been in love with the guy. They used to spend afternoons together listening to Al's older brother's leftover records from the early eighties: A Flock of Seagulls, Visage, Ultravox. The singers wore makeup, and their hair was swept up in whoopie curls and banglets, but the songs, Joe thought, were some songs. Longing vocals on top of wet, sparkly keyboards: "Ultraviolet, radio lights, telecommunication . . ."

One warm October evening, almost four years earlier, Joe's mom had taken Joe and Al to Scream in the Dark, a haunted house set up in two gaping, connected barns, across the Mississippi, in Algiers. Christian kids dressed from top to bottom in hunter-orange directed the parking, took admission money, and made you sign an injury-release form. It felt like summer: it was seventy-four degrees out in the early evening. Joe and Al wore matching, tartan-plaid, flimsy cotton shorts. Even their thin, hairless legs matched.

"What kind of movie is this?" Joe's mom asked, bending over a picnic table to sign her form. Despite Joe's warning, she'd got herself up in a long black dress.

Joe went first, on his hands and knees into the entrance tunnel. Al followed, and then Joe's mom, her knees bound up in the dress. At the end of the tunnel was a ladder. Joe climbed to the second level, a pitch-dark room of indeterminate size, at the far end of which flashed the strobe-lit entrance to the next room. He ventured forward; Al and Mom followed.

"I thought it was going to be a movie," Mom said, and they all laughed. Then, in the dark, someone touched Joe's shoulder.

He shouted, "Al! That's not funny."

"I didn't do anything," Al whispered.

"Someone touched me," Mom said. "Run!"

Joe hurried through the lightlessness, his forearms braced in front of him, into the following room. The floor and walls and ceiling were painted in a black-and-white checkerboard pattern; the strobe light worked its distortions. Joe looked over his shoulder at his mom and laughed. She chanced a smile. The kids in front of him were trying to get to the other side of the room, but they couldn't walk straight. The floor was a sharp pyramid, and you slid backward as you got closer to the peak. Joe looked over his shoulder. The wall behind his mother was moving. There was a man in a checkerboard costume, face painted white, sliding along the wall. He reached out to touch her. Joe took her hand and dragged her into the next room.

Here, in a hyped-up jungle, where the recorded sounds of squawking birds and giggling monkeys played deafeningly, Joe's mom disappeared; she had found the emergency exit and run out. Joe could hear her shouting, "I thought it was a movie!" The floor was made of foam rubber, and covered with rolling, shin-high hurdles. Al took Joe's hand. A gorilla watched them from behind a vivid palm tree, the outline of which was glowing purple.

Al could distinguish the hurdles from the flat stretches, but Joe, at first, couldn't; he perceived, instead, only the fluorescent foliage painted on the foam. Al shouted "Jump!" at each hurdle.

There was nothing like holding Al's warm, sweaty hand. At what looked to be the final hurdle, Joe made himself fall, and pulled Al with him. They wriggled to the wall, Joe's head propped on the foam hurdle, Al's head on Joe's chest. They watched the jumble of flapping shirts and jeans, listened to the screams and laughter.

Al touched Joe's face. "I like you," he said.

"I like you more than that," Joe said.

"How much?"

Their voices stayed in the space between their faces, and Joe found himself close to tears. "More than I like anyone," he said. "All day in school, I think about you." Birds called. The gorilla moved closer, then paused.

"Man, that makes me feel good," Al said. "Say it again."

And then there had been a kiss.

Now, spread out on his driveway, Joe shuddered and shut his eyes tight. The memory had returned with unwelcome carnal immediacy. Al Theim hadn't meant a word he said, Joe thought. Al Theim was just some wack softhearted guy who blew a few sentences out of his mouth. And so were the handful of guys he'd met since. Bullshitters. Maybe I'm not trying hard enough, he thought. Maybe tonight I'll talk to every person I see on Decatur Street, just bust up to them on the sidewalk and introduce myself. He shifted his head on its bed of grass clippings and loose gravel, and then he fell asleep.

He awoke to the whoop of an approaching car horn. He cracked open his eyes and just barely lifted his head to see who it was. A top-dollar car, reflecting sunlight, so he couldn't make out its color. Friends? Family? He dropped his head back and shut his eyes.

The car pulled onto the driveway beside him, purred for a moment, and then went silent.

The door opened, and his mother said, "Wake up, I'm home."

"Hey," Joe said.

She walked around the car, the soles of her low heels scratching the macadam. She came to his spot beside the mailbox and crouched down next to him. "Where you going tonight?"

"Out with friends."

"O.K., I won't ask." She settled onto her knees and smoothed her lemony cotton lap.

"I *said* out with friends."

"I *said* I won't ask."

Joe struggled to sit, propping himself up on one elbow. He looked at his mother's shoes, at her hose and her dress, at her knuckly hands and freckled arms—the freckles from long hours of weekend sunbathing. He knew why she liked the heat beating down on her, emptying her thoughts. He appreciated as much as she did the sensation of spilling a glass of iced tea down your throat as you lay, nearly still, on a chair in your own back yard.

Joe could tell that she was tired. It was Friday. It had been a long week. He put his hand on the side of her face. Her skin was soft, and cold from the car's A.C. "Stay with me a minute," he said. "Let's hang out for a minute."

She tilted her head to the side, catching his hand between her cheek and shoulder and holding it there. "You talk," she said. "I'd be so grateful."

(1994)

Here Come
the Maples

John Updike

They had always been a lucky couple, and it was just
their luck that, as they at last decided to part, the
Puritan Commonwealth in which they lived passed
a no-fault amendment to its creaking, overworked
body of divorce law. By its provisions a joint affidavit had to be filed. It went, "Now come Richard F.
and Joan R. Maple and swear under the penalties of
perjury that an irretrievable breakdown of the marriage exists." For Richard, reading a copy of the document in his Boston apartment, the wording
conjured up a vision of himself and Joan breezing
into a party hand in hand while a liveried doorman
trumpeted their names and a snow of confetti and
champagne bubbles exploded in the room. In the
two decades of their marriage, they had gone together to a lot of parties, and always with a touch

of excitement, a little hope, a little expectation of something lucky happening.

With the affidavit were enclosed various frightening financial forms and a request for a copy of their marriage license. Though they had lived in New York and London, on islands and farms and for one summer even in a log cabin, they had been married a few subway stops from where Richard now stood, reading his mail. He had not been in the Cambridge City Hall since the morning he had been granted the license, the morning of their wedding. His parents had driven him up from the Connecticut motel where they had all spent the night, on their way from West Virginia; they had risen at six, to get there on time, and for much of the journey he had had his coat over his head, hoping to get back to sleep. He seemed in memory now a sea creature, boneless beneath the jellyfish bell of his own coat, rising helplessly along the coast as the air grew hotter and hotter. It was June, and steamy. When, toward noon, they got to Cambridge, and dragged their bodies and boxes of wedding clothes up the four flights to Joan's apartment, on Avon Street, the bride was taking a bath. Who else was in the apartment Richard could not remember; his recollection of the day was spotty—legible patches on a damp gray blotter. The day had no sky and no clouds, just a fog of shadowless sunlight enveloping the bricks on Brattle Street, and the white spires of Harvard, and the fat cars baking in the tarry streets. He was twenty-one, and Eisenhower was President, and the bride was behind the door, shouting that he mustn't come in, it would be bad luck for him to see her. Someone was in there with her, giggling and splashing. Who? Her sister? Her mother? Richard leaned against the bathroom door, and heard his parents heaving themselves up the stairs behind him, panting but still chattering, and pictured Joan as she was when in the bath, her toes pink, her neck tendrils flattened, her breasts floating and soapy and slick. Then the memory dried up, and the next blot showed her and him side by side, driving together into the shimmering noontime traffic jam of Central Square. She wore a summer dress of sun-faded cotton; he kept his eyes on the traffic, to minimize the bad luck of seeing her before the ceremony. Other couples, he thought at the time, must have arranged to have their papers in order more than two hours before the wedding. But then, no doubt, other grooms didn't travel to the ceremony with their coats over their heads like children hiding from a thunderstorm. Hand in hand, smaller than Hänsel and Gretel in his mind's eye, they ran up the long flight of stairs into a gingerbread-brown archway and disappeared.

CAMBRIDGE CITY HALL, in a changed world, was unchanged. The rounded Richardsonian castle, red sandstone and pink granite, loomed as a gentle giant in its crass neighborhood. Its interior was varnished oak, pale and gleaming. Richard seemed to remember receiving the license at a grated window downstairs with a brass plate, but an arrow on cardboard directed him upward. His knees trembled and his stomach churned at the enormity of what he was doing. He turned a corner. A grandmotherly woman reigned within a spacious, idle territory of green-topped desks and great ledgers in steel racks. "Could I get a c-copy of a marriage license?" he asked her.

"Year?"

"Beg pardon?"

"What is the year of the marriage license, sir?"

"1953." Enunciated, the year seemed distant as a star, yet here he was again, feeling not a minute older, and sweating in the same summer heat. Nevertheless, the lady, having taken down the names and the date, had to leave him and go to another chamber of the archives, so far away in truth was the event he wished to undo.

She returned with a limp he hadn't noticed before. The ledger she carried was three feet wide when opened, a sorcerer's tome. She turned the vast pages carefully, as if the chasm of lost life and forsaken time they represented might at a slip leap up and swallow them both. She must once have been a flaming redhead, but her hair had dulled to apricot and had stiffened to permanent curls, lifeless as dried paper. She smiled, a crimpy little smile. "Yes," she said. "Here we are."

And Richard could read, upside down, on a single long red line, Joan's maiden name and his own. Her profession was listed as "Teacher" (she had been an apprentice art teacher; he had forgotten her spattered blue smock, the clayey smell of her fingers, the way she would bicycle to work on even the coldest days) and his own, inferiorly, as "Student." And their given addresses surprised him, in being different—the foyer on Avon Street, the entryway in Lowell House, forgotten doors opening on the corridor of shared addresses that stretched from then to now. Their signatures— He could not bear to study their signatures, even upside down. At a glance, Joan's seemed firmer, and bluer. "You want one or more copies?"

"One should be enough."

As fussily as if she had not done this thousands of times before, the former redhead, smoothing the paper and repeatedly dipping her antique pen, copied the information onto a standard form.

What else survived of that wedding day? There were a few slides, Richard remembered. A cousin of Joan's had posed the main members of the wedding on the sidewalk outside the church, all gathered around a parking meter. The meter, a slim silvery representative of the municipality, occupies the place of honor in the grouping, with his narrow head and scarlet tongue. Like the meter, the groom is very thin. He blinked simultaneously with the shutter, so the suggestion of a death mask hovers about his face. The dimpled bride's pose, tense and graceful both, has something dancerlike about it, the feet pointed outward on the hot bricks; she might be about to pick up the organdie skirts of her bridal gown and vault herself into a tour jeté. The four parents, not yet transmogrified into grandparents, seem dim in the slide, half lost in the fog of light, benevolent and lumpy like the stones of the building in which Richard was shelling out the three-dollar fee for his copy, his anti-license.

Another image was captured by Richard's college roommate, who drove them to their honeymoon cottage in a seaside town an hour south of Cambridge. A croquet set had been left on the porch, and Richard, in one of those stunts he had developed to mask unease, picked up three of the balls and began to juggle. The roommate, perhaps also uneasy, snapped the moment up; the red ball hangs there forever, blurred, in the amber slant of the dying light, while the yellow and green glint in Richard's hands and his face concentrates upward in a slack-jawed ecstasy.

"I have another problem," he told the grandmotherly clerk as she shut the vast ledger and prepared to shoulder it.

"What would that be?" she asked.

"I have an affidavit that should be notarized."

"That wouldn't be my department, sir. First floor, to the left when you get off the elevator, to the right if you use the stairs. The stairs are quicker, if you ask me."

He followed her directions and found a young black woman at a steel desk bristling with gold-framed images of fidelity and solidarity and stability, of children and parents, of a sombre brown boy in a brown military uniform, of a family laughing by a lakeside; there was even a photograph of a house—an ordinary little ranch house somewhere, with a green lawn. She read Richard's affidavit without comment. He suppressed his urge to beg her pardon. She asked to see his driver's license and compared its face with his. She handed him a pen and set a seal of irrevocability beside his signature. The red ball still hung in the air, somewhere in a box of slides he would never see again, and the luminous hush of the cottage when they were left alone in it still travelled, a capsule of silence, outward to the stars; but what grieved Richard more, wincing as he stepped from the brown archway into the summer glare, was a suspended detail of the wedding. In his daze, his sleepiness, in his wonder at the white creature trembling beside him at the altar, on the edge of his awareness like a rainbow in a fog, he had forgotten to seal the vows with a kiss. Joan had glanced over at him, smiling, expectant; he had smiled back, not remembering. The moment passed, and they hurried down the aisle as now he hurried, ashamed, down the City Hall stairs to the street and the tunnel of the subway.

AS THE SUBWAY racketed through darkness, he read about the forces of nature. A scholarly extract had come in the mail, in the same mail as the affidavit. Before he lived alone, he would have thrown it away without a second look, but now, as he slowly took on the careful habits of a Boston codger, he read every scrap he was sent, and even stooped in the alleys to pick up a muddy fragment of newspaper and scan it for a message. *Thus,* he read, *it was already known in 1935 that the natural world was governed by four kinds of force: in order of increasing strength, they are the gravitational, the weak, the electromagnetic, and the strong.* Reading, he found himself rooting for the weak forces; he identified with them. Gravitation, though negligible at the microcosmic level, *begins to predominate with objects on the order of magnitude of a hundred kilometres, like large asteroids; it holds together the moon, the earth, the solar system, the stars, clusters of stars within galaxies, and the galaxies themselves.* To Richard it was as if a fainthearted team overpowered at the start of the game was surging to triumph in the last, macrocosmic quarter; he inwardly cheered. The subway lurched to a stop at Kendall, and he remembered how, a few days after their wedding, he and Joan took a train north through New Hampshire, to summer jobs they had contracted for, as a couple. The train, long since discontinued, had wound its way north along the busy rivers sullied by sawmills and into evergreen mountains where ski lifts stood rusting. The seats had been purple plush, and the train incessantly, gently swayed. Her arms, pale against the plush, showed a pink shadowing of sunburn. Uncertain of how to have a honeymoon, yet certain that they must create memories to last till death did them part, they had played croquet naked, in the little yard that, amid the trees, seemed an eye of grass gazing upward at the sky. She beat him, every game. *The weak force,* Richard read, *does not appreciably affect the structure of the nucleus before the decay occurs; it is like a flaw in a bell of cast metal which has no effect on the ringing of the bell until it finally causes the bell to fall into pieces.*

The subway car climbed into light, to cross the Charles. Sailboats tilted on the glitter below. Across the river, Boston's smoke-colored skyscrapers hung like paralyzed fountains. The train had leaned around a bay of a lake and halted at The Weirs, a gritty summer place of ice cream dripped on asphalt, of a candy-apple scent wafted from the edge of childhood. After a wait of hours, they caught the mail boat to their island where they would work. The island was on the far side of Lake Winnipesaukee, with many other islands intervening, and many mail drops necessary. Before each docking, the boat blew its whistle—an immense noise. The Maples had sat on the prow, for the sun and scenery; once there, directly under the whistle, they felt they had to stay. The islands, the water, the mountains beyond the shore did an adagio of shifting perspectives around them and then—each time, astoundingly—the blast of the whistle would flatten their hearts and crush the landscape into a wad of noise; these blows assaulted their young marriage. He both blamed her and wished to beg her forgiveness for what neither of them could control. After each blast, the engine would be cut, the boat would sidle to a rickety dock, and from the dappled soft paths of this or that evergreen island tan children and counsellors in bathing trunks and moccasins would spill forth to receive their mail, their shouts ringing strangely in the deafened ears of the newlyweds. By the time they reached their own island, the Maples were exhausted.

Quantum mechanics and relativity, taken together, are extraordinarily restrictive and they, therefore, provide us with a great logical engine. Richard returned the pamphlet to his pocket and got off at Charles. He walked across the overpass toward the hospital, to see his arthritis man. His bones ached at night. He had friends who were dying, who were dead; it no longer seemed incredible that he would follow them. The first time he had visited this hospital, it had been to court Joan. He had climbed this same ramp to the glass doors and inquired within, stammering, for the whereabouts, in this grand maze of unhealth, of the girl who had sat, with a rubber band around her ponytail, in the front row of English 162b: "The English Epic Tradition, Spenser to Tennyson." He had admired the tilt of the back of her head for three hours a week all winter. He gathered up courage to talk in exam period as, together at a library table, they were mulling over murky photostats of Blake's illustrations to "Paradise Lost." They agreed to meet after the exam and have a beer. She didn't show. In that amphitheatre of desperately thinking heads, hers was absent. And, having put "The Faerie Queene" and "The Idylls of the King" to rest together, he called her dorm and learned that Joan had been taken to the hospital. A force of nature drove him to brave the long corridors and the wrong turns and the crowd of aunts and other suitors at the foot of the bed; he found Joan in white, between white sheets, her hair loose about her shoulders and a plastic tube feeding something transparent into the underside of her arm. In later visits, he achieved the right to hold her hand, trussed though it was with splints and tapes. Platelet deficiency had been the diagnosis. The complaint had been she couldn't stop bleeding. Blushing, she told him how the doctors and internes had asked her when she had last had intercourse, and how embarrassing it had been to confess, in the face of their polite disbelief, never.

The doctor removed the blood-pressure tourniquet from Richard's arm and smiled. "Have you been under any stress lately?"

"I've been getting a divorce."

"Arthritis, as you may know, belongs to a family of complaints with a psychosomatic component."

"All I know is that I wake up at four in the morning and it's very depressing to think I'll never get over this, this pain'll be inside my shoulder for the rest of my life."

"You will. It won't."

"When?"

"When your brain stops sending out punishing signals."

Her hand, in its little cradle of healing apparatus, its warmth unresisting and noncommittal as he held it at her bedside, rested high, nearly at the level of his eyes. On the island, the beds in the log cabin set aside for them were of different heights, and though Joan tried to make them into a double bed, there was a ledge where the mattresses met which either he or she had to cross, amid a discomfort of sheets pulling loose. But the cabin was in the woods and powerful moist scents of pine and fern swept through the screens with the morning chirrup of birds and the evening rustle of animals. There was a rumor there were deer on the island; they crossed the ice in the winter and were trapped when it melted in the spring. Though no one, neither camper nor counsellor, ever saw the deer, the rumor persisted that they were there.

Why then has no one ever seen a quark? Remembering this sentence as he walked along Charles Street toward his apartment, that no one has ever seen a quark, Richard fished in his pockets for the pamphlet on the forces of nature, and came up instead with a new prescription for painkiller, a copy of his marriage license, and the signed affidavit. *Now come . . .* The pamphlet had got folded into it. He couldn't find the sentence, and instead read, *The theory that the strong force becomes stronger as the quarks are pulled apart is somewhat speculative; but its complement, the idea that the force gets weaker as the quarks are pushed closer to each other, is better established.* Yes, he thought, that had happened. In life there are four forces: love, habit, time, and boredom. Love and habit at short range are immensely powerful, but time, lacking a minus charge, accumulates inexorably, and with its brother boredom levels all. He was dying; that made him cruel. His heart flattened in horror at what he had just done. How could he tell Joan what he had done to their marriage license? The very quarks in the telephone circuits would rebel.

In the forest, there had been a green clearing, an eye of grass, a meadow starred with microcosmic white flowers, and here one dusk the deer had come, the female slightly in advance, the male larger and darker, his rump still in shadow as his mate nosed out the day's last sun, the silhouettes of both haloed by the same light that gilded the meadow grass. A fleet of blank-faced motorcyclists roared by, a rummy waved to

Richard from a laundromat doorway, a girl in a seductive halter gave him a cold eye, the light changed from red to green, and he could not remember if he needed orange juice or bread, doubly annoyed because he could not remember if they had ever really seen the deer, or if he had imagined the memory, conjured it from the longing that it be so.

"I DON'T REMEMBER," Joan said over the phone. "I don't think we did, we just talked about it."

"Wasn't there a kind of clearing beyond the cabin, if you followed the path?"

"We never went that way, it was too buggy."

"A stag and a doe, just as it was getting dark. Don't you remember anything?"

"No. I honestly don't, Richard. How guilty do you want me to feel?"

"Not at all, if it didn't happen. Speaking of nostalgia—"

"Yes?"

"I went up to Cambridge City Hall this afternoon and got a copy of our marriage license."

"Oh dear. How was it?"

"It wasn't bad. The place is remarkably the same. Did we get the license upstairs or downstairs?"

"Downstairs, to the left of the elevator as you go in."

"That's where I got our affidavit notarized. You'll be getting a copy soon; it's a shocking document."

"I did get it, yesterday. What was shocking about it? I thought it was funny, the way it was worded. Here we come, there we go."

"Darley, you're so tough and brave."

"I assume I must be. No?"

"Yes."

Not for the first time in these two years did he feel an eggshell thinness behind which he crouched and which Joan needed only to raise her voice to break. But she declined to break it, either out of ignorance of how thin the shell was, or because she was hatching on its other side, just as, on the other side of that bathroom door, she had been drawing near to marriage at the same rate as he, and with the same regressive impulses. "What I don't understand," she was saying, "are we both supposed to sign the same statement, or do we each sign one, or what? And which one? My lawyer keeps sending me three of everything, and some of them are in blue covers. Are these the important ones or the unimportant ones that I can keep?"

In truth, the lawyers, so adroit in their accustomed adversary world of blame, of suit and countersuit, did seem confused by the no-fault provision. On the very morning of the divorce, Richard's greeted him on the courthouse steps with the possibility that he as plaintiff might be asked to specify what in the marriage had persuaded him of its irretrievable breakdown. "But that's the whole point of no-fault," Joan interposed, "that you don't have to say anything." She had climbed the courthouse steps beside Richard; indeed, they had come in the same car, because one of their children had taken hers.

The proceeding was scheduled for early in the day. Picking her up at a quarter after seven, he had found her standing barefoot on the lawn in the circle of their driveway, up to her ankles in mist and dew. She was holding her high-heeled shoes in her hand. The sight made him laugh. Opening the car door, he said, "So there *are* deer on the island!"

She was too preoccupied to make sense of his allusion. She asked him, "Do you think the judge will mind if I don't wear stockings?"

"Keep your legs behind his bench," he said. He was feeling fluttery, lightheaded. He had scarcely slept, though his shoulder had not hurt, for a change. She got into the car, bringing with her her shoes and the moist smell of dawn. She had always been an early riser, and he a late one. "Thanks for doing this," she said, of the ride, adding, "I guess."

"My pleasure," Richard said. As they drove to court, discussing their cars and their children, he marvelled at how light Joan had become; she sat on the side of his vision as light as a feather, her voice tickling his ear, her familiar intonations and emphases thoroughly musical and half unheard, like the patterns of a concerto that sets us to daydreaming. He no longer blamed her: that was the reason for the lightness. All those years, he had blamed her for everything—for the traffic jam in Central Square, for the blasts of noise on the mail boat, for the difference in the levels of their beds. No longer: he had set her adrift from omnipotence. He had set her free, free from fault. She was to him as Gretel to Hänsel, a kindred creature moving beside him down a path while birds behind them ate the bread crumbs.

Richard's lawyer eyed Joan lugubriously. "I understand that, Mrs. Maple," he said. "But perhaps I should have a word in private with my client."

The lawyers they had chosen were oddly different. Richard's was a big rumpled Irishman, his beige summer suit baggy and his belly straining his shirt, a melancholic and comforting father-type. Joan's was small, natty, and flip; he dressed in checks and talked from the side of his mouth, like a racing tout. Twinkling, chipper even at this sleepy hour, he emerged from behind a pillar in the marble temple of justice and led Joan away. Her head, slightly higher than his, tilted to give him her ear; she dimpled, docile. Richard wondered in amazement, Could this sort of man have been, all these years, the secret type of her desire? His own lawyer, breathing heavily, asked him, "If the judge does ask for a specific cause of the breakdown—and I don't say he will, we're all sailing uncharted waters here—what will you say?"

"I don't know," Richard said. He studied the swirl of marble, like a tiny wave breaking, between his shoe tips. "We had political differences. She used to make me go on peace marches."

"Any physical violence?"

"Not much. Not enough, maybe. You really think he'll ask this sort of thing? Is this no-fault or not?"

"No-fault is a *tabula rasa* in this state. At this point, Dick, it's what we make of it. I don't know what he'll do. We should be prepared."

"Well—aside from the politics, we didn't get along that well sexually."

The air between them thickened; with his own father, too, sex had been a painful topic. His lawyer's breathing became grievously audible. "So you'd be prepared to say there was personal and emotional incompatibility?"

It seemed profoundly untrue, but Richard nodded. "If I have to."

"Good enough." The lawyer put his big hand on Richard's arm and squeezed. His closeness, his breathiness, his air of restless urgency and forced cheer, his old-fashioned suit and the folder of papers tucked under his arm like roster sheets all came into focus: he was a coach, and Richard was about to kick the winning field goal, do the high-difficulty dive, strike out the heart of the batting order with the bases already loaded. Go.

They entered the courtroom two by two. The chamber was chaste and empty; the carved trim was painted forest green. The windows gave on an ancient river blackened by industry. Dead judges gazed alertly down. The two lawyers conferred, leaving Richard and Joan to stand awkwardly apart. He made his "What now?" face at her. She made her "Beats me" face back. "Oyez, oyez," a disembodied voice chanted, and the judge hurried in, smiling, his robes swinging. He was a little sharp-featured man with a polished pink face; his face declared that he was altogether good, and would never die. He stood and nodded at them. He seated himself. The lawyers went forward to confer in whispers. Richard inertly gravitated toward Joan, the only animate object in the room that did not repel him. "It's a Daumier," she whispered, of the tableau being enacted before them. The lawyers parted. The judge beckoned. He was so clean his smile squeaked. He showed Richard a piece of paper; it was the affidavit. "Is this your signature?" he asked him.

"It is," Richard said.

"And do you believe, as this paper states, that your marriage has suffered an irretrievable breakdown?"

"I do."

The judge turned his face toward Joan. His voice softened a notch. "Is this *your* signature?"

"It is." Her voice was a healing spray, full of tiny rainbows, in the corner of his eye.

"And do you believe that your marriage has suffered an irretrievable breakdown?"

A pause. She did not believe that, Richard knew. She said, "I do."

The judge smiled and wished them both good luck. The lawyers sagged with relief, and a torrent of merry legal chitchat—speculations about the future of no-fault, reminiscences of the old days of Alabama quickies—excluded Joan and Richard. Obsolete at their own ceremony, Joan and Richard stepped back from the bench in unison and stood side by side, uncertain of how to turn, until Richard at last remembered what to do; he kissed her.

(1976)

YOURS

MARY ROBISON

Allison struggled away from her white Renault, limping with the weight of the last of the pumpkins. She found Clark in the twilight on the twig- and leaf-littered porch, behind the house. He wore a tan wool shawl. He was moving up and back in a cushioned glider, pushed by the ball of his slippered foot.

Allison lowered a big pumpkin and let it rest on the porch floor.

Clark was much older than she—seventy-eight to Allison's thirty-five. They had been married for four months. They were both quite tall, with long hands, and their faces looked something alike. Allison wore a natural-hair wig. It was a thick blond hood around her face. She was dressed in bright-dyed denims today. She wore durable clothes, usually, for she volunteered afternoons at a children's day-care center.

She put one of the smaller pumpkins on Clark's long lap. "Now, nothing surreal," she told him. "Carve just a *regular* face. These are for kids."

In the foyer, on the Hepplewhite desk, Allison found the maid's chore list, with its cross-offs, which included Clark's supper. Allison went quickly through the day's mail: a garish coupon packet, a flyer advertising white wines at Jamestown Liquors, November's pay-TV program guide, and—the worst thing, the funniest—an already opened, extremely unkind letter from Clark's married daughter, up North. "You're an old fool," Allison read, and "You're being cruelly deceived." There was a gift check for twenty-five dollars, made out to Clark, enclosed—his birthday had just passed—but it was uncashable. It was signed "Jesus H. Christ."

Late, late into this night, Allison and Clark gutted and carved the pumpkins together, at an old table set out on the back porch. They worked over newspaper after soggy newspaper, using paring knives and spoons and a Swiss Army knife Clark liked for the exact shaping of teeth and eyes and nostrils. Clark had been a doctor—an internist—but he was also a Sunday watercolor painter. His four pumpkins were expressive and artful. Their carved features were suited to the sizes and shapes of the pumpkins. Two looked ferocious and jagged. One registered surprise. The last was serene and beaming.

Allison's four faces were less deftly drawn, with slits and areas of distortion. She had cut triangles for noses and eyes. The mouths she had made were all just wedges—two turned up and two turned down.

By 1 A.M., they were finished. Clark, who had bent his long torso forward to work, moved over to the glider again and looked out sleepily at nothing. All the neighbors' lights were out across the ravine. For the season and time, the Virginia night was warm. Most of the leaves had fallen and blown away already, and the trees stood unbothered. The moon was round, above them.

Allison cleaned up the mess.

"Your jack-o'-lanterns are much much better than mine," Clark said to her.

"Like hell," Allison said.

"Look at me," Clark said, and Allison did. She was holding a squishy bundle of newspapers. The papers reeked sweetly with the smell of pumpkin innards. "Yours are *far* better," he said.

"You're wrong. You'll see when they're lit," Allison said.

She went inside, came back with yellow vigil candles. It took her a while to get each candle settled into a pool of its own melted wax inside the jack-o'-lanterns, which were lined up in a row on the porch railing. Allison went along and relit each candle and fixed the pumpkin lids over the little flames. "See?" she said. They sat together a moment and looked at the orange faces.

"We're exhausted. It's good-night time," Allison said. "Don't blow out the candles. I'll put in new ones tomorrow."

In her bedroom, a few weeks earlier in her life than had been predicted, she began to die. "Don't look at me if my wig comes off," she told Clark. "Please." Her pulse cords were fluttering under his fingers. She raised her knees and kicked away the comforter. She said something to Clark about the garage being locked.

At the telephone, Clark had a clear view out back and down to the porch. He wanted to get drunk with his wife once more. He wanted to tell her, from the greater perspective he had, that to own only a little talent, like his, was an awful, plaguing thing; that being only a little special meant you expected too much, most of the time, and liked yourself too little. He wanted to assure her that she had missed nothing.

Clark was speaking into the phone now. He watched the jack-o'-lanterns. The jack-o'-lanterns watched him.

(1984)

Roses, Rhododendron

ALICE ADAMS

One dark and rainy Boston spring of many years ago, I spent all my after-school and evening hours in the living room of our antique-crammed Cedar Street flat, writing down what the Ouija board said to my mother. My father, a spoiled and rowdy Irishman, a sometime engineer, had run off to New Orleans with a girl, and my mother hoped to learn from the board if he would come back. Then, one night in May, during a crashing black thunderstorm (my mother was both afraid and much in awe of such storms), the board told her to move down South, to North Carolina, taking me and all the antiques she had been collecting for years, and to open a store in a small town down there. That is what we did, and shortly thereafter, for the first time in my life, I fell violently and permanently in love: with a house, with a family of three people, and with an area of countryside.

Perhaps too little attention is paid to the necessary preconditions of "falling in love"—I mean the state of mind or place that precedes one's first sight of the loved person (or house or land). In my own case, I remember the dark Boston afternoons as a precondition of love. Later on, for another important time, I recognized boredom in a job. And once the fear of growing old.

In the town that she had chosen, my mother, Margot (she picked out her own name, having been christened Margaret), rented a small house on a pleasant back street. It had a big surrounding screened-in porch, where she put most of the antiques, and she put a discreet sign out in the front yard: "Margot—Antiques." The store was open only in the afternoons. In the mornings and on Sundays, she drove around the countryside in our ancient and spacious Buick, searching for trophies among the area's country stores and farms and barns. (She is nothing if not enterprising; no one else down there had thought of doing that before.)

Although frequently embarrassed by her aggression—she thought nothing of making offers for furniture that was in use in a family's rooms—I often drove with her during those first few weeks. I was excited by the novelty of the landscape. The red clay banks that led up to the thick pine groves, the swollen brown creeks half hidden by flowering tangled vines. Bare, shaded yards from which rose gaunt, narrow houses. Chickens that scattered, barefoot children who stared at our approach.

"Hello there. I'm Mrs. John Kilgore—Margot Kilgore—and I'm interested in buying old furniture. Family portraits. Silver."

Margot a big brassily bleached blonde in a pretty flowered-silk dress and high-heeled patent sandals. A hoarse and friendly voice. Me a scrawny, pale, curious girl, about ten, in a blue linen dress with smocking across the bodice. (Margot has always had a passionate belief in good clothes, no matter what.)

On other days, Margot would say, "I'm going to look over my so-called books. Why don't you go for a walk or something, Jane?"

And I would walk along the sleepy, leafed-over streets, on the unpaved sidewalks, past houses that to me were as inviting and as interesting as unread books, and I would try to imagine what went on inside. The families. Their lives.

The main street, where the stores were, interested me least. Two-story brick buildings—dry-goods stores, with dentists' and lawyers' offices above. There was also a drugstore, with round marble tables and wire-backed chairs, at which wilting ladies sipped at their Cokes (this was to become a favorite haunt of Margot's). I preferred the civic monuments: a pre-Revolutionary Episcopal chapel of yellowish cracked plaster, and several tall white statues to the Civil War dead—all of them quickly overgrown with ivy or Virginia creeper.

These were the early nineteen-forties, and in the next few years the town was to change enormously. Its small textile factories would be given defense contracts (parachute silk); a Navy preflight school would be established at a neighboring university town. But at that moment it was a sleeping village. Untouched.

My walks were not a lonely occupation, but Margot worried that they were, and some curious reasoning led her to believe that a bicycle would help. (Of course, she turned out to be right.) We went to Sears, and she bought me a big new bike—blue, with balloon tires—on which I began to explore the outskirts of town and the countryside.

The house I fell in love with was about a mile out of town, on top of a hill. A small stone bank that was all overgrown with tangled roses led up to its yard, and pink and white roses climbed up a trellis to the roof of the front porch—the roof on which, later, Harriet and I used to sit and exchange our stores of erroneous sexual information. Harriet Farr was the daughter of the house. On one side of the house, there was what looked like a newer wing, with a bay window and a long side porch, below which the lawn sloped down to some flowering shrubs. There was a yellow rosebush, rhododendron, a plum tree, and beyond were woods—pines, and oak and cedar trees. The effect was rich and careless, generous and somewhat mysterious. I was deeply stirred.

As I was observing all this, from my halted bike on the dusty white hilltop, a small, plump woman, very erect, came out of the front door and went over to a flower bed below the bay window. She sat down very stiffly. (Emily, who was Harriet's mother, had some terrible, never diagnosed trouble with her back; she generally wore a brace.) She was older than Margot, with very beautiful white hair that was badly cut in that butchered nineteen-thirties way.

From the first, I was fascinated by Emily's obvious dissimilarity to Margot. I think I was also somehow drawn to her contradictions—the shapeless body held up with so much dignity, even while she was sitting in the dirt. The lovely chopped-off hair. (There were greater contradictions, which I learned of later—she was a Virginia Episcopalian who always voted for Norman Thomas, a feminist who always delayed meals for her tardy husband.)

Emily's hair was one of the first things about the Farr family that I mentioned to Margot after we became friends, Harriet and Emily and I, and I began to spend most of my time in that house.

"I don't think she's ever dyed it," I said, with almost conscious lack of tact.

Of course, Margot was defensive. "I wouldn't dye mine if I thought it would be a decent color on its own."

But by that time Margot's life was also improving. Business was fairly good, and she had finally heard from my father, who began to send sizable checks from New Orleans. He had found work with an oil company. She still asked the Ouija board if she would see him again, but her question was less obsessive.

THE SECOND TIME I rode past that house, there was a girl sitting on the front porch, reading a book. She was about my age. She looked up. The next time I saw her there, we both smiled. And the time after that (a Saturday morning in late June) she got up and slowly came out to the road, to where I had stopped, ostensibly to look at the view—the sweep of fields, the white highway, which wound down to the thick greenery bordering the creek, the fields and trees that rose in dim and distant hills.

"I've got a bike exactly like that," Harriet said indifferently, as though to deny the gesture of having come out to meet me.

For years, perhaps beginning then, I used to seek my antithesis in friends. Inexorably following Margot, I was becoming a big blonde, with some of her same troubles. Harriet was cool and dark, with long, gray eyes. A girl about to be beautiful.

"Do you want to come in? We've got some lemon cake that's pretty good."

Inside, the house was cluttered with odd mixtures of furniture. I glimpsed a living room, where there was a shabby sofa next to a pretty, "antique" table. We walked through a dining room that contained a decrepit mahogany table surrounded with delicate fruitwood chairs. (I had a horrifying moment of imagining Margot there, with her accurate eye—making offers in her harsh Yankee voice.) The walls were crowded with portraits and with nineteenth-century oils of bosky landscapes. Books overflowed from rows of shelves along the walls. I would have moved in at once.

We took our lemon cake back to the front porch and ate it there, overlooking that view. I can remember its taste vividly. It was light and tart and sweet, and a beautiful lemon color. With it, we drank cold milk, and then we had seconds and more milk, and we discussed what we liked to read.

We were both at an age to begin reading grownup books, and there was some minor competition between us to see who had read more of them. Harriet won easily, partly because her mother reviewed books for the local paper, and had brought home Steinbeck, Thomas Wolfe, Virginia Woolf, and Elizabeth Bowen. But we also found in common an enthusiasm for certain novels about English children. (Such snobbery!)

"It's the best cake I've ever had!" I told Harriet. I had already adopted something of Margot's emphatic style.

"It's very good," Harriet said judiciously. Then, quite casually, she added, "We could ride our bikes out to Laurel Hill."

We soared dangerously down the winding highway. At the bridge across the creek, we stopped and turned onto a narrow, rutted dirt road that followed the creek through woods as dense and as alien as a jungle would have been—thick pines with low sweeping branches, young leafed-out maples, peeling tall poplars, elms, brambles, green masses of honeysuckle. At times, the road was impassable, and we had to get off our bikes and push them along, over crevices and ruts, through mud or sand. And with all that we kept up our somewhat stilted discussion of literature.

"I love Virginia Woolf!"

"Yes, she's very good. Amazing metaphors."

I thought Harriet was an extraordinary person—more intelligent, more poised, and prettier than any girl of my age I had ever known. I felt that she could become anything at all—a writer, an actress, a foreign correspondent (I went to a lot of movies). And I was not entirely wrong; she eventually became a sometimes-published poet.

We came to a small beach, next to a place where the creek widened and ran over some shallow rapids. On the other side, large gray rocks rose steeply. Among the stones grew isolated, twisted trees, and huge bushes with thick green leaves. The laurel of Laurel Hill. Rhododendron. Harriet and I took off our shoes and waded into the warmish water. The bottom squished under our feet, making us laugh, like the children we were, despite all our literary talk.

MARGOT WAS ALSO making friends. Unlike me, she seemed to seek her own likeness, and she found a sort of kinship with a woman named Dolly Murray, a rich widow from Memphis who shared many of Margot's superstitions—fear of thunderstorms, faith in the Ouija board. About ten years older than Margot, Dolly still dyed her hair red; she was a noisy, biassed, generous woman. They drank gin and gossiped together, they met for Cokes at the drugstore, and sometimes they drove to a neighboring town to have dinner in a restaurant (in those days, still a daring thing for unescorted ladies to do).

I am sure that the Farrs, outwardly a conventional family, saw me as a neglected child. I was so available for meals and overnight visits. But that is not how I experienced my life—I simply felt free. And an important thing to be said about Margot as a mother is that she never made me feel guilty for doing what I wanted to do. And of how many mothers can that be said?

There must have been a moment of "meeting" Emily, but I have forgotten it. I remember only her gentle presence, a soft voice, and my own sense of love returned. Beautiful white hair, dark deep eyes, and a wide mouth, whose corners turned and moved to express whatever she felt—amusement, interest, boredom, pain. I have never since seen such a vulnerable mouth.

I amused Emily; I almost always made her smile. She must have seen me as something foreign—a violent, enthusiastic Yankee (I used forbidden words, like "God" and "damn"). Very unlike the decorous young Southern girl that she must have been, that Harriet almost was.

She talked to me a lot; Emily explained to me things about the South that otherwise I would not have picked up. "Virginians feel superior to everyone else, you know," she said, in her gentle Virginian voice. "Some people in my family were quite shocked when I married a man from North Carolina and came down here to live. And a Presbyterian at that! Of course, that's nowhere near as bad as a Baptist, but only Episcopalians really count." This was all said lightly, but I knew that some part of Emily agreed with the rest of her family.

"How about Catholics?" I asked her, mainly to prolong the conversation. Harriet was at the dentist's, and Emily was sitting at her desk answering letters. I was perched on the sofa near her, and we both faced the sweeping green view. But since my father, Johnny Kilgore, was a lapsed Catholic, it was not an entirely frivolous question. Margot was a sort of Christian Scientist (her own sort).

"We hardly know any Catholics." Emily laughed, and then she sighed. "I do sometimes still miss Virginia. You know, when we drive up there I can actually feel the difference as we cross the state line. I've met a few people from South Carolina," she went on, "and I understand that people down there feel the same way Virginians do." Clearly, she found this unreasonable.

"West Virginia? Tennessee?"

"They don't seem Southern at all. Neither do Florida and Texas—not to me."

("Dolly says that Mrs. Farr is a terrible snob," Margot told me, inquiringly.

"In a way." I spoke with a new diffidence that I was trying to acquire from Harriet.

"Oh.")

Once, I told Emily what I had been wanting to say since my first sight of her. I said, "Your hair is so beautiful. Why don't you let it grow?"

She laughed, because she usually laughed at what I said, but at the same time she looked surprised, almost startled. I understood that what I had said was not improper but that she was totally unused to attentions of that sort from anyone, including herself. She didn't think about her hair. In a puzzled way, she said, "Perhaps I will."

Nor did Emily dress like a woman with much regard for herself. She wore practical, seersucker dresses and sensible, low shoes. Because her body had so little shape, no indentations (this must have been at least partly due to the back brace), I was surprised to notice that she had pretty, shapely legs. She wore little or no makeup on her sun- and wind-weathered face.

And what of Lawrence Farr, the North Carolina Presbyterian for whom Emily had left her people and her state? He was a small, precisely made man, with fine dark features (Harriet looked very like him). A lawyer, but widely read in literature, especially the English nineteenth century. He had a courtly manner, and sometimes a wicked tongue; melancholy eyes, and an odd, sudden, ratchety laugh. He looked ten years younger than Emily; the actual difference was less than two.

"WELL," SAID MARGOT, settling into a Queen Anne chair—a new antique—on our porch one stifling hot July morning, "I heard some really interesting gossip about your friends."

Margot had met and admired Harriet, and Harriet liked her, too—Margot made Harriet laugh, and she praised Harriet's fine brown hair. But on some instinct (I am not sure whose) the parents had not met. Very likely, Emily, with her Southern social antennae, had somehow sensed that this meeting would be a mistake.

That morning, Harriet and I were going on a picnic in the woods to the steep rocky side of Laurel Hill, but I forced myself to listen, or half listen, to Margot's story.

"Well, it seems that some years ago Lawrence Farr fell absolutely madly in love with a beautiful young girl—in fact, the orphaned daughter of a friend of his. Terribly romantic. Of course, she loved him, too, but he felt so awful and guilty that they never did anything about it."

I did not like this story much; it made me obscurely uncomfortable, and I think that at some point both Margot and I wondered why she was telling it. Was she pointing out imperfections in my chosen other family? But I asked, in Harriet's indifferent voice, "He never kissed her?"

"Well, maybe. I don't know. But of course everyone in town knew all about it, including Emily Farr. And with her back! Poor woman," Margot added somewhat piously but with real feeling, too.

I forgot the story readily at the time. For one thing, there was some-thing unreal about anyone as old as Lawrence Farr "falling in love." But looking back to Emily's face, Emily looking at Lawrence, I can see that pained watchfulness of a woman who has been hurt, and by a man who could always hurt her again.

In those days, what struck me about the Farrs was their extreme cour-tesy to each other—something I had not seen before. Never a harsh word. Of course, I did not know then about couples who cannot afford a single harsh word.

POSSIBLY BECAUSE OF the element of danger (very slight—the slope was gentle), the roof over the front porch was one of the places Harriet and I liked to sit on warm summer nights when I was invited to stay over. There was a country silence, invaded at intervals by summer country sounds—the strangled croak of tree frogs from down in the glen; the crazy baying of a distant hound. There, in the heavy scent of roses, on the scratchy shingles, Harriet and I talked about sex.

"A girl I know told me that if you do it a lot your hips get very wide."

"My cousin Duncan says it makes boys strong if they do it."

"It hurts women a lot—especially at first. But I knew this girl from Santa Barbara, and she said that out there they say Filipinos can do it without hurting."

"Colored people do it a lot more than whites."

"Of course, they have all those babies. But in Boston so do Catholics!"

We are seized with hysteria. We laugh and laugh, so that Emily hears and calls up to us, "Girls, why haven't you-all gone to bed?" But her voice is warm and amused—she likes having us laughing up there.

And Emily liked my enthusiasm for lemon cake. She teased me about the amounts of it I could eat, and she continued to keep me sup-plied. She was not herself much of a cook—their maid, a young black girl named Evelyn, did most of the cooking.

Once, but only once, I saw the genteel and opaque surface of that family shattered—saw those three people suddenly in violent opposi-tion to each other, like shards of splintered glass. But what I have for-gotten is the cause—what brought about that terrible explosion?

The four of us, as so often, were seated at lunch. Emily was at what seemed to be the head of the table. At her right hand was the small silver bell that summoned Evelyn to clear, or to bring a new course. Harriet and I across from each other, Lawrence across from Emily. (There was always a tentativeness about Lawrence's posture. He could have been an honored guest, or a spoiled and favorite child.) We were talking in an easy way. I have a vivid recollection only of words that began to career and gather momentum, to go out of control. Of voices raised. Then Harriet rushes from the room. Emily's face reddens dangerously, the corners of her mouth twitch downward, and Lawrence, in an exquisitely icy voice, begins to lecture me on the virtues of reading Trollope. I am supposed to help him pretend that nothing has happened, but I can hardly hear what he is saying. I am in shock.

That sudden unleashing of violence, that exposed depth of terrible emotions might have suggested to me that the Farrs were not quite as I had imagined them, not the impeccable family in my mind—but it did not. I was simply and terribly—and selfishly—upset, and hugely relieved when it all seemed to have passed over.

DURING THAT SUMMER, the Ouija board spoke only gibberish to Margot, or it answered direct questions with repeated evasions:

"Will I ever see Johnny Kilgore again, in this life?"

"Yes no perhaps."

"Honey, that means you've got no further need of the board, not right now. You've got to think everything out with your own heart and instincts," Dolly said.

Margot seemed to take her advice. She resolutely put the board away, and she wrote to Johnny that she wanted a divorce.

I had begun to notice that these days, on these sultry August nights, Margot and Dolly were frequently joined on their small excursions by a man named Larry—a jolly, red-faced man who was in real estate and who reminded me considerably of my father.

I said as much to Margot, and was surprised at her furious reaction. "They could not be more different, they are altogether opposite. Larry is a Southern gentleman. You just don't pay any attention to anyone but those Farrs."

A word about Margot's quite understandable jealousy of the Farrs. Much later in my life, when I was unreasonably upset at the attachment of one of my own daughters to another family (unreasonable because her chosen group were all talented musicians, as she was), a wise friend told me that we all could use more than one set of parents—our relations with the original set are too intense, and need dissipating. But no one, certainly not silly Dolly, was around to comfort Margot with this wisdom.

The summer raced on. ("Not without dust and heat," Lawrence several times remarked, in his private ironic voice.) The roses wilted on the roof and on the banks next to the road. The creek dwindled, and beside it honeysuckle leaves lay limply on the vines. For weeks, there was no rain, and then, one afternoon, there came a dark torrential thunderstorm. Harriet and I sat on the side porch and watched its violent start—the black clouds seeming to rise from the horizon, the cracking, jagged streaks of lightning, the heavy, welcome rain. And, later, the clean smell of leaves and grass and damp earth.

Knowing that Margot would be frightened, I thought of calling her, and then remembered that she would not talk on the phone during storms. And that night she told me, "The phone rang and rang, but I didn't think it was you, somehow."

"No."

"I had the craziest idea that it was Johnny. Be just like him to pick the middle of a storm for a phone call."

"There might not have been a storm in New Orleans."

But it turned out that Margot was right.

The next day, when I rode up to the Farrs' on my bike, Emily was sitting out in the grass where I had first seen her. I went and squatted beside her there. I thought she looked old and sad, and partly to cheer her I said, "You grow the most beautiful flowers I've ever seen."

She sighed, instead of smiling as she usually did. She said, "I seem to have turned into a gardener. When I was a girl, I imagined that I would grow up to be a writer, a novelist, and that I would have at least four children. Instead, I grow flowers and write book reviews."

I was not interested in children. "You never wrote a novel?"

She smiled unhappily. "No. I think I was afraid that I wouldn't come up to Trollope. I married rather young, you know."

And at that moment Lawrence came out of the house, immaculate in white flannels.

He greeted me, and said to Emily, "My dear, I find that I have some rather late appointments, in Hillsboro. You won't wait dinner if I'm a trifle late?"

(Of course she would; she always did.)

"No. Have a good time," she said, and she gave him the anxious look that I had come to recognize as the way she looked at Lawrence.

SOON AFTER THAT, a lot happened very fast. Margot wrote to Johnny again that she wanted a divorce, that she intended to marry Larry. (I wonder if this was ever true.) Johnny telephoned—not once but several times. He told her that she was crazy, that he had a great job with some shipbuilders near San Francisco—a defense contract. He would come to get us, and we would all move out there. Margot agreed. We would make a new life. (Of course, we never knew what happened to the girl.)

I was not as sad about leaving the Farrs and that house, that town, those woods as I was to be later, looking back. I was excited about San Francisco, and I vaguely imagined that someday I would come back and that we would all see each other again. Like parting lovers, Harriet and I promised to write each other every day.

And for quite a while we did write several times a week. I wrote about San Francisco—how beautiful it was: the hills and pastel houses, the sea. How I wished that she could see it. She wrote about school and friends. She described solitary bike rides to places we had been. She told me what she was reading.

In high school, our correspondence became more generalized. Responding perhaps to the adolescent mores of the early nineteen-forties, we wrote about boys and parties; we even competed in making ourselves sound "popular." The truth (my truth) was that I was sometimes popular, often not. I had, in fact, a stormy adolescence. And at that time I developed what was to be a long-lasting habit. As I reviewed a situation in which I had been ill-advised or impulsive, I would reenact the whole scene in my mind with Harriet in my own role—Harriet, cool and controlled, more intelligent, prettier. Even more than I wanted to see her again, I wanted to *be* Harriet.

Johnny and Margot fought a lot and stayed together, and gradually a sort of comradeship developed between them in our small house on Russian Hill.

I went to Stanford, where I halfheartedly studied history. Harriet was at Radcliffe, studying American literature, writing poetry.

We lost touch with each other.

Margot, however, kept up with her old friend Dolly, by means of Christmas cards and Easter notes, and Margot thus heard a remarkable piece of news about Emily Farr. Emily "up and left Lawrence without so much as a by-your-leave," said Dolly, and went to Washington, D.C., to work in the Folger Library. This news made me smile all day. I was so proud of Emily. And I imagined that Lawrence would amuse himself, that they would both be happier apart.

By accident, I married well—that is to say, a man whom I still like and enjoy. Four daughters came at uncalculated intervals, and each is remarkably unlike her sisters. I named one Harriet, although she seems to have my untidy character.

From time to time, over the years, I would see a poem by Harriet Farr, and I always thought it was marvellous, and I meant to write her. But I distrusted my reaction. I had been (I was) so deeply fond of Harriet (Emily, Lawrence, that house and land) and besides, what would I say—"I think your poem is marvellous"? I have since learned that this is neither an inadequate nor an unwelcome thing to say to writers. Of course, the true reason for not writing was that there was too much to say.

Dolly wrote to Margot that Lawrence was drinking "all over the place." He was not happier without Emily. Harriet, Dolly said, was travelling a lot. She married several times and had no children. Lawrence developed emphysema, and was in such bad shape that Emily quit her job and came back to take care of him—whether because of feelings of guilt or duty or possibly affection, I didn't know. He died, lingeringly and miserably, and Emily, too, died, a few years later—at least partly from exhaustion, I would imagine.

THEN, AT LAST, I did write Harriet, in care of the magazine in which I had last seen a poem of hers. I wrote a clumsy, gusty letter, much too long, about shared pasts, landscapes, the creek. All that. And as soon as I had mailed it I began mentally rewriting, seeking more elegant prose.

When for a long time I didn't hear from Harriet, I felt worse and worse, cumbersome, misplaced—as too often in life I had felt before. It did not occur to me that an infrequently staffed magazine could be at fault.

Months later, her letter came—from Rome, where she was then living. Alone, I gathered. She said that she was writing it at the moment of receiving mine. It was a long, emotional, and very moving letter, out of character for the Harriet that I remembered (or had invented).

She said, in part: "It was really strange, all that time when Lawrence was dying, and God! so long! and as though 'dying' were all that he was doing—Emily, too, although we didn't know that—all that time the picture that moved me most, in my mind, that moved me to tears, was not of Lawrence and Emily but of you and me. On our bikes at the top of the hill outside our house. Going somewhere. And I first thought that that picture simply symbolized something irretrievable, the lost and irrecoverable past, as Lawrence and Emily would be lost. And I'm sure that was partly it.

"But they were so extremely fond of you—in fact, you were a rare area of agreement. They missed you, and they talked about you for years. It's a wonder that I wasn't jealous, and I think I wasn't only because I felt included in their affection for you. They liked me best with you.

"Another way to say this would be to say that we were all three a little less crazy and isolated with you around, and, God knows, happier."

An amazing letter, I thought. It was enough to make me take a long look at my whole life, and to find some new colors there.

A postscript: I showed Harriet's letter to my husband, and he said, "How odd. She sounds so much like you."

(1975)

INFLUENZA

DANIEL MENAKER

It was a New York I'd never seen at close range before. I'd known it only through the squibs in the papers, which reproduced what I imagined attending
society events must have been like: a background blur
out of which emerged one rich or famous mug after
another. The pictures that floated out of the inky
blackness above these name blurts always made the
people look abnormal—prognathous, narcoleptic,
Tourettic, or as vacant as unlaid storm-drain pipes.
This was strange, because when some of these same
people drove in their limos or 190 SLs over to the
West Side, to drop their sons off at the Coventry
School, they were handsome and cheerful, the dads
in slim business suits, the moms in pricey jeans and
burgundy or wintergreen sweaters or sweatshirts.
Every head of hair with a suave streak or swath of

gray; good skin, with crinkles instead of wrinkles; amphitheatrically perfect white teeth. Maybe the combination of dusk and engraved invitations threw them into a gargoyle phase. I taught English in the Upper School at Coventry in the late sixties and seventies, and for the first three of those years, when I was in neurotic despair and was on the outs with the school's autocratic headmaster, W. C. H. Proctor—a socialite not only because of his capital-campaign obligations but out of native hobnobbery—the world of penthouses and summers at Niantic or Hyannis or Bar Harbor and of dressage and mixed doubles and poached salmon and charity bashes seemed as distant to me as a cloud to a clam.

In the early spring of my fourth year at Coventry, my gloom began to lighten. I'd tried to stop a fight in the locker room and got knifed, and Proctor saw it as some kind of courageous act. He began to call me "Jake" instead of "Singer" or "you." As time went on, he put me on this committee and that committee, and asked me to speak on behalf of the school to parents and prospective parents and groups of alumni. I found it uncomfortable under his wing, but I also began to feel more present in my life, at least my professional life, as if some psychic clutch had finally engaged and the neurasthenic idling—

Now, really, Mr. Singer—it is most embarrassing to listen to this narrative masturbation. I know that you had a good rhythm going as you flipped through the pages of your dictionary to find all your impressive words, and I'm so sorry to interrupt, but perhaps you could try a little harder to get to the point!

This would be the voice of Dr. Ernesto Morales, the psychoanalyst I saw three times a week for all but the first of my seven years as a teacher. I internalized his Spanish accent and speech patterns and the machete-like sarcasm that he wielded in the slash-and-burn process he tried to pass off as "interpretation," and I guess such internalization is part of the point of analysis. It's true that life improved for me as I went to him, but whether if I could do it all over again I would actually choose to have the homunculus of an insane, bodybuilding, black-bearded Cuban Catholic Freudian shouting at me from inside my own head I am not sure.

> *Dr. M. (*clearing his throat, his audible for boredom*): Please let me know when you are sure of something, Mr. Singer.*
> *Me: Sorry.*

Dr. M.: I'm surprised that you didn't say that you <u>guessed</u> you were sorry.
Me: Sorry.
Dr. M.: (Silence).
Me: What's wrong now, for Christ's sake? I said I was getting better—
  you should take it as a compliment.
Dr. M.: So you ask me to kiss your ass in gratitude as you waste my time
  with this interminable prehahmble? Even an analyst's patience has—
Me: Preamble.
Dr. M.: Pree-ahmble. Even an analyst's patience has some limit, Mr.
  Singer.
Me: O.K., O.K.

So anyway, at school, things were going well. I gave these talks to groups of parents who were considering Coventry for their boys, and I seemed to be convincing a lot of them. Of course, I'd be so nervous I'd spend a half hour on the shitter beforehand, but—

Dr. M.: Ah, honesty. It is always so refreshing, like a breeze through the
  palmettos in Havana. It is a pity we are still ninety miles off the
  shore of your subject.

Anyway, there was a day in the middle of April when the air in New York was as cool and clear as—

Dr. M.: And now we have the weather report! Isn't the news supposed
  to come first, Mr. Singer?

As a day in October, while—

Dr. M.: What about the rich and famous people?
Me: I'm getting there. I'm just setting this up, trying to give the whole
  picture.
Dr. M.: This giving of the entire picture, as you say, is your character-
  istic way of putting painful matters on the shelf for a while longer,
  preferably until they are stale and unappetizing. I would wager that
  you wish to speak of the problems that brought you to me in the first
  place—your rage at your mother for dying when you were six years

old, the fact that months and months elapsèd when no woman even so much as glimpsèd your penis, the estrangement between you and your father, the compromises involved in your profession. Here they all are, still preying on your mind as if they were the eagle at the livers of Prometheus, no? This is what happens when a patient terminates the treatment before he should.

Me: But—

Dr. M.: But most of all you wish to avoid the recognition of the crucial role I played in your life. You cling still to the belief—no, the delusion—that one can be his own man, create himself, and as it were have no parent of any sort.

Me: But that's what this is about. If you'd just give me a chance to get started, you'd—

Dr. M.: Mr. Singer, you would put off the sunrise if you were not quite ready for breakfast.

Me: But—

Dr. M.: But if we could not make progress in this area in our real work together, what chance is there, I ask you, of our getting anywhere in this absurd imaginary dialogue of yours? So proceed with your meteorology, if you feel that you must, but you must also forgive me if I catch forty huinks while you do.

THERE WAS A Sunday in the middle of April when the air in New York was as cool and clear as it is in late October. The trees in Central Park had gone blurry with buds, the Great Lawn had begun to lose the look of an old blanket thrown down to protect the earth, and the water in the Reservoir had a fine chop, like a miniature sea. A few people—the avant-garde of the jogging movement—beetled around the gravel path. It was all down there and I was up here, fifteen stories above Fifth Avenue, on the terrace of an apartment that occupied the top two floors of a magnificent Deco building between Eighty-third and Eighty-fourth Streets. To my left, in his usual blue blazer and gray slacks, stood Coventry's headmaster, nautical in appearance and demeanor.

"Ah, fresh air, Jake," Proctor said, putting his hand on my shoulder. Fresh air was his universal restorative. "There's nothing like it, even in New York City."

To my right stood Allegra Marshall, the hostess of this Coventry fund-raising lunch. Luncheon. My first point-blank encounter with the Manhattan of pure wealth and glamour. Five round tables of eight in a huge dining room with wainscoting and a "Close Encounters" chandelier. White maids in black uniforms and white, lace-edged aprons. Cutlery, linen, chased silver. Not a bell-bottom in sight, no ankhs, no zoris, no peasant blouses. It could have been the fifties. It could have been now.

Before I escaped to the terrace, one sleek fellow, the grandfather of a student of mine, asked me where I was going over spring break, and I said, "Nowhere," and he said, "Well, what a good idea!" He and I then discussed the Yankees' prospects for the coming season, and he pointed out a relative of Jacob Ruppert's across the vast living room or parlor or whatever it was. "This is a man who won't touch a drop of anything," the sleek fellow said. "I've heard that he's ashamed of his fortune." My other conversation was with the mother of one of my advanced-placement seniors who simply could not get *over* how wonderfully *detailed* my comments were on her son's papers.

When Proctor and I arrived, Mrs. Marshall gave me an automatic smile but a firm handshake—the kind that a girl's rich, manly dad or independent-minded mom tries to install at an early age. She was wearing a short black dress and a black wristband. Her husband— Coventry '59—had died, of cancer, on New Year's Day, leaving her with a six-year-old son—in first grade at the school—an infant daughter, and his millions to add to hers. The apartment was beautiful and tasteful to the point of hilarity, and its mistress, with her tall, willowy stature, pale complexion, bright-blue eyes, and long, dark, ironed-looking hair, and her aristocratic imperfection of feature—a real nose with a real bump in it, one very white front tooth slightly overlapping the other—also seemed comically perfect for her role of young society personage gamely pressing on. Now, out on the terrace, in the presence of Proctor and his bromides, she seemed sad, and her perfection looked frayed at the edges, and after a fellow-blazer-and-gray-flannelsman hailed the headmaster back inside, I thought I saw her roll her eyes.

"Sometimes I think he'd make a better admiral than a headmaster," I said. "Do you ever see any muggings down there?"

"You're Mr. Springer?" she asked.

"Singer. Jake Singer."

"You're the one who is going to do the sales pitch."

"Yes. I've done something like this three or four times now, but I keep getting stagefright. Especially here. I mean, I feel sort of out of place. And it's for money this time, not just to try to get people to send their kids."

"Proctor says you do it very well. When we set this thing up, he told me the applications pour in after you talk."

"You know, a year ago he was barely speaking to me."

"Why?"

"Oh, I was always arguing with him, always mouthing off. Nothing better to do, I guess."

"What do you mean?"

"You know, just trouble with authority."

"But he certainly likes you now."

"I just calmed down, I suppose."

"Just like that?"

"No, it probably has something to do with being in analysis, though I'm not supposed to talk about it and I don't like to give my lunatic analyst any credit."

"I'm in it, too, so you're safe."

"But you have a real reason, not just the vapors, like me. Anyway, one thing I am sure of is that it isn't Proctor who changed. He'd prescribe fresh air for you if your husband had died." Good work, Jake. "Oh, Mrs. Marshall, I'm so sorry. What an idiot I am."

"It's all right. I've discovered it's like having two heads. But when you collect yourself I hope you'll call me Allegra. And, by the way, these things make me as uncomfortable as they make you." She went back inside, leaving me alone with my clumsy self.

At lunch, Proctor and I sat on either side of our hostess, and I said how delicious the consommé was. "Actually, it's turtle soup," she said. It was difficult to eat the rest of the meal, with my foot so far in my mouth and the butterflies in my stomach. But I nodded and smiled and chewed as best I could, and I made what seemed to me an English teacher's joke—something feeble about cashing in Mr. Chips. Mrs. Marshall's frozen smile thawed into a real laugh—very musical—and I felt as if I'd done her a good turn. "Great chicken," I said when the veal chop was served, and she looked at me in proto-discomfiture until I shrugged, whereupon she got it and smiled a real smile again. Before dessert and after a trip to the bathroom, I made my speech: To afford the kind of diversity in our student body. All the way from catcher's mitts to calculators. Provide the brand of leadership that seems so sorely lacking in our nation. Instill the values, stem the rising tide of drugs. To defray cost of mandatory haircuts and install narrower and quieter ties. *(Polite laughter.)* To pay for the polish Proctor uses for his brass blazer buttons and his bald bean.

THIS LAST I said to Dr. Morales in his cold, cluttered office the next morning as I lay on the slab-flat couch with the cervically inimical jelly-roll headrest. It was a chilly, drizzly day, the bad side of spring. I had already told him about Allegra Marshall and my high anxiety and various faux pas. "You did not really say this about the polish, Mr. Singer," he said.

"No—it's a joke."

"I have asked you to tell me what you said in your speech and first you drone like an old priest and then you become saracastic—sarcastic and rude, if I may say, since I, too, am bald. Why do you suppose you cry in fear before the hand?"

"Beforehand. Who said anything about crying?"

"These attacks of cramps and diarrhea—you are weeping like a frightened child, but since you are a man you must do it through your asshole. And I shall ask the questions here. Why are you so frightened of something so boring and contemptible, Mr. Singer?"

"If I don't know the drill here by now, I really should be ashamed of myself. It's *not* boring and stupid. I act that way only because I care about it so much and want so badly to do well, to appease the spirit of my dead mother, whom I magically think I must have killed when I was six, and to earn the respect of my father, who thinks I am a failure and wishes I had been a doctor like him, and to please you. Always to please you, of course."

"Again this same sequence—dull recitation with following it the scorn. Ho-hum and fuck you, is it not?"

"Well, I mean four years of—"

"No, it is thirty-two meenoose six years, Mr. Singer—twenty-six years of preventing yourself from genuine involvement in your feelings and your life. I swear to Christ that if Marilyn Monroe came to you with no clothes on and a wet pussy you would not know what to do with her. Now please listen to me. If you joke, I shall kill you and spare you the effort of this slow suicide. Is this school of yours a good school?"

"Yes. It could be—"

"*Is it a good school?*"

"Yes."

"Do your students respect you?"

"Yes." Satisfaction, as surprising as a twenty-dollar bill on the sidewalk, came to me with this answer.

"Tell me one important thing you have done for the school besides the teaching."

"Well—"

"It is dry, Mr. Singer."

"I'm helping to get scholarships for poor kids," I said, more proudly than I meant to.

"Good, there is feeling in your words at last. Anything else?"

"I'm convincing more people to apply, and now I'm helping to raise money. As of yesterday."

"Ah, your voice has fallen here. Why?"

"I don't know—the whole idea of raising money, being with rich people, glad-handing and putting on a show."

"*It is a good school!*" thundered Dr. Morales. "You are trying to make it better according to your convictions! Making a speech is not selling eslaves or torturing cute lambs! A President of the United Estates has attended this school, three or four *Nobelistas*, many professors and doctors, the director of the Peace Corps, I believe, the head of Sloan-Kettering, the man who designed—"

"How do you know all this?" I asked.

"I have looked it up. I should not have revealed this, perhaps—it is bad technique—but just maybe you will take a leaf from my tree, Mr. Singer. I am *interested* in my work. You are my work. I am *interested* in you. And one more thing—if there are rich people in the world, why should you not be among them? You yourself are hardly from the road of tobacco. If there is a rich young widow making goggle eyes at you, why should you not fuck her, I ask you. Why should you not marry her, when I come to think of it. Why didn't you mention how she looked when you were speaking of her?"

"Less Marilyn Monroe than Ali McGraw," I said. "But beautiful enough. Quite beautiful, in fact."

"In fact? I did not think it was in fiction. I do not know who is this Alice McGraw."

"She's the one in 'Love Story'—the girl who dies."

"Ah, yes. This is interesting. We must stop now, Mr. Singer, but have you by any chance happened to notice the corpses that have littered our conversation this morning like a battlefield, as if it were? Your mother, the husband of the hostess, the character of this movie."

"Marilyn Monroe."

"Very good, Mr. Singer. You are quite right, I have joined in this necrophilia. But it is *spring*, Mr. Singer. Time for the new beginnings, for the birds to tweeter and among the twigs to build their nests."

DR. MORALES'S CRUDE incitement concerning Allegra Marshall at the end of the session had not come out of nowhere. Near the beginning, when I mentioned her widowhood and the opulence of her apartment, I could feel him coming to attention like a setter behind me. I was surprised and annoyed to feel myself coming to attention the following week, when I was in the nurse's office at school, getting a Band-Aid for a wound inflicted by the staples that had interfered with my reading of "Hester Prynne: Hawthorn's Revolutionary Heroin." A little kid was lying on the cot looking green around the gills, and the nurse, a clinical type with a neurosurgeon's hauteur and the name Gladys Knight, of all things, was on the phone saying, "You and the babysitter probably have the same organism that George has, Mrs. Marshall, with the nausea and the vertigo. I'd bring him over for you myself, but George is the fourth incidence today, so I really should stay here."

I asked if it was Allegra Marshall she was talking to and she covered the phone and scowled at me. "This is important, Mr. Singer, if you don't mind," she said. "This child *and* his mother *and* the babysitter have all come down with gastroenteritis, and we're trying to figure out how to get him home."

"I met Mrs. Marshall last week. I'd be glad to take him home—I've got two free periods. Tell Mrs. Marshall it's me."

In another five minutes, George Marshall and I went out into the April sunshine and hailed a cab on West End Avenue, after a parting advisory from Miss Knight: "One of the other children had projectile vomiting." As we drove across the park, yellow with forsythia and daffodils, George sat still and regarded me. He was small for his age but built solidly, with blond hair and a turned-up nose with a few freckles sprinkled over it—he looked nothing like his mother. "My dad died," he said when we stopped for a red light at Ninety-sixth Street and Fifth Avenue. "I know," I said. "It's very sad for you and your family." "My sister doesn't realize it," he said. "She's too little. Are you a teacher in the upper school?" I told him I was. "I thought I saw you," he said.

The taxi started up again, and George faced forward, looking sick and unhappy. His feet didn't quite reach the floor. Even though I'd never met this boy before, I knew for a fact that he believed that he had done something to cause what had happened to his family, and I wanted to reach over with both hands and shake the innocent truth into him before the guilt worked itself too deep into his heart.

George said he could go up in the elevator by himself, but the doorman said that Mrs. Marshall had asked me to take him upstairs, if it wasn't too much trouble. So up in the elaborately scrolled and panelled elevator we went. When the door opened onto the apartment's foyer, Mrs. Marshall was standing there looking very sick and forlorn herself, plain and ashen and lank-haired, so that the elegant dark-blue Chinesey housecoat she had on seemed as beside the point as the Aubusson on the floor and the modest Corot on the wall behind her. "I'm tired, Mom," George said, and he tottered away down the long hallway. "I'm going to lie down for a while."

"I'll be right there," Mrs. Marshall said.

"I hope your daughter's all right," I said. "The nurse told me your babysitter is sick, too."

"Emily is fine. And George's mother will be here in half an hour. She lives just over on Park. We'll be O.K."

"George's mother?"

"My husband's mother. My late husband's mother. Georgie is George Junior."

"Oh."

"It was nice of you to bring him home. Thank you."

"It was nothing. He's a sweet kid."

"Let me pay you for the taxi."

"Oh, no. That's all right." I looked over her shoulder at the living room, glowing with perfection in the morning light. "I know this is silly," I said, "but I wish there was something else I could do for you."

"Why is that silly?"

"I mean, I've only met you once, and—"

"Is it silly because I'm rich?"

"Yes."

"Ah—honesty. But it shows what you know." Tears were in her eyes now, and her nose looked more broken than distinguished, and she seemed skinny rather than slender and pathetic rather than tragic; and I felt ridiculous instead of gallant, and furious at Dr. Morales for his careless manipulations, and for regarding this woman so lubriciously and so lightly, like a personal ad, like a sitting duck. "I'm sorry if I've upset you," I said. "Don't worry about it," she said, pushing the elevator button.

"AND I THINK you should be ashamed of yourself," I said to Dr. Morales the next morning, after telling him as calmly as I could what had happened with George Marshall and his mother the day before.

"I am," Dr. Morales replied. "I am truly ashamed." He rattled some papers around and cleared his throat a few times.

I sat up and put my feet on the floor and looked at him. He had a tax form over the yellow pad he used for taking what I assumed were scathing notes about me and his other victims.

"Filing late?" I said. "I hope you applied for the automatic two-month extension."

"This is against the rules, Mr. Singer."

"You mean the New York Psychoanalytic Society has an actual rule against doing your taxes during sessions with your patients? Why, that's positively draconian."

"I shall not explain myself to you, Mr. Singer. This is as forbidden to me as sitting up is to you. But God and Freud will pardon me, I feel certain, for occupying myself with other matters when a patient enters my office in an inappropriate rage, insults me further by thinking to disguise it, and then has the amazing condescension to tell me that I should be ashamed of myself, as if I were a four-year-old child who has deliberately belchèd during Communion."

"I would never have made such a fool of myself if you hadn't—"

"Had not what, Mr. Singer? Had not held a pistol at your head to force you to volunteer to take the boy home? Had not squeezèd your heart in the taxi to make you recognize his psychological situation and sympathize with him? Had not transformed you into Sharlie Mc-Carthy and then like Edgar Burgeon thrown my voice into you standing there in front of the mother and to diminish her humanity on account of her wealth? By the way, Mr. Singer, will you please lie down."

"You want it both ways," I said, continuing to face him. "You want me to behave the way you think I should, and then when I try and then fail you disavow any part in the matter. 'My advice is to jump, Mr. Singer, but if you break your neck, don't blame me.'"

"Had not, in general, as I was saying, miraculously reached into your soul and poured into it the poison that you are convinced is so powerful as to threaten also anyone whom you might love. Like your mother, your father, like a woman. Like me. You are not Siva, Mr. Singer, nor Attila nor Hitler, nor even Sharles Starkweather. You are not so lethal as you wish to believe. Now please lie down."

"No. I don't feel well. I'm going home."

"You know, I truly *am* ashamed that after four years of our work together you can still busy your mind with any amount of anger at yourself and at me to ignore what is really going on in your life—for example, the possibility that from the start this woman has taken some interest in you, and that this was why I tried gently and humorously to encourage your interest in her."

"*Gently?*"

"Why else would a person divulge within five minutes of meeting someone the highly intimate knowledge that she was in analysis, as you divulgèd it to her also—why else would she say this if she did not feel immediate trust and confidentiality? And why else would she have asked you to accompany her son in the elevator if not because she wished to see you again, and being in a very unattractive and weakened condition, what is more. Now please do lie down and try to address these matters."

"No, I really do feel ill," I said. "I'm leaving."

"So now the regression and withdrawal will be complete."

I CALLED IN sick and spent the rest of the day in or very near the bathroom in my apartment. From time to time I hazarded a walk into the living room to watch TV. I would doze on the couch, wake up to a soap opera or a game show, whose gaudiness the flu rendered almost hallucinatory, get up and turn it off. And before stumbling toiletward again, I once or twice looked around my place and took stock. In January, as my responsibilities grew at school, I had through an effort of will upgraded my domestic situation. I discarded the bricks and boards and sofa *trouvé* and card table, and the bottom half of a bunk bed sold to me by the building's gaunt Croatian super for thirty-five dollars, and the dieseling vintage refrigerator, which I called the Serf of Ice Cream—another English teacher's joke—and replaced them with Door Store merchandise and new appliances. A captain's bed, a blond wall unit or two, a big, round, tan hooked rug in the living room, an oak table with a chrome base, even a Zurbarán print and a Magritte poster—that kind of thing. All in all, it had become a decent bachelor's place on the eleventh floor of a nice building on West End Avenue—plenty of light and a nice breeze in the spring and summer—just around the corner from Coventry. Rent-controlled, which you could still get back then, especially on the fringe of a bad neighborhood. But so what? It was still a pocket of isolation—especially in illness, when you'd like to be able to call on someone—and I felt like a penny in the pocket. Whatever progress I'd made was in baby steps, or in a marionette's artificial, hinged gait, with Dr. Morales pulling the strings. I felt far less desperate than I had four years earlier, but the absence of desperation is not life.

The flu subsided. I took a longer, deeper nap, looked in listlessly as Thurman Munson and his teammates braved chilly April conditions at Yankee Stadium, ate a little chicken soup, drank a lot of water, stayed on my feet, barely, in the shower, and collapsed onto my bed into an even deeper sleep, which lasted the night.

. . .

I FELT MUCH better in the morning but couldn't face the red-letter discussion looming in my Advanced Placement class or the concluding negotiations over "A Separate Peace" in my regular junior courses, to say nothing of playing pepper with the baseball team in Riverside Park after school, so I called in sick again and read and dozed on the sofa. I was brought out of a semi-dream, in which Dr. Morales lobbied the halls of Congress on behalf of Cuban cigars, by the ringing of the doorbell. It hadn't rung in so long that I'd forgotten when the last time was. I opened it without using the little burglar scope or asking who was there. What can anyone do to me, after all, I said to myself in the self-pitying aftermath of my stock-taking and influenza.

It was Allegra Marshall, well beyond influenza and its aftermath—looking very beautiful once again, in fact, if nervous.

"I'm sorry, I should have called," she said. "I know you're sick, but you live so close to the school that I thought I would just stop by. And then the doorman said he didn't need to announce me or anything."

"It's the super," I said. "My friend the super."

"So here I am. I hope I'm not disturbing you."

"I'm much better," I said. "It's O.K. Is George all right?"

"I took him back to school yesterday, and I asked for you and they told me you were out sick. And when they told me you were out again today I felt even more guilty. You probably got this from George, or maybe even from me."

"Oh, it's going around."

"But that isn't why I was looking for you at school in the first place," she said. "I wanted to apologize for being so rude to you the other morning. Here you had done me this kindness."

"I was rude first—worse than rude," I said. "You caught me out. I asked for it."

"Well, I'm sorry anyway. Now I really should leave you alone."

She turned away and started back toward the elevator, and as she did I heard that insinuating voice, which had already installed itself in my mind, say, "Now, Mr. Singer, I ask you—what do you wish this woman to do, take out a full-page advertisement in the New York *Times?*" I drew a deep breath and said, just as she was about to push the "Down" button, "Wait, um, Allegra, as long as we're apologizing." She turned again, to face me. "I wasn't really doing you a kindness. I offered to take George home so I could see you. It was just an excuse. And my analyst sort of put me up to the whole thing anyway."

"You mean you *didn't* really want to see me?"

"No, I did, I probably did, or I would have, but this doctor of mine gets himself in the middle of everything, so it's hard to tell. He egged me on. He said *you* were interested in *me*."

"He was right."

"What?"

"He was right."

"He was right?"

"He was right."

II—MOTHER'S DAY

They wanted to have children right away, but she didn't get pregnant. The specialist she saw couldn't find anything wrong. Still, she and her husband had sex by the chart, she took hormones, they went on tense "relaxed" vacations. None of it worked. At length, her husband said maybe he was the one with the problem—she had to give him credit for that. The specialist he saw, who wore a bright-red toupee, said "Whee" when he looked through the microscope at the semen sample, and the subsequent, more scientific assay found nothing wrong. Now they had both no one and each other to blame. It was an open field. It's like a poison in a well that you're both drinking from, Allegra told me. They kept trying to conceive a child but meanwhile adopted a baby boy through Spence-Chapin. They gave up on biology, and on sex, a couple of years later, and a few years after that, in the midst of growing strain and louder silence between them, which they managed to hide from the Spence-Chapin social worker, they adopted another baby—a girl this time—in the hope that this would somehow solve their problems. Three months after that, her husband was diagnosed with pancreatic cancer, and three months after that he died. Their parents were friends. She had known him all her life, through Brearley for her and Coventry for him, Radcliffe for her and Yale and Wharton for him, summers at Sag Harbor, winters skiing out West. They went out with other people from time to time, but nothing came of that. They thought they were comfortable with each other. They got married when she was twenty-three and he was twenty-five. The comfort seemed to evaporate overnight. Even without all the reproductive trouble, there would have been trouble, she was sure. She should have learned something from the way the dark skinny boys with the scraggly beards and the banjos and their protest songs à la Phil Ochs attracted her in Cambridge. She should have gone to graduate school in English at Berkeley and thrown herself into the free-speech upheaval out there. She should have done a lot of things. Until her husband died, she felt as though her life had been written down before she was born, in a novel so boring and pre-dictable that even the writer realized it and put the manuscript in some drawer and left it there. Now she had despair to add to the tedium. No one would come near her in her grief. Or maybe she pushed them away. And she *was* grieving—you can miss someone you don't much like, she had discovered. This was depressing all by itself. Men stayed away out of propriety, and just as well, in most cases. Her family and her hus-band's family seemed afraid of her. She loved her son and daughter so much and so feared what would happen to them if she couldn't give them what they needed that she felt it almost guaranteed that she wouldn't be able to. She sometimes had nightmares about having them taken away. Her husband had been a good father—she had to give him credit for that, too. As good as his long hours at Thomson & McKin-non, Auchincloss permitted. He hadn't had to work but he did, and that was really the only other thing she would give him credit for. Though she realized it was not a bad list and he was not a bad guy. Just the wrong guy. And she had found herself wondering, out there on the terrace when we first spoke, whether—dark and thin as I was and scraggly as my beard might be if I grew one—I played the banjo.

"Now I should leave you alone," she had said in the doorway after confirming Dr. Morales's conjecture. "I wanted to get another look at you—that's why I asked you to come up with George when you took him home. I could have just written you a note, after all."

"Well, would you like to come in?" I had said.

"Are you really feeling all right?"

"Yes."

"Then yes, I'll come in for a little while."

And that was when she sat down on my Door Store sofa and told me about herself. And then she asked me about myself. It got to be eleven-thirty, and I found I was hungry, for the first time in a couple of days, so I excused myself and went to the kitchen and wolfed down a bowl of cereal. When I went back, Allegra stood up and said, "I thought that talking to someone new or doing something different might help me out of this trap I feel I'm in."

"I'm flattered that you think of me as new and different. I feel more or less like the same old thing."

"I really should go now," she said, pulling at one of her cuticles.

"You don't have to."

"Then would you please kiss me?"

I went over to her and put my arms around her and kissed her. She tilted her head back a little and looked at me. She was so tall: eye to eye with me.

"Cheerios," she said. "Would you please really kiss me?"

I did my best.

"Good," she said. "Give me your hand." She took my hand and put it on her breast. She tilted her head back and looked me in the eye again, as if she were measuring something. "That feels very good," she said. "You don't know how long it has been."

"Yes, I do," I said. "But I think I can take it from here. I'm getting tired of people telling me what to do."

IT TURNED OUT that she wasn't really directorial about sex but, as in that firm handshake when we met, just well mannered. "May I suck your cock?" she asked, with that unnerving look in the eye, and when I said "Sure" she said "Thank you." "Would you mind if we stopped for a second so that I can get on my hands and knees?" "Could you please hold my shoulders down?" "Would you put your finger in my ass." She sprinkled these courtesies among other, much more pre-verbal utterances, and the whole effect was wonderfully, almost overwhelmingly lewd. After a while, she didn't really have to ask but I let her every now and then anyway, for the pleasure of hearing her.

"Socialite widow Allegra Marshall, after copulating with prep-school pedagogue Jake Singer," I said, while we rested.

"What?"

"You know—those society-party pictures in the papers. I've probably seen you in them and had no idea who you were. And now here you are. And you turn out to be a regular human being. So regular that you probably came over to the West Side just to use me. But if you did, I must say that I can't understand why women are always objecting to being used."

"After we fuck a few more times and then I tell you I don't care about you, you'll find out," Allegra said.

"Is that likely to happen?"

"The fucking? Oh, yes, I hope so. Right now, in fact, if you can, please. But I'll have to be discreet. I am a widow, you know. As for the rest, I have no idea. Maybe your analyst does. He seems very smart. All mine says is 'Why is that, do you think?' and 'What does this bring to mind?' "

"That sounds pretty good to me. I don't know why you need analysis—you're so direct."

"The closer I am to people, the more distant I feel, it turns out. And don't you think it's just a little bit strange for someone to tell all her secrets to someone she has had maybe fifteen minutes of conversation with before? And then beg for sex?"

"You didn't exactly beg," I said. "And anyway I don't think it's strange."

"Well, you should."

THREE WEEKS LATER, after coaching third base in the varsity's last game, against Collegiate, I went down to Tiffany's and bought Allegra a silver-and-onyx bracelet for Mother's Day. She had discreetly come to my place again a week after the first time. And I discreetly had supper once at her apartment, late one night. She cooked some kind of chicken and I made some salad. Her kids were asleep. I dried the dishes afterward—I could hardly bear to use the dish towel, it was so exquisitely folded. I left just as the sun was hitting the tops of the buildings on Central Park West. Proctor told me I looked tired when he stopped by my classroom to ask if I would say a few words at graduation. He suggested I get some fresh air after school. Luckily, all I had to do that day was give final exams.

"Mother's Day is Sunday," I said to Dr. Morales when I lay down on the couch the morning after the trip to Tiffany's. "Too bad I don't have one."

"It is indeed too bad, Mr. Singer. It is not funny."

"Well, at least I don't have to buy a present or anything," I said. "So, do you think Nixon will be impeached or not?"

"For permitting you to employ him as a red herring, do you mean?"

"For abusing his power," I said, as pointedly as I could.

"I don't know, Mr. Singer. Can we return to Mother's Day? I know you were just being humorous, but here so sadly, as you know, there are no jokes."

"Why should we talk about it? What's the point? I remember making a card for my mother when I was in first grade in Bronxville, and she loved it. And then she died. Now I don't believe in it—it's just commercial. I think that's probably because my mother is dead. Just bitter, I suppose."

"Remove the 'probably' and 'suppose.' "

"Well, so there you are."

"What about your new lover? She has children."

"So? I'm not one of them."

"I shall tell you what, Mr. Singer. I shall make a bargain with you, not because I am feeling magnanimous toward you, the good Christ knows, but because my heart goes out to this woman, this poor woman who cannot have children naturally, this woman whose husband has died, this woman who is trying to fight her way out of depression and make changes in her life, this woman who would be cut to the quicks if she could hear you speak so coldly and callously about her, this woman who has what suddenly appears to be the further misfortune of taking you into her bed. The bargain is this, Mr. Singer: Take the fee for this session and get your narrow and self-absorbèd ass off my couch and go to Tiffany's and with the money buy this woman something beautiful. And then give it to her. And do not come back here until you do."

"Free advice—a first for you," I said. "Well, even the analyst can have a breakthrough, I guess." I reached down to my briefcase, which was on the floor next to the backbuster, and took out the little blue box tied with a white ribbon and held it up over my head.

Dr. Morales was silent for a full minute. Then he said, "Why did you feel the need to tease me in this way, Mr. Singer? Could you not bear the idea that I have helped you to take such a step for once without having to get in the back of you and push?"

"I think you hit the nail on the head," I said. "When I went to buy this, I wouldn't have been surprised to find you driving the No. 4 bus down Fifth Avenue, and when I went into the store I could hear you whispering, 'Now, don't be a cheapskates, Mr. Singer,' and the only thing that almost kept me from going ahead was knowing how much satisfaction this whole thing would bring you." In the middle of this I had started crying, though my voice didn't break. Tears just ran out of my eyes as if from a spillway.

"Think instead of the person who will receive this gift and how pleased she will be."

"We even came up with the exact same store. You know, I could accept help from you a lot more easily if you were less constantly critical of me, less sarcastic about it all, and if I didn't suspect that you were getting some kind of perverted kick from disparaging me and trying to run my life."

"I think this is the *only* way you can accept help, Mr. Singer. I think I am doing what is right. I do have my own life, you may be certain of that. I am not living through you or my other patients, much as you wish to believe it so."

"Are you sure?" I said. "Was there an ounce too much protest in there somewhere?"

I WALKED BACK to the West Side through Central Park, trying to calm down. The morning was soft and warm; flowers were everywhere. I heard a padding behind me and the next thing I knew I was flat on my face and someone was running away with my briefcase. The next thing I knew, I was running after him and then catching up with him and knocking him flat on his face and taking my briefcase back. He got up and ran away. He was just a kid, a druggie in jeans and a black T-shirt, with a peace symbol hanging from a little chain on his narrow, sallow chest.

"HE PICKED THE wrong guy," I told Allegra, late on Sunday night. We were in her kitchen again, eating leftovers from the sumptuous meal the cook had prepared for her and her parents and in-laws that afternoon. She had a cook. She was wearing the bracelet I'd just given her, and she paid me the compliment of saying that getting through the day had been much easier because she could look forward to seeing me at night. It was also kind of her to be so enthusiastic about my present, I thought, when she probably owned enough jewelry to sink a yacht. I went on bragging. "He couldn't have known about my blazing speed or all-around athleticism, I guess."

"I did," she said. "Proctor told me when he told me about you before the dinner last month. Did you know that the white-haired man you were talking to, Alex Something—I forget his last name—gave the school a hundred thousand dollars the next week?"

"Yes, Proctor told me. How did you hear about it?"

"In the thank-you letter Proctor sent me. He said wasn't the school lucky to have you as a spokesman, and he thinks you have a brilliant future in education."

"What would he know about education?" I said. I ate a forkful of little potatoes as perfect as pearls. "You have a *cook*."

"You know, I can see where you could be a little scary."

"But you like me," I said.

"*And* I like you," Allegra said, standing up and taking my hand. "Will you come with me now?"

"Shouldn't we clean up first?"

"Leave it for the maid this time. I really can't wait."

"You have a *maid*."

Her bedroom was huge and looked like a chamber in an English country house, with a frayed but magnificent tapestry on the wall, a washstand in front of it, a vast mahogany wardrobe against the opposite wall, and a quiet Oriental rug the size of the Caspian Sea. The bed itself seemed a Yankee interloper; a thin and complex patchwork quilt

covered it, and underneath was an off-white down comforter and pillows as yielding as fresh snow. I, too, felt like an intruder there, for all
of Dr. Morales's reassurances. I folded my clothes into small dimen-
sions and put them in a little pile on a wing chair with flowered uphol-
stery. Then I put my wallet and keys and change in a tiny pile on top of
the self-effacing clothes pile. I turned off the marble-based lamp that
sat on a delicate little table next to the bed.

When Allegra came out of the bathroom, I could see by the moonlight pouring in the tall window from over Central Park that she had
nothing on. She stood in front of me and turned the lamp back on and
said, "Do you like me, too?" She was thin, but her breasts were full and
her hips curved just widely enough to escape boyishness. It occurred to
me that there is something to be said for motherhood without childbearing, and the luxury of my immediate material and sexual circumstances came home to me and seemed less like a stroke than an assault
of luck.

"Yes, I like you," I said.

"If it's O.K., I'd like to get astride you," Allegra said.

"All right."

After this rearrangement, she leaned over and turned the light back
on again. "Would you mind talking for a few minutes while we're like
this?" she asked.

"Fine with me. You are like an erotic dream come true, you know."

"I swear I've never acted like this before. I wish you could stay with
me in the morning."

"I wish I could, too," I said. "But there's your children, and the
babysitter. And the cook. The maid. And my classes start at 8:30."

"I don't even know what a job is like. Is that awful?"

"Teaching is wonderful when it goes well."

"But you have to do it even when you don't want to."

"That's one of the good things about a job."

"That sounds puritanical."

"I think it's just middle class."

"I don't have to do anything I don't want to do."

"Of course you do," I said. "You have to take care of sick children even when you're sick yourself."

"That's love—it's different. Speaking of love—" she said.

"So this is love," I said when she was still again. To keep myself from coming I had been trying to think about how it would feel not to have to work. This beat my dusty old delaying tactic of mowing an imaginary lawn, even though in the middle of my reverie of wealth I felt Dr. Morales's influence seep into the room like swamp gas. "*Mr. Singer, I suspect and fear that you are about to open this gifted horse's mouth and inspect its teeth, is it not?*" I could hear him say. "*Can you not resist your impulse to piss on your good fortune?*"

"It might be," Allegra said. "I feel as though we would always get along well."

"But you don't know me at all," I was about to say, before Dr. Morales whinnied mockingly in my head to warn me away from honesty. "Would you mind if we turned the tables here again?" I said instead. "Because if it's all right with you I'd like to finish this off as if I were in control, pretty please."

Allegra laughed. "You're making fun of me," she said.

"Yes, but I really would like to do that."

"All right, turn me over now, and we can come at the same time. Let's watch each other, O.K.?"

"Sure," I said. "It would be a pleasure." And like an eight-year-old boy who has succumbed to wearing a tie for the first time, I silently added to the Dr. Morales inside my head, You win. I'll try to throw my lot in with this rich and interesting woman—who happens also to be a staggering piece of ass—and her wainscoted world. What would that world make of me, a neurotic school-teaching Jew without a Corot, Herreshoff, or nine iron to his name, I wondered—if it ever got to that point. Oh, well, I went on, I have nothing to lose. And I might have told myself that lie and forgotten about it and everything else for a little while if Allegra, holding me in her direct and at that point hectic gaze, hadn't said, "Jake, Jake, not yet, please" and I hadn't believed, for a split second, that she was begging me to cancel the calculating decision I'd just made. I did have something to lose, I realized then, as I tried to oblige Allegra— whether more for fun or strategy I was suddenly no longer sure. In fact, some part of myself had just gone out the window and was hurtling down to the sidewalk below, although I couldn't put a name to it. "Now, Jake," Allegra said, and, just before ardor obliterated all further thought, I heard my indwelling Dr. Morales say, "It is your innocence that you have lost, Mr. Singer, and for that it is a high time."

(1995)

How Old, How Young

John O'Hara

You did not often see a woman crying on the street. You sometimes saw one in the neighborhood where the doctors had their offices, coming out of an office with another woman or a man and crying from pain. Sometimes they would be coming from a dentist's office, but they would be holding bloodstained handkerchiefs to their mouths. Doctor's office or dentist's office, they would usually get in a waiting car or a taxi and not be on the street very long, and anyway their crying was easily explained. You just about never were walking along the street and saw a young woman crying out of emotional anguish, weeping tears that were tears of sorrow and not caring that she might be making a spectacle of herself. But on this particular afternoon a long while ago James H. Choate, who had a summer job as runner

for the family bank, was on an errand to a law office, and coming
toward him he saw this young woman, and if he had not known her he
would have said she was plastered. She was wearing white shoes with
brown wing tips and medium-high heels, and yet she walked as if she
had on ski boots. She was wearing a simple dark-blue linen one-piece
dress with a thin black belt and a white collar, and a straw hat that was
varnished black—pretty much of a uniform among certain types of
girls in those days. But she was walking like a drunken tart. Then when
she got closer he saw that it was Nancy Liggett and that she was weeping without any self-restraint and leaving her misery naked for people
to stare at. Jamie Choate wanted to cover her, as though her nakedness
were the real thing. He stopped and stood in her uncertain path, but
she walked around him. "Nancy!" he said. She kept on going and he
watched her indecisively until she reached her car. She got in, and he
was glad that it was a coupé; it offered her some shelter from the mys-
tified stares of people, including himself. It was twenty minutes of
three, and he had to get to the lawyers' office and back to the bank before closing time. He had not been told the nature of the envelope he
was to pick up, but he had been ordered to get it back before three,
without fail. He was very unimportant at the bank; they did not think
much of him there. He made a special effort on this errand. He got
back in plenty of time—five minutes to spare—as much because he
wanted to see if Nancy's car was still in the block as to make a good impression at the bank. The car was gone.

There was a swimming-party picnic that night that Nancy Liggett
should have been at but wasn't. Some people had a boathouse at a dam
in the woods about fifteen miles out of town. The water was always very
cold and so was the air, and even though the bank thermometer that
day had registered above ninety degrees, people at the picnic were
drinking straight rye to keep off the chill. Quite a few people got tight.
It was a Friday, the beginning of the weekend for most of the people,
but Saturday morning was a very busy time at the bank, and Jamie
Choate stayed sober. His cousin Walker Choate was at the picnic to remind him, in case he forgot. Walker was an assistant paying teller and
a regular member of the staff. Very patronizing toward Jamie. "Remember, you have all those blotters to change in the morning," said
Walker. "Need a steady hand and a clear mind for that."

"Oh, go to hell," said Jamie. "I wonder why Nancy Liggett isn't here tonight."

"Why the sudden interest in Nancy?" said Walker.

"Because I've fallen in love with her," said Jamie.

"Then why didn't you bring her?"

"I don't know. I was hoping you would and then I'd take her away from you."

"If I ever brought Nancy to anything, it wouldn't be hard to take her away from me. Even you could. Why don't you go take a look in the woods. Maybe she's here and forgot to check in with you."

"Walker, you *are* a wet smack," said Jamie.

"Yeah, and you're not dry behind the ears," said Walker.

It was a fairly large party and included people who were still in prep school and people who had children of their own, and a greater number of those in between. It would have been possible for Nancy to have arrived at the boathouse, stayed there a few minutes, and vanished in the woods without Jamie's having seen her. To make sure she hadn't, he went to the hostess-chaperon, Gwen Lloyd, and said, "I've been looking all over for Nancy Liggett."

"She isn't here," said Gwen. "She called up and said she wasn't coming. Offered no excuse, and she was supposed to help out with the food."

"Oh, you spoke to her? How did she seem?" said Jamie.

"How did she seem? She seemed rude and inconsiderate," said Gwen. "She was supposed to bring three dozen ears of corn for corn-on-the-cob, and when I started to ask her about them, she just hung up."

"Not like her," said Jamie.

"Well, it'll be a long time before I count on *her* again. I don't know what's got into her lately. Don't tell me you have a sneaker for her, Jamie."

"What if I did?" said Jamie.

"Well, that's your business, but you'd do better with someone your own age."

"Nancy's the same age. Exactly the same age. We were both born in 1904."

"Girls mature earlier," said Gwen. "You're still in college, and she's been home two or three years."

"What are you not saying that you're kind of hinting at?"

"Just that she's older than you, even if you were born the same year."

"Well, at least she called up and said she wasn't coming," said Jamie.

"Yes, you do have a sneaker for her," said Gwen.

"I'm not as naïve as you'd make me out to be," he said.

"You're away most of the time. I just hope you don't fall for Nancy Liggett," said Gwen.

"I think maybe I have."

"Then forget everything I've said," said Gwen. "Heaven knows she needs someone she can depend on. And that's *all* I'm going to *say*."

"You married people! You'd think you had some monopoly on how people react."

"In certain things we have more experience," said Gwen.

"I'll say you have," said Jamie. "Who's going to chaperon the chaperons, that's what we always say."

"Uncalled for, that remark," said Gwen. "If you're not having a good time, nobody's asking you to stay."

"Then I bid you a fond adieu," said Jamie. It was close to eleven o'clock and from his point of view the party had been a frost. Some of the people had paired off and vanished; the singers were going through their repertory; two tables of bridge had settled down in the boathouse; Walker Choate was trying to persuade an out-of-town girl to go canoeing with him. It was all very much like every other swimming-party picnic the Lloyds had given, except that on this one Jamie had had no fun, no fun at all.

On his way home he slowed down as he passed the Liggetts' house. There was a light on in the room that he knew to be Nancy's bedroom, but Mr. and Mrs. Liggett were not the kind of people who sanctioned midnight visitors. At home Jamie went to the icebox and got a glass of milk, to the cakebox and got a couple of brownies. He sat on the kitchen table with his feet resting on a chair and pondered the newest mystery in his life: why had he never fallen in love with Nancy Liggett until he had seen her good looks washed away by tears, her face made plain by misery? Ah, well, it was not much of a mystery, really. Her good looks had always kept him away, and now she was just like anyone else—except that he was in love with her. And he would never be the same again. A new organ had come to life, somewhere in his chest, and it was pumping something warm and sweet through the rest of him. Nancy Liggett, who needed someone she could depend on.

He had a ladder match to play the next afternoon, and he thought of defaulting, but his best chance of seeing Nancy would be at the club pool. He played the match and won, had a ginger ale with the kid he had beaten, took a shower and put on his bathing suit and went to the pool. She was there, sitting by herself with her chin on her knees and her arms clasping her legs. She looked up at him as he dropped his towel and sat beside her. "Hello," she said.

"Do you mind?" he said.

"I'm not being very conversational," she said.

"Well, that makes two of us," he said. "You didn't go to the Lloyds'."

"No," she said.

"I left fairly early. It was still going strong, but the only person I wanted to talk to wasn't there."

"No?"

"No," he said.

"I warned you I wasn't being very conversational," she said. She picked up her bathing cap and pulled it on, tucking in wisps of her blond hair, cocking her head as she did, and unconsciously being extremely feminine and attractive. She stood up and went to the edge of the pool, hesitated, and dived in. He waited to see her when she got out, with her wet bathing suit sticking to her body, but he also wanted to see if she would return to their place. He had quite a while to wait. She swam very slowly up and down the length of the pool, floated a bit, and finally climbed out.

"You weren't going to get rid of me that way," he said.

"It was worth a try," she said. She took off her cap and dried the back of her neck and ran her fingers through her hair. She lit a cigarette and lowered herself to the concrete.

"How's the water?" he said.

"Very damp," she said. "You ought to investigate it."

"All right. Will you be here when I get back?"

"Why not? I was here first," she said.

He dived in and repeated her slow swim and float, and climbed out. "Can I have one of your butts?"

She pushed the pack and matches toward him. He lit one and took a couple of drags. "Don't be sore at me, Nancy. I didn't do anything. I just happened to *be* there, coming out of the bank."

"I'm not sore at you—just as long as you don't ask any questions," she said.

"I want to know, though. And it isn't just idle curiosity."

"What else is it?"

"Do you really want to know?" he said.

She turned and faced him. "Yes."

"It's love," he said.

"Oh, for Jesus' sake," she said.

"You said you wanted to know, and I told you," he said.

"I certainly didn't want to know that," she said.

"It doesn't put you under any obligation."

"I'll say it doesn't," she said.

"I just found out myself, last night."

"Because you saw me blubbering on the public street, you came to the conclusion that you're in love with me. You'd change your mind pretty quickly if you knew *why* I was crying," she said. "And you'll know soon enough. Everybody will. All of you. Everybody at this pool. Old Mr. Griffiths down there on the eighth tee. Johnny Wells, Mr. Charlton, Stanley Griffiths. The fussy foursome. You'd better get away before they all see you with me."

"What's the matter, Nancy?"

"Oh, for God's sake leave me alone," she said. She pulled up her knees again and rested her chin on them, and wept.

"What *is* it? I *love* you, Nancy."

"Oh, Christ almighty, Jamie. I want to die. I want to *die.*"

"Let's go someplace. Get dressed and we'll go for a ride," he said. She looked at him and she was not pretty, but there was the beginning of trust in her eyes.

"Where will you take me?" she said.

"Anywhere you say."

She put her towel to her face and sniffled. "Where's your car?"

"In the second row, halfway down the hill."

"I'll be there in ten minutes," she said. "Don't you come with me. I'll meet you in your car."

. . .

IT TOOK THEM longer than ten minutes, but she was there waiting when he got to his car. She was pretty again, in a flowery print sleeveless dress and a necklace of tiny Tecla pearls.

"Any place you want to go?"

She shook her head, and with her fingers only she waved to the clubhouse. "Goodbye, club," she said. "Nice to have known you."

They passed through two towns before either of them said anything. "Are you thirsty? I am," he said.

"Very," she said.

He stopped the car at a roadside stand and got a couple of mugs of root beer. "This is all they had," he said. "Out of everything else."

"I love root beer," she said. "Remember those picnics when we were very little? At the Griffiths' farm? I got stung by yellow jackets one year."

"I was there. You were certainly a mess. All puffed up."

"And Mrs. Griffiths put clay all over me, supposed to take the sting out but it didn't."

"The wrong kind of clay, I guess."

"I minded that worse than the sting, that mud all over my face and arms," she said. "Well, I should have gotten used to it. The mud's going to fly thick and fast."

"You don't have to talk about it, Nance," he said.

"Oh, I can now. We're not even in the same county, so I can talk, and I want to." She handed him her mug, and he returned it to the refreshment stand. They drove away.

"Do you think I'm pregnant, Jamie? Is that what you think it is?"

"The possibility occurred to me."

"Well, it might be a possibility but it doesn't happen to be what I was crying about," she said. "It's my father."

"Your father?"

"They came and arrested him this morning. It'll be in the paper this afternoon. Judge McDermott released him on bail, but he's going to have to go to prison."

"For what?"

"Misappropriation of funds. Daddy is a thief. He stole over sixty thousand dollars in three years."

"At the Trust Company?"

"Yes. When you saw me yesterday he had just signed a confession. I was there when he signed it. I went to his office to ask him for some money. Poor Daddy. He hated to refuse me anything, and didn't very often. But there I was, and some lawyers and a detective—although I didn't know that that's what they were. 'Gentlemen, my daughter is here to ask me for some money. Shall I tell her what my excuse is for turning her down?' One of the men said no, it would be cruel. But Daddy said I had to find out sometime. Sixty thousand dollars, and he doesn't know where it all went. He told me to go home and be with Mother when she got the bad news. Today I went to the club for the last time ever. Monday I start looking for a job."

"Your mother has some money, hasn't she?"

"Some. Enough for her to live on, I guess, but not in our house."

"I wondered why you said 'Goodbye, club.' I had a feeling it meant something."

"And you were right," she said. "About *that*. You weren't right in suspecting I was pregnant. I'm much too careful for that."

"I wouldn't know," he said.

"No, and the only person that would know—I don't expect to see *him* any more. Not after he hears about Daddy. So I guess I'm going to start being virtuous, for a change."

"Oh, stop trying to be so sophisticated. You make me sick. Whoever the guy is—and I'll bet I could guess—you don't know *what* he's going to do."

"Don't I? He's quaking in his boots right now, terrified that he'd somehow get mixed up in this."

"If that's your opinion of him, why did you have an affair with him?"

"Oh, Jamie, what a question. I knew what I was letting myself in for, but that didn't stop me."

"Well, at least his wife doesn't know. Although she is sore at you."

"How do you know?"

"Because you were supposed to bring three dozen ears of corn to her picnic last night," he said.

"Oh," she said.

"Who else could it be? As soon as I knew I was in love with you, I spent all last night figuring out all the possibilities. I finally narrowed it down to two."

"Who was the other?" said Nancy.

"That wet-smack cousin of mine, Walker," he said.

"No. Not Walker."

"I'm glad of that, anyway," he said.

"He is a wet smack, isn't he? And his wife is so unattractive. At least Gwen is pretty. A bitch, but pretty. At least I never felt that I was taking candy from a baby."

"Gwen thinks you ought to have someone you can depend on," he said.

"How touching."

"I think so, too," he said.

"And so do I. That makes three of us."

"Why don't you marry me?" he said.

"Let me find a job first," she said. "What do they pay you at the bank?"

"Fifteen dollars a week."

"Which is probably what I'll get, if I'm lucky. We could be gloriously happy on thirty a week, you and I."

"I'll have some money when I'm twenty-five."

"Yes, but what do we do in the meantime? Thanks for the offer, Jamie. But you have another year in college, and then I suppose they'll pack you off to the Harvard Business School, and then you ought to have a year or two in Wall Street. You and I are exactly the same age, but do you see how young you are? And how old I am?"

"I didn't like the sound of that when I heard it from Gwen," he said.

"Ask me again four years from now," she said.

"I don't want to have to wait that long," he said.

"We don't have to wait, for everything," she said.

(1967)

Eyes of a
Blue Dog

Gabriel García Márquez

Then she looked at me. I thought that she was looking at me for the first time. But when she turned
around behind the candlestick and I kept feeling her
slippery and oily look in back of me, over my shoulder, I understood that it was I who was looking at
her for the first time. I lit a cigarette. I took a drag of
the harsh, strong smoke before spinning in my chair,
balancing on one of the rear legs. After that I saw her
there, as if she'd been standing beside the candlestick
looking at me every night. For a few brief minutes
that's all we did: look at each other. I looked from the
chair, balancing on one of the rear legs. She stood,
with a long and quiet hand on the candlestick, looking at me. I saw her eyelids lit up as on every night.
It was then that I remembered the usual thing, when
I said to her, "Eyes of a blue dog." Without taking

her hand off the candlestick she said to me, "That. We'll never forget that." She left the circle of light, sighing. "Eyes of a blue dog. I've written it everywhere."

I saw her walk over to the dressing table. I watched her appear in the circular glass of the mirror, looking at me now in a measured exchange. I watched her keep on looking at me with her great hot-coal eyes: looking at me while she opened the little box covered with pink mother-of-pearl. I saw her powder her nose. When she finished, she closed the box, stood up again, and walked over to the candlestick, once more saying, "I'm afraid that someone is dreaming about this room and revealing my secrets." And over the flame she held the same long and tremulous hand that she had been warming before sitting down at the mirror. She said, "You don't feel the cold." I said to her, "Sometimes." And she said to me, "You must feel it now."

And then I understood why I couldn't have been alone in the room. It was the cold that had been giving me the certainty of my solitude. "Now I feel it," I said. "And it's strange, because the night is quiet. Maybe the sheet fell off."

She didn't answer. Again she began to move toward the mirror, and I turned again in the chair, keeping my back to her. Without seeing her, I knew what she was doing. I knew that she was sitting in front of the mirror again, seeing my back, which had had time to reach the depths of the mirror and be caught by her look, which had also had just enough time to reach the depths and return before her hand returned to her lips, anointed now with crimson from the first turn of her hand in front of the mirror. I saw, opposite me, the smooth wall, which was like another blind mirror. I couldn't see her—sitting behind me—but could imagine her as if a mirror had been hung in place of the wall.

"I see you," I told her. And on the wall I saw her as if she had raised her eyes and had seen me in the depths of the mirror, with my back turned toward her, my face turned toward the wall. Then I saw her lower her eyes again and keep them on her brassiere, not talking. And I said to her again, "I see you."

She raised her eyes from her brassiere. "That's impossible," she said. I asked her why. And she said, with her eyes quiet and on her brassiere again, "Because your face is turned toward the wall." Then I spun the chair around. I had my cigarette clenched in my mouth. When I remained facing the mirror, she went back by the candlestick. Now she had her hands open over the flame, like the two wings of a hen, toasting herself, and with her face shaded by her own fingers. "I think I'm going to catch cold," she said. "This must be a city of ice." She turned her face to profile and her skin, going from copper to red, suddenly appeared sad. "Do something about it," she said. And she began to get undressed, item by item, starting at the top with the brassiere.

I told her, "I'm going to turn back to the wall." She said, "No. In any case, you'll see me the way you did when your back was turned." And no sooner had she said it than she was almost completely undressed, with the flame licking her long copper skin.

I said, "I've always wanted to see you like that, with the skin of your belly full of deep pits, as if you'd been beaten." And before I realized that my words had become clumsy at the sight of her nakedness she became motionless, warming herself on the globe over the candlestick, and she said, "Sometimes I think I'm made of metal." She was silent for an instant. The position of her hands over the flame varied slightly.

I said, "Sometimes, in other dreams, I've thought you were only a little bronze statue in the corner of some museum. Maybe that's why you're cold." And she said, "Sometimes, when I sleep on my heart, I can feel my body growing hollow and my skin is like plate. Then, when the blood beats inside of me, it's as if someone were calling by knocking on my stomach and I can feel my own copper sound in the bed. It's like—what do you call it—laminated metal." She drew closer to the candlestick.

"I would have liked to hear you," I said. And she said, "If we find each other sometime, put your ear to my ribs when I sleep on the left side and you'll hear me echoing. I've always wanted you to do it sometime." I heard her breathe heavily as she talked. And she said that for years she'd done nothing different. Her life had been dedicated to finding me in reality, through that identifying phrase "Eyes of a blue dog." She went along the street saying it aloud, as a way of telling the only person who could have understood her, "I'm the one who comes into your dreams every night and tells you, 'Eyes of a blue dog.' "

She said that she went into restaurants and before ordering said to the waiters, "Eyes of a blue dog." But the waiters bowed reverently, without remembering ever having said that in their dreams. Then she would write on the napkins and scratch on the varnish of the tables with a knife, "Eyes of a blue dog." And on the steamed-up windows of hotels, stations, all public buildings she would write with her forefinger, "Eyes of a blue dog." She said that once she went into a drugstore and noticed the same smell that she had smelled in her room one night after having dreamed about me. He must be near, she thought, seeing the clean, new tiles of the drugstore. Then she went over to the clerk and said to him, "I always dream—about a man who says to me, 'Eyes of a blue dog.'" And she said that the salesman had looked at her eyes and told her, "As a matter of fact, Miss, you do have eyes like that." And she said to him, "I have to find the man who told me those very words in my dreams." The clerk started to laugh and moved to the other end of the counter. She kept on looking at the clean tile and smelling the odor. And she opened her purse and on the tiles, with her crimson lipstick, she wrote in red letters, "Eyes of a blue dog." The clerk came back from where he had been. He told her, "Madam, you have dirtied the tiles." He gave her a damp cloth, saying, "Clean it up." And she said, still by the candlestick, that she had spent the whole afternoon on all fours, washing the tiles and saying, "Eyes of a blue dog," until people gathered at the door and said she was crazy.

Now, when she finished speaking, I remained in the corner, sitting, rocking in the chair. "Every day I try to remember the phrase with which I am to find you," I said. "Now I don't think I'll forget it tomorrow. Still, I've always said the same thing and when I wake up I've always forgotten what the words I can find you with are." And she said, "You invented them yourself on the first day." I said to her, "I invented them because I saw your eyes of ash. But I never remember the next morning." And she, with clenched fists, beside the candlestick, breathed deeply. "If you could at least remember now what city I've been writing it in," she said.

Her clenched teeth gleamed over the flame. "I'd like to touch you now," I said. She raised her face, which had been looking at the light; she raised her stare—burning, roasting, too, just like her, like her hands—and I felt that she saw me, in the corner where I was sitting, rocking in the chair. "You never told me that before," she said. I said, "I tell you now and it's the truth." From the other side of the candlestick she asked for a cigarette. The butt had disappeared between my fingers.

I'd forgotten that I was smoking. She said, "I don't know why I can't remember where I wrote it." And I said to her, "For the same reason that tomorrow I won't be able to remember the words." And she said sadly, "No. It's just that sometimes I think that I've dreamed that, too."

I stood up and walked toward the candlestick. She was a little beyond, and I kept on walking with the cigarettes and matches in my hand, which would not go beyond the candlestick. I held the cigarette out to her. She squeezed it between her lips and leaned over to reach the flame before I had time to light the match. "In some city in the world, on all the walls, those words have to appear in writing: 'Eyes of a blue dog,'" I said. "If I remembered them tomorrow I could find you."

She raised her head again, and now the glowing cigarette was between her lips. "Eyes of a blue dog," she sighed, remembered, with the cigarette drooping over her chin and one eye half closed. Then, with the cigarette between her fingers, she sucked in the smoke and exclaimed, "This is something else now. I'm warming up." And she said it with her voice a little lukewarm and fleeting, as if she hadn't really said it but had written it on a piece of paper and had brought the paper close to the flame while I read "I'm warming . . ." and had continued holding the paper between her thumb and forefinger, turning it around as it was being consumed, so that I just read ". . . up" before the paper was completely consumed and dropped all wrinkled to the floor, diminished, converted into light ash dust. "That's better," I said. "Sometimes it frightens me to see you that way. Trembling beside a candlestick."

WE HAD BEEN seeing each other for several years. Sometimes when we were already together, somebody would drop a spoon outside and we would wake up. Little by little, we'd been coming to understand that our friendship was subordinated to things, to the simplest of happenings. Our meetings always ended that way, with the fall of a spoon early in the morning.

Now, next to the candlestick, she was looking at me. I remembered that she had also looked at me in that way in the past, in that remote dream where I made the chair spin on its back leg and remained facing a strange woman with ashen eyes. It was in that dream that I asked her for the first time, "Who are you?" And she said to me, "I don't remember." I said to her, "But I think we've seen each other before." And she said, indifferently, "I think I dreamed about you once, about this same room." I told her, "That's it. I'm beginning to remember now." And she said, "How strange. It's certain that we've met in other dreams."

She took two drags on the cigarette. I was still standing, facing the candlestick, when suddenly I was looking at her. I looked her up and down and she was still copper—no longer hard and cold metal but soft, malleable copper. "I'd like to touch you," I said again. And she said, "You'll ruin everything." I said, "It doesn't matter now. All we have to do is turn the pillow over in order to meet again." And I held my hand out over the candlestick. She didn't move. "You'll ruin everything," she said again before I could touch her. "Maybe, if you came around behind the candlestick, we'd wake up frightened in who knows what part of the world." But I insisted. "It doesn't matter," I said. And she said, "If we turned over the pillow, we'd meet again. But when you wake up you'll have forgotten." I began to move toward the corner. She stayed behind, warming her hands over the flame. And I still wasn't beside the chair when I heard her say behind me, "When I wake up at midnight, I keep turning in bed, with the fringe of the pillow burning my knee, and repeating until dawn, 'Eyes of a blue dog.'"

Then I remained with my face toward the wall. "It's already dawning," I said without looking at her. "When it struck two I was awake, and that was a long time back." I went to the door. When I had the knob in my hand, I heard her voice again, the same, invariable. "Don't open that door," she said. "The hallway is full of difficult dreams." And I asked her, "How do you know?" She told me, "Because I was there a moment ago and I had to come back when I discovered I was sleeping on my heart." I had the door half opened. I moved it a little and a cold, thin breeze brought me the fresh smell of vegetable earth, damp fields. She spoke again. I turned, still moving the door, mounted on silent hinges, and I told her, "I don't think there's any hallway outside here. I'm getting the smell of country." And she, a little distant, told me, "I know that better than you. What's happening is that there's a woman outside dreaming about the country." She crossed her arms over the flame. She continued speaking. "It's that woman who always wanted to have a house in the country and was never able to leave the city." I remembered having seen the woman in some previous dream, but I knew, with the door ajar now, that within half an hour I would have to go down for breakfast. And I said, "In any case, I have to leave here in order to wake up."

Outside, the wind fluttered for an instant, then remained quiet, and the breathing of someone sleeping who had just turned over in bed could be heard. The wind from the fields had ceased. There were no more smells. "Tomorrow I'll recognize you from that," I said. "I'll recognize you when on the street I see a woman writing 'Eyes of a blue dog' on the walls." And she, with a sad smile, which was already a smile of surrender to the impossible, the unreachable, said, "Yet you won't remember anything during the day." And she put her hands back over the candlestick, her features darkened by a bitter cloud. "You're the only man who doesn't remember anything of what he's dreamed after he wakes up."

(Translated, from the Spanish, by Gregory Rabassa.)

(1978)

WE

MARY GRIMM

We all got married—Suzanne and Virginia and I—
and it was all we ever wanted to be at the time. I
fought with my parents to get married, and Suzanne
ran away from home with her boyfriend to get married, and Virginia saved her money for a year and
eight months, eating a bag lunch at work every day
and walking up from the square to save the five cents
for the transfer and making her own clothes and only
seeing movies when they came to the drive-in—all
to get married.

And then we had done it and we were married.
Sex all the time. Our own houses (rented). A whole
list of things that would not have been gathered together except for us: toasters, glassware, unbreakable
dinner sets with a rim of gold around the white
plates, towels we were going to paint the bathroom

to match. It was heaven. Every day we woke up to different clock radios all set to the same rock station, and we had breakfast with our husbands, except for Suzanne, who said goodbye to hers at two-thirty in the morning, unless he tried very hard not to wake her and only kissed her on the forehead before he left. Then maybe we did the dishes or made the bed or put something out to defrost for dinner. I would get this really happy feeling as I was putting on my coat if I could look around and everything was nice: the glasses turned upside down and shining, the carpet speckless and smooth like a mowed lawn, the pillows on the bed fat and undented. Or maybe we only had time to put on eyeliner and go. We went to work and at lunch (still a bag lunch for Virginia, because of saving for their future house) we told stories about our husbands. Then we went home and (a) fixed dinner from a new recipe, or (b) called out for pizza, or (c) went to a sit-down restaurant that wasn't too expensive. Later, at home, we watched TV with our husbands, with our arms around each other, or somebody would come over and we'd play gin rummy or pinochle with the tape player turned up loud. We could have done anything we wanted to do, that was the thing.

And then (we still didn't know each other yet, although Suzanne lived only one house away from me) we'd been married for a while and there was something funny about it. I didn't want to have sex every night, for instance. This was awful, after how it had been. Sometimes I wanted to watch the end of a movie or one of my favorite shows instead of having sex. I didn't tell him, but I felt sick. Then I got used to it. Suzanne says it was the other way for her: she could tell sometimes he wanted to listen to the ballgame on the radio instead. Virginia didn't say much about this, but she's shier than Suzanne and me. And also when he and I were at home together, alone, one of us would always be calling up someone to come over. He would call up his buddies to come over and work on the car. Or I would call up my sister and her husband to come over and watch a movie. I had a feeling like "What's next?"

Right here was when I met Suzanne, in the supermarket. I'd seen her around before, in the yard or driving up her driveway in her car or hanging up bedspreads on the clothesline in her back yard, so I thought what the hell and I said hello. The thing is I probably wouldn't have said hello earlier on because then I had everything I wanted. But on this day—it was April—there was a wind scooting little pieces of paper around the supermarket parking lot and a feeling in the air that you should be driving fast someplace, and I didn't know it but I was pregnant. I wanted something, and Suzanne looked as if she had some of what I wanted. She was wearing a new miniskirt and mirror shades, and she had a way of walking as if she was in a commercial. She was pregnant, too, but she already knew and had gone right from the doctor's to buy the miniskirt so she could wear it for a couple of months before her stomach pushed out.

But whatever we thought we wanted or thought each other was like didn't matter—was forgotten, even—because from the first words we said to each other we knew we were going to be friends. I had thought that wouldn't happen anymore now that I was married. I went back from the supermarket to her house for coffee (I felt like my mother—having coffee and doughnuts with a neighbor) and we talked for two hours while my groceries melted and slumped in the car. I can't remember what we talked about. Everything. Suzanne said it was like being in love, which I found upsetting when she said it. But it was true. We leaned across the table toward each other, that morning and other mornings, drinking cups of coffee (later Sanka) and eating and smoking until we had to quit, and told each other stories about our pasts, our families, our school loves, our hopes for adventure. It wasn't like a conversation, which sounds too stiff and polite; it was more like a piece of music where we each had parts that overlapped, or a play where the actors say what is closest to their hearts.

And then when we were about five months along Virginia and her husband moved into the house on the other side of Suzanne. If Suzanne and I hadn't gotten to be good friends so fast, things might have been difficult or different. There might have been jealousy or misunderstandings or whatever. But as it was we knew each other so well already that there was room for Virginia, who was nice and really not a demanding sort anyway. She wasn't pregnant but was planning to be, and in two months she was.

FOR A WHILE we didn't have to worry about the thing of being married. For quite a long while. There was all the business of doctor visits, baby showers, maternity clothes, painting the extra bedroom. And then the hospital, the drive home with the baby looking so cute in the infant seat for the first time, the adoring grandparents waiting at home with giant panda bears and potty seats that played a tune. And then the long plunge into babyness. All of life was baby life: baby food, baby clothes, baby wipes, the baby changing table, baby's schedule, baby's nap, baby's bad time with breast-feeding/colic/teething. All our stories were baby stories: how baby had thrown up yellow, how baby had pulled the pierced earrings right out of our ears, how baby had rolled over for the first time while we were out of the room and almost fallen off the bed, how baby would not go to sleep until a certain song was played on the tape player.

Suzanne and I both had two, Virginia only one: she seemed shy and not very definite, but she was a planner. And for three years we were submerged together. We woke up at seven and sank into our lives, making breakfast/lunch/dinner, cutting food up into tiny bites, taking slow walks pushing strollers or with a staggering child hanging on to our hands, slipping the top diaper off towering stacks of whiteness, pulling out the potty chair, holding someone else's eager flesh in our arms, holding it back from destruction by fire, cars, household pets, electric sockets. Our husbands visited every day, between work and going out and going to bed, but we scarcely noticed. And every night we went to bed later than we wanted and as soon as we touched the sheets found ourselves rising up into sleep and dreams, as light as birds.

And then there was a change. At first we thought it was just because Virginia had gone back to work. Her little girl was three—old enough for day care, Virginia said. We were amazed that she had had the strength to think ahead—she had been on the waiting list for the school for months. She went back to the phone company—not at her old job but at a new one they found for her. This made Suzanne and me discontented. Our younger children were only one and a half and two—too young, we thought, for day care. And we had no jobs to go back to. Suzanne had gone to college for a while but had quit when her money ran out, and her family refused to lend her any. Come back home and get married was not what they said, but they might as well have. I had never been to college at all. Virginia, though, had her B.A. For a while we couldn't like her as well as we had, and we looked for signs that her little girl was suffering from day care. Was she thin? Was she more quarrelsome and whiny? Was a career more important, Suzanne and I asked ourselves, than your child's happiness? Could you have a career at the phone company?

We got together more and more often to discuss this and then other things. We were surprised to find ourselves thinking again, it had been so long. And then we realized that the change was in the kids, too, and that that change had made it possible for us to think, to put our heads above water, to begin to float again on the surface of the world. They, the kids, were becoming people, sometimes responsible for themselves, capable of wishes that were not dictated or instigated by us, wanting to be on their own. The older kids had been like this for a while but we hadn't noticed.

And we noticed other things, too: that our husbands were still there, but that things between us were not quite the same. That we were not as young as we still thought of ourselves as being. That we looked different—older, or maybe just not taken care of. It's a wonder we didn't lynch Virginia for having had only one child and being already out in the world. Suzanne and I knew that we would have to wait—did we ever discuss this?—we would have to wait until the little kids were older. It would be at least a year, but probably more like two. We couldn't afford Virginia's day care, so it would have to be the church day play, where they took only four-year-olds. But what to do in the meantime, now that we were conscious again?

You might have thought we would have taken a look at our husbands again. But things with them had gotten into a different way, and maybe we thought that was the way it was supposed to be, or maybe we thought it would do no good to change things. We had things we did with our husbands on the weekends, and we went out sometimes, but really we had separate lives. I had a memory of how I had thought before we got married that we would spend all our time together, that we would go places together and do things as ordinary as shopping for the fun of it, but now I knew how dumb that was. We didn't think of getting divorced; we knew we were married, and that was that. But that feeling from the day in April came back, worse than ever, and Suzanne and I put our heads together to do something about it. It was hard to even think of change when things had been the same for so long.

Oh, we were so bored. Nothing ever happened on our street, except the regular visits of the mailmen and the meter men and the teen-agers who stuck flyers into our mailboxes or rubber-banded them to the bannisters of the porch. Nothing happened at the supermarket except that you heard from the cashiers about who had died in the neighborhood. Nothing happened at church except you could see who had new clothes or was pregnant. But we were determined to look for what there was.

The first thing we tried was new recipes. For a while we cooked something new every day. We got cookbooks out of the library—Hawaiian cookbooks, make-your-own-bread cookbooks, tomato cookbooks, dinner-in-an-hour cookbooks. We bugged our aunts and grandmothers for family recipes, which we wrote out and exchanged on file cards. At every dinner we tried them on our husbands and children. Every morning when we had coffee, instead of buying doughnuts from Snow White the way we used to, one of us made something: chocolate-chip kuchen, apricot-sour-cream coffee cake, banana bran muffins with lemon glaze. Instead of Oreos and chips, our kids ate snacks of prune-peanut crunch, sesame breadsticks, carrot and cheese-cubes on a stick. We made ice cubes with single grapes and cherries frozen inside, we candied violets in the spring and rose petals in the summer. We had gala dinners to which our husbands and children and Virginia and her husband and child came, uncomfortable and surprised to find themselves all together in one house or the other. But that was no good, and it was back to meat loaf and macaroni and cheese. I still make Spanish rice, though.

Next: sewing. I had a sewing machine that I had hardly ever used, bought from a high-pressure salesman in the first months of our marriage. My husband and I were so dumb, and the salesman was so powerful and certain. We sat before him on the couch holding each other's hands behind a cushion and we said yes to everything—yes to the cross-stitching attachment, yes to the five-year service contract. The sewing machine sat in the hall between the bedrooms, sometimes with things stacked on it, sometimes next to a stool or a stepladder for one of the kids. But now we dragged it out, Suzanne and I, and we got a pattern that was marked "Easy-Sew" and we picked out cloth at the Sewtex Fabric store, with the kids rampaging up and down the aisles and begging for cards of buttons and long curling strips of ribbons and lace. We looked at but cautiously did not buy the patterns for baby and children's clothes—little rompers with duck appliqués, little dresses with ruffled sleeves and hems. We planned how we might make all our clothes except for coats and bathing suits and underwear. The cloth was wonderful to carry home, heavy and bright-colored, smooth to touch, folding over and over on itself without wrinkling. Mine was golden yellow and full of light. Suzanne's was silver, a gray as pale and shining as the moon.

And all that month we pinned the thin crumpled tissues of the pattern to the cloth with sharp, glittery pins and flashed the metal of the scissors through the folded layers and attached the pieces to each other under the whir of the machine's needle. They were simple dresses: a panel for the front and one for the back, attached at the shoulders by slender strips of cloth that were meant to be tied in a bow. But we sweated and swore over them, sewed pieces backward, stabbed our fingers with pins until they bled. The kids ate cookies and pickles and M&M's and Popsicles unheeded for the last two days before we were done. We tried the dresses on in Suzanne's bedroom, pulling the shades in the middle of the day and standing on her bed unsteadily, laughing and holding on to each other, to see if they looked good in the back. The ties tied, we exclaimed to each other. They were real dresses, wearable, that we could go out in and no one would be able to tell that we had bled on them. But never again, I said, and Suzanne agreed—never again would I sew another thing except a button on or a hem up.

And then we joined a book club. Once a month the members met to discuss a book that had been agreed on beforehand. Suzanne and I were conscious that we had not used our minds much for a while. We went to the library and got out the book, a very long novel by a famous South American writer, and read it in tandem, borrowing it back and forth. What do you think it means, I would ask Suzanne between loads of laundry, when the old guy comes back and looks just the same but he should have been dead for about a hundred years? How about that blood, she asked me when we were giving the kids peanut-butter sandwiches for lunch, letting them spread their own so they would learn to be independent, even though it took so long and was so hard to clean up. What did you think when that blood dripped and flowed like a stream down the street to the house of the murdered man's mother? We didn't know. We went to the meeting, held at a member's house, and sat waiting for enlightenment, but no one asked the questions we were interested in, and we were afraid to ask them. The other members were teachers, mostly, and they argued with each other and harangued and pounded the arms of their chairs and were so terrifying to Suzanne and me that we could hardly eat the pasta salad and brownies afterward. Did we have suggestions for the next book, one of the teachers asked us nicely when we sat balancing our plates and glasses. We said no.

IT WAS SUMMER again now: longer nights, warm sweet air. It seemed like a long time since we had had any fun. We sat in the mornings drinking countless cups of coffee while the kids drove up the driveway and down the driveway on their Big Wheels. We sat on Suzanne's back steps watching the kids play with dirt and water under the apple trees. We lay on a blanket in my back yard while Suzanne's husband mowed the lawn. And we moaned and we moped. Why didn't we see any fun people anymore? Why didn't we ever get to go anyplace? Why didn't anyone we knew have a party? Why didn't we? We could. It would be an outdoor party, we planned, with lights in the trees and a speaker hooked up outside. While the kids threw sand at each other we made a guest list, a food list, a decorations list, a music list. Twenty times we decided what to wear, and twenty times we changed our minds. On the night of the party, we carted the kids off to Grandma's, harried our husbands to make the electrical and musical preparations. We combed the silken lengths of each other's hair, applied layers of scarlet and heather and ivory bisque to the smooth skin of our faces. "You look wonderful," we said to each other.

Virginia came early, with a goose-liver pâté and her husband. How is work, we said. She told us about the feud between her supervisor and the most senior operator, about the new system being installed that would require them to learn a new form of data entry, about the new coffee machine that she and her co-workers had chipped in to buy. She said that she was thinking of getting her own car and had found three new places to eat lunch and wanted to update her wardrobe to a more office look. What's new, she asked us. We looked at each other, and then away. Our kids had new teeth, new scrapes and bruises, new words learned from illicit television and unapproved friends. Suzanne had new eyeshadow. I had just gotten a new bra and had found a more efficient way to pack the freezer. Nothing much, we said.

And then we set out to have fun. Fun was drinking new combinations of liquor and mix, drinking out of other people's glasses, perching on the arms of chairs and saying outrageous things, letting someone light our cigarette and looking into his eyes with the flame between us, talking about things that our mothers would have been shocked to hear said aloud, playing the music as loud as possible but not so loud that the neighbors would call the police. It was fun to sing along with the music from where we lay in the grass under the rocking, bobbing lanterns that hung in the apple trees, and to race back and forth between our two houses for more drinks, more cookies, more celery stuffed with peanut butter. We were glad to go to the store for more ginger ale, recruiting someone to go with us who was not our husband, walking down the street in the welcome dark and into the dead daylight of the street lights. We thought it might make us finally and forever happy to kiss someone in the kitchen leaning against the sink, one hand on the cool, smooth curve of the enamel and the other touching the weave of a shirt that we had never washed or ironed or sewed a button on. The morning after the party, though, was just the same, filled with cornflakes and daytime television, and there were the dirty glasses and erupting ashtrays as well.

We enrolled in a class. We made a list of places to take the kids and we took them there: fast-food lunches, swimming, the park with the jungle gym or the park with the hiking trails, for walks, to story hour. We took up badminton and played for weeks with anyone who showed up on a court marked on my lawn with white spray paint, waiting our turn lounging on the old car that my husband thought he might get around to fixing someday, our backs against the front window, legs stretched out on the metal of the hood, heads thrown back to the sky. We played on into the dark, until we could see nothing except the small white blur of the shuttlecock arcing across the yard, and then not even that, so that we struck out at it on faith.

It was fall. And then maybe, we thought, if we go out together. Just the girls, since our husbands didn't want to go anyway. We could go to movies, to plays, to dinner. We went out with an old friend of mine, still unmarried, whom we envied and felt superior to. It was more fun to go out with Janine because she was single and we were not and we could do anything because we were not involved in the game the way she was. You guys, she would say, I can't believe you guys. Will you cut it out, she would say. We went to dinner and ate unfamiliar foods, spicy and fragrant. We went to plays and strained forward in our seats the better to enter another world. We went to a Tupperware party when we were high as kites. We went to bars where we met podiatry students who claimed to be amazed when we said how old we were and some of whom got sentimental and clingy when it was time to leave. But when we went out, no matter how immensely silly we became, or how high we got, no matter how many places we went and how late we stayed out, drinking cup after cup of coffee at an all-night restaurant while we talked and talked about our lives and how they disappointed us and how they might gladden us, when we went back it was still the same.

And then I got the flu, a long, lingering flu. I was sick as a dog—so sick that my husband had to do for the kids, get their dinners and put them in and take them out of the bathtub and read them the same book over and over again. And Suzanne was invited to join her cousin's bowling team while I was sick. Twice a week I watched her from my front window, where I was lying on the couch using up Kleenex as she got picked up by a carful of women wearing satin team jackets. And when I was well she came over and told me she'd stayed after one night and made out with the bartender. I thought I'd never get over it.

SO WHAT HAPPENED? Nothing, really. Everything went on a little while longer, until we got to the end of this period in our lives, until we stopped looking for something that we didn't have or know. But we didn't stop because of despair, or because we were tired of looking, but because it was time. Suzanne got a job at an office. I started college. We began meeting Virginia downtown for lunch. We threw our jeans and T-shirts to the back of the closet and bought new clothes: suits and blouses for Suzanne, slacks and sweaters and a denim jacket for me. There was new stuff on our minds: day care, timesaving appliances, comfortable yet attractively businesslike shoes, notebooks for shorthand and for notes on Dutch medieval art. And we were still married. We had never been able to completely forget about being married, so our husbands were still there. They still came home and called up their friends to work on their cars and didn't want to go anyplace, but it didn't matter so much anymore. We smiled at them over breakfast and bragged about them at lunch. And at night we thought about sex again and did something about it. Janine got married and we all went to the wedding and we cried, every one of us—even Virginia, who had just met her.

Now we're too busy to think or to remember the time when Suzanne and I sat in one of our kitchens with the kids milling around while we talked on, oblivious, or cooked together, or sat under the apple trees; how we were pulled together like magnets every morning after our husbands went to work; how we spent the whole day together; how our kids had lunch together, took naps and went to the bathroom together.

Which is O.K. But do we miss it, what we had together when there was no one else in the world but mothers and children? And do we miss it, the soft solid feel of our children's bodies under our hands, the sweet smell of their breath, their voices in our ears singing the alphabet and the names of trees, puddings, television characters; the look of their bodies asleep, arms and legs flung out like a star or wound in a tight breathing ball; their questions asking why and what and how the world is made and ordered and laid out before us? No. Not every day.

(1988)

THE DARK STAGE

DAVID PLANTE

From his seat in the stalls, Sir Edward was aware, more than of anything else in the play, of the saliva spurting from the mouth of a raging actor, of the way the high heel of the younger actress caught in the hem of her long dress, of the earring that fell from the lobe of the matronly actress when she swung around quickly. Though the actors ignored these wayward happenings—didn't wipe off the saliva, delivered the impassioned speech balanced unsteadily on one foot while the other was still caught in the hem, stepped over the earring—to Sir Edward these were the most interesting moments in the play. During the final scene, his concentration was focussed on a moth flying high over the actors' heads, zigzagging through a cloud of brightly lit dust.

That moth was still flying above the actors' heads when they came out to bow, and Edward told himself he mustn't stare at it. He was pretty sure the matronly actress, who stood at the center of the bowing line, saw him in the audience, and he tried to clap hard and fast when she left the line and came forward to bow alone, but he could only clap slowly, his large hands making soft sounds, if any. She was wearing a wide-brimmed hat with feathers, and a dress that revealed her high, pointed shoes, and she wore a brooch in the middle of the ruff of her rounded bodice. She left the stage first, then the others, and the stage went dark. For a moment, Edward saw the age spots and veins on the backs of his hands, still raised against the darkness.

He waited. The safety curtain came down as he walked along the now empty row of seats to the aisle, where an usherette was picking up a program someone had dropped on the red carpet.

TO GET TO the stage door, he had to go through the lobby and out under the illuminated portico, with its high white pillars, and along the wet pavement of St. James's to the first side street, and around the block to a narrow, deserted cul-de-sac at the back of the theatre. "STAGE DOOR" was painted in white letters on a square blue lamp over the double doors, one of which was open; through it Edward saw a floor of wide, un-painted planks and a dim passage, and, just to the side, a little room, like a cupboard, where a man with his shirtsleeves rolled up to his elbows was sitting on a chair tilted back against a wall and staring down. He looked up when Edward approached and asked for Dame Hilary West's dressing room, and, pointing to the stairs at the end of the passage, he told Edward, "That'll be No. 8."

The treads were wooden and the stairs steep. The pale-yellow walls were bare and shone in the electric light. It seemed to Edward that there was no one in the theatre. He knocked on the painted door and, hearing "Come in," he opened the door by its white porcelain knob.

Hilary, changed from her costume into a suit, was standing at a table; with her hands placed flat on it, she was leaning forward, as if to study closely the white plastic head that held the wig she had worn on-stage. On the table next to the head was the hat with the feathers. She was in profile to Edward, and she remained that way for a moment; then she turned to him, raised her hands, clapped them together, and laughed.

"I was sure I saw you in the stalls," she said. "Why didn't you let me know you'd be here?"

He laughed lightly. "The fact is, I decided only this afternoon."

"I know your way of deciding to do something suddenly," she said. She went to him and hugged him and, stretching out her long, thin neck, offered him a cheek to kiss. Then, impulsively, she hugged him more tightly and kissed his cheek before she let him go.

He said, "The man at the stage door didn't even ask my name."

"Oh, you can't have visited an actress in her dressing room in a very, very long time. Leaving off your card disappeared at about the same time the man who kept the coal fires in the dressing rooms disappeared—and the woman who brought round tea."

She kicked her shoe toward the grate of a small fireplace, behind which was a modern electric fire, and gestured at the table, where there was an electric kettle and mugs.

"I suppose it has been some time," Edward said.

Hilary turned away from him so that the long silver chains around her neck clinked against one another. She always moved quickly and smoothly. She said, "It's a terrible play, isn't it?"

He laughed in a way that was also a shrug. In a corner of the room was a narrow bed with a red coverlet and square pillows in white, crocheted slips. The bed sagged in the middle.

With her hands to her hair, Hilary turned back to Edward and said, "Terrible, terrible."

He shrugged again. "I noticed a lot of things seemed to go wrong tonight."

"There are always things going wrong."

"I like the way you all ignore what would be immediately corrected if it were real life—someone would pick up the fallen earring."

Hilary waved her hands. She didn't want to talk about the play or the production. She came up close to Edward once more, and then, drawing back a little, she remembered to ask, "But where is Diane?"

He said, "Diane died two weeks ago."

Hilary's hands fluttered about her mouth, and she spoke through her fingers. "Died? But why didn't I know?" She lowered her hands. "Why didn't someone tell me? I don't read the papers, I wouldn't have seen the obit—but surely someone could have told me."

"*I* could have."

"Darling, you would have been too upset to do anything but sit in a darkened room. I know you. But don't we have any friends any longer who could have let me know?"

"Evidently not."

"Evidently," she said, "not."

"This is my first evening out since," Edward said.

"And to such a terrible play."

"Not really so terrible."

"It is. It is." She went to the table with the plastic head and the wig, and she seemed to look into the white face of the head, with its very fine nose and lips and big, blank eyes.

"Tell me," Edward asked. "Are you free?"

As if she were silently but intently communicating with the head, she didn't answer. Then, with a girlish swing of her hips, she faced him and asked, "Free?"

"For supper?"

"Yes, I am. I'm always free after performances. Always."

"I bought a game pie today for my supper. There's enough for two."

"I'd love that. I have a car. Do you?"

"I don't."

"Then we'll go in my car. The driver should be waiting just outside. He's always waiting just outside to take me home, alone, alone." Edward smiled at her, and she, recognizing that he had caught her acting, smiled gently back at him. "It's true," she said.

As they were descending the stairs, Hilary put her arm in Edward's and went on, "I'm very touched, you know, that you should want to see me your first night out."

The driver, a slim young Indian man, opened the back door of the car for them. The car went from the West End to St. John's Wood, where the trees, dark in the light of the street lamps, were losing their leaves.

"I never go to the theatre anymore," Hilary said. "Never. Why should I expect anyone else to go?"

. . .

WHILE EDWARD SET places with plates and silver from a cupboard in the basement dining room of the large house, Hilary walked the length of the table, bending her knees so that with each step her body dipped and then rose, and she ran a finger along the edge. At the end she examined the finger to see if it had collected any crumbs.

She said, "It's silly to ask, and it can't now mean anything, but did Diane ever know about"—she delicately twiddled her fingers as though to get rid of crumbs, if there were any, and looked at Edward, her eyelids wrinkled and her lashes thick with mascara—"you and me?"

Edward nodded. "She did, yes."

Hilary did another of her dips, bending her knees slightly, and said, "And so all those times I saw her, and she was as friendly as friendly could be, she knew."

"She knew."

"Why didn't you tell me she did?"

"She made me swear I wouldn't tell you. She—"

"I know, she would have been humiliated by my knowing she did and that she put up with it. I know. I know. I know."

Edward pointed to a place setting at one end of the table, and Hilary sat. Then he went into the kitchen and came out with a large wedge of game pie on a serving dish.

He ate leaning over his food, and when he drank from his glass of wine he hardly raised it off the table but leaned even farther forward. Hilary sat up straight, bringing the silver forkfuls up higher than her mouth and then lowering them, and she raised her glass almost higher than her nose each time she drank. She held her chin and bosom out.

Finally she said, "I don't think Gregory ever knew."

Edward hesitated. "I think he did."

"He told you he did?"

"Yes."

"And he told you not to tell me?"

"He did."

Hilary pressed the tips of her fingers to her eyebrows and lowered her head.

"Are you all right?" Edward asked.

She threw her hands out and raised her head and, after a deep breath, said, "I would like to say yes, that I'm all right, that you're all right—Are you all right?"

"I don't know."

"Nor do I, nor do I."

Edward got up and took the empty serving dish into the kitchen, and when he came back he found Hilary with her eyes closed. He said, "Hilary."

She opened her eyes and asked, "Please, may I spend the night?"

"Of course you may."

She got up and came to him and put her hand, which was freckled with brown spots, on one of his arms. "Go tell my driver to go and come back for me in the morning."

He did, and returned to the basement dining room, where he and Hilary sat at the table, silent again.

"I—" Hilary began, but her face went stark, and she said, "There's someone in the house, upstairs."

A flash passed through Edward.

Hilary began again: "I—" And again she stopped. She was motionless for a moment, and then, thrusting her chair so it fell backward with a bang, she stood. "There is someone upstairs," she said. "I know there is."

Edward went to the dining-room door, which led to the passage and the stairs, and he opened it, about to go up.

"No, no," Hilary said, reaching out a hand that clutched a white napkin. "You mustn't go up."

"Then what shall I do?"

Shaking the napkin, Hilary tilted her head back and laughed a strange, wild laugh; then she threw the napkin down.

Startled, Edward went around to Hilary's end of the table and set her chair upright. He said, "You must go to bed."

"Yes, yes," she said. "You're right."

As he helped her up the stairs, she leaned a little against him.

On the landing outside the room where she was to sleep, he opened an airing cupboard and took out a folded nightgown. As he handed it to her, one of the arms fell. Hilary raised the sleeve and said, "I would never have known Diane went in for such pretty nightgowns. Look at the lace around the cuff." She bit her lower lip, and, tears welling in her eyes, she smiled. "Shall I use the loo first?"

He kissed her on both cheeks and went into his bedroom and shut the door. He undressed, put on his pajamas, and lay on the bed to wait for Hilary to finish in the bathroom.

When he closed his eyes, he saw only darkness. Quickly, he opened them, and looked for a moment at the lit lamp, with a blue shade, next to his bed. He reached out and switched the lamp off, and when he closed his eyes again he saw the outline of the lamp shade, bright about the round edge, in the darkness. But it gradually faded and vanished, and once more the darkness was blank.

He wasn't falling asleep; he was fully aware, and his awareness widened out on all sides. He opened his eyes and saw a hand appear in the darkness.

It was a young woman's hand. He saw the curve of her shoulder appear, and a cheek. He saw a nipple appear, and a breast. He saw long hair fall out of the darkness, and an exposed ear, and the smooth side of a neck. A young woman was emerging, detail by detail. He saw her navel, the soft fold below her tummy, the pubic tuft. He saw her eyes, her nose, her full-lipped mouth. She was smiling, and as she smiled she turned toward him so that her long hair swung through space. She was no one he had ever seen.

(1995)

Song of Roland

Jamaica Kincaid

His mouth was like an island in the sea that was his
face; I am sure he had ears and nose and eyes and all
the rest, but I could see only his mouth, which I
knew could do all the things that a mouth usually
does, such as eat food, purse in approval or disap-
proval, smile, twist in thought; inside were his teeth
and behind them was his tongue. Why did I see him
that way, how did I come to see him that way? It was
a mystery to me that he had been alive all along and
that I had not known of his existence and I was perfectly fine—I went to sleep at night and I could wake
up in the morning and greet the day with indifference if it suited me, I could comb my hair and
scratch myself and I was still perfectly fine—and he
was alive, sometimes living in a house next to mine,
sometimes living in a house far away, and his exis-

tence was ordinary and perfect and parallel to mine, but I did not know of it, even though sometimes he was close enough to me for me to notice that he smelt of cargo he had been unloading; he was a stevedore.

His mouth really did look like an island, lying in a twig-brown sea, stretching out from east to west, widest near the center, with tiny, sharp creases, its color a shade lighter than that of the twig-brown sea in which it lay, the place where the two lips met disappearing into the pinkest of pinks, and even though I must have held his mouth in mine a thousand times, it was always new to me. He must have smiled at me, though I don't really know, but I don't like to think that I would love someone who hadn't first smiled at me. It had been raining, a heavy downpour, and I took shelter under the gallery of a dry-goods store along with some other people. The rain was an inconvenience, for it was not necessary; there had already been too much of it, and it was no longer only outside, overflowing in the gutters, but inside also, roofs were leaking and then falling in. I was standing under the gallery and had sunk deep within myself, enjoying completely the despair I felt at being myself. I was wearing a dress; I had combed my hair that morning; I had washed myself that morning. I was looking at nothing in particular when I saw his mouth. He was speaking to someone else, but he was looking at me. The someone else he was speaking to was a woman. His mouth then was not like an island at rest in a sea but like a small patch of ground viewed from high above and set in motion by a force not readily seen.

When he saw me looking at him, he opened his mouth wider, and that must have been the smile. I saw then that he had a large gap between his two front teeth, which probably meant that he could not be trusted, but I did not care. My dress was damp, my shoes were wet, my hair was wet, my skin was cold, all around me were people standing in small amounts of water and mud, shivering, but I started to perspire from an effort I wasn't aware I was making; I started to perspire because I felt hot, and I started to perspire because I felt happy. I wore my hair then in two plaits and the ends of them rested just below my collarbone; all the moisture in my hair collected and ran down my two plaits, as if they were two gutters, and the water seeped through my dress just below the collarbone and continued to run down my chest, only stopping at the place where the tips of my breasts met the fabric, revealing, plain as a new print, my nipples. He was looking at me and talking to someone else, and his mouth grew wide and narrow, small and large, and I wanted him to notice me, but there was so much noise: all the people standing in the gallery, sheltering themselves from the strong rain, had something they wanted to say, something not about the weather (that was by now beyond comment) but about their lives, their disappointments most likely, for joy is so short-lived there isn't enough time to dwell on its occurrence. The noise, which started as a hum, grew to a loud din, and the loud din had an unpleasant taste of metal and vinegar, but I knew his mouth could take it away if only I could get to it; so I called out my own name, and I knew he heard me immediately, but he wouldn't stop speaking to the woman he was talking to, so I had to call out my name again and again until he stopped, and by that time my name was like a chain around him, as the sight of his mouth was like a chain around me. And when our eyes met, we laughed, because we were happy, but it was frightening, for that gaze asked everything: who would betray whom, who would be captive, who would be captor, who would give and who would take, what would I do. And when our eyes met and we laughed at the same time, I said, "I love you, I love you," and he said, "I know." He did not say it out of vanity, he did not say it out of conceit, he only said it because it was true.

HIS NAME WAS Roland. He was not a hero, he did not even have a country; he was from an island, a small island that was between a sea and an ocean, and a small island is not a country. And he did not have a history; he was a small event in somebody else's history, but he was a man. I could see him better than he could see himself, and that was because he was who he was and I was myself but also because I was taller than he was. He was unpolished, but he carried himself as if he were precious. His hands were large and thick, and for no reason that I could see he would spread them out in front of him and they looked as if they were the missing parts from a powerful piece of machinery; his legs were straight from hip to knee and then from the knee they bent at an angle as if he had been at sea too long or had never learnt to walk properly to begin with. The hair on his legs was tightly curled as if the hairs were pieces of thread rolled between the thumb and the forefinger in preparation for sewing and so was the hair on his arms, the hair in his underarms, and the hair on his chest; the hair in those places was black and grew sparsely; the hair on his head and the hair between his legs was black and tightly curled also, but it grew in such abundance that it was impossible for me to move my hands through it. Sitting, standing, walking, or lying down, he carried himself as if he were something precious, but not out of vanity, for it was true, he was something precious; yet when he was lying on top of me he looked down at me as if I were the only woman in the world, the only woman he had ever looked at in that way—but that was not true, a man only does that when it is not true. When he first lay on top of me I was so ashamed of how much pleasure I felt that I bit my bottom lip hard—but I did not bleed, not from biting my lip, not then. His skin was smooth and warm in places I had not kissed him; in the places I had kissed him his skin was cold and coarse, and the pores were open and raised.

Did the world become a beautiful place? The rainy season eventually went away, the sunny season came, and it was too hot; the riverbed grew dry, the mouth of the river became shallow, the heat eventually became as wearying as the rain, and I would have wished it away if I had not become occupied with this other sensation, a sensation I had no single word for. I could feel myself full of happiness, but it was a kind of happiness I had never experienced before, and my happiness would spill out of me and run all the way down a long, long road and then the road would come to an end and I would feel empty and sad, for what could come after this? How would it end?

Not everything has an end, even though the beginning changes. The first time we were in a bed together we were lying on a thin board that was covered with old cloth, and this small detail, evidence of our poverty—people in our position, a stevedore and a doctor's servant, could not afford a proper mattress—was a major contribution to my satisfaction, for it allowed me to brace myself and match him breath for breath. But how can it be that a man who can carry large sacks filled with sugar or bales of cotton on his back from dawn to dusk exhausts himself within five minutes inside a woman? I did not then and I do not now know the answer to that. He kissed me. He fell asleep. I bathed my face then between his legs; he smelt of curry and onions, for those were the things he had been unloading all day; other times when

I bathed my face between his legs—for I did it often, I liked doing it—
he would smell of sugar, or flour, or the large, cheap bolts of cotton
from which he would steal a few yards to give me to make a dress.

WHAT IS THE everyday? What is the ordinary? One day, as I was walking toward the government dispensary to collect some supplies—one of
my duties as a servant to a man who was in love with me beyond anything he could help and so had long since stopped trying, a man I ignored except when I wanted him to please me—I met Roland's wife,
face to face, for the first time. She stood in front of me like a sentry—
stern, dignified, guarding the noble idea, if not noble ideal, that was her
husband. She did not block the sun, it was shining on my right; on my
left was a large black cloud; it was raining way in the distance; there was
no rainbow on the horizon. We stood on the narrow strip of concrete
that was the sidewalk. One section of a wooden fence that was supposed
to shield a yard from passersby on the street bulged out and was broken,
and a few tugs from any careless party would end its usefulness; in that
yard a primrose bush bloomed unnaturally, its leaves too large, its flowers showy, and weeds were everywhere, they had prospered in all the
wet. We were not alone. A man walked past us with a cutlass in his
knapsack and a mistreated dog two steps behind him; a woman walked
by with a large basket of food on her head; some children were walking
home from school, and they were not walking together; a man was leaning out a window, spitting, he used snuff. I was wearing a pair of mod-
estly high heels, red, not a color to wear to work in the middle of the day,
but that was just the way I had been feeling, red with a passion, like that
hibiscus that was growing under the window of the man who kept spitting from the snuff. And Roland's wife called me a whore, a slut, a pig,
a snake, a viper, a rat, a lowlife, a parasite, and an evil woman. I could see
that her mouth formed a familiar hug around these words—poor thing,
she had been used to saying them. I was not surprised. I could not have
loved Roland the way I did if he had not loved other women. And I was
not surprised; I had noticed immediately the space between his teeth. I
was not surprised that she knew about me; a man cannot keep a secret,
a man always wants all the women he knows to know each other.

I believe I said this: "I love Roland; when he is with me I want him to love me; when he is not with me I think of him loving me. I do not love you. I love Roland." This is what I wanted to say, and this is what I believe I said. She slapped me across the face; her hand was wide and thick like an oar; she, too, was used to doing hard work. Her hand met the side of my face: my jawbone, the skin below my eye and under my chin, a small portion of my nose, the lobe of my ear. I was then a young woman in my early twenties, my skin was supple, smooth, the pores invisible to the naked eye. It was completely without bitterness that I thought as I looked at her face, a face I had so little interest in that it would tire me to describe it, Why is the state of marriage so desirable that all women are afraid to be caught outside it? And why does this woman, who has never seen me before, to whom I have never made any promise, to whom I owe nothing, hate me so much? She expected me to return her blow but, instead, I said, again completely without bitterness, "I consider it beneath me to fight over a man."

I was wearing a dress of light-blue Irish linen. I could not afford to buy such material, because it came from a real country, not a false country like mine; a shipment of this material in blue, in pink, in lime green, and in beige had come from Ireland, I suppose, and Roland had given me yards of each shade from the bolts. I was wearing my blue Irish-linen dress that day, and it was demure enough—a pleated skirt that ended quite beneath my knees, a belt at my waist, sleeves that buttoned at my wrists, a high neckline that covered my collarbone—but underneath my dress I wore absolutely nothing, no undergarments of any kind, only my stockings, given to me by Roland and taken from yet another shipment of dry goods, each one held up by two pieces of elastic that I had sewn together to make a garter. My declaration of what I considered beneath me must have enraged Roland's wife, for she grabbed my blue dress at the collar and gave it a huge tug; it rent in two from my neck to my waist. My breasts lay softly on my chest, like two small pieces of unrisen dough, unmoved by the anger of this woman; not so by the touch of her husband's mouth, for he would remove my dress, by first patiently undoing all the buttons and then pulling down the bodice, and then he would take one breast in his mouth, and it would grow to a size much bigger than his mouth could hold, and he would let it go and turn to the other one; the saliva evaporating from the skin on that breast was an altogether different sensation from the sensation of my other breast in his mouth, and I would divide myself in two, for I could not decide which sensation I wanted to take dominance over the other. For an hour he would kiss me in this way and then exhaust himself on top of me in five minutes. I loved him so. In the dark I couldn't see him clearly, only an outline, a solid shadow; when I saw him in the daytime he was fully dressed. His wife, as she rent my dress, a dress made of material she knew very well, for she had a dress made of the same material, told me his history: it was not a long one, it was not a sad one, no one had died in it, no land had been laid waste, no birthright had been stolen; she had a list, and it was full of names, but they were not the names of countries.

What was the color of her wedding day? When she first saw him was she overwhelmed with desire? The impulse to possess is alive in every heart, and some people choose vast plains, some people choose high mountains, some people choose wide seas, and some people choose husbands; I chose to possess myself. I resembled a tree, a tall tree with long, strong branches; I looked delicate, but any man I held in my arms knew that I was strong; my hair was long and thick and deeply waved naturally, and I wore it braided and pinned up, because when I wore it loosely around my shoulders it caused excitement in other people—some of them men, some of them women, some of them it pleased, some of them it did not. The way I walked depended on who I thought would see me and what effect I wanted my walk to have on them. My face was beautiful, I found it so.

And yet I was standing before a woman who found herself unable to keep her life's booty in its protective sack, a woman whose voice no longer came from her throat but from deep within her stomach, a woman whose hatred was misplaced. I looked down at our feet, hers and mine, and I expected to see my short life flash before me; instead, I saw that her feet were without shoes. She did have a pair of shoes, though, which I had seen: they were white, they were plain, a round toe and flat laces, they took shoe polish well, she wore them only on Sundays and to church. I had many pairs of shoes, in colors meant to attract attention and dazzle the eye; they were uncomfortable, I wore them every day, I never went to church at all.

. . .

MY STRONG ARMS reached around to caress Roland, who was lying on my back naked; I was naked also. I knew his wife's name, but I did not say it; he knew his wife's name, too, but he did not say it. I did not know the long list of names that were not countries that his wife had committed to memory. He himself did not know the long list of names; he had not committed this list to memory. This was not from deceit, and it was not from carelessness. He was someone so used to a large fortune that he took it for granted; he did not have a bankbook, he did not have a ledger, he had a fortune—but still he had not lost interest in acquiring more. Feeling my womb contract, I crossed the room, still naked; small drops of blood spilt from inside me, evidence of my refusal to accept his silent offering. And Roland looked at me, his face expressing confusion. Why did I not bear his children? He could feel the times that I was fertile, and yet each month blood flowed away from me, and each month I expressed confidence at its imminent arrival and departure, and always I was overjoyed at the accuracy of my prediction. When I saw him like that, on his face a look that was a mixture—confusion, dumbfoundedness, defeat—I felt much sorrow for him, for his life was reduced to a list of names that were not countries, and to the number of times he brought the monthly flow of blood to a halt; his life was reduced to women, some of them beautiful, wearing dresses made from yards of cloth he had surreptitiously removed from the bowels of the ships where he worked as a stevedore.

At that time I loved him beyond words; I loved him when he was standing in front of me and I loved him when he was out of my sight. I was still a young woman. No small impressions, the size of a child's forefinger, had yet appeared on the soft parts of my body; my legs were long and hard, as if they had been made to take me a long distance; my arms were long and strong, as if prepared for carrying heavy loads; I was not beautiful, but if I could have been in love with myself I would have been. I was in love with Roland. He was a man. But who was he really? He did not sail the seas, he did not cross the oceans, he only worked in the bottom of vessels that had done so; no mountains were named for him, no valleys, no nothing. But still he was a man, and he wanted something beyond ordinary satisfaction—beyond one wife, one love, and one room with walls made of mud and roof of cane leaves, beyond the small plot of land where the same trees bear the same fruit year following year—for it would all end only in death, for though no history yet written had embraced him, though he could not identify the small uprisings within himself, though he would deny the small uprisings within himself, a strange calm would sometimes come over him, a cold stillness, and since he could find no words for it, he was momentarily blinded with shame.

One night Roland and I were sitting on the steps of the jetty, our backs facing the small world we were from, the world of sharp, dangerous curves in the road, of steep mountains of recent volcanic formations covered in a green so humble no one had ever longed for them, of three hundred and sixty-five small streams that would never meet up to form a majestic roar, of clouds that were nothing but large vessels holding endless days of water, of people who had never been regarded as people at all; we looked into the night, its blackness did not come as a surprise, a moon full of dead white light travelled across the surface of a glittering black sky; I was wearing a dress made from another piece of cloth he had given me, another piece of cloth taken from the bowels of a ship without permission, and there was a false pocket in the skirt, a pocket that did not have a bottom, and Roland placed his hand inside the pocket, reaching all the way down to touch inside of me; I looked at his face, his mouth I could see and it stretched across his face like an island and like an island, too, it held secrets and was dangerous and could swallow things whole that were much larger than itself; I looked out toward the horizon, which I could not see but knew was there all the same, and this was also true of the end of my love for Roland.

(1993)

THE MAN
IN THE MOON

WILLIAM MAXWELL

In the library of the house I grew up in there was a box of photographs that I used to look through when other forms of entertainment failed me. In this jumble there was a postcard of my mother's brother, my Uncle Ted, and a young woman cozying up together in the curve of a crescent moon. I would have liked to believe that it was the real moon they were sitting in, but you could see that the picture was taken in a photographer's studio. Who she was it never occurred to me to ask. Thirty or forty years later, if his name came up in conversation, women who were young at the same time he was would remark how attractive he was. He was thin-faced and slender, and carried himself well, and he had inherited the soft brown eyes of the Kentucky side of the family.

In the small towns of the Middle West at that time—I am speaking of, roughly, the year 1900—it was unusual for boys to be sent away to school. My uncle was enrolled in a military academy in Gambier, Ohio, and flunked out. How much education he had of a kind that would prepare him for doing well in one occupation or another I have no idea. I would think not much. Like many young men born into a family in comfortable circumstances, he felt that the advantages he enjoyed were part of the natural order of things. What the older generation admired and aspired to was dignity, resting on a firm basis of accomplishment. I think what my uncle had in mind for himself was the life of a classy gent, a spender—someone who knows, from experience, which pleasures to seek out and which to avoid as not worth the bother, and who gives off the glitter of privilege. And he behaved as if this kind of life was within his reach. Which it wasn't. There was a period—I don't know how long it was, perhaps a few months, perhaps a year or so— when if he was strapped and couldn't think of anybody to put the bite on, he would write out a check to himself and sign it with the name of one of his sisters or of a friend.

I don't think anything on earth would have induced my father to pass a bad check, but then his family was poor when he was a child, and lived on the street directly behind the jail. Under everything he did, and his opinions about human behavior, was the pride of the self-made man. He blamed my uncle's shameless dodges on his upbringing. When my Grandfather Blinn would try to be strict with his son, my father said, my grandmother would go behind his back and give Teddy the money. My grandmother's indulgence, though it may have contributed to my uncle's lapses from financial probity, surely wasn't the only cause of them. In any case, the check forging didn't begin until both my grandparents were dead.

My grandfather was brought up on a cattle farm in Vermont not far from the Canadian border. He left home at eighteen to work as a bookkeeper in a pump factory in Cincinnati. Two years later he began to read law in a law office there. More often than not, he read on an empty stomach, but he mastered Blackstone's "Commentaries" and Chitty's "Pleadings," and at the age of twenty-one was admitted to the bar. What made him decide to move farther west to Illinois I don't know. Probably there were already too many lawyers in Ohio. When he was still in his early thirties he tried to run for Congress on the Republican ticket and was nosed out by another candidate. Some years later the nomination was offered to my grandfather at a moment when there was no serious Democratic opposition, and he chose not to run because it would have taken him away from the practice of law. By the time he was forty he had a considerable reputation as a trial lawyer, and eventually he argued cases before the Supreme Court. Lawyers admired him for his ability in the courtroom, and for his powers of close reasoning. People in general saw in him a certain largeness of mind that other men didn't have. From the way my mother spoke of him, it was clear that—to her—there never had been and never could be again a man quite so worthy of veneration. My uncle must often have felt that there was no way for him to stand clear of his father's shadow.

Because my grandfather had served a term on the bench of the Court of Claims, he was mostly spoken of as Judge Blinn. His fees were large but he was not interested in accumulating money and did not own any land except the lot his house stood on. He was not at all pompous, but when he left his office and came home to his family he did not entirely divest himself of the majesty of the law, about which he felt so deeply. From a large tinted photograph that used to hang over the mantelpiece in my Aunt Annette's living room, I know that he had a fine forehead, calm gray eyes, and a drooping mustache that partly concealed the shape of his mouth.

There were half a dozen imposing houses in Lincoln but my grandfather's house wasn't one of them. It stood on a quiet elm-shaded street and was a two-story flat-roofed house with a wide porch extending all across the front and around the sides. It was built in the eighteen-seventies and is still there, well over a hundred years old—what passes for an old house in the Middle West. My father worked for a fire-insurance company and was gone three days out of the middle of the week, drumming up business in small-town agencies all over the state, and so we were at my grandfather's house a good deal. Though I haven't been in it for sixty years, I can still move around in it in my mind. Sliding doors, which I liked to ease in and out of their recesses, separated the back parlor, where the family tended to congregate around my grandmother's chair, from the front parlor, where nobody ever sat. There it was always twilight because the velvet curtains shut out the sun. If I stood looking into the pier glass between the two front windows I saw the same heavy walnut and mahogany furniture in an even dimmer light. Whether this is an actual memory or an attempt on the part of my mind to adjust the past to my feelings about it I am not altogether sure. The very words "the past" suggest lowered window shades and a withdrawal from brightness of any kind. Orpheus in the Underworld. The end of my grandparents' life cast a shadow backwards over what had gone before, but in point of fact it was not a gloomy house, and the life that went on in it was not withdrawn or melancholy.

My Aunt Edith was the oldest. Then came my mother. Then Annette. Between Annette and my uncle there was another child, who didn't live very long. My grandmother was morbidly concerned for my uncle's safety when he was little, and Annette was told that she must never let him out of her sight when they were playing together. She was not much older than he was, and used to have nightmares in which something happened to him. They remained more or less in this relationship to each other during the whole of their lives.

My mother and her sisters had a certain pride of family, but it had nothing to do with a feeling of social superiority, and was, actually, so unexamined and metaphysical that I never understood the grounds for it. It may have been something my grandmother brought with her from Kentucky and passed on to her children. That branch of the family didn't go in for genealogy, and the stories that have come down are vague and improbable.

When I try the name Youtsey on a Southerner, all the response I ever get is a blank look. There appear to have been no statesmen in my grandmother's family, no colonial governors, no men or women of even modest distinction. That leaves money and property. My grandmother's father, John Youtsey, owned a hundred acres of land on the Licking River, where he raised strawberries for the markets of Cincinnati. He was also a United States marshal—that is to say, he had been appointed to carry out the wishes of the judicial district in which he lived, and had duties similar to those of a sheriff. Three of his sons fought in the Civil War, on the side of the North. Shortly before the war broke out, he began to build a new house with bricks fired on the place. I saw it once. I was taken there by one of my mother's cousins. The farm had passed out of the family and was now owned by a German couple. My grandmother used to take her children to Kentucky every summer and when the July term of court was over, my grandfather joined them. My mother told me that the happiest days of her childhood were spent here, playing in the attic and the hayloft and the water meadows, with a multitude of her Kentucky cousins. But as I looked around I saw nothing that I could accept as a possible backdrop for all that excitement and mirth and teasing and tears. There wasn't even a child's swing. The farmer's wife told us to look around as much as we liked, and went back to her canning. We paused in the doorway of a long empty room. I concluded from the parquet floors that it must have been the drawing room. Since my mother's cousin had gone to some trouble to bring me here, I felt that I ought to say something polite, and remarked, "In my great-grandfather's time this must have been a beautiful room," and he said with a smile, "Grandfather kept his wheat in it." My uncle may have inherited his *folie des grandeurs* from some improvident ancestor but it wasn't, in any event, the bewhiskered old gentleman farmer who built and lived in this house.

The lessons that hardship had taught my Grandfather Blinn he was unable to pass on to his son. He must have had many talks with Ted about his future, and the need to apply himself, and what would happen to him if he didn't. Hunger that is only heard about is not very real. My uncle had a perfect understanding of how one should conduct oneself after one has arrived; it was the getting there that didn't much interest him. The most plausible explanation is that he was a changeling.

FROM A HISTORY of Logan County published in 1911 I learned that Edward D. Blinn, Jr.—that is, my Uncle Ted—was the superintendent of the Lincoln Electric Street Railway. My grandfather must have put him there, since he was a director and one of the incorporators of this enterprise. One spur of the streetcar tracks went from the courthouse square to the Illinois Central Railroad depot, another to a new subdivision in the northwest part of town, and still another to the cemeteries. In the summertime the cars were open on the sides, and in warm weather pleasanter than walking. Except during the Chautauqua season, they were never crowded. The conductor stomped on a bell in the floor beside him to make pedestrians and farm wagons get out of the way, and from time to time showers of sparks would be emitted by the overhead wires. What did the superintendent have to do? Keep records, make bank deposits, be there if something went wrong, and in an emergency run one of the cars himself (with his mind on the things he would do and the way he would live when he had money). The job was only a stopgap, until something more appropriate offered itself. *But what if nothing ever did?*

When my grandfather's back was turned, Ted went to Chicago and made some arrangements that he hoped would change the course of his life; for a thousand dollars (which, of course, he did not have), a firm in Chicago agreed to supply him with an airplane and, in case my uncle didn't choose to fly it, a pilot. It was to be part of the Fourth of July celebration. The town agreed to pay him two thousand dollars if the plane went up.

Several years ago the contract was found tucked between the pages of a book that had been withdrawn from the Lincoln College library—God knows how it got there. It is dated June 27, 1911—to my surprise; for it proves that I was a few weeks less than three years old at the time, and I had assumed that to be able to remember the occasion as vividly as I do I must have been at least a year older than that.

The plane stood in a wheat field out beyond the edge of town. The wheat had been harvested and the stubble pricked my bare legs. My father held me by the hand so I would not get lost in the crowd. Very few people there had ever seen an airplane before, and all they asked was to see this one leave the ground and go up into the air like a bird. Several men in mechanic's coveralls were clustered around the plane. Now and then my uncle climbed into the cockpit and the place grew still with expectation. The afternoon wore on slowly. The sun beat down out of a brassy sky. Word must have passed through the crowd that the plane was not going to go up, for my father said suddenly, "We're going home now." Looking back over my shoulder I saw the men still tinkering with the airplane engine. My father told me a long time later that while all this was going on my grandfather was pacing the floor in his law office, thinking about the thousand dollars he would have to raise somehow if the plane failed to go up, and that if it did go up there was a very good chance his only son might be killed.

Using what arguments I find it hard to imagine (except that a courtroom is one thing and home is another, and drops of water wear away stone), Ted persuaded my grandfather to buy a motorcar. The distance from my grandfather's house to his law office was less than a mile, and the roads around Lincoln were unpaved, with deep ruts. Even four or five years later, when motorcars were beginning to be more common, an automobile could sink and sink into a mudhole until it was resting on its rear axle. But anyway, there it was, a Rambler, with leather straps holding the top down, brass carriage lamps, and the emergency brake, the gearshift, and the horn all on the outside above the right-hand running board. It stood in front of my grandfather's house on Ninth Street, more like a monument than a means of locomotion. It is unlikely that anyone but Ted ever drove it, and it must have given a certain dash to his courtship of a charming red-headed girl named Alma Haller. I have pursued her and her family through three county histories and come up with nothing of any substance. Her father served several terms as a city alderman, he was a director of the streetcar company, and he owned a farm west of Lincoln, but there is no biography, presumably because he was not coöperative. Anyway, the soft brown eyes, the understanding of what is pleasing to women, assiduousness, persistence, something, did the trick. They were engaged to be married. And if either family was displeased by the engagement I never heard of it.

My uncle had the reputation in Lincoln of being knowledgeable about motors, and a friend who had arranged to buy an automobile in Chicago asked Ted to go with him when he picked it up. On the way down to Lincoln the car skidded and went out of control and turned over. My uncle was in the seat beside the driver. His left arm was crushed and had to be amputated. My grandmother's premonitions were at last accounted for. What I was kept from knowing about and seeing because I was a small child it does not take very much imagination to reconstruct. He is lying in a hospital bed with his upper chest heavily bandaged. There are bruises on his face. He is drowsy from morphine. Sometimes he complains to the nurse or to Annette, sitting in a chair beside his bed, about the pain he feels in the arm that he has lost. Sometimes he lies there rearranging the circumstances that led up to the accident so that he is at the wheel of the car. Or better still, not in the car at all. When the morphine wore off and his mind was more clear, what can he have thought except that it was somebody else's misfortune that came to him by mistake?

When he left the hospital, and forever afterward, he carried himself stiffly, as if he were corseted. He did not let anyone help him if he could forestall it, and was skillful at slipping his overcoat on in such a way that it did not call attention to the fact that his left arm was immovable and ended in a gray suède glove.

A few years ago, one of Alma Haller's contemporaries told me that she had realized she was not in love with Ted and was on the point of breaking off the engagement but after the accident felt she had to go through with it. They went through with it with style. All church weddings that I have attended since have seemed to me a pale imitation of this one. In a white corduroy suit that my mother had made for me, I walked down the aisle of the Episcopal church beside my cousin Peg, who was a flower girl. I assume that I didn't drop the ring and that the groom put it on the fourth finger of the bride's left hand, but that part I have no memory of; though the movie camera kept on whirring there was no film in it. What was he thinking about as he watched the bridal procession coming toward him? That there would be no more sitting in the moon with girls who had no reason to expect anything more of him than a good time? That there, in satin and lace, was his heart's desire? That people were surreptitiously deciding which was the real arm and which the artificial one? All these things, perhaps, or none of them. The next thing I remember (the camera now having film in it again) is my mother depositing me on a gilt chair, at the wedding reception, and saying that she would be right back. Her idea of time and mine were quite different. The bride's mother, in a flame-colored velvet dress, interested me briefly; my grandmother always wore black. I had never before seen footmen in knee breeches and powdered wigs passing trays of champagne glasses. Or so many people in one house. And I was afraid I would never see my mother again. Just when I had given up all hope, my Aunt Edith, who had no children of her own, appeared with a plate of ice cream for me.

In the next reel, it is broad daylight and I am standing—again with my father holding my hand—on a curb on College Avenue. But this time it is so I will not step into the street and be run over by the fire engines. As before, there is a crowd. It is several months after the wedding. There is a crackling sound and yellow flames flow out of the upstairs windows and lick the air above the burning roof of the house where the wedding reception took place. The gilt furniture is all over the lawn, and there is talk about defective wiring. The big three-story house is as inflammable as a box of kitchen matches.

In the hit-or-miss way of children's memories, I recall being in a horse and buggy with my aunt and uncle, on a snowy night, as they drove around town delivering Christmas presents. And on my sixth birthday our yard is full of children. All the children I know have come bringing presents, and when London Bridge falls I am caught in the arms of my red-haired aunt, and pleased that this has happened. Then suddenly she was not there anymore. She divorced my uncle and I never saw her again. After a couple of years she remarried and moved away, and she didn't return to Lincoln to live until she was an old woman.

As OFTEN HAPPENED with elderly couples during that period, my grandmother's funeral followed my grandfather's within the year. Because she had insisted on it, my grandfather had named his son as his executor, and Ted quit his job with the streetcar company in order to devote himself to settling the estate. My grandfather did not leave anything like as much as people thought he would. He was in the habit of going on notes with young men who needed to borrow money and had no collateral. When the notes came due, more often than not my grandfather had to make good on them, the co-signer being unable to. He also made personal loans, which his family knew about but which he didn't bother to keep any record of since they were to men he considered his friends, and after his death they denied that there was any such debt. Meanwhile, it became clear to anyone with eyes in his head that my uncle was spending a lot of money that could only have come from the estate. My mother and my aunts grew alarmed, and asked my father to step in and represent their interests. He found that Ted had already spent more than half of the money my grandfather left. Probably he didn't mean to take more than his share. It just slipped through his fingers. He would no doubt have run through everything, and with nothing to show for it, if my father hadn't stopped him. My father was capable of the sort of bluntness that makes people see themselves and their conduct in a light unsoftened by excuses of any kind. I would not have wanted to be my uncle when my father was inquiring into the details of my grandfather's estate, or have had to face his contempt. There was nothing more coming to Ted when the estate was finally settled, and, finding himself backed into a corner, he began forging checks. The fact that it didn't lead to his being arrested and sent to prison suggests that the sums involved were not large. I once heard my mother say to my Aunt Edith (who had stopped having anything to do with him) that when she wrote to Ted she was always careful not to sign her full name. The friends whose names he forged were young, in their twenties like my uncle, and poor as Job's turkey. How he justified doing that to them it would be interesting to know. When it comes to self-deception we are all vaudeville magicians. In any case, forging checks for small amounts of money relieved his immediate embarrassment but did not alter his circumstances.

Children as they pass through one stage of growth after another are a kind of anthology of family faces. At the age of four I looked very much like one of my mother's Kentucky cousins. Holding my chin in her hand, she used to call me by his name. Then for a while I looked like her. At the age of eleven or twelve I suddenly began to look like my Uncle Ted. When people remarked on this, I saw that it made my father uneasy. The idea that if I continued to look like him I would end up forging checks amused me, but faulty logic is not necessarily incompatible with the truth, which in this case was that when, because of Christmas or my birthday, I had ten or fifteen dollars, I could always think of something to spend it on. All my life I have tended to feel that money descends from heaven like raindrops. I also understood that it doesn't rain a good deal of the time, and when I couldn't afford to buy something I wanted I have been fairly content to do without it. My uncle was not willing, is what it amounted to.

When my mother died during the influenza epidemic of 1918–19, I turned to the person who was closest to her for comfort and understanding. I am not sure whether this made things harder for Annette or not. Her marriage was rocky, and more than once appeared to be on the point of breaking up but never did. Nearly every day, my Uncle Will Bates drove out to one of his farms to make sure that the tenant farmer was not putting anything over on him. When he came home he would pass through the living room, leaving behind him a sense of strain between my aunt and him, but as far as I could make out it had nothing to do with my being there. Sometimes I found my Uncle Ted there, too. I didn't know, and didn't ask, where he was living and what he was doing to support himself. I think it was probably the low point of his life. There was no color in his face. His eyes never lit up or looked inquiringly or with affection at any of the people seated around the dining-room table. If he spoke, it was to answer yes or no to a question from my aunt. That when he and Annette were alone he opened his heart to her as freely as I did I have no doubt.

Defeat is a good teacher, Hazlitt said. What it teaches some people is to stop trying.

EXCEPT FOR THE very old, nothing, good or bad, remains the same very long. My father remarried, and was promoted, and moved us to Chicago. I went to high school there, and my older brother went off to college, at the University of Illinois, in Champaign-Urbana. On the strength of his experience with the streetcar company, my uncle had managed to get a job in Champaign, working for a trolley line that meandered through various counties in central and southern Illinois. Nobody knew him there, or anything about him. He was simply Ed Blinn, the one-armed man at the ticket counter. He kept this job for many years, from which I think it can be inferred that he didn't help himself to the petty cash or falsify the bookkeeping. During the five years that my brother was in college and law school they would occasionally have dinner together. He tried to borrow money from my brother, whose monthly allowance was adequate but not lavish, and my brother stopped seeing him. Once, when Ted came up to Chicago, he invited me to have dinner with him at the Palmer House. Probably he felt that it was something my mother would have wanted him to do, but this idea didn't occur to me; adolescents seldom have any idea why older people are being nice to them. He was about forty and I was fifteen or sixteen, and priggishly aware that, in taking me to a restaurant that was so expensive, he was again doing things in a way he couldn't afford. He had an easier time chatting with the headwaiter than he did in getting any conversation out of me. After we got up from the table he gave me a conducted tour of a long corridor in the hotel that was known as Peacock Alley. I could see that he was in his natural element. I would have enjoyed it more if there had been peacocks. When I followed my brother down to the university I didn't look my uncle up, and he may not even have known I was there.

Some years later, from a thousand miles away, I learned that he had married again. He married a Lincoln woman, the letter from home said. Edna Skinner. He and his wife were running a rental library in Chicago, and she was expecting a baby. Then I heard that the baby died, and they had moved back to Lincoln, and she was working at the library, and somebody had found him a job running the elevator in the courthouse—where (as people observed with a due sense of the irony of it) his father had practiced law.

By that time my father had retired from business and he and my stepmother were living in Lincoln again. When I went back to Illinois on a visit, I saw my Aunt Annette. She was angry at Ted for marrying. Though she did not say so, what she felt, I am sure, was that there were now two children she couldn't let out of her sight. And she disliked his new wife. She said, "Edna only married him because she was impressed with his family." All this, however, didn't prevent my aunt from doing what she could for them. The grocer was given to understand that they could charge things to her account. She did this knowing that my Uncle Will was bound to notice that the grocery bills were padded, and would be angry with her. As he was. She refused to tell the grocer that her brother and his wife were not to charge things anymore, and my Uncle Will, not being sure what the consequences would be if he put a stop to it, allowed it to continue. Also, living in a small town, there is always the question of what people will think. One would not want to have it said that, with the income off several farms and a substantial balance at the bank, one had let one's brother-in-law and his wife go hungry.

I did not meet Edna until I brought my own wife home to Lincoln for the first time. We had only been married three or four months. When we were making the round of family visits, it struck me as not quite decent not to take her to meet Ted and the aunt I had never seen. My father didn't think that this was necessary. He and my stepmother had given a party for us, and invited all the friends of the family who had known me when I was a boy. They didn't ask Ted and Edna. I doubt if it even occurred to them. Though they all lived in the same small town, my father never had any reason to be in the courthouse or the library, and he hadn't had anything to do with Ted since the days, thirty years before, when he had to step in and straighten out the handling of my grandfather's estate. But I saw no reason I shouldn't follow my own instincts, which were not to leave anybody out. I was thirty-six and so grateful to have escaped from the bachelor's solitary existence that all my feelings were close to the surface. I couldn't call Ted, because they had no telephone, but somebody told me where they were living and we went there on a Sunday morning and knocked on the screen door. As my uncle let us in, I saw that he was pleased we had come. The house looked out across the college grounds and was very small, hardly big enough for two people. Overhanging trees filtered out the sunlight. I found that I had things I wanted to say to him. It was as if we had been under a spell and now it was broken. There was a kind of easy understanding between us that I was not prepared for. I felt the stirring of affection, and I think he may have as well.

Edna I took to on sight. She had dark eyes and a gentle voice. She was simple and open with my wife, and acted as if meeting me was something she had been hoping would happen. Looking around, I could see that they didn't have much money, but neither did we.

I wrote to them when we got home, and heard from her. After my uncle died, she continued to write, and she sent us a small painting that she had done.

Not long ago, by some slippage of the mind, I was presented with a few moments out of my early childhood: My grandfather's house, so long lived in by strangers, is ours again. The dining-room table must have several leaves in it, for there are six or eight people sitting around it. My mother is not in the cemetery but right beside me. She is talking to Granny Blinn about . . . about . . . I don't know what about. If I turn my head I will see my grandfather at the head of the table. The windows are there, and look out on the side yard. The goldfish are swimming through their castle at the bottom of the fishbowl. The door to the back parlor is there. Over the sideboard there is a painting of a watermelon and grapes. No one stops me when I get down from my chair and go out to the kitchen and ask the hired girl for a slice of raw potato. I like the greenish taste. When I come back into the dining room I go and stand beside my uncle. He finishes what he is saying and then notices that I am looking with curiosity at his glass of beer. He holds it out to me, and I take a sip and when I make a face he laughs. His left hand is resting on the white damask tablecloth. He can move his fingers. The catastrophe hasn't happened. I would have liked to linger there with them, but it was like trying to breathe underwater. I came up for air, and lost them.

THE VIEW FROM the seventies is breathtaking. What is lacking is someone, *anyone*, of the older generation to whom you can turn when you want to satisfy your curiosity about some detail of the landscape of the past. There is no longer any older generation. You have become it, while your mind was mostly on other matters.

I wouldn't know anything more about my uncle's life except for a fluke. A boy I used to hang around with when I was a freshman in Lincoln High School—John Deal—had a slightly older sister named Margaret. Many years later I caught up with her again. My wife and I were on Nantucket, and wandered into a shop full of very plain old furniture and beautiful china, and there she was. She was married to a Russian émigré, a bearlike man with a cast in one eye and huge hands. He was given to patting her affectionately on the behind, and perfectly ready to be fond of anyone who turned up from her past. I learned afterward that he had been wounded in the First World War and had twice been decorated for bravery. Big though his hands were, he made ship's models—the finest I have ever seen. That afternoon, as we were leaving, she invited us to their house for supper. The Russian had made a huge crock of vodka punch, which he warned us against, and as we sat around drinking it, what came out, in the course of catching up on the past, was that Margaret and Edna Blinn were friends.

Remembering this recently, I looked up Margaret's telephone number in my address book. The last letter I had had from her was years ago, and I wasn't sure who would answer. When she did, I said, "I want to know about my Uncle Ted Blinn and Edna. How did you happen to know her?"

"We were both teaching in the public schools," the voice at the other end of the line said. "And we used to go painting together."

"Who was she? I mean, where was she from?"

"I don't know."

"Was she born in Lincoln?"

"I kind of think not," the voice said. "I do know where they met. At your grandfather's farm, Grassmere."

"My grandfather didn't have a farm."

"Well, that's where they met."

"My grandfather had a client, one of the Gilletts, who owned a farm near Elkhart—I think it was near Elkhart. Anyway, she moved East and he managed the farm for her. It was called Gracelands. Could it have been there that they met?"

"No. Grassmere."

Oral history is a tangle of the truth and alterations on it.

"They had a love affair," Margaret said. "And Edna got pregnant and lost her job because of it."

"Even though they got married?"

"Yes. It was more than the school board could countenance, and she was fired. He quit his job in Champaign and they went to Chicago and opened a rental library."

"I know. . . . What did the baby die of?"

"It was born dead."

Looking back on my uncle's life, it seems to me to have been a mixture of having to lie in the bed he had made and the most terrible, undeserved, outrageous misfortune. The baby was born dead. He lost his arm in that automobile accident and no one else was even hurt. They put whatever money they had into that little rental library in Chicago just in time to have it go under in the Depression.

THE OLDEST COUNTY history mentions an early pioneer, Thomas R. Skinner, who came to that part of Illinois in 1827, cleared some land near the town of Mount Pulaski, and was the first county surveyor and the first county judge. Edna was probably a direct or a collateral descendant. She may also have been the daughter of W. T. Skinner, who was superintendent and principal of the Mount Pulaski high school. Whatever her background may have been, she was better educated and more cultivated than any of the women in my family, and if she had had money would, I think, have been treated quite differently.

From that telephone call and the letter that followed I learned a good deal that I hadn't known before. Edna worshipped my uncle, Margaret said. She couldn't get over how wonderful, how distinguished, he was. He was under no illusions whatever about himself but loved her. He called her "Baby."

She never spoke about things they lacked, and never seemed to realize how poor they were. She lived in a world of art and music and great literature. He had a drinking problem.

They lived in many different houses—in whatever was vacant at the moment, and cheap. For a while they lived in what had been a one-room Lutheran schoolhouse. They even lived in the country, and Ted drove them into town to work in a beat-up Ford roadster. Whatever house they were living in was always clean and neat. Annette gave them some of my Grandmother Blinn's English bone china, and Edna had some good furniture that had come down in her family—two Victorian chairs and a walnut sofa upholstered in mustard-colored velvet.

Annette and my Uncle Will Bates went to Florida for several months every winter, and while they were away Ted and Edna lived in their house. She loved my Aunt Annette, and was grateful to her for all she had done for them, and didn't know that the affection was not returned.

Margaret found Ted interesting to talk to and kind, but aloof. She had no idea what he was paid for running the elevator in the courthouse. Edna's salary at the library was seventy-five dollars a month. He made a little extra money by selling cigarettes out of the elevator cage, until some town official put a stop to it because he didn't have a license.

My uncle always dressed well. (Clothes of the kind he would have thought fit to put on his back do not wear out, if treated carefully.) Edna had one decent dress, which she washed when she got home from the library, and ironed, and wore the next day. She loved clothes. When she wanted to give herself a treat she would buy a copy of *Harper's Bazaar* and thumb through the pages with intense interest, as if she were dealing with the problem of her spring wardrobe.

She was a Christian Scientist and tended to look on the bright side even of things that didn't have any bright side. She would be taken with sudden enthusiasms for people. When she started in on the remarkable qualities of someone who wasn't in any way remarkable, Ted would poke fun at her. The grade-school and high-school students who came to the library looking for facts for their essays on compulsory arbitration or whales or whatever found her helpful. She encouraged them to develop the habit of reading, and to make something of their lives. Some of them came to think of her as a friend, and remained in touch with her after they left school. At the end of the day, Ted came to the library to pick her up and walk home with her. Margaret didn't think that he had any men friends.

They had a dog, a mutt that had attached himself to them. Whatever Ted asked the dog to do he would try to do, even if it was, for a dog, impossible. Or when he had, in fact, no clear idea of what was wanted of him. He made my uncle laugh. Not much else did.

He must have been in his early sixties when he got pneumonia. He didn't put up much of a fight against it. Edna believed that he willed himself to die.

"Sometimes she would invite me for lunch on Sunday," Margaret said. "Your uncle ate by himself in the other room—probably because there weren't enough knives and forks for three. Having fed him, Edna would get out the card table and spread a clean piece of canvas on it or an old painting, and set two places with the Blinn china. The forks were salad forks, so small that they tended to get lost on the plates. And odd knives and spoons, jelly glasses, and coffee cups from the ten-cent store. Then she would bring on, in an oval silver serving dish, an eggplant casserole, or something she had invented. She was a superb cook, and she did it all on a two-burner electric plate. After the lunch dishes were washed and put away we would go off painting together. There was nothing unusual about her watercolors but her oils were odd in an interesting way. She couldn't afford proper canvas and used unsized canvas or cardboard, and instead of a tube of white lead she had a small can of house paint. She had studied at the Art Institute when they lived in Chicago. I think now that she saw her life as being like that of Modigliani or some other bohemian starving in a garret on the Left Bank. Ted was ashamed of the way they lived. . . . Only once did she ask me for help. She had seen a coat that she longed for, and it was nine dollars. Or it may have been that she needed nine dollars to make up the difference, with what she had. At that time you could buy a Sears, Roebuck coat for that. Anyway, she asked if I would take two paintings in exchange for the money. . . . When I saw her after her heart attack she was lovely and slender—much as she must have looked when she and Ted first knew each other. She spent the last year or so of her life living in what had been a doctor's office. . . . That nine-dollar coat continues to haunt me."

SHE WAS BURIED beside Ted, in the Blinn family plot. My grandfather's headstone is no higher than the sod it is embedded in, and therefore casts no shadow over the grave of his son.

(1984)

THE KUGELMASS EPISODE

WOODY ALLEN

Kugelmass, a professor of humanities at City College, was unhappily married for the second time. Daphne Kugelmass was an oaf. He also had two dull sons by his first wife, Flo, and was up to his neck in alimony and child support.

"Did I know it would turn out so badly?" Kugelmass whined to his analyst one day. "Daphne had promise. Who suspected she'd let herself go and swell up like a beach ball? Plus she had a few bucks, which is not in itself a healthy reason to marry a person, but it doesn't hurt, with the kind of operating nut I have. You see my point?"

Kugelmass was bald and as hairy as a bear, but he had soul.

"I need to meet a new woman," he went on. "I need to have an affair. I may not look the part, but

I'm a man who needs romance. I need softness, I need flirtation. I'm not getting younger, so before it's too late I want to make love in Venice, trade quips at '21,' and exchange coy glances over red wine and candlelight. You see what I'm saying?"

Dr. Mandel shifted in his chair and said, "An affair will solve nothing. You're so unrealistic. Your problems run much deeper."

"And also this affair must be discreet," Kugelmass continued. "I can't afford a second divorce. Daphne would really sock it to me."

"Mr. Kugelmass—"

"But it can't be anyone at City College, because Daphne also works there. Not that anyone on the faculty at C.C.N.Y. is any great shakes, but some of those coeds . . ."

"Mr. Kugelmass—"

"Help me. I had a dream last night. I was skipping through a meadow holding a picnic basket and the basket was marked 'Options.' And then I saw there was a hole in the basket."

"Mr. Kugelmass, the worst thing you could do is act out. You must simply express your feelings here, and together we'll analyze them. You have been in treatment long enough to know there is no overnight cure. After all, I'm an analyst, not a magician."

"Then perhaps what I need is a magician," Kugelmass said, rising from his chair. And with that he terminated his therapy.

A couple of weeks later, while Kugelmass and Daphne were moping around in their apartment one night like two pieces of old furniture, the phone rang.

"I'll get it," Kugelmass said. "Hello."

"Kugelmass?" a voice said. "Kugelmass, this is Persky."

"Who?"

"Persky. Or should I say The Great Persky?"

"Pardon me?"

"I hear you're looking all over town for a magician to bring a little exotica into your life? Yes or no?"

"Sh-h-h," Kugelmass whispered. "Don't hang up. Where are you calling from, Persky?"

Early the following afternoon, Kugelmass climbed three flights of stairs in a broken-down apartment house in the Bushwick section of Brooklyn. Peering through the darkness of the hall, he found the door he was looking for and pressed the bell. I'm going to regret this, he thought to himself.

Seconds later, he was greeted by a short, thin, waxy-looking man.

"*You're* Persky the Great?" Kugelmass said.

"The Great Persky. You want a tea?"

"No, I want romance. I want music. I want love and beauty."

"But not tea, eh? Amazing. O.K., sit down."

Persky went to the back room, and Kugelmass heard the sounds of boxes and furniture being moved around. Persky reappeared, pushing before him a large object on squeaky roller-skate wheels. He removed some old silk handkerchiefs that were lying on its top and blew away a bit of dust. It was a cheap-looking Chinese cabinet, badly lacquered.

"Persky," Kugelmass said, "what's your scam?"

"Pay attention," Persky said. "This is some beautiful effect. I developed it for a Knights of Pythias date last year, but the booking fell through. Get into the cabinet."

"Why, so you can stick it full of swords or something?"

"You see any swords?"

Kugelmass made a face and, grunting, climbed into the cabinet. He couldn't help noticing a couple of ugly rhinestones glued onto the raw plywood just in front of his face. "If this is a joke," he said.

"Some joke. Now, here's the point. If I throw any novel into this cabinet with you, shut the doors, and tap it three times, you will find yourself projected into that book."

Kugelmass made a grimace of disbelief.

"It's the emess," Persky said. "My hand to God. Not just a novel, either. A short story, a play, a poem. You can meet any of the women created by the world's best writers. Whoever you dreamed of. You could carry on all you like with a real winner. Then when you've had enough you give a yell, and I'll see you're back here in a split second."

"Persky, are you some kind of outpatient?"

"I'm telling you it's on the level," Persky said.

Kugelmass remained skeptical. "What are you telling me—that this cheesy homemade box can take me on a ride like you're describing?"

"For a double sawbuck."

Kugelmass reached for his wallet. "I'll believe this when I see it," he said.

Persky tucked the bills in his pants pocket and turned toward his bookcase. "So who do you want to meet? Sister Carrie? Hester Prynne? Ophelia? Maybe someone by Saul Bellow? Hey, what about Temple Drake? Although for a man your age she'd be a workout."

"French. I want to have an affair with a French lover."

"Nana?"

"I don't want to have to pay for it."

"What about Natasha in 'War and Peace'?"

"I said French. I know! What about Emma Bovary? That sounds to me perfect."

"You got it, Kugelmass. Give me a holler when you've had enough." Persky tossed in a paperback copy of Flaubert's novel.

"You sure this is safe?" Kugelmass asked as Persky began shutting the cabinet doors.

"Safe. Is anything safe in this crazy world?" Persky rapped three times on the cabinet and then flung open the doors.

Kugelmass was gone. At the same moment, he appeared in the bedroom of Charles and Emma Bovary's house at Yonville. Before him was a beautiful woman, standing alone with her back turned to him as she folded some linen. I can't believe this, thought Kugelmass, staring at the doctor's ravishing wife. This is uncanny. I'm here. It's her.

Emma turned in surprise. "Goodness, you startled me," she said. "Who are you?" She spoke in the same fine English translation as the paperback.

It's simply devastating, he thought. Then, realizing that it was he whom she had addressed, he said, "Excuse me. I'm Sidney Kugelmass. I'm from City College. A professor of humanities. C.C.N.Y.? Uptown. I—oh, boy!"

Emma Bovary smiled flirtatiously and said, "Would you like a drink? A glass of wine, perhaps?"

She is beautiful, Kugelmass thought. What a contrast with the troglodyte who shared his bed! He felt a sudden impulse to take this vision into his arms and tell her she was the kind of woman he had dreamed of all his life.

"Yes, some wine," he said hoarsely. "White. No, red. No, white. Make it white."

"Charles is out for the day," Emma said, her voice full of playful implication.

After the wine, they went for a stroll in the lovely French country-side. "I've always dreamed that some mysterious stranger would appear and rescue me from the monotony of this crass rural existence," Emma said, clasping his hand. They passed a small church. "I love what you have on," she murmured. "I've never seen anything like it around here. It's so . . . so modern."

"It's called a leisure suit," he said romantically. "It was marked down." Suddenly he kissed her. For the next hour they reclined under a tree and whispered together and told each other deeply meaningful things with their eyes. Then Kugelmass sat up. He had just remembered he had to meet Daphne at Bloomingdale's. "I must go," he told her. "But don't worry, I'll be back."

"I hope so," Emma said.

He embraced her passionately, and the two walked back to the house. He held Emma's face cupped in his palms, kissed her again, and yelled, "O.K., Persky! I got to be at Bloomingdale's by three-thirty."

There was an audible pop, and Kugelmass was back in Brooklyn.

"So? Did I lie?" Persky asked triumphantly.

"Look, Persky, I'm right now late to meet the ball and chain at Lexington Avenue, but when can I go again? Tomorrow?"

"My pleasure. Just bring a twenty. And don't mention this to any-body."

"Yeah. I'm going to call Rupert Murdoch."

Kugelmass hailed a cab and sped off to the city. His heart danced on point. I am in love, he thought, I am the possessor of a wonderful secret. What he didn't realize was that at this very moment students in various classrooms across the country were saying to their teachers, "Who is this character on page 100? A bald Jew is kissing Madame Bovary?" A teacher in Sioux Falls, South Dakota, sighed and thought, Jesus, these kids, with their pot and acid. What goes through their minds!

Daphne Kugelmass was in the bathroom-accessories department at Bloomingdale's when Kugelmass arrived breathlessly. "Where've you been?" she snapped. "It's four-thirty."

"I got held up in traffic," Kugelmass said.

. . .

KUGELMASS VISITED PERSKY the next day, and in a few minutes was again passed magically to Yonville. Emma couldn't hide her excitement at seeing him. The two spent hours together, laughing and talking about their different backgrounds. Before Kugelmass left, they made love. "My God, I'm doing it with Madame Bovary!" Kugelmass whispered to himself. "Me, who failed freshman English."

As the months passed, Kugelmass saw Persky many times and developed a close and passionate relationship with Emma Bovary. "Make sure and always get me into the book before page 120," Kugelmass said to the magician one day. "I always have to meet her before she hooks up with this Rodolphe character."

"Why?" Persky asked. "You can't beat his time?"

"Beat his time. He's landed gentry. Those guys have nothing better to do than flirt and ride horses. To me, he's one of those faces you see in the pages of *Women's Wear Daily*. With the Helmut Berger hairdo. But to her he's hot stuff."

"And her husband suspects nothing?"

"He's out of his depth. He's a lacklustre little paramedic who's thrown in his lot with a jitterbug. He's ready to go to sleep by ten, and she's putting on her dancing shoes. Oh, well . . . See you later."

And once again Kugelmass entered the cabinet and passed instantly to the Bovary estate at Yonville. "How you doing, cupcake?" he said to Emma.

"Oh, Kugelmass," Emma sighed. "What I have to put up with. Last night at dinner, Mr. Personality dropped off to sleep in the middle of the dessert course. I'm pouring my heart out about Maxim's and the ballet, and out of the blue I hear snoring."

"It's O.K., darling. I'm here now," Kugelmass said, embracing her. I've earned this, he thought, smelling Emma's French perfume and burying his nose in her hair. I've suffered enough. I've paid enough analysts. I've searched till I'm weary. She's young and nubile, and I'm here a few pages after Léon and just before Rodolphe. By showing up during the correct chapters, I've got the situation knocked.

Emma, to be sure, was just as happy as Kugelmass. She had been starved for excitement, and his tales of Broadway night life, of fast cars and Hollywood and TV stars, enthralled the young French beauty.

"Tell me again about O.J. Simpson," she implored that evening, as she and Kugelmass strolled past Abbé Bournisien's church.

"What can I say? The man is great. He sets all kinds of rushing records. Such moves. They can't touch him."

"And the Academy Awards?" Emma said wistfully. "I'd give anything to win one."

"First you've got to be nominated."

"I know. You explained it. But I'm convinced I can act. Of course, I'd want to take a class or two. With Strasberg maybe. Then, if I had the right agent—"

"We'll see, we'll see. I'll speak to Persky."

That night, safely returned to Persky's flat, Kugelmass brought up the idea of having Emma visit him in the big city.

"Let me think about it," Persky said. "Maybe I could work it. Stranger things have happened." Of course, neither of them could think of one.

"WHERE THE HELL do you go all the time?" Daphne Kugelmass barked at her husband as he returned home late that evening. "You got a chippie stashed somewhere?"

"Yeah, sure, I'm just the type," Kugelmass said wearily. "I was with Leonard Popkin. We were discussing Socialist agriculture in Poland. You know Popkin. He's a freak on the subject."

"Well, you've been very odd lately," Daphne said. "Distant. Just don't forget about my father's birthday. On Saturday?"

"Oh, sure, sure," Kugelmass said, heading for the bathroom.

"My whole family will be there. We can see the twins. And Cousin Hamish. You should be more polite to Cousin Hamish—he likes you."

"Right, the twins," Kugelmass said, closing the bathroom door and shutting out the sound of his wife's voice. He leaned against it and took a deep breath. In a few hours, he told himself, he would be back in Yonville again, back with his beloved. And this time, if all went well, he would bring Emma back with him.

At three-fifteen the following afternoon, Persky worked his wizardry again. Kugelmass appeared before Emma, smiling and eager. The two spent a few hours at Yonville with Binet and then remounted the Bovary carriage. Following Persky's instructions, they held each other tightly, closed their eyes, and counted to ten. When they opened them, the carriage was just drawing up at the side door of the Plaza Hotel, where Kugelmass had optimistically reserved a suite earlier in the day.

"I love it! It's everything I dreamed it would be," Emma said as she swirled joyously around the bedroom, surveying the city from their window. "There's F.A.O. Schwarz. And there's Central Park, and the Sherry is which one? Oh, there—I see. It's too divine."

On the bed there were boxes from Halston and Saint Laurent. Emma unwrapped a package and held up a pair of black velvet pants against her perfect body.

"The slacks suit is by Ralph Lauren," Kugelmass said. "You'll look like a million bucks in it. Come on, sugar, give us a kiss."

"I've never been so happy!" Emma squealed as she stood before the mirror. "Let's go out on the town. I want to see 'Chorus Line' and the Guggenheim and this Jack Nicholson character you always talk about. Are any of his flicks showing?"

"I cannot get my mind around this," a Stanford professor said. "First a strange character named Kugelmass, and now she's gone from the book. Well, I guess the mark of a classic is that you can reread it a thousand times and always find something new."

THE LOVERS PASSED a blissful weekend. Kugelmass had told Daphne he would be away at a symposium in Boston and would return Monday. Savoring each moment, he and Emma went to the movies, had dinner in Chinatown, passed two hours at a discothèque, and went to bed with a TV movie. They slept till noon on Sunday, visited SoHo, and ogled celebrities at Elaine's. They had caviar and champagne in their suite on Sunday night and talked until dawn. That morning, in the cab taking them to Persky's apartment, Kugelmass thought, It was hectic, but worth it. I can't bring her here too often, but now and then it will be a charming contrast with Yonville.

At Persky's, Emma climbed into the cabinet, arranged her new boxes of clothes neatly around her, and kissed Kugelmass fondly. "My place next time," she said with a wink. Persky rapped three times on the cabinet. Nothing happened.

"Hmm," Persky said, scratching his head. He rapped again, but still no magic. "Something must be wrong," he mumbled.

"Persky, you're joking!" Kugelmass cried. "How can it not work?"

"Relax, relax. Are you still in the box, Emma?"

"Yes."

Persky rapped again—harder this time.

"I'm still here, Persky."

"I know, darling. Sit tight."

"Persky, we *have* to get her back," Kugelmass whispered. "I'm a married man, and I have a class in three hours. I'm not prepared for anything more than a cautious affair at this point."

"I can't understand it," Persky muttered. "It's such a reliable little trick."

But he could do nothing. "It's going to take a little while," he said to Kugelmass. "I'm going to have to strip it down. I'll call you later."

Kugelmass bundled Emma into a cab and took her back to the Plaza. He barely made it to his class on time. He was on the phone all day, to Persky and to his mistress. The magician told him it might be several days before he got to the bottom of the trouble.

"How was the symposium?" Daphne asked him that night.

"Fine, fine," he said, lighting the filter end of a cigarette.

"What's wrong? You're as tense as a cat."

"Me? Ha, that's a laugh. I'm as calm as a summer night. I'm just going to take a walk." He eased out the door, hailed a cab, and flew to the Plaza.

"This is no good," Emma said. "Charles will miss me."

"Bear with me, sugar," Kugelmass said. He was pale and sweaty. He kissed her again, raced to the elevators, yelled at Persky over a pay phone in the Plaza lobby, and just made it home before midnight.

"According to Popkin, barley prices in Kraków have not been this stable since 1971," he said to Daphne, and smiled wanly as he climbed into bed.

THE WHOLE WEEK went by like that. On Friday night, Kugelmass told Daphne there was another symposium he had to catch, this one in Syracuse. He hurried back to the Plaza, but the second weekend there was nothing like the first. "Get me back into the novel or marry me," Emma told Kugelmass. "Meanwhile, I want to get a job or go to class, because watching TV all day is the pits."

"Fine. We can use the money," Kugelmass said. "You consume twice your weight in room service."

"I met an Off Broadway producer in Central Park yesterday, and he said I might be right for a project he's doing," Emma said.

"Who is this clown?" Kugelmass asked.

"He's not a clown. He's sensitive and kind and cute. His name's Jeff Something-or-Other, and he's up for a Tony."

Later that afternoon, Kugelmass showed up at Persky's drunk.

"Relax," Persky told him. "You'll get a coronary."

"Relax. The man says relax. I've got a fictional character stashed in a hotel room, and I think my wife is having me tailed by a private shamus."

"O.K., O.K. We know there's a problem." Persky crawled under the cabinet and started banging on something with a large wrench.

"I'm like a wild animal," Kugelmass went on. "I'm sneaking around town, and Emma and I have had it up to here with each other. Not to mention a hotel tab that reads like the defense budget."

"So what should I do? This is the world of magic," Persky said. "It's all nuance."

"Nuance, my foot. I'm pouring Dom Pérignon and black eggs into this little mouse, plus her wardrobe, plus she's enrolled at the Neighborhood Playhouse and suddenly needs professional photos. Also, Persky, Professor Fivish Kopkind, who teaches Comp Lit and who has always been jealous of me, has identified me as the sporadically appearing character in the Flaubert book. He's threatened to go to Daphne. I see ruin and alimony jail. For adultery with Madame Bovary, my wife will reduce me to beggary."

"What do you want me to say? I'm working on it night and day. As far as your personal anxiety goes, that I can't help you with. I'm a magician, not an analyst."

By Sunday afternoon, Emma had locked herself in the bathroom and refused to respond to Kugelmass's entreaties. Kugelmass stared out the window at the Wollman Rink and contemplated suicide. Too bad this is a low floor, he thought, or I'd do it right now. Maybe if I ran away to Europe and started life over . . . Maybe I could sell the *International Herald Tribune*, like those young girls used to.

The phone rang. Kugelmass lifted it to his ear mechanically.

"Bring her over," Persky said. "I think I got the bugs out of it."

Kugelmass's heart leaped. "You're serious?" he said. "You got it licked?"

"It was something in the transmission. Go figure."

"Persky, you're a genius. We'll be there in a minute. Less than a minute."

Again the lovers hurried to the magician's apartment, and again Emma Bovary climbed into the cabinet with her boxes. This time there was no kiss. Persky shut the doors, took a deep breath, and tapped the box three times. There was the reassuring popping noise, and when Persky peered inside, the box was empty. Madame Bovary was back in her novel. Kugelmass heaved a great sigh of relief and pumped the magician's hand.

"It's over," he said. "I learned my lesson. I'll never cheat again, I swear it." He pumped Persky's hand again and made a mental note to send him a necktie.

THREE WEEKS LATER, at the end of a beautiful spring afternoon, Persky answered his doorbell. It was Kugelmass, with a sheepish expression on his face.

"O.K., Kugelmass," the magician said. "Where to this time?"

"It's just this once," Kugelmass said. "The weather is so lovely, and I'm not getting any younger. Listen, you've read 'Portnoy's Complaint'? Remember The Monkey?"

"The price is now twenty-five dollars, because the cost of living is up, but I'll start you off with one freebie, due to all the trouble I caused you."

"You're good people," Kugelmass said, combing his few remaining hairs as he climbed into the cabinet again. "This'll work all right?"

"I hope. But I haven't tried it much since all that unpleasantness."

"Sex and romance," Kugelmass said from inside the box. "What we go through for a pretty face."

Persky tossed in a copy of "Portnoy's Complaint" and rapped three times on the box. This time, instead of a popping noise there was a dull explosion, followed by a series of crackling noises and a shower of sparks. Persky leaped back, was seized by a heart attack, and dropped dead. The cabinet burst into flames, and eventually the entire house burned down.

Kugelmass, unaware of this catastrophe, had his own problems. He had not been thrust into "Portnoy's Complaint," or into any other novel, for that matter. He had been projected into an old textbook, "Remedial Spanish," and was running for his life over a barren, rocky terrain as the word "*tener*" ("to have")—a large and hairy irregular verb—raced after him on its spindly legs.

(1970)

THE CINDERELLA WALTZ

ANN BEATTIE

Milo and Bradley are creatures of habit. For as long as I've known him, Milo has worn his moth-eaten blue scarf with the knot hanging so low on his chest that the scarf is useless. Bradley is addicted to coffee and carries a thermos with him. Milo complains about the cold, and Bradley is always a little edgy. They come out from the city every Saturday—this is not habit but loyalty—to pick up Louise. Louise is even more unpredictable than most nine-year-olds; sometimes she waits for them on the front step, sometimes she hasn't even gotten out of bed when they arrive. One time she hid in a closet and wouldn't leave with them.

Today Louise has put together a shopping bag full of things she wants to take with her. She is taking my whisk and my blue pottery bowl, to make Sunday breakfast for Milo and Bradley; Beckett's "Happy Days," which she has carried around for weeks, and which she looks through, smiling—but I'm not sure she's reading it; and a coleus growing out of a conch shell. Also, she has stuffed into one side of the bag the fancy Victorian-style nightgown her grandmother gave her for Christmas, and into the other she has tucked her octascope. Milo keeps a couple of dresses, a nightgown, a toothbrush, and extra sneakers and boots at his apartment for her. He got tired of rounding up her stuff to pack for her to take home, so he has brought some things for her that can be left. It annoys him that she still packs bags, because then he has to go around making sure that she has found everything before she goes home. She seems to know how to manipulate him, and after the weekend is over she often calls tearfully to say that she has left this or that, which means that he must get his car out of the garage and drive all the way out to the house to bring it to her. One time, he refused to take the hour-long drive, because she had only left a copy of Tolkien's "The Two Towers." The following weekend was the time she hid in the closet.

"I'll water your plant if you leave it here," I say now.

"I can take it," she says.

"I didn't say you couldn't take it. I just thought it might be easier to leave it, because if the shell tips over the plant might get ruined."

"O.K.," she says. "Don't water it today, though. Water it Sunday afternoon."

I reach for the shopping bag.

"I'll put it back on my windowsill," she says. She lifts the plant out and carries it as if it's made of Steuben glass. Bradley bought it for her last month, driving back to the city, when they stopped at a lawn sale. She and Bradley are both very choosy, and he likes that. He drinks French-roast coffee; she will debate with herself almost endlessly over whether to buy a coleus that is primarily pink or lavender or striped.

"Has Milo made any plans for this weekend?" I ask.

"He's having a couple of people over tonight, and I'm going to help them make crêpes for dinner. If they buy more bottles of that wine with the yellow flowers on the label, Bradley is going to soak the labels off for me."

"That's nice of him," I say. "He never minds taking a lot of time with things."

"He doesn't like to cook, though. Milo and I are going to cook. Bradley sets the table and fixes flowers in a bowl. He thinks it's frustrating to cook."

"Well," I say, "with cooking you have to have a good sense of timing. You have to coördinate everything. Bradley likes to work carefully and not be rushed."

I wonder how much she knows. Last week she told me about a conversation she'd had with her friend Sarah. Sarah was trying to persuade Louise to stay around on the weekends, but Louise said she always went to her father's. Then Sarah tried to get her to take her along, and Louise said that she couldn't. "You could take her if you wanted to," I said later. "Check with Milo and see if that isn't right. I don't think he'd mind having a friend of yours occasionally."

She shrugged. "Bradley doesn't like a lot of people around," she said.

"Bradley likes you, and if she's your friend I don't think he'd mind."

She looked at me with an expression I didn't recognize; perhaps she thought I was a little dumb, or perhaps she was just curious to see if I would go on. I didn't know how to go on. Like an adult, she gave a little shrug and changed the subject.

AT TEN O'CLOCK Milo pulls into the driveway and honks his horn, which makes a noise like a bleating sheep. He knows the noise the horn makes is funny, and he means to amuse us. There was a time just after the divorce when he and Bradley would come here and get out of the car and stand around silently, waiting for her. She knew that she had to watch for them, because Milo wouldn't come to the door. We were both bitter then, but I got over it. I still don't think Milo would have come into the house again, though, if Bradley hadn't thought it was a good idea. The third time Milo came to pick her up after he'd left home, I went out to invite them in, but Milo said nothing. He was standing there with his arms at his sides like a wooden soldier, and his eyes were as dead to me as if they'd been painted on. It was Bradley whom I reasoned with. "Louise is over at Sarah's right now, and it'll make her feel more comfortable if we're all together when she comes in," I said to him, and Bradley turned to Milo and said, "Hey, that's right. Why don't we go in for a quick cup of coffee?" I looked into the back seat of the car and saw his red thermos there; Louise had told me about it. Bradley meant that they should come in and sit down. He was giving me even more than I'd asked for.

It would be an understatement to say that I disliked Bradley at first. I was actually afraid of him, afraid even after I saw him, though he was slender, and more nervous than I, and spoke quietly. The second time I saw him, I persuaded myself that he was just a stereotype, but someone who certainly seemed harmless enough. By the third time, I had enough courage to suggest that they come into the house. It was embarrassing for all of us, sitting around the table—the same table where Milo and I had eaten our meals for the years we were married. Before he left, Milo had shouted at me that the house was a farce, that my playing the happy suburban housewife was a farce, that it was unconscionable of me to let things drag on, that I would probably kiss him and say, "How was your day, sweetheart?," and that he should bring home flowers and the evening paper. "Maybe I would!" I screamed back. "Maybe it would be nice to do that, even if we were pretending, instead of you coming home drunk and not caring what had happened to me or to Louise all day." He was holding on to the edge of the kitchen table, the way you'd hold on to the horse's reins in a runaway carriage. "I care about Louise," he said finally. That was the most horrible moment. Until then, until he said it that way, I had thought that he was going through something horrible—certainly something was terribly wrong—but that, in his way, he loved me after all. "*You don't love me?*" I had whispered at once. It took us both aback. It was an innocent and pathetic question, and it made him come and put his arms around me in the last hug he ever gave me. "I'm sorry for you," he said, "and I'm sorry for marrying you and causing this, but you know who I love. I told you who I love." "But you were kidding," I said. "You didn't mean it. You were kidding."

When Bradley sat at the table that first day, I tried to be polite and not look at him much. I had gotten it through my head that Milo was crazy, and I guess I was expecting Bradley to be a horrible parody—Craig Russell doing Marilyn Monroe. Bradley did not spoon sugar into Milo's coffee. He did not even sit near him. In fact, he pulled his chair a little away from us, and in spite of his uneasiness he found more things to start conversations about than Milo and I did. He told me about the ad agency where he worked; he is a designer there. He asked if he could go out on the porch to see the brook—Milo had told him about the stream in the back of our place that was as thin as a pencil but still gave us our own watercress. He went out on the porch and stayed there for at least five minutes, giving us a chance to talk. We didn't say one word until he came back. Louise came home from Sarah's house just as Bradley sat down at the table again, and she gave him a hug as well as us. I could see that she really liked him. I was amazed that I liked him, too. Bradley had won and I had lost, but he was as gentle and low-key as if none of it mattered. Later in the week, I called him and asked him to tell me if any free-lance jobs opened in his advertising agency. (I do a little free-lance artwork, whenever I can arrange it.) The week after that, he called and told me about another agency, where they were looking for outside artists. Our calls to each other are always brief and for a purpose, but lately they're not just calls about business. Before Bradley left to scout some picture locations in Mexico, he called to say that Milo had told him that when the two of us were there years ago I had seen one of those big circular bronze Aztec calendars and I had always regretted not bringing it back. He wanted to know if I would like him to buy a calendar if he saw one like the one Milo had told him about.

Today, Milo is getting out of his car, his blue scarf flapping against his chest. Louise, looking out the window, asks the same thing I am wondering: "Where's Bradley?"

Milo comes in and shakes my hand, gives Louise a one-armed hug.

"Bradley thinks he's coming down with a cold," Milo says. "The dinner is still on, Louise. We'll do the dinner. We have to stop at Gristede's when we get back to town, unless your mother happens to have a tin of anchovies and two sticks of unsalted butter."

"Let's go to Gristede's," Louise says. "I like to go there."

"Let me look in the kitchen," I say. The butter is salted, but Milo says that that will do, and he takes three sticks instead of two. I have a brainstorm and cut the cellophane on a leftover Christmas present from my aunt—a wicker plate that holds nuts and foil-wrapped triangles of cheese—and, sure enough: one tin of anchovies.

"We can go to the museum instead," Milo says to Louise. "Wonderful."

But then, going out the door, carrying her bag, he changes his mind. "We can go to America Hurrah, and if we see something beautiful we can buy it," he says.

They go off in high spirits. Louise comes up to his waist, almost, and I notice again that they have the same walk. Both of them stride forward with great purpose. Last week, Bradley told me that Milo had bought a weathervane in the shape of a horse, made around 1800, at America Hurrah, and stood it in the bedroom, and then was enraged when Bradley draped his socks over it to dry. Bradley is still learning what a perfectionist Milo is, and how little sense of humor he has. When we were first married, I used one of our pottery casserole dishes to put my jewelry in, and he nagged me until I took it out and put the dish back in the kitchen cabinet. I remember his saying that the dish looked silly on my dresser because it was obvious what it was and people would think we left our dishes lying around. It was one of the things that Milo wouldn't tolerate, because it was improper.

WHEN MILO BROUGHT Louise back on Sunday night they were not in a good mood. The dinner had been all right, Milo said, and Griffin and Amy and Mark had been amazed at what a good hostess Louise had been, but Bradley hadn't been able to eat.

"Is he still coming down with a cold?" I ask. I was still a little shy about asking questions about Bradley.

Milo shrugs. "Louise made him take megadoses of Vitamin C all weekend."

Louise says, "Bradley said that taking too much Vitamin C was bad for your kidneys, though."

"It's a rotten climate," Milo says, sitting on the living-room sofa, scarf and coat still on. "The combination of cold and air pollution . . ."

Louise and I look at each other, and then back at Milo. For weeks now, he has been talking about moving to San Francisco, if he can find work there. (Milo is an architect.) This talk bores me, and it makes Louise nervous. I've asked him not to talk to her about it unless he's actually going to move, but he doesn't seem to be able to stop himself.

"O.K.," Milo says, looking at us both. "I'm not going to say anything about San Francisco."

"*California* is polluted," I say. I am unable to stop myself, either.

Milo heaves himself up from the sofa, ready for the drive back to New York. It is the same way he used to get off the sofa that last year he lived here. He would get up, dress for work, and not even go into the kitchen for breakfast—just sit, sometimes in his coat as he was sitting just now, and at the last minute he would push himself up and go out to the driveway, usually without a goodbye, and get in the car and drive off either very fast or very slowly. I liked it better when he made the tires spin in the gravel when he took off.

He stops at the doorway now, and turns to face me. "Did I take all your butter?" he says.

"No," I say. "There's another stick." I point into the kitchen.

"I could have guessed that's where it would be," he says, and smiles at me.

WHEN MILO COMES the next weekend, Bradley is still not with him. The night before, as I was putting Louise to bed, she said that she had a feeling he wouldn't be coming.

"I had that feeling a couple of days ago," I said. "Usually Bradley calls once during the week."

"He must still be sick," Louise said. She looked at me anxiously. "Do you think he is?"

"A cold isn't going to kill him," I said. "If he has a cold, he'll be O.K."

Her expression changed; she thought I was talking down to her. She lay back in bed. The last year Milo was with us, I used to tuck her in and tell her that everything was all right. What that meant was that there had not been a fight. Milo had sat listening to music on the phonograph, with a book or the newspaper in front of his face. He didn't pay very much attention to Louise, and he ignored me entirely. Instead of saying a prayer with her, the way I usually did, I would say to her that everything was all right. Then I would go downstairs and hope that Milo would say the same thing to me. What he finally did say one night was "You might as well find out from me as some other way."

"Hey, are you an old bag lady again this weekend?" Milo says now, stooping to kiss Louise's forehead.

"Because you take some things with you doesn't mean you're a bag lady," she says primly.

"Well," Milo says, "you start doing something innocently, and before you know it it can take you over."

He looks angry, and acts as though it's difficult for him to make conversation, even when the conversation is full of sarcasm and double-entendres.

"What do you say we get going?" he says to Louise.

In the shopping bag she is taking is her doll, which she has not played with for more than a year. I found it by accident when I went to tuck in a loaf of banana bread that I had baked. When I saw Baby Betsy, deep in the bag, I decided against putting the bread in.

"O.K.," Louise says to Milo. "Where's Bradley?"

"Sick," he says.

"Is he too sick to have me visit?"

"Good heavens, no. He'll be happier to see you than to see me."

"I'm rooting some of my coleus to give him," she says. "Maybe I'll give it to him like it is, in water, and he can plant it when it roots."

When she leaves the room, I go over to Milo. "Be nice to her," I say quietly.

"I'm nice to her," he says. "Why does everybody have to act like I'm going to grow fangs every time I turn around?"

"You were quite cutting when you came in."

"I was being self-deprecating." He sighs. "I don't really know why I come here and act this way," he says.

"What's the matter, Milo?"

But now he lets me know he's bored with the conversation. He walks over to the table and picks up a *Newsweek* and flips through it. Louise comes back with the coleus in a water glass.

"You know what you could do," I say. "Wet a napkin and put it around that cutting and then wrap it in foil, and put it in water when you get there. That way, you wouldn't have to hold a glass of water all the way to New York."

She shrugs. "This is O.K.," she says.

"Why don't you take your mother's suggestion," Milo says. "The water will slosh out of the glass."

"Not if you don't drive fast."

"It doesn't have anything to do with my driving fast. If we go over a bump in the road, you're going to get all wet."

"Then I can put on one of my dresses at your apartment."

"Am I being unreasonable?" Milo says to me.

"I started it," I say. "Let her take it in the glass."

"Would you, as a favor, do what your mother says?" he says to Louise. Louise looks at the coleus, and at me.

"Hold the glass over the seat instead of over your lap, and you won't get wet," I say.

"Your first idea was the best," Milo says.

Louise gives him an exasperated look and puts the glass down on the floor, pulls on her poncho, picks up the glass again and says a sullen goodbye to me, and goes out the front door.

"Why is this my fault?" Milo says. "Have I done anything terrible? I—"

"Do something to cheer yourself up," I say, patting him on the back.

He looks as exasperated with me as Louise was with him. He nods his head yes, and goes out the door.

Was everything all right this weekend?" I ask Louise.

"Milo was in a bad mood, and Bradley wasn't even there on Saturday," Louise says. "He came back today and took us to the Village for breakfast."

"What did you have?"

"I had sausage wrapped in little pancakes and fruit salad and a rum bun."

"Where was Bradley on Saturday?"

She shrugs. "I didn't ask him."

She almost always surprises me by being more grownup than I give her credit for. Does she suspect, as I do, that Bradley has found another lover?

"Milo was in a bad mood when you two left here Saturday," I say.

"I told him if he didn't want me to come next weekend, just to tell me." She looks perturbed, and I suddenly realize that she can sound exactly like Milo sometimes.

"You shouldn't have said that to him, Louise," I say. "You know he wants you. He's just worried about Bradley."

"So?" she says. "I'm probably going to flunk math."

"No, you're not, honey. You got a C-plus on the last assignment."

"It still doesn't make my grade average out to a C."

"You'll get a C. It's all right to get a C."

She doesn't believe me.

"Don't be a perfectionist, like Milo," I tell her. "Even if you got a D, you wouldn't fail."

Louise is brushing her hair—thin, shoulder-length, auburn-colored hair. She is already so pretty and so smart in everything except math that I wonder what will become of her. When I was her age, I was plain and serious and I wanted to be a tree surgeon. I went with my father to the park and held a stethoscope—a real one—to the trunks of trees, listening to their silence. Children seem older now.

"What do you think's the matter with Bradley?" Louise says. She sounds worried.

"Maybe the two of them are unhappy with each other right now."

She misses my point. "Bradley's sad, and Milo's sad that he's unhappy."

I drop Louise off at Sarah's house for supper. Sarah's mother, Martine Cooper, looks like Shelley Winters, and I have never seen her without a glass of Galliano on ice in her hand. She has a strong candy smell. Her husband has left her, and she professes not to care. She has emptied her living room of furniture and put up ballet bars on the walls, and dances in a purple leotard to records by Cher and Mac Davis. I prefer to have Sarah come to our house, but her mother is adamant that everything must be, as she puts it, "fifty-fifty." When Sarah visited us a week ago and loved the chocolate pie I had made, I sent two pieces home with her. Tonight, when I left Sarah's house, her mother gave me a bowl of jello fruit salad.

The phone is ringing when I come in the door. It is Bradley.

"Bradley," I say at once, "whatever's wrong, at least you don't have a neighbor who just gave you a bowl of maraschino cherries in green jello with a Reddi Wip flower squirted on top."

"Jesus," he says. "You don't need me to depress you, do you?"

"What's wrong?" I say.

He sighs into the phone. "Guess what?" he says.

"What?"

"I've lost my job."

It wasn't at all what I was expecting to hear. I was ready to hear that he was leaving Milo, and I had even thought that that would serve Milo right. Part of me still wanted him punished for what he did. I was so out of my mind when Milo left me that I used to go over and drink Galliano with Martine Cooper. I even thought seriously about forming a ballet group with her. I would go to her house in the afternoon, and she would hold a tambourine in the air and I would hold my leg rigid and try to kick it.

"That's awful," I say to Bradley. "What happened?"

"They said it was nothing personal—they were laying off three people. Two other people are going to get the axe at the agency within the next six months. I was the first to go, and it was nothing personal. From twenty thousand bucks a year to nothing, and nothing personal, either."

"But your work is so good. Won't you be able to find something again?"

"Could I ask you a favor?" he says. "I'm calling from a phone booth. I'm not in the city. Could I come talk to you?"

"Sure," I say.

It seems perfectly logical that he should come alone to talk—perfectly logical until I actually see him coming up the walk. I can't entirely believe it. A year after my husband has left me, I am sitting with his lover—a man, a person I like quite well—and trying to cheer him up because he is out of work. ("Honey," my father would say, "listen to Daddy's heart with the stethoscope, or you can turn it toward you and listen to your own heart. You won't hear anything listening to a tree." Was my persistence willfulness, or belief in magic? Is it possible that I hugged Bradley at the door because I'm secretly glad he's down and out, the way I used to be? Or do I really want to make things better for him?)

He comes into the kitchen and thanks me for the coffee I am making, drapes his coat over the chair he always sits in.

"What am I going to do?" he asks.

"You shouldn't get so upset, Bradley," I say. "You know you're good. You won't have trouble finding another job."

"That's only half of it," he says. "Milo thinks I did this deliberately. He told me I was quitting on him. He's very angry at me. He fights with me, and then he gets mad that I don't enjoy eating dinner. My stomach's upset, and I can't eat anything."

"Maybe some juice would be better than coffee."

"If I didn't drink coffee, I'd collapse," he says.

I pour coffee into a mug for him, coffee into a mug for me.

"This is probably very awkward for you," he says. "That I come here and say all this about Milo."

"What does he mean about your quitting on him?"

"He said . . . he actually accused me of doing badly deliberately, so they'd fire me. I was so afraid to tell him the truth when I was fired that I pretended to be sick. Then I really *was* sick. He's never been angry at me this way. Is this always the way he acts? Does he get a notion in his head for no reason and then pick at a person because of it?"

I try to remember. "We didn't argue much," I say. "When he didn't want to live here, he made me look ridiculous for complaining when I knew something was wrong. He expects perfection, but what that means is that you do things his way."

"I *was*. I never wanted to sit around the apartment, the way he says I did. I even brought work home with me. He made me feel so bad all week that I went to a friend's apartment for the day on Saturday. Then he said I had walked out on the problem. He's a little paranoid. I was listening to the radio, and Carole King was singing that song 'It's Too Late,' and he came into the study and looked very upset, as though I had planned for the song to come on. I couldn't believe it."

"Whew," I say, shaking my head. "I don't envy you. You have to stand up to him. I didn't do that. I pretended the problem would go away."

"And now the problem sits across from you drinking coffee, and you're being nice to him."

"I know it. I was just thinking we look like two characters in some soap opera my friend Martine Cooper would watch."

He pushes his coffee cup away from him with a grimace.

"But anyway, I like you now," I say. "And you're exceptionally nice to Louise."

"I took her father," he says.

"Bradley—I hope you don't take offense, but it makes me nervous to talk about that."

"I don't take offense. But how can you be having coffee with me?"

"You invited yourself over so you could ask that?"

"Please," he says, holding up both hands. Then he runs his hands through his hair. "Don't make me feel illogical. He does that to me, you know. He doesn't understand it when everything doesn't fall right into line. If I like fixing up the place, keeping some flowers around, therefore I can't like being a working person, too, therefore I deliberately sabotage myself in my job." Bradley sips his coffee.

"I wish I could do something for him," he says in a different voice.

This was not what I have expected, either. We have sounded like two wise adults, and then suddenly he has changed and sounds very tender. I realize the situation is still the same. It is two of them on one side and me on the other, even though Bradley is in my kitchen.

"Come and pick up Louise with me, Bradley," I say. "When you see Martine Cooper, you'll cheer up about your situation."

He looks up from his coffee. "You're forgetting what I'd look like to Martine Cooper," he says.

MILO IS GOING to California. He has been offered a job with a new San Francisco architectural firm. I am not the first to know. His sister, Deanna, knows before I do, and mentions it when we're talking on the phone. "It's middle-age crisis," Deanna says sniffily. "Not that I need to tell you." Deanna would drop dead if she knew the way things are. She is scandalized every time a new scene is put up in Bloomingdale's window. ("Those mannequins had eyes like an Egyptian princess, and *rags*. I swear to you, they had mops and brooms and ragged gauze dresses on, with whores' shoes—stiletto heels that prostitutes wore in the fifties.")

I hang up from Deanna's call and tell Louise I'm going to drive to the gas station for cigarettes. I go there to call New York on their pay phone.

"Well, I only just knew," Milo says. "I found out for sure yesterday, and last night Deanna called and so I told her. It's not like I'm leaving tonight."

He sounds elated, in spite of being upset that I called. He's happy in the way he used to be on Christmas morning. I remember him once running into the living room in his underwear and tearing open the gifts we'd been sent by relatives. He was looking for the eight-slice toaster he was sure we'd get. We'd been given two-slice, four-slice, and six-slice toasters, but then we got no more. "Come out, my eight-slice beauty!" Milo crooned, and out came an electric clock, a blender, and an expensive electric pan.

"When are you leaving?" I ask him.

"I'm going out to look for a place to live next week."

"Are you going to tell Louise yourself this weekend?"

"Of course," he says.

"And what are you going to do about seeing Louise?"

"Why do you act as if I don't like Louise?" he says. "I will occasionally come back East, and I will arrange for her to fly to San Francisco on her vacations."

"It's going to break her heart."

"No it isn't. Why do you want to make me feel bad?"

"She's had so many things to adjust to. You don't have to go to San Francisco right now, Milo."

"It happens, if you care, that my own job here is in jeopardy. This is a real chance for me, with a young firm. They really want me. But anyway, all we need in this happy group is to have you bringing in a couple of hundred dollars a month with your graphic work and me destitute and Bradley so devastated by being fired that of course he can't even look for work."

"I'll bet he is looking for a job," I say.

"Yes. He read the want ads today and then fixed a crab quiche."

"Maybe that's the way you like things, Milo, and people respond to you. You forbade me to work when we had a baby. Do you say anything encouraging to him about finding a job, or do you just take it out on him that he was fired?"

There is a pause, and then he almost seems to lose his mind with impatience.

"I can hardly *believe*, when I am trying to find a logical solution to all our problems, that I am being subjected, by telephone, to an unflattering psychological analysis by my ex-wife." He says this all in a rush.

"All right, Milo. But don't you think that if you're leaving so soon you ought to call her, instead of waiting until Saturday?"

Milo sighs very deeply. "I have more sense than to have important conversations on the telephone," he says.

. . .

MILO CALLS ON Friday and asks Louise whether it wouldn't be nice if both of us came in and spent the night Saturday and if we all went to brunch together Sunday. Louise is excited. I never go into town with her.

Louise and I pack a suitcase and put it in the car Saturday morning. A cutting of ivy for Bradley has taken root, and she has put it in a little green plastic pot for him. It's heartbreaking, and I hope that Milo notices and has a tough time dealing with it. I am relieved I'm going to be there when he tells her, and sad that I have to hear it at all.

In the city, I give the car to the garage attendant, who does not remember me. Milo and I lived in the apartment when we were first married, and moved when Louise was two years old. When we moved, Milo kept the apartment and sublet it—a sign that things were not going well, if I had been one to heed such a warning. What he said was that if we were ever rich enough we could have the house in Connecticut *and* the apartment in New York. When Milo moved out of the house, he went right back to the apartment. This will be the first time I have visited there in years.

Louise strides in in front of me, throwing her coat over the brass coatrack in the entranceway—almost too casual about being there. She's the hostess at Milo's, the way I am at our house.

He has painted the walls white. There are floor-length white curtains in the living room, where my silly flowered curtains used to hang. The walls are bare, the floor has been sanded, a stereo as huge as a computer stands against one wall of the living room, and there are four speakers.

"Look around," Milo says. "Show your mother around, Louise."

I am trying to remember if I have ever told Louise that I used to live in this apartment. I must have told her, at some point, but I can't remember it.

"Hello," Bradley says, coming out of the bedroom.

"Hi, Bradley," I say. "Have you got a drink?"

Bradley looks sad. "He's got champagne," he says, and looks nervously at Milo.

"No one *has* to drink champagne," Milo says. "There's the usual assortment of liquor."

"Yes," Bradley says. "What would you like?"

"Some bourbon, please."

"Bourbon." Bradley turns to go into the kitchen. He looks different; his hair is different—more wavy—and he is dressed as though it were summer, in straight-legged white pants and black leather thongs.

"I want Perrier water with strawberry juice," Louise says, tagging along after Bradley. I have never heard her ask for such a thing before. At home, she drinks too many Cokes. I am always trying to get her to drink fruit juice.

Bradley comes back with two drinks and hands me one. "Did you want anything?" he says to Milo.

"I'm going to open the champagne in a moment," Milo says. "How have you been this week, sweetheart?"

"O.K.," Louise says. She is holding a pale-pink, bubbly drink. She sips it like a cocktail.

Bradley looks very bad. He has circles under his eyes, and he is ill at ease. A red light begins to blink on the phone-answering device next to where Bradley sits on the sofa, and Milo gets out of his chair to pick up the phone.

"Do you really want to talk on the phone right now?" Bradley asks Milo quietly.

Milo looks at him. "No, not particularly," he says, sitting down again. After a moment, the red light goes out.

"I'm going to mist your bowl garden," Louise says to Bradley, and slides off the sofa and goes to the bedroom. "Hey, a little toadstool is growing in here!" she calls back. "Did you put it there, Bradley?"

"It grew from the soil mixture, I guess," Bradley calls back. "I don't know how it got there."

"Have you heard anything about a job?" I ask Bradley.

"I haven't been looking, really," he says. "You know."

Milo frowns at him. "Your choice, Bradley," he says. "I didn't ask you to follow me to California. You can stay here."

"No," Bradley says. "You've hardly made me feel welcome."

"Should we have some champagne—all four of us—and you can get back to your bourbons later?" Milo says cheerfully.

We don't answer him, but he gets up anyway and goes to the kitchen. "Where have you hidden the tulip-shaped glasses, Bradley?" he calls out after a while.

"They should be in the cabinet on the far left," Bradley says.

"You're going with him?" I say to Bradley. "To San Francisco?"

He shrugs, and won't look at me. "I'm not quite sure I'm wanted," he says quietly.

The cork pops in the kitchen. I look at Bradley, but he won't look up. His new hairdo makes him look older. I remember that when Milo left me I went to the hairdresser the same week and had bangs cut. The next week, I went to a therapist who told me it was no good trying to hide from myself. The week after that, I did dance exercises with Martine Cooper, and the week after that the therapist told me not to dance if I wasn't interested in dancing.

"I'm not going to act like this is a funeral," Milo says, coming in with the glasses. "Louise, come in here and have champagne! We have something to have a toast about."

Louise comes into the living room suspiciously. She is so used to being refused even a sip of wine from my glass or her father's that she no longer even asks. "How come I'm in on this?" she asks.

"We're going to drink a toast to me," Milo says.

Three of the four glasses are clustered on the table in front of the sofa. Milo's glass is raised. Louise looks at me, to see what I'm going to say. Milo raises his glass even higher. Bradley reaches for a glass. Louise picks up a glass. I lean forward and take the last one.

"This is a toast to me," Milo says, "because I am going to be going to San Francisco."

It was not a very good or informative toast. Bradley and I sip from our glasses. Louise puts her glass down hard and bursts into tears, knocking the glass over. The champagne spills onto the cover of a big art book about the Unicorn Tapestries. She runs into the bedroom and slams the door.

Milo looks furious. "Everybody lets me know just what my insufficiencies are, don't they?" he says. "Nobody minds expressing himself. We have it all right out in the open."

"He's criticizing me," Bradley murmurs, his head still bowed. "It's because I was offered a job here in the city and I didn't automatically refuse it."

I turn to Milo. "Go say something to Louise, Milo," I say. "Do you think that's what somebody who isn't brokenhearted sounds like?"

He glares at me and stumps into the bedroom, and I can hear him talking to Louise reassuringly. "It doesn't mean you'll *never* see me," he says. "You can fly there, I'll come here. It's not going to be that different."

"You lied!" Louise screams. "You said we were going to brunch."

"We are. We are. I can't very well take us to brunch before Sunday, can I?"

"You didn't say you were going to San Francisco. Where *is* San Francisco, anyway?"

"I just said so. I bought us a bottle of champagne. You can come out as soon as I get settled. You're going to like it there."

Louise is sobbing. She has told him the truth and she knows it's futile to go on.

BY THE NEXT morning, Louise acts the way I acted—as if everything were just the same. She looks calm, but her face is small and pale. She looks very young. We walk into the restaurant and sit at the table Milo has reserved. Bradley pulls out a chair for me, and Milo pulls out a chair for Louise, locking his finger with hers for a second, raising her arm above her head, as if she were about to take a twirl.

She looks very nice, really. She has a ribbon in her hair. It is cold, and she should have worn a hat, but she wanted to wear the ribbon. Milo has good taste: the dress she is wearing, which he bought for her, is a hazy purple plaid, and it sets off her hair.

"Come with me. Don't be sad," Milo suddenly says to Louise, pulling her by the hand. "Come with me for a minute. Come across the street to the park for just a second, and we'll have some space to dance, and your mother and Bradley can have a nice quiet drink."

She gets up from the table and, looking long-suffering, backs into her coat, which he is holding for her, and the two of them go out. The waitress comes to the table, and Bradley orders three Bloody Marys and a Coke, and eggs Benedict for everyone. He asks the waitress to wait awhile before she brings the food. I have hardly slept at all, and having a drink is not going to clear my head. I have to think of things to say to Louise later, on the ride home.

"He takes so many *chances*," I say. "He pushes things so far with people. I don't want her to turn against him."

"No," he says.

"Why are you going, Bradley? You've seen the way he acts. You know that when you get out there he'll pull something on you. Take the job and stay here."

Bradley is fiddling with the edge of his napkin. I study him. I don't know who his friends are, how old he is, where he grew up, whether he believes in God, or what he usually drinks. I'm shocked that I know so little, and I reach out and touch him. He looks up.

"Don't go," I say quietly.

The waitress puts the glasses down quickly and leaves, embarrassed because she thinks she's interrupted a tender moment. Bradley pats my hand on his arm. Then he says the thing that has always been between us, the thing too painful for me to envision or think about.

"I love him," Bradley whispers.

We sit quietly until Milo and Louise come into the restaurant, swinging hands. She is pretending to be a young child, almost a baby, and I wonder for an instant if Milo and Bradley and I haven't been playing house, too—pretending to be adults.

"Daddy's going to give me a first-class ticket," Louise says. "When I go to California we're going to ride in a glass elevator to the top of the Fairman Hotel."

"The Fairmont," Milo says, smiling at her.

Before Louise was born, Milo used to put his ear to my stomach and say that if the baby turned out to be a girl he would put her into glass slippers instead of bootees. Now he is the prince once again. I see them in a glass elevator, not long from now, going up and up, with the people below getting smaller and smaller, until they disappear.

(1979)

EXPERIMENT

JULIAN BARNES

His story didn't always begin in the same way. In the preferred version, my Uncle Freddy was in Paris on business, traveling for a firm that produced authentic wax polish. He went into a bar and ordered a glass of white wine. The man standing next to him asked what his area of activity was, and he replied, "*Cire réaliste.*"

But I also heard my uncle tell it differently. For instance, he had been taken to Paris by a rich patron to act as navigator in a motor rally. The stranger in the bar (we are now at the Ritz, by the way) was refined and haughty, so my uncle's French duly rose to the occasion. Asked his purpose in the city, he replied, "*Je suis, sire, rallyiste.*" In a third, and it seemed to me most implausible, version—but then the quotidian is often preposterous, and so the preposterous may in return be plausible—the white wine in front of my uncle was a Reuilly. This, he would explain, came from a small appellation in the Loire, and was not unlike Sancerre in style. My uncle was new to Paris, and had already ingested several glasses (the location having shifted to a *petit zinc* in the *quartier latin*), so that when the stranger (who this time was not haughty) asked what he was drinking, he felt that panic which occurs when a foreign idiom escapes the mind, and the further panic when an English expression is desperately translated. The idiomatic model he chose was "I'm on the beer," and so he said, "*Je suis sur Reuillys.*" Once, when I rebuked my uncle for the contradictoriness of his memories, he gave a contented little smile. "Marvellous, the subconscious, isn't it?" he replied. "So inventive."

If the neighboring drinker came in several physical forms, he likewise introduced himself variously as Tanguy, Prévert, Duhamel, and Unik; once, even as Breton himself. We can, at least, be sure of the date of this evanescent encounter: March, 1928. Further, my Uncle Freddy, as even the most cautious commentators have agreed, is—was—none other than the mildly disguised "T.F." who appears in Session 5(a) of the Surrealist group's famously un-Platonic dialogues about sex. The transcript of this session was published for the first time in 1990, as an appendix to "Recherches sur la Sexualité, Janvier 1928–Août 1932." The notes state that my uncle was almost certainly introduced to the group by Pierre Unik and that "T.F.," contrary to the subsequent meanderings of his subconscious, was actually in Paris on holiday.

We shouldn't be too skeptical about my uncle's undeserved entrée to the Surrealist circle. They did, after all, admit occasional outsiders—a defrocked priest, a passing vagabond—to their discussions. And perhaps they thought a twenty-nine-year-old Englishman of conventional appearance, brought to them by a linguistic misunderstanding, might usefully broaden their terms of reference. My uncle was fond of attributing his permitted presence to the French dictum that within every lawyer there lurks the remnants of a poet. I am not of either world, you understand (and neither was my uncle). Is this piece of wisdom any truer than its opposite: that within every poet there lurks the remnants of a lawyer?

Uncle Freddy maintained that the session he attended took place in the apartment of the man he met in the bar, which limits it to five possible locations. There were about a dozen participants according to my uncle; nine according to the "Recherches." I should make it clear that since Session 5(a) was not published until 1990, and my uncle died in 1985, he was only ever faced with self-inflicted inconsistencies. Further, the tale of Uncle Freddy and the Surrealists was strictly for the smoking room, where narrative libertarianism was more acceptable. After swearing listeners never to mention it to Aunt Kate, he would enlarge on the frank licentiousness of what had taken place back in 1928. At times, he would claim to have been shocked, and maintain that he had heard more filth in one evening among Parisian intellectuals than he had in three years of barrack-room life during the last war. At others, his self-presentation was as the English man-about-town, the card, the dandy, all too willing to pass on a few tips, a few handy refinements of technique, to this gathering of Frenchmen whose cerebral intensity, in his view, hampered their normal sensual responses.

The published Session, needless to say, confirms neither version. Those who have read the "Recherches" will be familiar with its strange mixture of pseudoscientific inquiry and frank subjective response. The truth is that everyone talks about sex in a different way, just as everyone, we naturally assume, does it in a different way. André Breton, animator of the group, is a lofty Socratic figure, austere and at times repellent ("I don't like anyone to caress me. I hate that"). The others are variously benign to cynical, self-mocking to boastful, candid to satirical. The dialogues are happily full of humor; occasionally of the unintended sort, inflicted by posterity's frigid judgment; but more often intended, issuing from a rueful acknowledgment of our human frailty. In the third Session, for instance, Breton is catechizing his four male companions about whether they would allow a woman to touch their sex when it was not erect. Marcel Noll replies that he hates it. Benjamin Péret says that if a woman did that to him, he would feel diminished. Breton agrees: "diminished" is exactly the right word for how he would feel. To which Louis Aragon rejoins, "If a woman touched my sex only when it was erect, it wouldn't get that way very often."

I am straying from the point. I'm probably also trying to put off the admission that my uncle's participation in Session 5(a) is for most of its extent frankly disappointing. Perhaps there was a false democracy in the assumption that an Englishman picked up in a bar because of a ver-

bal mistake would have important testimony to offer this probing tri-
bunal. "T.F." is asked many of the usual questions: under what conditions he prefers to have sex; how he lost his virginity; whether and how
he can tell if a woman has reached orgasm; how many people he has
had sexual relations with; how recently he has masturbated; how many
times in succession he is capable of orgasm; and so on. I shall not
bother to relate my uncle's responses, because they are either banal or, I
suspect, not wholly truthful. When asked by Breton the characteristi-
cally compendious question "Apart from ejaculating in the vagina,
mouth, or anus, where do you like to ejaculate in order of preference: 1)
Armpit 2) Between the breasts 3) On the stomach?" Uncle Freddy answers—and here I have to retranslate from the French, so do not offer
these as his exact words—"Is the cupped palm permitted?" Quizzed
about which sexual position he prefers, my uncle replies that he likes to
be lying on his back, with the woman sitting on top of him. "Ah," says
Benjamin Péret, "the so-called 'lazy position.'"

My uncle is then interrogated about the British propensity for
sodomy, about which he is defensive, until it transpires that homosexu-
ality is not the topic but, rather, sodomy between men and women.
Then my uncle is baffled. "I have never done it," he replies, "and I have
never heard of anyone doing it." "But do you dream of doing it?" asks
Breton. "I have never dreamed of doing it," T.F. doggedly responds.
"Have you ever dreamed of fucking a nun in a church?" is Breton's next
question. "No, never." "What about a priest or a monk?" asks Queneau.
"No, not that either" is the reply.

I am not surprised that Session 5(a) is relegated to an appendix. The
interrogators and fellow-confessors are in a lethargic or routine mood,
while the surprise witness keeps pleading the Fifth. Then, toward the
end of the evening, there comes a moment when the Englishman's
presence seems briefly justified. I feel I should at this point give the
transcript in full:

ANDRÉ BRETON: What is your opinion of love?
T.F.: When two people get married . . .
ANDRÉ BRETON: No, no, no! The word "marriage" is anti-Surrealist.
JEAN BALDENSPERGER: What about sexual relations with animals?
T.F.: What do you mean?

JEAN BALDENSPERGER: *Sheep. Donkeys.*

T.F.: *There are very few donkeys in Ealing. We had a pet rabbit.*

JEAN BALDENSPERGER: *Did you have relations with the rabbit?*

T.F.: *No.*

JEAN BALDENSPERGER: *Did you dream of having relations with the rabbit?*

T.F.: *No.*

ANDRÉ BRETON: *I cannot believe that your sexual life can possibly be as empty of imagination and Surrealism as you make it appear.*

JACQUES PRÉVERT: *Can you describe to us the principal differences between sexual relations with an Englishwoman and those with a Frenchwoman?*

T.F.: *I only arrived in France yesterday.*

JACQUES PRÉVERT: *Are you frigid? No, do not take offense. I am not serious.*

T.F.: *Perhaps I can make a contribution by describing something I used to dream about.*

JEAN BALDENSPERGER: *To do with donkeys?*

T.F.: *No. There used to be a pair of twin sisters in my street.*

JEAN BALDENSPERGER: *You wanted to have sexual relations with both of them at the same time?*

RAYMOND QUENEAU: *How old were they? Were they young girls?*

PIERRE UNIK: *You are excited by lesbianism? You like to watch women caress one another?*

ANDRÉ BRETON: *Please, gentlemen, let our guest speak. I know we are Surrealists, but this is chaos.*

T.F.: *I used to look at these twin sisters, who were in all visible respects identical, and ask how far that identity continued.*

ANDRÉ BRETON: *You mean, if you were having sexual relations with one, how could you tell it was she and not the other?*

T.F.: *Exactly. At the beginning. And this in turn provoked a further question. What if there were two people—women who in their . . .*

ANDRÉ BRETON: *In their sexual movements . . .*

T.F.: *In their sexual movements were exactly the same, and yet in all other respects were completely different.*

PIERRE UNIK: *Erotic doppelgängers yet social disparates.*

ANDRÉ BRETON: *Precisely. That is a valuable contribution. Even, if I*
may say so to our English guest, a quasi-Surrealist contribution.
JACQUES PRÉVERT: *So you have not yet been in bed with a French-*
woman?
T.F.: *I told you, I arrived yesterday.*

This is the end of Uncle Freddy's documented participation in Session 5(a), which then returned to matters such as the distinction between orgasm and ejaculation, and the relation between dreams and masturbatory desire. My uncle evidently had little to contribute on these subjects.

I HAD, OF course, no suspicion of this future corroboration when I saw my uncle for the last time. This was in November of 1984. Aunt Kate was dead by then, and my visits to "T.F." (as I am inclined to think of him nowadays) had become increasingly dutiful. Nephews tend to prefer aunts to uncles. Aunt Kate was dreamy and indulgent; there was something gauzy-scarved and secretive about her. Uncle Freddy was indecently foursquare; he seemed to have his thumbs in his waistcoat pockets even when wearing a two-piece suit. His stance, both moral and physical, had the bullying implication that he truly understood what manhood consisted of, that his generation had miraculously caught the elusive balance between earlier repression and subsequent laxness, and that any deviation from this *beau idéal* was regrettable, if not actively perverse. As a result, I was never quite at ease with the future "T.F." He once announced that it was his avuncular responsibility to teach me about wine, but his pedantry and assertiveness put me off the subject until quite recently.

It had become a routine after Aunt Kate's death that I would take Uncle Freddy out to dinner on his birthday, and that afterward we would return to his flat, off the Cromwell Road, and drink ourselves stupid. The consequences mattered little to him; but I had my patients to think of, and would annually try to avoid getting as drunk as I had the previous year. I can't say I ever succeeded, because though each year my resolution was stronger, so was the countervailing force of my uncle's tediousness. In my experience, there are various good but lesser motives—guilt, fear, misery, happiness—for indulging in a certain excess of drink, and one larger motive for indulging in a great excess: boredom. At one time I knew a clever alcoholic who insisted that he drank because things then happened to him such as never did when he was sober. I half believed him, though to my mind drink does not really make things happen, it simply helps you bear the pain of things not happening. For instance, the pain of my uncle being exceptionally boring on his birthdays.

The ice would fissure as it hit the whiskey, the casing of the gas fire would clunk, Uncle Freddy would light what he claimed was his annual cigar, and the conversation would turn yet again to what I now think of as Session 5(a).

"So remind me, Uncle, what you were really doing in Paris."

"Trying to make ends meet. What all young men do." We were on our second half bottle of whiskey; a third would be required before a welcome enough form of anesthesia developed. "Task of the male throughout history, wouldn't you say?"

"And did you?"

"Did I what?"

"Make ends meet?"

"You've a filthy mind for one of your age," he said, with the sudden sideways aggression that liquor imparts.

"Chip off the old block, Uncle Freddy." I didn't, of course, mean it.

"Did I ever tell you . . ." and he was launched, if that verb doesn't give too vivid an impression of directness and purpose. This time he had again chosen to be in Paris as map reader and mechanic to some English milord.

"What sort of car was it? Just out of interest."

"Panhard," he answered sniffily. It always was a Panhard when he told this version. I used to divert myself by wondering whether such consistency on my uncle's part made this element of his story more likely to be true, or more likely to be false.

"And where did the rally go?"

"Up hill and down dale, my boy. Round and about. From one end of the land to the other."

"Trying to make ends meet."

"Wash your mouth out."

"Chip off the old . . ."

"So I was in this bar. . . ."

I caressed him with the questions he needed, until he reached the normal climax to his story, one of the few points at which he agreed with the subsequently published Session 5(a).

"So Fellow-me-lad says to me, 'Have you done it with a French lass yet?' and I say, 'Give us time, only got off the boat yesterday!' "

I would normally have feigned a run of dying chuckles, poured some more Scotch, and waited for Uncle Freddy's next topic. This time, for some reason, I declined his ending.

"So did you?"

"Did I what?"

"Do it with a French lass?"

I was breaking the rules, and his reply was a kind of rebuke; or, at least, I took it as such. "Your Aunt Kate was as pure as driven snow," he announced with a hiccup. "The missing doesn't get any the less, you know, for all the years. I can't wait to join her."

"Never say die, Uncle Freddy." This is not the sort of expression I normally use. I practically added "Life in the old dog yet," such was the infectious, indeed pestiferous, influence of my uncle. Instead, I repeated, "So—did you do it with a French lass?"

"Thereby hangs a tale, my boy, and it's one I've never told a living soul." I think if I'd shown genuine interest at this point I might have scared him off, but I was slumped in the oppressive reflection that my uncle was not just an old bore but a parody of an old bore. Why didn't he strap on a peg leg and start capering round some inglenooked pub waving a clay pipe? "Thereby hangs a tale, and it's one I've never told a living soul." People don't say that anymore. Except my uncle just had.

"They fixed me up, you see."

"Who fixed you up?"

"The Surrealist boys. My newfound chums."

"You mean, they found you a job?"

"Are you stupid tonight or just normal? I'm not sure I can tell. They fixed me up with a woman. Well, two, to be precise."

I began to pay attention at this point. Needless to say, I did not believe my uncle. He was probably fed up with the lack of impact made by the umpteenth retelling of How I Met the Surrealists and had been working up some new embellishment.

"You see, in my considered opinion, those get-togethers . . . They all wanted to meet up and talk smut, but couldn't admit it, so they said there was some scientific purpose behind it all. Fact is, they weren't very good at talking smut. Inhibited, really, I suppose I'd say. Intellectuals. No fire in their veins, just ideas. Why, in my three years in the army . . ."

I will spare you this ritual diversion.

"So I could sense what they were after, but I wasn't going to provide it. Almost like betraying your country, talking smut to a group of foreigners. Unpatriotic, don't you think?"

"Never tried it, Uncle."

"Ha. You've got a tongue on you tonight. Never tried it. That was just like them, wanting to know what I'd never tried. Trouble with their sort is, if you say you've never wanted to do so-and-so, they don't believe you. In fact, just because you say you *don't* want to do so-and-so, they assume that deep down this is what you're bursting to do. Cockeyed, eh?"

"Could be."

"So I thought it incumbent upon me to raise the tone of the gathering. Don't laugh, I know what I'm saying. You wait till *you* find yourself sitting around with a lot of intellectuals all talking about John Thomas. So I said, here's one to think about. What if there were two lasses who made love in the same way. Exactly the same way, so that if you closed your eyes you couldn't tell the difference. Wouldn't that be a thing, I said. And with all their brains they hadn't turned up that conundrum before. It set them by the ears, I don't mind telling you."

I'm not surprised. It's one of those questions you tend not to ask. Neither about yourself (is there somebody else out there who does it in a way indistinguishable from me?), nor about others. In sex we note distinctiveness, not similarity. She/he is/was good/not so good/wonderful/bit boring/fakey, or whatever; but we don't as a rule think, Oh, being in bed with her was much like being in bed with So-and-So a couple of years ago. In fact, if I were to close my eyes . . . We don't, on the whole, think that way. Courtesy, in part, I expect; a desire to maintain the individuality of others. And perhaps a fear that if you do that to them, they might start thinking the same back about you.

"So my new chums fixed me up."

"...?"

"They wanted to thank me for my contribution to their discussions. Seeing as I'd been so useful. Chappie I'd met in the bar said he'd be in touch."

"Surely the rally was about to start, Uncle?" Well, it was hard to resist.

"The next day he turned up and said the group was offering me what he called a Surrealist gift. They were touched by the fact that I had not as yet enjoyed the favors of a French lass, and they were prepared to right this wrong."

"Remarkably generous." A remarkable fantasy is what I really thought.

"He said they'd booked a room for me at three o'clock the next afternoon in a hotel off Saint Sulpice. He said he'd be there, too. I thought this a bit strange, but, on the other hand, never look a gift horse and all that.

" 'What are you going to be there for?' I asked. 'I think I'm up to managing on my own.' So he explained the arrangement. They wanted me to take part in a test. They wanted to know if sex with a Frenchwoman was different from sex with an Englishwoman. I said why did they need me to help them find that out. They said they thought I'd have a more straightforward response. Meaning, I suppose, that I wouldn't sit around and think about it all the time like they would.

"I said, 'Let me get this straight. You want me to have a couple of hours with a French lass and then come round the next day and tell you what I thought of it?' 'No,' Chappie says. 'Not the next day, day after. The *next* day we've booked you the same room with another girl.' 'That's handsome,' I say. 'Two French lasses for the price of one.' 'Not quite,' he says. 'One of them is English. You have to tell which is which.' 'Well,' I say, 'I can tell that just by saying "*bonjour*" and looking at them.' 'That's why,' he says, 'you aren't allowed to say "*bonjour*" and you aren't allowed to look at them. I'll be there when you arrive and blindfold you, then I'll let the girl in. When she's gone and you hear the door shut, you can take the blindfold off. How do you feel about that?'

"How did I feel about that? Well, it was a bit of a surprise. I'd just been thinking, Don't look a gift horse in the mouth, and now it was a question of not looking *two* gift horses in the mouth, or anywhere else. How did I feel? Man to man, I felt like a couple of Christmases had come round at the same time. Part of me wasn't too partial to the blindfold business: though, man to man, another part of me rather was."

Isn't it pathetic how old men lie about the sex they had in earlier days? What could be more transparently an invention? Paris, youth, a woman, *two* women, a hotel room in the afternoon, all set up and paid for by someone else? Pull the other one, Uncle. Twenty minutes in an *hôtel de passe* with a rough hand towel and a subsequent dose of clap is more like it. Why do old men need this sort of comfort? And what banal scenarios they drool out to themselves. O.K., Uncle, fast-forward with the soft porn. We'll forget about navigating in the rally.

"So I said, Count me in. And then next afternoon I went to this hotel behind Saint Sulpice. It came on to rain, and I had to run from the Métro station and got there in a muck sweat." This wasn't bad—I'd been expecting a brilliant spring day with accordionists serenading him through the Jardin du Luxembourg. "I got to the room, Chappie was there, took off my hat and coat. Wasn't planning to get starkers in front of mine host, as you might imagine. He said, 'Don't worry, she'll do the rest.' He just sat me down on the bed, wrapped this scarf around my head, knotted it twice, made me promise as an Englishman not to do any peeping, and left the room. A couple of minutes later, I heard the door open."

My uncle put down his whiskey, set his head back, and closed his eyes, closing them to remember something he had not in any case seen. Indulgently, I let him drag out the pause. At last, he said, "And then the next day. Again. Raining again, too."

The gas fire noisily held its breath, the ice cubes trilled promptingly in my glass. But Uncle Freddy didn't seem to want to continue. Or perhaps he'd really stopped. That wouldn't do. It was—how shall I put it?—like narrative cock-teasing.

"So?"

"So," my uncle repeated softly. "Just so."

We sat quietly for a minute or two until I couldn't avoid the question. "And what *was* the difference?"

Uncle Freddy put his head back, closed his eyes, and uttered a noise between a sigh and a whimper. Eventually, he said, "The French lass licked the raindrops from my face." He opened his eyes again, and showed me his tears.

I was strangely moved. I was also wearily suspicious, but this didn't stop me being moved. *The French lass licked the raindrops from my face.* I gave my uncle—whether plausible liar or sentimental remembrancer—the gift of my envy.

"You could tell?"

"Tell what?" He seemed half absent, being tweaked and tickled by his memories.

"Which one was English and which one was French?"

"Oh yes, I could tell."

"How?"

"How do you think?"

"Smell of garlic?"

He chuckled. "No. They both wore scent, as a matter of fact. Quite strong scent. Not the same, of course."

"So . . . they did different things? Or was it the way they did it?"

"Trade secret." Now he was beginning to look smug again.

"Come off it, Uncle Freddy."

"Always made it a rule never to snitch on my lady friends."

"Uncle Freddy, you never set eyes on them. They were provided for you. They weren't your lady friends."

"They were to me. Both of them. That's what they felt like. That's what I've always considered them."

This was exasperating, not least because I'd been drawn into giving credence to my uncle's fantasy. And what was the point of inventing a story and then withdrawing the key facts?

"But you can tell me, Uncle, because you told them."

"Them?"

"The group. You reported to them the next day."

"Well, an Englishman's word is his bond except when it isn't. You've lived long enough to know that. And besides . . . the truth is I had a feeling, not so much the first time but more strongly the second, that I was being watched."

"Someone in the wardrobe?"

"I don't know. How, where. Just sensed it, somehow. It made me feel a bit grubby. And as I say, I made it a rule never to snitch on my lady friends. So I took the boat train home the next day."

Forgetting about the motor rally, or the career in authentic wax polish, or whatever else it might have been.

"And *that*," my uncle continued, "was the cleverest thing I ever did." He looked at me as if his whole story had been aimed at this moment. "Because that's where I met your Aunt Kate. On the boat train."

"I never knew that."

"No reason why you should. Engaged within the month, married within three."

A busy spring indeed. "And what did *she* think of your adventure?"

His face shut down again. "Your Aunt Kate was as pure as driven snow. I'd no more have talked about that than . . . pick my teeth in public."

"You never told her?"

"Never breathed a word. Anyway, imagine it from her side. She meets a likely fellow, gets a bit soft on him, asks what he's been up to in Paris, and he tells her he's been knocking off lasses at the rate of one a day after promising to go back afterwards and talk smut about them. She'd not be soft on him for long, would she?"

In my limited observation, Aunt Kate and Uncle Freddy, despite their different natures, had been a devoted couple. His grief at her death, even when exaggerated into melodrama by drink, had seemed quite genuine. The fact that he survived her by six years I attributed to no more than the enforced habit of living. Two months after this final birthday evening, he gave up that habit. The funeral was the usual sparse and awkward business: a Surrealist wreath with an obscene motif might have helped.

Five years later the "Recherches sur la Sexualité" appeared, and my uncle's story was partly corroborated. My curiosity and frustration were also revived; I was left staring at the same old questions. I resented the fact that my uncle had clammed up, leaving me with nothing but *The French lass licked the raindrops from my face.*

As I have mentioned, my uncle's encounter with the Surrealist group was relegated to a mere appendix. The "Recherches" are of course extensively annotated: preface, introduction, text, appendices, footnotes to text, footnotes to appendices, footnotes to footnotes. Probably I am the only person to have spotted something that is at most only of family interest. Footnote 23 to Session 5(a) states that the Englishman referred to as T.F. was on one occasion the subject of what is described as an "attempted vindication of Surrealist theory (cf. note 12 to Appendix VI)," but that no record of the results obtained has survived. Footnote 12 to Appendix VI describes these "attempted vindications" and mentions that in a few of them there was an Englishwoman involved. This woman is referred to simply as "K."

I have only two final reflections on the matter. The first is that when scientists employ volunteers to help with their research projects, they often withhold from these participants the true purpose of the test, for fear such knowledge might, wittingly or unwittingly, affect the purity of the process and the accuracy of the result.

The second thought came to me only quite recently. I may have mentioned that I take a novice interest in wine. I belong to a small group that meets twice a month: we each take along a bottle, and the wines are tasted blind. Usually we get them wrong, sometimes we get them right, though what is wrong and what is right in this matter is a complicated business. If a wine tastes to you like a young Australian Chardonnay, then that, in a sense, is what it is. The label may subsequently declare it to be an expensive Burgundy, but if it hasn't been that in your mouth, then that is what it can never truly become.

This isn't quite what I meant to say. I meant to say that a couple of weeks ago we had a guest tutor. She was a well-known Master of Wine, and she told us an interesting fact. Apparently if you take a magnum and decant it into two separate bottles and put them into a blind tasting, then it's extremely rare for even wily drinkers to guess that the wine in those two particular bottles is in fact the same one. People expect all the wines to be different, and their palates therefore insist that they are. She said it was a most revealing experiment, and that it almost always works.

(1995)

Scarves, Beads, Sandals

Mavis Gallant

After three years, Mathilde and Theo Schurz were divorced, without a mean thought, and even Theo says she is better off now, married to Alain Poix. (Or "Poids." Or "Poisse." Theo may be speaking the truth when he says he can't keep in mind every facet of the essential Alain.) Mathilde moved in with Alain six months before the wedding, in order to become acquainted with domestic tedium and annoying habits, should they occur, and so avoid making the same mistake (marriage piled onto infatuation) twice. They rented, and are now gradually buying, a two-bedroom place on Rue Saint-Didier, in the Sixteenth Arrondissement. In every conceivable way it is distant from the dispiriting south fringe of Montparnasse, where Theo continues to reside, close to several of the city's grimmest hospitals, and always under some threat or other—eviction, plagues of mice, demolition of the whole cul-de-sac of sagging one-story studios. If Theo had been attracted by her "physical aspect"—Mathilde's new, severe term for beauty—Alain accepts her as a concerned and contributing partner, intellectually and spiritually. This is not her conclusion. It is her verdict.

Theo wonders about "spiritually." It sounds to him like a moist west wind, ready to veer at any minute, with soft alternations of sun and rain. Whatever Mathilde means, or wants to mean, even the idea of the partnership should keep her fully occupied. Nevertheless, she finds time to drive across Paris, nearly every Saturday afternoon, to see how Theo is getting along without her. (Where is Alain? In close liaison with a computer, she says.) She brings Theo flowering shrubs from the market on Île de la Cité, still hoping to enliven the blighted yard next to the studio, and food in covered dishes—whole, delicious meals, not Poix leftovers—and fresh news about Alain.

Recently, Alain was moved to a new office—a room divided in two, really, but on the same floor as the Minister and with part of an eighteenth-century fresco overhead. If Alain looks straight up, perhaps to ease a cramp in his neck, he can take in Apollo—just Apollo's head—watching Daphne turn into a laurel tree. Owing to the perspective of the work, Alain has the entire Daphne—roots, bark, and branches, and her small pink Enlightenment face peering through leaves. (The person next door has inherited Apollo's torso, dressed in Roman armor, with a short white skirt, and his legs and feet.) To Theo, from whom women manage to drift away, the situation might seem another connubial bad dream, but Alain interprets it as an allegory of free feminine choice. If he weren't so pressed with other work, he might write something along that line: an essay of about a hundred and fifty pages, published between soft white covers and containing almost as many colored illustrations as there are pages of print; something a reader can absorb during a weekend and still attend to the perennial border on Sunday afternoon.

He envisions (so does Mathilde) a display on the "recent nonfiction" table in a Saint-Germain-des-Prés bookshop, between stacks of something new about waste disposal and something new about Jung. Instead of writing the essay, Alain applies his trained mind and exacting higher education to shoring up French values against the Anglo-

Saxon mud slide. On this particular Saturday, he is trying to batter into proper French one more untranslatable expression: "airbag." It was on television again the other day, this time spoken by a woman showing black-and-white industrial drawings. Alain would rather take the field against terms that have greater resonance, are more blatantly English, such as "shallow" and "bully" and "wishful thinking," but no one, so far, has ever tried to use them in a commercial.

So Mathilde explains to Theo as she sorts his laundry, starts the machine, puts clean sheets on the bed. She admires Theo, as an artist—it is what drew her to him in the first place—but since becoming Mme. Poix she has tended to see him as unemployable. At an age when Theo was still carrying a portfolio of drawings up and down and around Rue de Seine, looking for a small but adventurous gallery to take him in, Alain has established a position in the cultural apparat. It may even survive the next elections: he is too valuable an asset to be swept out and told to find a job in the private sector. Actually, the private sector could ask nothing better. Everyone wants Alain. Publishers want him. Foreign universities want him. Even America is waiting, in spite of the uncompromising things he has said about the hegemony and how it encourages well-bred Europeans to eat pizza slices in the street.

Theo has never heard of anybody with symbolic imagery, or even half an image, on his office ceiling outlasting a change of government. The queue for space of that kind consists of one ravenous human resource after the other, pushing hard. As for the private sector, its cultural subdivisions are hard up for breathing room, in the dark, stalled between floors. Alain requires the clean horizons and rich oxygen flow of the governing class. Theo says none of this. He removes foil from bowls and dishes, to see what Mathilde wants him to have for dinner. What can a Theo understand about an Alain? Theo never votes. He has never registered, he forgets the right date. All at once the campaign is over. The next day familiar faces, foxy or benign, return to the news, described as untested but eager to learn. Elections are held in spring, perhaps to make one believe in growth, renewal. One rainy morning in May, sooner or later, Alain will have to stack his personal files, give up Apollo and Daphne, cross a Ministry courtyard on the first lap of a march into the private sector. Theo sees him stepping along cautiously, avoiding the worst of the puddles. Alain can always teach, Theo tells himself. It is what people say about aides and assistants they happen to know, as the astonishing results unfold on the screen.

ALAIN KNOWS THEO, of course. Among his mixed feelings, Alain has no trouble finding the esteem due to a cultural bulwark: Theo and his work have entered the enclosed space known as "time-honored." Alain even knows about the Poids and Poisse business, but does not hold it against Theo; according to Mathilde, one no longer can be sure when he is trying to show he has a sense of humor or when he is losing brain cells. He was at the wedding, correctly dressed, suit, collar, and tie, looking distinguished—something like Braque at the age of fifty, Alain said, but thinner, taller, blue-eyed, lighter hair, finer profile. By then they were at the reception, drinking champagne under a white marquee, wishing they could sit down. It was costing Mathilde's father the earth—the venue was a restaurant in the Bois de Boulogne—but he was so thankful to be rid of Theo as a son-in-law that he would have hired Versailles, if one could.

The slow, winding currents of the gathering had brought Theo, Alain, and Mathilde together. Theo with one finger pushed back a strayed lock of her hair; it was reddish gold, the shade of a persimmon. Perhaps he was measuring his loss and might even, at last, say something embarrassing and true. Actually, he was saying that Alain's description—blue-eyed, etc.—sounded more like Max Ernst. Alain backtracked, said it was Balthus he'd had in mind. Mathilde, though not Alain, was still troubled by Theo's wedding gift, a botched painting he had been tinkering with for years. She had been Mme. Poix for a few hours, but still felt responsible for Theo's gaffes and imperfections. When he did not reply at once, she said she hoped he did not object to being told he was like Balthus. Balthus was the best-looking artist of the past hundred years, with the exception of Picasso.

Alain wondered what Picasso had to do with the conversation. Theo looked nothing like him: he came from Alsace. He, Alain, had never understood the way women preferred male genius incarnated as short, dark, and square-shaped. "Like Celtic gnomes," said Theo, just to fill in. Mathilde saw the roses in the restaurant garden through a blur which was not the mist of happiness. Alain had belittled her, on their wedding day, in the presence of her first husband. Her first husband had implied she was attracted to gnomes. She let her head droop. Her hair slid over her cheeks, but Theo, this time, left it alone. Both men looked elsewhere—Alain because tears were something new, Theo out of habit. The Minister stood close by, showing admirable elegance of manner—not haughty, not familiar; careful, kind, like the Archbishop of Paris at a humble sort of funeral, Theo said, thinking to cheer up Mathilde. Luckily, no one overheard. Her mood was beginning to draw attention. Many years before, around the time of the Algerian War, a relative of Alain's mother had married an aunt of the Minister. The outer rims of the family circles had quite definitely overlapped. It was the reason the Minister had come to the reception and why he had stayed, so far, more than half an hour.

Mathilde was right; Theo must be losing brain cells at a brisk rate now. First Celtic gnomes, then the Archbishop of Paris; and, of course, the tactless, stingy, offensive gift. Alain decided to smile, extending greetings to everyone. He was attempting to say, I am entirely happy on this significant June day. He was happy, but not entirely. Perhaps Mathilde was recalling her three years with Theo and telling herself nothing lasts. He wished Theo would do something considerate, such as disappear. A cluster of transparent molecules, the physical remainder of the artist T. Schurz, would dance in the sun, above the roses. Theo need not be dead—just gone.

"Do you remember, Theo, the day we got married," said Mathilde, looking up at the wrong man, by accident intercepting the smile Alain was using to reassure the Minister and the others. "Everybody kept saying we had made a mistake. We decided to find out how big a mistake it was, so in the evening we went to Montmartre and had our palms read. Theo was told he could have been an artist but was probably a merchant seaman. His left hand was full of little shipwrecks." She may have been waiting for Alain to ask, "What about you? What did your hand say?" In fact, he was thinking just about his own. In both palms he had lines that might be neat little roads, straight or curved, and a couple of spidery stars.

AT FIRST, THEO had said he would give them a painting. Waiting, they kept a whole wall bare. Alain supposed it would be one of the great recent works; Mathilde thought she knew better. Either Alain had forgotten about having carried off the artist's wife or he had decided it didn't matter to Theo. That aside, Theo and Theo's dealer were tight as straitjackets about his work. Mathilde owned nothing, not even a crumpled sketch saved from a dustbin. The dealer had taken much of the earlier work off the market, which did not mean Theo was allowed to give any away. He burned most of his discards and kept just a few unsalable things in a shed. Speaking of his wedding gift, Theo said the word "painting" just once and never again: he mentioned some engravings— falling rain or falling snow—or else a plain white tile he could dedicate and sign. Mathilde made a reference to the empty wall. A larger work, even unfinished, even slightly below Theo's dealer's exacting standards, would remind Mathilde of Theo for the rest of her life.

Five days later, the concierge at Rue Saint-Didier took possession of a large oil study of a nude with red hair—poppy red, not like Mathilde's— prone on a bed, her face concealed in pillows. Mathilde recognized the studio, as it had been before she moved in and cleaned it up. She remembered the two reproductions, torn out of books or catalogues, askew on the wall. One showed a pair of Etruscan figures, dancing face to face, the other a hermit in a landscape. When the bed became half Mathilde's, she took them down. She had wondered if Theo would mind, but he never noticed—at any rate, never opened an inquiry.

"Are you sure this thing is a Schurz?" said Alain. Nothing else bothered him. He wondered, at first, if Theo had found the picture at a junk sale and had signed it as a joke. The true gift, the one they were to cherish and display, would come along later, all the more to be admired because of the scare. But Theo never invented jokes; he blundered into them.

"I am not that woman," Mathilde said. Of course not. Alain had never supposed she was. There was the crude red of the hair, the large backside, the dirty feet, and then the date—"1979"—firm and black and in the usual place, to the right of "T. Schurz." At that time, Mathilde was still reading translations of Soviet poetry, in love with a teacher of Russian at her lycée, and had never heard of "T. Schurz." In saying this, Alain showed he remembered the story of her life. If she'd had a reason to forgive him, about anything, she would have absolved him on the spot; then he spoiled the moment by declaring that it made no difference. The model was not meant to be anyone in particular.

Mathilde thought of Emma, Theo's first long-term companion (twelve years), but by '79 Emma must have been back in Alsace, writing cookery books with a woman friend. Julita (six years) fit the date but had worn a thick yellow braid down her back. She was famous for having tried to strangle Theo, but her hands were too small—she could not get a grip. After the throttling incident, which had taken place in a restaurant, Julita had packed a few things, most of them Theo's, and moved to the north end of Paris, where she would not run into him. Emma left Theo a microwave oven, Julita a cast-iron cat, standing on its hind legs, holding a tray. She had stolen it from a stand at the flea market, Theo told Mathilde, but the story sounded unlikely: the cat was heavy to lift, let alone be fetched across a distance. Two people would have been needed; perhaps one had been Theo. Sometimes, even now, some old friend from the Julita era tells Theo that Julita is ill or hard up and that he ought to help her out. Theo will say he doesn't know where she is or else, yes, he will do it tomorrow. She is like art taken off the market now, neither here nor there. The cat is still in the yard, rising out of broken flowerpots, empty bottles. Julita had told Theo it was the one cat that would never run away. She hung its neck with some amber beads Emma had overlooked in her flight, then pocketed the amber and left him the naked cat.

When Mathilde was in love with Theo and jealous of women she had never met, she used to go to an Indian shop, in Montparnasse, where first Emma, then Julita had bought their flat sandals and white embroidered shifts and long gauzy skirts, black and pink and indigo. She imagined what it must have been like to live, dress, go to parties, quarrel, and make up with Theo in the seventies. Emma brushed her brown hair upside down, to create a great drifting mane. A woman in the Indian store did Julita's braid, just because she liked Julita. Mathilde bought a few things, skirts and sandals, but never wore them. They made her look alien, bedraggled, like the Romanian Gypsy women begging for coins along Rue de Rennes. She did not want to steal from a market or fight with Theo in bistros. She belonged to a generation of women who showed a lot of leg and kept life smooth, tight-fitting, close-woven. Theo was right: she was better off with Alain.

Still, she had the right to know something about the woman she had been offered as a gift. It was no good asking directly; Theo might say it was a journalist who came to tape his memoirs or the wife of a Lutheran dignitary or one of his nieces from Alsace. Instead, she asked him to speak to Alain; out of aesthetic curiosity, she said, Alain acquired the facts of art. Theo often did whatever a woman asked, unless it was important. Clearly, this was not. Alain took the call in his office; at that time, he still had a cubicle with a bricked-up window. Nobody recalled who had ordered the bricks or how long ago. He worked by the light of a neon fixture that flickered continually and made his eyes water. Summoned by an aide to the Minister, on propitious afternoons by the Minister himself (such summonses were more and more frequent), he descended two flights, using the staircase in order to avoid a giddy change from neon tube to the steadier glow of a chandelier. He brought with him only a modest amount of paperwork. He was expected to store everything in his head.

Theo told Alain straight out that he had used Julita for the pose. She slept much of the day and for that reason made an excellent model: was never tired, never hungry, never restless, never had to break off for a cigarette. The picture had not worked out and he had set it aside. Recently he had looked at it again and decided to alter Julita from the neck up. Alain thought he had just been told something of consequence; he wanted to exchange revelations, let Theo know he had not enticed Mathilde away but had merely opened the net into which she could jump. She had grabbed Theo in her flight, perhaps to break the fall. But Alain held still; it would be unseemly to discuss Mathilde. Theo was simply there, like an older relative who has to be considered and mollified, though no one knows why. There was something flattering about having been offered an unwanted and unnecessary explanation; few artists would have bothered to make one. It was as though Theo had decided to take Alain seriously. Alain thanked him.

Unfortunately, the clarification had made the painting even less interesting than it looked. Until then, it had been a dud Schurz but an honest vision. The subject, a woman, entirely womanly, had been transfigured by Schurz's reactionary visual fallacy (though honest, if one accepted the way his mind worked) into a hefty platitude; still, it was art. Now, endowed with a name and, why not, an address, a telephone number, a social-security number, and a personal history, Theo's universal statement dwindled to a footnote about Julita—second long-term companion of T. Schurz, first husband of Mathilde, future first wife of Alain Poix. A white tile with a date and a signature would have shown more tact and common sense.

All this Alain said to Mathilde that night, as they ate their dinner next to the empty wall. Mathilde said she was certain Theo had gone to considerable trouble to choose something he believed they would understand and appreciate and that would enhance their marriage. It was one of her first lies to Alain: Theo had gone out to the shed where he kept his shortfalls and made a final decision about a dead loss. Perhaps he guessed they would never hang it and so damage his reputation, although as a rule he never imagined future behavior more than a few minutes away. Years ago, in a bistro on Rue Stanislas, he had drawn a portrait of Julita on the paper tablecloth, signed and dated it, torn it off, even made the edges neat. It was actually in her hands when he snatched it back, ripped it to shreds, and set the shreds on fire in an ashtray. It was then that Julita had tried to get him by the throat.

YESTERDAY, FRIDAY, AN April day, Theo was awakened by a hard beam of light trained on his face. There was a fainter light at the open door, where the stranger had entered easily. The time must have been around five o'clock. Theo could make out an outline, drawn in gray chalk: leather jacket, close-cropped head. (Foreign Legion deserter? Escaped prisoner? Neo-Nazi? Drugs?) He spoke a coarse, neutral, urban French—the old Paris accent was dying out—and told Theo that if he tried to move or call he, the intruder, might hurt him. He did not say how. They all watch the same programs, Theo told himself. He is young and he repeats what he has seen and heard. Theo had no intention of moving and there was no one to call. His thoughts were directed to the privy, in the yard. He hoped the young man would not take too long to discover there was nothing to steal, except a small amount of cash. He would have told him where to find it, but that might be classed as calling out. His checkbook was in a drawer of Emma's old desk, his bank card behind the snapshot of Mathilde, propped on the shelf above the sink. The checkbook was no good to the stranger, unless he forced Theo to sign all the checks. Theo heard him scuffing about, heard a drawer being pulled. He shut his eyes, opened them to see the face bent over him, the intent and watchful expression, like a lover's, and the raised arm and the flashlight (probably) wrapped in one of Mathilde's blue-and-white tea towels.

He came to in full daylight. His nose had bled all over the pillows, and the mattress was sodden. He got up and walked quite steadily, barefoot, over the stones and gravel of the yard; returning to the studio, he found some of yesterday's coffee still in the pot. He heated it up in a saucepan, poured in milk, drank, and kept it down. Only when that was done did he look in a mirror. He could hide his blackened eyes behind sunglasses but not the raw bruise on his forehead or his swollen nose. He dragged the mattress outside and spread it in the cold April sunlight. By four o'clock, Mathilde's announced arrival time—for it seemed to him today could be Saturday—the place was pretty well cleaned up, mattress back on the bed, soiled bedclothes rolled up, pushed in a corner. He found a banquet-size tablecloth, probably something of Emma's, and drew it over the mattress. Only his cash had vanished; the checkbook and bank card lay on the floor. He had been attacked, for no reason, by a man he had never seen before and would be unable to recognize: his face had been neutral, like his voice. Theo turned on the radio and, from something said, discovered this was still Friday, the day before Mathilde's habitual visiting day. He had expected her to make the mattress dry in some magical and efficient, Mathilde-like way. He kept in the shed a couple of sleeping bags, for rare nights when the temperature fell below freezing. He got one of them out, gave it a shake, and spread it on top of the tablecloth. It would have to do for that night.

Today, Saturday, Mathilde brought a meal packed in a black-and-white bag from Fauchon: cooked asparagus, with the lemon-and-oil sauce in a jar, cold roast lamb, and a gratin of courgettes and tomatoes—all he has to do is turn on Emma's microwave—a Camembert, a round loaf of that moist and slightly sour bread, from the place on Rue du Cherche-Midi, which reminds Schurz of the bread of his childhood, a carton of thick cream, and a bowl of strawberries, washed and hulled. It is too early for French strawberries. These are from Spain, picked green, shipped palely pink, almost as hard as radishes, but they remind one that it is spring. Schurz barely notices seasons. He works indoors. If rain happens to drench the yard when he goes outside to the lavatory, he puts on the Alpine beret that was part of his uniform when he was eighteen and doing his military service.

Mathilde, moving out to live with Alain, took with her a picture of Theo from that period, wearing the beret and the thick laced-up boots and carrying the heavy skis that were standard issue. He skied and shot a rifle for eighteen months, even thought he might have made it a permanent career, if that was all there was to the Army. No one had yet fallen in love with him, except perhaps his mother. His life was simple then, has grown simpler now. The seasons mean nothing, except that green strawberries are followed by red. Weather means crossing the yard bareheaded or covered up.

Mathilde has noticed she is starting to think of him as "Schurz." It is what his old friends call Theo. This afternoon, she had found him looking particularly Schurz-like, sitting on a chair he had dragged outside, drinking tea out of a mug, with the string of the tea bag trailing. He had on an overcoat and the regimental beret. He did not turn to the gate when she opened it or get up to greet her or say a word. Mathilde had to walk all round him to see his face.

"My God, Schurz, what happened?"

"I tripped and fell in the dark and struck my head on the cat."

"I wish you'd get rid of it," she said.

She took the mug from his hands and went inside, to unpack his dinner and make fresh tea. The beret, having concealed none of the damage, was useless now. He removed it and hung it rakishly on the cat, on one ear. Mathilde returned with, first, a small folding garden table (her legacy), then with a tray and teacups and a teapot and a plate of sliced gingerbread, which she had brought him the week before. She poured his tea, put sugar in, stirred it, and handed him the cup.

She said, "Theo, how long do you think you can go on living here, alone?" (It was so pathetic, she rehearsed, for Alain. Theo was like a child; he had made the most absurd attempt at covering up the damage, and instead of putting the mattress out to dry he had turned the wet side down and slept on top of it, in a sleeping bag. Who was that famous writer who first showed signs of senility and incontinence on a bridge in Rome? I kept thinking of him. Schurz just sat there, like a guilty little boy. He caught syphilis when he was young and gave it to Emma; he said it was from a prostitute, in Montmartre, but I believe it was a married woman, the wife of the first collector to start buying his work. He can't stay there alone now. He simply can't. His checkbook and bank card were lying next to the trash bin. He must have been trying to throw them away.)

Her picture had been on the floor, too, the one taken the day she married Theo. Mathilde has a small cloud of red-gold hair and wears a short white dress and a jacket of the eighties, with shoulders so wide that her head seems unnaturally small, like a little ball of reddish fluff. Theo is next to her, not too close. He could be a relative or a family friend or even some old crony who heard the noise of the party and decided to drop in. The photograph is posed here, in the yard. One can see a table laden with bottles, and a cement-and-stucco structure—the privy, with the door shut, for a change—and a coldwater tap and a bucket lying on its side. You had to fill the bucket and take it in with you.

Schurz never tried to improve the place or make it more comfortable. His reason was, still is, that he might be evicted at any time. Any month, any day, the police and the bailiffs will arrive. He will be rushed off the premises, with just the cast-iron cat as a relic of his old life.

"I'll tell you what happened," he said, showing her his mess of a face. "Yesterday morning, while I was still asleep, a man broke in, stole some money, and hit me with something wrapped in a towel. It must have been his flashlight."

(Oh, if you had heard him! she continued to prepare for Alain. A comic-strip story. The truth is he is starting to miss his footing and to do himself damage, and he pees in his sleep, like a baby. What kind of doctor do we need for him? What sort of specialist? A geriatrician? He's not really old, but there's been the syphilis, and he has always done confused and crazy things, like giving us that picture, when we really wanted a plain, pure tile.)

Schurz at this moment is thinking of food. He would like to be handed a plate of pork *ragoût* with noodles, swimming in gravy; but nobody makes that now. Or stewed eels in red wine, with the onions cooked soft. Or a cutlet of venison, browned in butter on both sides, with a purée of chestnuts. What he does not want is clear broth with a poached egg in it, or any sort of a salad. When he first came to Paris the cheapest meals were the heartiest. His mother had said, "Send me a Paris hat," not meaning it; though perhaps she did. His money, when he had any, went to supplies for his work or rent or things to eat.

Only old women wore hats now. There were hats in store windows, dusty windows, in narrow streets—black hats, for funerals and widows. But no widow under the age of sixty ever bought one. Young women wore hats at the end of summer, tilted straw things, that they tried on just for fun. When they took the hats off, their hair would spring loose. The face, freed of shadow, took on a different shape, seemed fuller, unmysterious, as bland as the moon. There was a vogue for bright scarves, around the straw hats, around the hair, wound around the neck along with strings of bright beads, loosely coiled—sand-colored or coral or a hard kind of blue. The beads cast colored reflections on the skin of a throat or on a scarf of a different shade, like a bead diluted in water. Schurz and his friends ate cheap meals in flaking courtyards and on terraces where the tables were enclosed in a hedge of brittle, unwatered shrubs. Late at night, the girls and young women would suddenly find that everything they had on was too tight. It was the effect of the warm end-of-summer night and the food and the red wine and the slow movement of the conversation. It slid without wavering from gossip to mean gossip to art to life-in-art to living without boundaries. A scarf would come uncoiled and hang on the back of a chair or a twig of the parched hedge; as it would hang, later, over the foot of someone's bed. Not often Schurz's (not often enough), because he lived in a hotel near the Café Mabillon, long before all those places were renovated and had elevators put in and were given a star in some of the guidebooks. A stiff fine had to be paid by any client caught with a late-night visitor. The police used to patrol small hotels and knock on doors just before morning, looking for French people in trouble with the law and for foreigners with fake passports and no residence permits. When they found an extra guest in the room, usually a frantic young woman trying to pull the sheet over her face, the hotelkeeper was fined, too, and the tenant thrown out a few hours later. It was not a question of sexual morality but just of rules.

When dinner was almost finished, the women would take off their glass beads and let them drop in a heap among the ashtrays and coffee cups and on top of the wine stains and scribbled drawings. Their high-heeled sandals were narrow and so tight that they had to keep their toes crossed; and at last they would slip them off, unobserved, using first one foot, then the other. Scarfless, shoeless, unbound, delivered, they waited for the last wine bottle to be emptied and the last of the coffee to be drunk or spilled before they decided what they specifically wanted or exactly refused. This was not like a memory to Theo but like part of the present time, something that unfolded gradually, revealing mysteries and satisfactions.

In the studio, behind him, Mathilde was making telephone calls. He heard her voice but not her words. On a late Saturday afternoon, she would be recording her messages on other people's machines: he supposed there must be one or two to doctors, and one for the service that sends vans and men to take cumbersome objects away, such as a soiled mattress. Several brief inquiries must have been needed before she could find Theo a hotel room, free tonight, at a price he would accept and on a street he would tolerate. The long unbroken monologue must have been for Alain, explaining that she would be much later than expected, and why. On Monday she would take Theo to the Bon Marché department store and make him buy a mattress, perhaps a whole new bed. Now here was a memory, a brief, plain stretch of the past: love apart, she had married him because she wanted to be Mme. T. Schurz. She would not go on attending parties and gallery openings as Schurz's young friend. Nobody knew whether she was actually living with him or writing something on his work or tagging along for the evening. She did not have the look of a woman who would choose to settle for a studio that resembled a garage or, really, for Schurz. It turned out she could hardly wait to move in, scrape and wax whatever he had in the way of furniture, whitewash the walls. She trained climbing plants over the wire fence outside, even tried to grow lemon trees in terra-cotta tubs. The tubs are still there.

She came toward him now, carrying the bag she had packed so that he would have everything he needed at the hotel. "Don't touch the bruise," she said, gently, removing the hand full of small shipwrecks. The other thing she said today, which he is bound to recall later on, was "You ought to start getting used to the idea of leaving this place. You know that it is going to be torn down."

Well, it is true. At the entrance to the doomed and decaying little colony there is a poster, damaged by weather and vandals, on which one can still see a depiction of the structure that will cover the ruin, once it has finally been brought down: a handsome biscuit-colored multipurpose urban complex comprising a library, a crèche, a couple of munici-pal offices, a screening room for projecting films about Bedouins or whales, a lounge where elderly people may spend the whole day playing board games, a theatre for amateur and professional performances, and four low-rent work units for painters, sculptors, poets, musicians, and photographers. (A waiting list of two thousand names was closed some years ago.) It seems to Theo that Julita was still around at the time when the poster was put up. The project keeps running into snags—aesthetic, political, mainly economic. One day the poster will have been his view of the future for more than a third of his life.

Mathilde backed out of the cul-de-sac, taking care (he does not like being driven), and she said, "Theo, we are near all these hospitals. If you think you should have an X-ray at once, we can go to an emergency ser-vice. I can't decide, because I really don't know how you got hurt."

"Not now." He wanted today to wind down. Mathilde, in her mind, seemed to have gone beyond dropping him at his hotel. He had agreed to something on Rue Delambre, behind the Coupole and the Dôme. She was on the far side of Paris, with Alain. As she drove on, she asked Theo if he could suggest suitable French for a few English expressions: "divided attention" and "hard-driven" and "matchless perfection," the latter in one word.

"I hope no one steals my Alpine beret," he said. "I left it hanging on the cat."

Those were the last words they exchanged today. It is how they said goodbye.

(1995)

Ten Miles West of Venus

Judy Troy

After Marvelle Lyle's husband, Morgan, committed suicide—his body being found on an April evening in the willows that grew along Black Creek—Marvelle stopped going to church. Franklin Sanders, her minister at Venus United Methodist, drove out to her house on a Sunday afternoon in the middle of May to see if he could coax her back. Her house was ten miles west of Venus—seven miles on the highway and three on a two-lane road that cut through the open Kansas wheat fields and then wound back through the forest preserve. The woods at this time of year were sprinkled with white blooming pear trees.

Franklin had his radio tuned to Gussie Dell's weekly "Neighbor Talk" program. Gussie was a member of his congregation, and Franklin wanted to see what embarrassing thing she would choose to say today. The week before, she had told a story about her grandson, Norman, drawing a picture of Jesus wearing high heels. "I have respect for Norman's creativity," she had said. "I don't care if Norman puts Jesus in a garter belt."

Today, though, she was on the subject of her sister, whom Franklin had visited in the hospital just the day before. "My sister has cancer," Gussie said. "She may die or she may not. My guess is she won't. I just wanted to say that publicly."

Franklin pulled into Marvelle's driveway and turned off the radio too soon to hear whatever Gussie was going to say next; he imagined it was something unfavorable about her sister's husband, who, for years now, had been sitting outside in his chicken shed, watching television. "One of these days I'm going to dynamite him out of there," Gussie liked to say. She was generally down on marriage, which Franklin couldn't argue with—his own marriage being unhappy, and that fact not a secret among his parishioners.

Franklin parked his new Ford Taurus between Marvelle's old pickup and the ancient Jeep Morgan had driven. Hanging from the Jeep's rearview mirror were Morgan's military dog tags. He'd been in the Vietnam War, though Franklin had never known any details about it. Morgan Lyle had never been forthcoming about himself, and the few times Franklin had seen him at church Morgan had spent the length of the sermon and most of the service smoking outside. "You have to accept him as he is," Marvelle had once told Franklin. "Otherwise, well, all I'm saying is he doesn't mean anything by what he says and does."

Also in the driveway—just a big gravel clearing, really, between the house and the garage where Morgan had had his motorcycle repair shop—was the dusty van their son, Curtis, drove. He was thirty-one and still living at home. Franklin, who was sixty-three, could remember Curtis as the blond-headed child who had once, in Sunday School, climbed out of a window in order to avoid reciting the Lord's Prayer. Now the grownup Curtis, in faded pants and no shirt, his thinning hair pulled back into a ponytail, opened the door before Franklin had a chance to knock. "Well, come on in, I guess," Curtis said. Behind him, Marvelle appeared in the kitchen doorway.

The house was built haphazardly into a hill, and was so shaded with oak and sweetgum trees that the inside—in spring and summer, anyway—was dark during the day. The only light in the room was a small lamp on a desk in the corner, shining down on iridescent feathers and other fly-tying materials. Curtis sat down at the desk and picked up a hook.

"I'll make coffee," Marvelle told Franklin, and he followed her into the kitchen, which was substantially brighter. An overhead light was on, and the walls were painted white. "I thought Sunday afternoons were when you visited the sick," Marvelle said.

"It was, but I do that on Saturdays now. I find other reasons to get out of the house on Sundays." Franklin sat at the kitchen table and watched her make coffee. She was a tall, muscular woman, and she'd lost weight since Morgan's death. Her jeans looked baggy on her; her red hair was longer than it used to be, and uncombed. "You could stand to eat more," Franklin told her.

"You men complain when we're fat and then worry when we're thin."

"When did I ever say you were fat?" Franklin said.

Marvelle turned toward him with the coffeepot in her hand. "You're right. You never did."

Franklin looked down at the table. This afternoon, with his mind on Morgan, and not on himself or his marriage, he'd managed to push aside the memory of an afternoon years ago, when he and Marvelle had found themselves kissing in the church kitchen. "Found themselves" was just how it had seemed to him. It was, like this day, a Sunday afternoon in spring; Marvelle and his wife and two other parishioners had been planting flowers along the front walk. Marvelle had come into the kitchen for coffee just when he had. He wasn't so gray-haired then or so bottom-heavy, and they walked toward each other and kissed passionately, as if they had planned it for months.

"You've always been an attractive woman," he said quietly.

"Don't look so guilty. It was a long time ago." Marvelle sat down across from him as the coffee brewed. "The amazing thing is that it only happened once."

"No," Franklin said, "it's that I allowed it to happen at all."

"Where was God that day? Just not paying attention?" Marvelle asked.

"That was me not paying attention to God," Franklin told her.

Curtis had turned on the radio in the living room, and Franklin could faintly hear a woman singing. Louder was the sound of the coffee brewing. The kitchen table was next to a window that overlooked a sloping wooded hill and a deep ravine. These woods, too, Franklin noticed, had their share of flowering pear trees. "It looks like snow has fallen in a few select places," he said.

"Doesn't it? I saw two deer walking down there this morning. For a moment, I almost forgot about everything else."

Franklin looked at her face, which was suddenly both bright and sad.

"That's interesting," he said carefully, "because that's what church services do for me."

"Sure they do. Otherwise, you'd lose your place," Marvelle said.

"You don't realize something," Franklin told her. "I'd rather not be the one conducting them. I feel that more and more as I get older. I'd like to sit with the congregation and just partake."

"Would you? Well, I wouldn't. I wouldn't want to do either one." She got up and poured coffee into two mugs and handed one to Franklin. "How do you expect me to feel?" she asked him, standing next to the window. "Do you see God taking a hand in my life? There are people in that congregation who didn't want to see Morgan buried in their cemetery."

"You're talking about two or three people out of a hundred and twenty."

"I bet you felt that way yourself," Marvelle told him.

"You know me better than to think that," Franklin said.

Marvelle sat down and put her coffee on the table in front of her. "All right, I do. Just don't make me apologize."

"When could anybody make you do anything you didn't want to do?" Franklin said to her.

FRANKLIN LEFT LATE in the afternoon, saying goodbye to Curtis after admiring Curtis's fly-tying abilities. Marvelle accompanied him to his car, walking barefoot over the gravel. "You'll be walking over coals next," Franklin said, joking.

"Are you trying to sneak God back into the conversation?" Marvelle asked him. She had her hand on his car door as he got in, and she closed the door after him.

"I'm talking about the toughness of your feet," Franklin said through the open window. "I don't expect that much from God. Maybe I used to. But the older I get, the easier I am on him. God's getting older, too, I figure."

"Then put on your seat belt," Marvelle said. She stepped back into a patch of sunlight, so the last thing he saw as he drove away was the sun on her untidy hair and on her pale face and neck.

The woods he passed were gloomier now, with the sun almost level with the tops of the tallest oaks; it was a relief to him to drive out of the trees and into the green wheat fields. The radio was broadcasting a Billy Graham sermon, which Franklin found he couldn't concentrate on. He was wondering about Gussie's sister and if she'd live, and for how long, and what her husband might be thinking, out in that chicken shed. When Franklin was at the hospital the day before, Gussie's sister hadn't mentioned her husband. She'd wanted to know exactly how Franklin's wife had redecorated their bedroom.

"Blue curtains and a flowered bedspread," he had told her, and that was all he could remember—nothing about the new chair or the wallpaper or the lamps, all of which he took note of when he went home afterward.

He was also thinking, less intentionally, about Marvelle, who was entering his thoughts as erratically as the crows flying down into the fields he was passing. She was eight or nine years older than when he'd kissed her, but those years had somehow changed into days. When Franklin tried to keep his attention on her grief, it wandered off to her hair, her dark eyes—to every godless place it could. It wasn't until he heard Billy Graham recite, "He maketh me to lie down in green pastures: He leadeth me beside the still waters," that Franklin's mind focussed back on Morgan lying in the willows. From that point on he paid attention to the words, falling apart a little when he heard, "Surely goodness and mercy shall follow me all the days of my life," because he didn't know anything more moving, except maybe love, which he didn't feel entitled to; he never had.

(1994)

THE CIRCLE

VLADIMIR NABOKOV

In the second place, because he was possessed by a sudden mad hankering after Russia. In the third place, finally, because he regretted those years of youth and everything associated with it—the fierce resentment, the uncouthness, the ardency, and the dazzlingly green mornings when the coppice deafened you with its golden orioles. As Innokentiy sat in the café and kept diluting with syphoned soda the paling sweetness of his cassis, he recalled the past with a constriction of the heart, with melancholy— what kind of melancholy?—well, a kind not yet sufficiently investigated. All that distant past rose with his breast, raised by a sigh, and slowly his father ascended from the grave, squaring his shoulders: Ilya Ilyich Bychkov, *"le maître d'école chez nous au village,"* in flowing black tie picturesquely knotted and tussah jacket, the buttons of which began, in the old fashion, high on the breastbone but stopped also at a high point, letting the diverging coat flaps reveal the watch chain across the waistcoat. His complexion was reddish, his head bald yet covered with a tender down resembling the velvet of a deer's vernal antlers. There were lots of little folds along his cheeks, and a fleshy wart next to the nose, producing the effect of an additional volute described by the fat nostril. In his high-school and college days, Innokentiy used to travel from town on holidays to visit his father at Leshino. Diving still deeper, he could remember the demolition of the old school at the end of the village, the clearing of the ground for its successor, the foundation-stone ceremony, the religious service in the wind, Count Konstantin Godunov-Cherdyntsev throwing the traditional gold coin, the coin sticking edgewise in the clay. The new building was of a grainy granitic gray on its outside; its inside for several years and then for another long spell (that is, when it joined the staff of memory) sunnily smelled of glue. The classes were graced with glossy educational appliances, such as enlarged portraits of insects injurious to field or forest. But Innokentiy found even more irritating the stuffed birds provided by Godunov-Cherdyntsev. Flirting with the common people! Yes, he saw himself as a stern plebeian: hatred (or so it seemed) suffocated him when as a youth he used to look across the river at the great manorial park, heavy with ancient privileges and imperial grants, casting the reflection of its black amassments onto the green water (with the creamy blur of a *Padus racemosa* blooming here and there among the fir trees).

The new school was built on the threshold of this century, at a time when Godunov-Cherdyntsev had returned from his fifth expedition to Central Asia and was spending the summer at Leshino, his estate in the Government of St. Petersburg, with his young wife. (At forty he was twice as old as she.) To what a depth one has plunged, good God! In a melting crystalline mist, as if it were all taking place underwater, Innokentiy saw himself as a boy of three or four entering the manor house and floating through marvellous rooms, with his father moving on tiptoe, a damp nosegay of lilies of the valley bunched in his fist so tight that they squeaked. And everything around seemed moist too—a luminous, squeaking, quivering haze, which was all one could distinguish. But in later years it turned into a shameful recollection, his father's flowers, tiptoeing progress, and sweating temples darkly symbolizing grateful servility—especially after Innokentiy was told by an old peasant that Ilya Ilyich had been disentangled by "our good master" from a trivial but tacky political affair, for which he would have been banished to the backwoods of the empire had the Count not interceded.

Tanya used to say that the Godunov-Cherdyntsevs had relatives not only in the animal kingdom but also among plants and minerals. And, indeed, Russian and foreign naturalists had described under the specific name of "*godunovi*" a new pheasant, a new antelope, a new rhododendron, and there was even a whole Godunov Range. The Count himself described only insects. Those discoveries of his, his outstanding contributions to zoology, and a thousand perils (for disregarding which he was famous) could not, however, make people indulgent to his high descent and great wealth. Furthermore, let us not forget that certain sections of our intelligentsia had always held nonapplied scientific research in contempt, and therefore Godunov was rebuked for showing more interest in "Sinkiang bugs" than in the plight of the Russian peasant. Young Innokentiy readily believed the tales (actually idiotic) told about the Count's travelling concubines, his Chinese-style inhumanity, and the secret errands he discharged for the Tsar—to spite the English. The reality of his image remained dim: an ungloved hand throwing a gold piece (and, in the still earlier recollection, that visit to the manor house, the lord of which got confused by the child with a Kalmuck, dressed in sky blue, met on the way through a reception hall). Then Godunov departed again, to Samarkand or to Vernyi (towns from which he usually started his fabulous strolls), and was gone a long time. Meanwhile his family summered in the south, preferring, apparently, their Crimean country place to their Petropolitan one. Their winters were spent in the capital. There on the Quay stood their house, a two-floor private residence, painted an olive hue. Innokentiy sometimes happened to walk by; his memory retained the feminine forms of a statue showing its dimpled sugar-white buttock through the patterned gauze on a whole-glassed window. Olive-brown atlantes with strongly arched ribs supported a balcony: the strain of their stone muscles and their agonizingly twisted mouths struck our hotheaded uppergrader as an allegory of the enslaved proletariat. Once or twice, on that Quay, in the beginning of the gusty Neva spring, he glimpsed the little Godunov girl with her fox terrier and governess—they positively whirled by, yet were so vividly outlined: Tanya wore boots laced up to the knee and a short navy-blue coat with knobbed brass buttons, and she slapped the pleats of her short navy-blue-skirt—with what? I think with the dog leash she carried—and the Ladoga wind tossed the ribbons of her sailor cap, and a little behind her sped her governess, karakul-jacketed, her waist flexed, one arm thrown out, the hand encased in a muff of tight-curled black fur.

He lodged with his aunt, a seamstress, in an Okhta tenement. He was morose, unsociable, applied ponderous, groaning efforts to his studies whilst limiting his ambition to a passing mark, but to every-body's astonishment finished school brilliantly and at the age of eigh-teen entered St. Petersburg University as a medical student—at which point his father's worship of Godunov-Cherdyntsev mysteriously in-creased. He spent one summer as a private tutor with a family in Tver. By May of the following year, 1914, he was back in the village of Leshino—and discovered not without dismay that the manor across the river had come alive.

More about that river, about its steep bank, about its old bathhouse. This was a wooden structure standing on piles; a stepped path, with a toad on every other step, led down to it, and not everyone could have found the beginning of that clayey descent in the alder thicket at the back of the church. His constant companion in riparian pastimes was Vasiliy, the blacksmith's son, a youth of indeterminable age (he could not say himself whether he was fifteen or a full twenty), sturdily built, ungainly, in skimpy, patched trousers, with huge bare feet, dirty carrot in color, and as gloomy in temper as was Innokentiy at the time. The pinewood piles cast concertina-shaped reflections that wound and un-wound on the water. Gurgling and smacking sounds came from under the rotten planks of the bathhouse. In a round, earth-soiled tin box de-picting a horn of plenty—it had once contained cheap fruit drops—worms wriggled listlessly. Vasiliy, taking care that the point of the hook would not stick through, pulled a plump segment of worm over it, leav-ing the rest to hang free; then seasoned the rascal with sacramental spittle and proceeded to lower the lead-weighted line over the outer railing of the bathhouse. Evening had come. Something resembling a broad fan of violet-pink plumes or an aerial mountain range with lateral spurs spanned the sky, and the bats were already flitting, with the overstressed soundlessness and evil speed of membraned beings. The fish had begun to bite, and, scorning the use of a rod, simply holding the tensing and jerking line between finger and thumb, Vasiliy tugged at it ever so slightly to test the solidity of the underwater spasms—and suddenly landed a roach or a gudgeon. Casually, and even with a kind of devil-may-care crackling snap, he would wrench the hook out of the toothless round little mouth and place the frenzied creature (rosy blood oozing from a torn gill) in a glass jar, where already a chevin was swimming, its lower lip stuck out. Angling was especially good in warm, overcast weather, when rain, invisible in the air, covered the water with mutually intersecting widening circles, among which appeared here and there a circle of different origin, with a sudden center: the jump of a fish that vanished at once or the fall of a leaf that immediately sailed away with the current. And how delicious it was to go bathing beneath that tepid drizzle, on the blending line of two homogeneous but differently shaped elements—the thick river water and the slender celestial one! Innokentiy took his dip intelligently and indulged afterward in a long rubdown with a towel. The peasant boys, on the other hand, kept floundering till complete exhaustion; finally, shivering, with chattering teeth and a turbid snot trail from nostril to lip, they would hop on one foot to pull their pants up their wet thighs.

That summer Innokentiy was gloomier than ever, and scarcely spoke to his father, limiting himself to mumbles and "hmm"s. Ilya Ilyich, on his part, experienced an odd embarrassment in his son's presence— mainly because he assumed, with terror and tenderness, that Innokentiy lived wholeheartedly in the pure world of the underground, as he had himself at that age. Schoolmaster Bychkov's room: motes of dust in a slanting sunbeam; lit by that beam, a small table he had made with his own hands, varnishing the top and adorning it with a pyrographic design; on the table a photograph of his wife in a velvet frame—so young, in such a nice dress, with a little pelerine and a corset-belt, charmingly oval-faced (that ovality coincided with the idea of feminine beauty in the eighteen-nineties); next to the photograph a crystal paperweight with a mother-of-pearl Crimean view inside, and a cockerel of cloth for wiping pens; and on the wall above, between two casement windows, a portrait of Leo Tolstoy, entirely composed of the text of one of his stories printed in microscopic type. Innokentiy slept on a leathern couch in an adjacent smaller chamber. After a long day in the open air he slept soundly; sometimes, however, a dream image would take an erotic turn, the force of its thrill would carry him out of the sleep circle, and for several moments he would remain lying as he was, squeamishness preventing him from moving.

In the morning he would go to the woods, a medical manual under his arm and both hands thrust under the tasselled cord girting his white Russian blouse. His university cap, worn askew in conformance to left-wing custom, allowed locks of brown hair to fall on his bumpy forehead. His eyebrows were knitted in a permanent frown. He might have been quite good-looking, had his lips been less blubbery. Once in the forest, he seated himself on a thick birch bole, which had been felled not long before by a thunderstorm (and still quivered with all its leaves from the shock), and smoked, and obstructed with his book the trickle of hurrying ants or lost himself in dark meditation. A lonely, impressionable, and touchy youth, he felt overkeenly the social side of things. He loathed the entire surroundings of the Godunovs' country life, such as their menials—"menials," he repeated, wrinkling his nose in voluptuous disgust. In their number he included the plump chauffeur, with his freckles, corduroy livery, orange-brown leggings, and starched collar propping a fold of his russet neck that used to flush purple when, in the carriage shed, he cranked up the no less revolting convertible upholstered in glossy red leather; and the senile flunky with gray side-whiskers who was employed to bite off the tails of newborn fox terriers; and the English tutor who could be seen striding across the village, hatless, raincoated, white-trousered—which caused the village boys to allude wittily to underpants and bareheaded religious processions; and the peasant girls, hired to weed the avenues of the park morning after morning under the supervision of one of the gardeners, a deaf little hunchback in a pink shirt, who, in conclusion, would sweep the sand near the porch with particular zest and ancient devotion. Innokentiy, with the book still under his arm, which hindered his crossing his arms—something he would have liked to do—stood leaning against a tree in the park and considered sullenly various items, such as the shiny roof of the white manor, which was not yet astir.

The first time he saw the Godunovs that summer was in late May (Old Style) from the top of a hill. A cavalcade appeared on the road curving around its base: Tanya in front, astraddle, boylike, on a bright bay; next, Count Godunov-Cherdyntsev himself, an insignificant-looking person riding an oddly small mouse-gray pacer; behind them the breeched Englishman; then some cousin or other; and, coming last, Tanya's brother, a boy of thirteen or so, who suddenly spurred his mount, overtook everybody, and dashed up the steep bit to the village, working his elbows jockey-fashion.

After that there followed several other chance encounters, and finally—all right, here we go. Ready? On a hot day in mid-June—

On a hot day in mid-June the mowers went swinging along on both sides of the path leading to the manor, and each mower's shirt stuck in alternate rhythm now to the right shoulder blade, now to the left. "May God assist you!" said Ilya Ilyich, in a passerby's traditional salute to men at work. He wore his best hat, a panama, and carried a bouquet of mauve bog orchids. Innokentiy walked alongside in silence, his mouth in circular motion (he was cracking sunflower seeds between his teeth and munching at the same time). They were nearing the manor park. At one end of the tennis court the deaf pink dwarf gardener, now wearing a workman's apron, soaked a brush in a pail and, bent in two, walked backward as he traced a thick creamy line on the ground. "May God assist you," said Ilya Ilyich in passing.

The table was laid in the main avenue; Russian dappled sunlight played on the tablecloth. The housekeeper, wearing a gorget, her steely hair smoothly combed back, was already in the act of ladling out chocolate, which the footmen were serving in dark-blue cups. At close range the Count looked his age; there were ashy streaks in his yellowish beard, and wrinkles fanned out from eye to temple. He had placed his foot on the edge of a garden bench and was making a fox terrier jump: the dog jumped not only very high, trying to hap the already wet ball the Count was holding, but actually contrived, while hanging in midair, to jerk itself still higher by an additional twist of its entire body. Countess Elizaveta Godunov, a tall rosy woman in a big wavery hat, was coming up from the garden with another lady, to whom she was vivaciously talking and making the Russian two-hand splash gesture of uncertain dismay. Ilya Ilyich stood with his bouquet and bowed. In this varicolored haze (as perceived by Innokentiy, who, despite having briefly rehearsed on the eve an attitude of democratic scorn, was overcome by the greatest embarrassment) there flickered young people, running children, somebody's black shawl embroidered with gaudy poppies, a second fox terrier, and above all, above all, those eyes gliding through shine and shade, those features still indistinct but already threatening him with fatal fascination, the face of Tanya, whose birthday was being feted.

Everybody was now seated. He found himself at the shade end of the long table, at which end convives did not so much indulge in mutual conversation as keep looking, all their heads turned in the same direction, at the brighter end, where there was loud talk and laughter, and a magnificent pink cake with a satiny glaze and sixteen candles, and the exclamations of children, and the barking of both dogs that had all but jumped onto the table—whilst here, at this end, the garlands of linden shade linked up people of the meanest rank: Ilya Ilyich, smiling in a sort of daze; an ethereal but ugly damsel whose shyness expressed itself in onion sweat; a decrepit French governess with nasty eyes, who held in her lap under the table a tiny invisible creature that now and then emitted a tinkle; and so forth. Innokentiy's direct neighbor happened to be the estate steward's brother—a blockhead, a bore, and a stutterer. Innokentiy talked to him only because silence would have been worse, so that, despite the paralyzing nature of the conversation, he desperately tried to keep it up. Later, however, when he became a frequent visitor at the manor and chanced to run into the poor fellow, Innokentiy never spoke to him, shunning him as a kind of snare or shameful memory.

Rotating in slow descent, the winged fruit of a linden lit on the tablecloth.

At the nobility's end, Godunov-Cherdyntsev raised his voice, speaking across the table to a very old lady in a lacy gown, and as he spoke encircled with one arm the graceful waist of his daughter, who stood near and kept tossing up a rubber ball on her palm. For quite a time Innokentiy tussled with a luscious morsel of cake that had come to rest beyond the edge of his plate. Finally, following an awkward poke, the damned raspberry stuff rolled and tumbled under the table (where we shall leave it). His father either smiled vacantly or licked his mustache; somebody asked him to pass the biscuits—he burst into happy laughter and passed them. All at once, right above Innokentiy's ear, there came a rapid, gasping voice: unsmilingly, and still holding that ball, Tanya was asking him to join her and her cousins; all hot and confused, he struggled to rise from table, pushing against his neighbor in the process of disengaging his right leg from under the shared garden bench.

When speaking of her, people exclaimed, "What a pretty girl!" She had light-gray eyes, velvet-black eyebrows, a largish, pale, tender mouth, and sharp incisors, and when she was unwell or out of humor one could distinguish the dark little hairs above her lip. She was inordinately fond of all summer games—tennis, badminton, croquet—doing everything deftly, with a kind of charming concentration. And, of course, that was the end of the artless afternoons of fishing with Vasiliy, who was greatly perplexed by the change and would pop up in the vicinity of the school toward evening, beckoning Innokentiy with a hesitating grin and holding up at face level a canful of worms—and at such moments Innokentiy shuddered inwardly as he sensed his betrayal of the people's cause. Meanwhile he derived not much joy from the company of his new friends. He was not really admitted to the center of their existence, being kept on its green periphery, taking part in open-air amusements but never being invited into the house. This infuriated him; he longed to be asked for lunch or dinner just to have the pleasure of haughtily refusing; and, in general, he remained constantly on the alert—sullen, suntanned, and shaggy, the muscles of his clenched jaws twitching—and feeling that every word Tanya said to her playmates cast an insulting little shadow in his direction, and, good God, how he hated them all: her boy cousins, her girl friends, the frolicsome dogs.

Abruptly, everything dimmed in noiseless disorder and vanished, and there he was, in the deep blackness of an August night, sitting on a bench at the bottom of the park and waiting, his breast prickly because of his having stuffed between shirt and skin the note which—as in an old novel—a barefoot little girl had brought him from the manor. The laconic style of the assignation led him to suspect a humiliating practical joke; yet he succumbed to the summons—and rightly: a light crunch of footfalls detached itself from the even rustle of the night. Her arrival, her incoherent speech, her nearness struck him as miraculous; the sudden intimate touch of her cold nimble fingers amazed his chastity. A huge, rapidly ascending moon burned through the trees. Shedding torrents of tears and blindly nuzzling him with salt-tasting lips, Tanya told him that on the following day her mother was taking her to the Crimea, that everything was finished, and—oh, how could he have been so obtuse! "Don't go anywhere, Tanya!" he pleaded, but a gust of wind drowned his words, and she sobbed even more violently. When she had hurried away, he remained on the bench without moving, listening to the hum in his ears, and presently walked back in the direction of the bridge, along the country road that seemed to stir in the dark, and then came the war years—ambulance work, his father's death—and after that, a general disintegration of things, but gradually life picked up again, and by 1920 he was already the assistant of Professor Behr at a spa in Bohemia, and three or four years later worked, under the same lung specialist, in Savoy, where one day, somewhere near Chamonix, Innokentiy happened to meet a young Soviet geologist. They got into conversation, and the latter mentioned that it was here, half a century ago, that Fedchenko, the great explorer of Fergana, had died the death of an ordinary tourist. How strange (the geologist added) that it should always turn out that way: death gets so used to pursuing fearless men in wild mountains and deserts that it also keeps coming at them in jest, without any special intent to harm, in all other circumstances, and to its own surprise catches them napping. Thus perished Fedchenko, and Severtsev, and Godunov-Cherdyntsev, as well as many foreigners of classic fame—Speke, Dumont d'Urville; and after several years more spent in medical research, far from the cares and concerns of political expatriation, Innokentiy happened to be in Paris for a few hours for a business interview with a colleague, and was already running down the stairs, gloving one hand, when, on one of the landings, a tall stoop-shouldered lady emerged from the lift—and he at once recognized Countess Elizaveta Godunov-Cherdyntsev. "Of course I remember you; how could I not remember?" she said, gazing not at his face but over his shoulder, as if somebody were standing behind him. (She had a slight squint.) "Well, come in, my dear," she continued, recovering from a momentary trance, and with the point of her shoe turned back a corner of the thick doormat, replete with dust, to get the key. Innokentiy entered after her, tormented by the fact that he could not recall what he had been told exactly about the how and the when of her husband's death.

And a few moments later Tanya came home, all her features fixed more clearly now by the etching needle of years, with a smaller face and kinder eyes. She immediately lit a cigarette, laughing, and without the least embarrassment recalling that distant summer, whilst he kept marvelling that neither Tanya nor her mother mentioned the dead explorer, and spoke so simply about the past, instead of bursting into the awful sobs that he, a stranger, kept fighting back—or were those two displaying, perhaps, the self-control peculiar to their class? They were soon joined by a pale, dark-haired little girl about ten years of age: "This is my daughter—come here, darling," said Tanya, putting her cigarette butt, now stained with lipstick, into a seashell that served as an ashtray. Then her husband, Ivan Ivanovich Kutaysov, came home, and the Countess, meeting him in the next room, was heard to identify their visitor, in her domestic French brought over from Russia, as "*le fils du maître d'école chez nous au village*," which reminded Innokentiy of Tanya's saying once in his presence to a girl friend of hers whom she wanted to notice his very shapely hands: "*Regarde ses mains.*" And now, listening to the melodious, beautifully idiomatic Russian in which the child replied to Tanya's questions, he caught himself thinking, malevolently and quite absurdly, Aha, there is no longer the money to teach kids foreign languages! For it did not occur to him at that moment that in those émigré times, in the case of a Paris-born child going to a French school, this Russian language represented *the* idlest and best luxury.

The Leshino topic was falling apart. Tanya, getting it all wrong, insisted that he used to teach her the pre-Revolution songs of radical students, such as the one about "The despot who feasts in his rich palace hall while destiny's hand has already begun to trace the dread words on the wall." "In other words, our first *stengazeta* [Soviet wall gazette]," remarked Kutaysov, a great wit. Tanya's brother was mentioned; he lived in Berlin, and the Countess started to talk about him. Suddenly, Innokentiy grasped a wonderful fact: nothing is lost, nothing whatever; memory accumulates treasures, stored-up secrets grow in darkness and dust, and one day a transient visitor at a lending library wants a book that has not once been asked for in twenty-two years. He got up from his seat, made his adieus, was not detained overeffusively. How strange that his knees should be trembling. That was really a shattering experience. He crossed the square, entered a café, ordered a drink, briefly rose to remove his own squashed hat from under him. What a dreadful feeling of uneasiness. He felt that way for several reasons. In the first place, because Tanya had remained as enchanting and as invulnerable as she had been in the past.

(Translated, from the Russian, by Dmitri Nabokov, in collaboration with the author.)

(1972)

The Profumo Affair

Ethna Carroll

—————

"He's a friend of the family's and a friend of Daddy's," my sister said on the telephone from London on the night that I was to go to the King's Inn with Pat Dolan. "He's a barrister."

"I don't care, that won't stop me," I felt like saying to her. I knew he was going to want to get off with me, just the way I used to sense that situation with some boy when I was a teen-ager. But I was not a teen-ager now. I was thirty-eight years old, but I felt the way I did when I was a teen-ager. I was running around the house getting ready to go out. The air was quite cool; it was October, Halloween. My mother had died only ten days before. I had come back to Dublin from America, where I lived, when I heard how ill she was, and I had been there for her last two days. It was extraordinary for me to be looking at other people looking at my mother in a coffin. Little boys staring at her, fiddling with the brass handles of her coffin. Little boys who were not crying—second cousins I had never met. I wanted to say, "That is my mother, why don't you cry?" But I just looked at them. Strange the way children are so heartless.

Death is sexual: that's strange, too. I'd actually had waves of sexual feeling, following the hearse from the hospital to the chapel. Now I was in my mother's bedroom. My mother's suitcases were on the floor with her papers in them. I felt excited. Could you believe that my mother had died and I felt excited? This was my first night alone in the house since my mother had died. A few days earlier, my sister had returned to London. Then this morning, my husband, who had come over to Dublin for the funeral, went back home to America. We emigrated from Ireland together long ago. When I was leaving for the States originally, my friends gave me a present of a bracelet and composed a poem for me. I remember how it ended:

> When you've made your first million and are up and away,
> Don't forget tribal days back in old Dublin Bay.

That was fourteen years ago.

I was looking in the mirror. The house was quiet, no ghosts coming up the stairs. The mirror was big, a big square mirror almost filling one wall. Above the fireplace near the mirror was a picture of the Agony in the Garden. *Into thy hands, Lord, I commend my spirit.* My mother probably said those words every night going to sleep alone for the last twenty years of her life. *Jesus, Mary, and Joseph, I give you my heart and my soul.* That's the way the prayers began when I was a child. In this same house, I'd walk up the stairs carrying a hot-water bottle in a pillowcase. I was about four years old. I was sitting in bed waiting for my mother to come up and say prayers with me. At the end of the prayers we had to bless everyone—my mother, my father (who lived somewhere overseas), my sister (who was away at school), all my relations, and everybody else in the whole whole world.

This was the big back room of the house. It was the first room where I remember sleeping alone, although my mother had slept in the front room when I was small. She told me that I used to sleep with her then.

My father was a photograph on the mantelpiece downstairs in the sitting room, a dot on a map somewhere. The house had been newly decorated over the past few years. I could remember the various layers in this house. Before the Agony in the Garden picture there was a crucifix on the wall of my room, a Communion present from my sister, and before that again there was a picture of the Sacred Heart.

I won the Sacred Heart in a raffle in school. It was the kind of raffle in which everyone gets a prize. I finished next-to-last in my class, and I was given a choice between two holy pictures for my prize. I hardly saw them, so blinded with disappointment was I that I'd missed the chocolates. My mother put the picture on the wall in my room after I brought it home. The Sacred Heart had scorching eyes that followed me around the room. But every time I opened my eyes when I was trying to sleep, I could still see it, by the light coming in from the street outside. It dimly glimmered, reminding me of the way I looked when I put a torch underneath my chin and looked in the mirror in the dark. Some nights, I used to jump out of bed and turn the picture to the wall. Then I imagined that the picture was turning slowly back again, on its own. The Sacred Heart stared out at me, more like a devil than like Christ.

At lunchtime, when I ran up to my room to get something, my mother had sometimes turned the picture back facing outward, and I had to leap down the stairs in case He threw daggers in my back. Finally my mother had taken it down. She had laughed at the Sacred Heart with His face turned to the wall like a dunce. I had forgotten all about Him.

One spring, my sister and I decided that we would keep snails as pets. We kept them on the kitchen roof, which could be reached through the back spare-room window. One day I ran up the stairs with a lovely, big snail, holding him carefully by the shell and watching him wave his feelers blindly in the air, and into the spare room. The Sacred Heart was there, staring out from the wall. I screamed. I accused my mother of having done it on purpose. "I hate the Sacred Heart!" I cried. After that, He vanished completely. Sometimes, even now, I wonder what has become of Him. I imagine myself searching for something in a trunk in the garage and finding Him under a pile of old clothes. I imagine Him floating up the stairs as I'm doing my hair and appearing behind me in the mirror, the way women see criminals coming into their rooms in movies. He'll be there with that flame like a dagger.

Nothing like that happened. I was brushing my hair, getting ready to meet Pat Dolan. The light was soft. My mother had hugged me the night before she died, from her hospital bed, a really strong hug. *I gave you life, now live it*—that's what it felt like. That was what I said to my son, who was eighteen, one day when I saw him in a room reading Samuel Beckett. "That man Beckett had the life of Riley when he was your age," I said to him. "Don't let him depress you. Don't."

I was putting on my makeup. "Say a little prayer for you"—that's how that song goes. I ran from the bathroom to the bedroom mirror. *"Before you I stand, sinful and sorrowful. . . ."* Those were the lines I liked from the Memorare. And *"poor banished children of Eve."* This reminded me of the final part of "Paradise Lost," where Adam and Eve are walking out the gates of Eden. I found those lines moving, but I couldn't recall them properly. There was something about the world was all before them, late and soon, and the idea was that they were walking together, I thought hand in hand, and yet they were separate, because there was some mention of their solitary way, and the whole theme was of exile and the loneliness of mankind, and that of course led me back to someone like Beckett. I wanted to get away from that man.

Then, there was the man who played the organ in the church for my mother's funeral. He was crying when my sister and I were making the arrangements. His brother had died recently, he told us. He still talked to him, walking around the house. The man who played the organ was in his sixties or so, and looked a bit dishevelled but in a nice way, a sort of artistic way, and he had that temperament, too. He cried but was able to keep talking, and he was not ashamed of his emotions. He took a photo of himself as a young man out of his pocket and showed it to me and my sister. He was a young man standing against a fence, somewhere in Dublin. He was posed a bit like that photo everyone sees of James Joyce. The hands in the pockets.

The phone rang again. It was my sister once more, from London, wondering if I had reminded my uncle about spending the night in the house with me. It would be desperate, she said, if he forgot and I was alone in the house at a time like this. I felt like saying, "I won't be alone, I'll be sleeping with Pat Dolan." But I didn't. I said that I would call my uncle in a few minutes. No, she said, I was too busy getting ready to go out, she'd call him for me. I was feeling annoyed at the way she was interfering. I wanted to tell her to mind her own business. But I couldn't, really. My sister was the one who introduced Pat Dolan to the family, who made him our friend, and if anyone had an original claim to him it was my sister, if there is such a thing as actually being able to claim another human being. My sister was divorced, but she had a boyfriend, so there was no reason to feel sorry for her. She had always denied anything romantic between herself and Pat Dolan.

"He isn't your husband, is he?"—I could have said that to her. I didn't. I felt that she would try and persuade me from what I wanted to do. I'd be in for all sorts of lectures from her. I got on well with her. She was only a few years older than I, but she hovered over me like a little mother. Chiefly I'd have to undergo her womanizer conversation. She was always going on about terrible womanizers to me. Usually I thought she was hinting about my husband. I always ignored her and walked around busily saying nothing, as if I couldn't possibly imagine whom she might be referring to. Just because a man wasn't sleeping with her, she thought of him as a womanizer. Another reason I didn't say anything to my sister was that she genuinely got depressed about womanizers. After Christina Onassis's death I read things from the newspaper to my sister. She was visiting me at the time, in Detroit. Christina Onassis had said that what she remembered of her childhood was "all the neglect." I still often thought of that remark. I could have saved the life of someone like Christina Onassis.

Anyway, I thanked my sister for her consideration, and put down the phone. Then I phoned a taxi for myself. I ran upstairs and got my bag and put my coat on and waited at the end of the stairs for the taxi to come.

EVEN THOUGH I'D heard about this man for years, I'd never met him until the funeral. "Kind Remembrance, Pat," he'd put on the flowers. A few days later he invited my sister and me to lunch. We had a great time. We all had a good bit of wine to drink. On the way back in the taxi he was running his fingers through the curls of my permed hair and pulling me toward him and kissing my hair and pressing the side of one of my breasts. The whole scene was more suited to London than to Dublin, I thought. He reminded me of the way I'd imagine a Member of Parliament would be coming back from lunch. I was thinking what a shock it must be to suddenly see cameras flashing in a window, and then the picture splashed across some newspaper.

I turned out to be right. Pat Dolan wanted to sleep with me. "How did you know?" he asked me later. "I wasn't absolutely positive," I said. "I wasn't sure how far you'd want to go."

FIRST I MEET him at the law library and we walk through the dark back streets of Dublin to get to the King's Inn. He's talking about what he does and doesn't like. He's talking about an opera festival he's been to. I'm saying that I like popular-opera songs by people like Verdi and that I like "Carmen." We are walking up the path to the King's Inn. The night reminds me of the time, years ago, when I decided to surrender my virginity. I was happy to have made up my mind. I remember standing under a railway bridge halfway into town. The evening was wet, and I could hear car tires going through the water on the road, and their headlights were flaring. I was with a young man I knew, a quantity surveyor, and he was undoing the buckle of his belt. And then I changed my mind. Later I regretted my decision, because I didn't see him again for about six weeks. I had just turned eighteen. In those days I kept myself to a mental timetable of where and how things should happen.

Next, Pat Dolan and myself are walking in the door of the King's Inn. We're in a room with high ceilings. We're at a reception, and people are talking and drinking sherry and there is a roaring fire in the grate. I'm being introduced to other people. "A pretty woman for you," Pat Dolan adds when I am talking to another barrister. There are two other women across the room. We smile at each other but never actually speak. I'm not used to this huge building; usually when I'm in a place like this, I'm walking around a museum. We go into the dining room. Chief barristers are walking about and we bow to them. Everyone is nice. They are serving me dishes. I'm sitting at a table with three barristers, counting Pat Dolan. I'm telling them about my life as a Montessori teacher in America. One of my barristers is talking about his college days. He had a professor who had only one eye, he says, but he could see around corners with it. Next, everyone is talking about the Presidential elections here in Ireland. A scandal has broken out about one of the candidates. There is going to be a rally for him, downtown. Everything remains very jovial.

We leave early. Pat Dolan tells the taxi-driver to go straight home. I'm afraid to say that my uncle is in the house, in case he says what of it or something. Still, I announce the news about my uncle as we are getting out of the taxi. I feel very strange that at this hour of my life I have the same level of chaperoning as I did when I was a fifteen-year-old. I say the news about my uncle as if I am delighted, and I sort of amaze myself.

"Is that a fact?" Pat Dolan says.

My uncle is watching the television when we come in. I leave Pat Dolan with my uncle while I go out to make some tea. I arrange cups and saucers on the tray. I am feeling sad that I may lose my chance with Pat Dolan. This event may never happen. When I bring in the tray, the three of us have tea together. My uncle and Pat Dolan are talking about the news. This uncle is my father's brother. My father was involved in my life when I was a teen-ager. He was very strict with me then. I was in a lot of trouble with him later on, not only because I walked up to the altar pregnant but because I was young and the person I was marrying was poor. My father came from a part of Dublin similar to my husband's, but my father had worked all his life away in Brisbane, trying to rise from that kind of place. My husband and I moved to America for the same reason, but I could never admit things to my father or say anything was the matter.

Pat Dolan does something brainy. "Let me help you with that tray to the kitchen," he says. He gets up and carries the tray out. I follow him, saying whoever heard of the visitor having to carry out the tray, and start to wash up the dishes. He puts the tray down on the kitchen table and turns around. "Can I stay the night?" he says.

I'm not expecting this question at this moment and I say nothing.

"How long will he be here?" he says, referring to my uncle.

"All night, but you can stay another night."

"Then you agree?" He sounds surprised, as if he didn't expect me to be the sort of married woman whom other men enjoy. We are both laughing in the kitchen. Pat Dolan is hugging me.

"What about tomorrow?" he says. That will be fine, because I'm meant to be clearing out the house, and my friends won't even call because I've told them I'm so busy that I'll have to be the one to contact them. He will come back then, he says. He wonders what we can do immediately and suggests a walk. It is almost midnight and I think it's too peculiar a thing to do now. My uncle will wonder what's going on, and I don't want him to know my business. He may even be wondering what all the whispering is in the kitchen.

"I'll outsit him," Pat Dolan says.

We go back into the room to my uncle and continue talking. Pat Dolan and I sit side by side on the couch, with our hands in our laps, listening to my uncle. He already has his electric blanket switched on, he says. After a while he thinks that his bed will be warm enough and he says good night.

My uncle will be leaving the house at nine-thirty in the morning, and Pat Dolan says that he will come back at ten. He thinks that may be a little awkward if my uncle hasn't left the house, but he has his briefcase with him and now he takes out a paper from it and puts it on the couch. He explains that he can say to my uncle that he forgot the paper. He opens a page to make it appear that we have been discussing legal matters.

I'm laughing, not so much at what Pat Dolan is doing but because my husband happens to have a similar briefcase. My husband isn't a barrister, he's a carpenter. He's a lovely-looking carpenter. Sometimes he reminds me of someone from a gang out of "West Side Story." Whenever I think of him that way I know I am being possessive. Once, we had an argument and he said to me, "Let go or I'll hit you and I won't be responsible for the strength of my fist." Later, he said he was sorry. But sometimes I go around thinking that I will be responsible for the strength of mine.

I sleep in the front bedroom tonight—not the room I was in earlier. I keep tossing and turning the whole night, it seems. There's a picture on the wall of this room, too, on the wall above the fireplace. It's a reproduction of Raphael's Madonna and child, and it was my mother's favorite picture. It's in a hexagonal gold frame and I can see the shape of it even in this light. Every so often I can hear my uncle, in the small front bedroom, talking in his sleep in a deep voice.

. . .

THE NEXT MORNING, everything goes according to schedule. My uncle and I have breakfast together. He leaves the house and Pat Dolan comes back shortly after ten. We have a cup of tea together in the kitchen. I'm standing with my back to the window and the kitchen sink, looking at Pat Dolan sitting on a chair at the table. It's strange watching this man I hardly know. I'm looking forward to the day. Other people will be doing mundane things, as I am meant to be doing, but I won't be. It's great, really. I have this whole free day ahead of me. When I'm rinsing cups Pat Dolan goes into the sitting room and puts his contract or whatever in his briefcase. Then he runs up the stairs. I can hear his footsteps across the landing. He moves quickly and is sort of energetic. There are other things in life, I suppose, but other people can do them today.

We are both quiet taking our clothes off. I feel quite casual, considering this is a first situation of this type for me. It's as if I'd been planning it for a long time and hadn't got the right opportunity. What might be trivial to other people is often a big deal to me. The air feels cool, even though the heat is on, and the sheets are cold. My breasts are just the right distance apart, according to Pat Dolan. I get all sorts of compliments (not that I suppose I would cease to exist if I didn't), but still it's nice to hear that I'm a beautiful woman. Pat Dolan talks to me a lot that way, and that's the main difference between this man and my husband, but I don't say anything. I don't feel the need to talk, even though loads of things have happened to me—loads of sad things, not just my mother's death but other things in life. They are the sort of things that might even make other people cry. All sorts of failures have accumulated in my life, all sorts of things that I don't want to think about, but this morning isn't one of them.

We don't even have a glass of water, the whole day. We have lots of conversations. Pat Dolan lies in bed with his hands behind his head and he talks toward the ceiling a lot, as if people have not been listening to him for a long time. He talks about the meaning of his life, and he speaks about his wife a good bit, really, and describes her in a flattering way, appearance-wise. But something happened in their lives ten years ago, he says, and things have not been the same, and it's hard to regain someone's trust once you lose it. "But I will not beg," he says.

"Will you not?"

"No," he says.

Pat Dolan's wife doesn't sleep with other men, even though it would do her good, Pat Dolan says, because it's good for a woman to feel desired. But she worries all the time about Pat Dolan's reputation. "Your reputation, Pat, your reputation," she's always saying. She's a terrible woman for reputations, and rightly so, Pat Dolan says, because some days he even sits across from the Attorney General of Ireland, in the law library of the Four Courts. But divorce is not always the answer, and Pat Dolan believes in salvaging the good. And he speaks about his college-age sons—about one he hits it off with particularly well, and how that son once described him, Pat Dolan, as a man fond of his desserts. He said that at the dinner table and it made Pat laugh. But I don't worry about Pat Dolan's wife. I've already enough on my hands without adding Pat Dolan's wife. She gets fifty per cent of all that belongs to Pat Dolan. That's enough.

"What turns you on?" That is one question that Pat Dolan asks me several times. Whatever it is, he wants to do it for me. I am saying that plain ordinary straightforward sex is enough for me. I will probably go down in history as one of the most unusual people of the twentieth century. But I am a bit insulted by the question, as if Pat Dolan were just using this situation with me so that he can go home and try to turn on his wife. I think about the situation for a while, and I decide that I will say something.

"Jealousy."

"Jealousy turns you on? And is that why you sleep with married men?"

"I don't, except for my husband and now you."

I explain that I don't even think of my husband as a married man and that it's jealousy the other way around—that when my husband sleeps with other women it makes me jealous. My husband isn't a dessert person. He's a main-course person.

"And do you not like ever to look around at a table and say to yourself, 'I've had them all'?" Pat Dolan wants to know.

But I never think that way. Now I do. I'm wondering what Pat Dolan's mother might be like.

We talk about life in America. Pat Dolan wants to know what my life is like there. I say that some sad things have happened to me and that living with an Irish carpenter is not always easy, and that emotionally I have probably survived, like one of the Kennedys but without the glamor or the consolation prizes. But I don't want to talk about things that have happened, in case it ruins our day together.

"Fair enough," says Pat Dolan.

Shortly before he goes he makes a telephone call. He says to the person that he can be reached at this number for the next half hour. He's feeling the flesh on one of my thighs and talking in such a businesslike manner about land contracts that I have to put my hand over my mouth to stop myself laughing. When he puts down the phone he looks at his watch. He'll have to go. The courts will be closed, he says.

"Is that where you're meant to be?"

"Yes."

It's about four o'clock. The sun is shining in on the wall at the end of the bed. I can hear children playing outside on the road. It feels like one of those long days when I was a child and was ill in bed all day. Next, I'm listening to Pat Dolan taking a shower. Usually there's just been my mother and my sister and me in this house. My father came home in the summers sometimes, when I was a teen-ager. I never remember my father and mother sleeping in the same room. Once my father had left his pajamas on my mother's bed, and she threw them out the door at him. I used to say to her that if she could have been nicer to my father he wouldn't have gone away.

Then I'm watching Pat Dolan getting dressed. He's saying that he might visit me in America if he can think up a good enough excuse to get away. He's wondering if I ever think of coming back to live in Ireland permanently. I say that I do think of coming back to Ireland but I'm not sure how I can do that and live decently. "If I came back to Ireland, would I be your mistress?" I ask.

"There's a strong possibility, a strong possibility."

I begin to imagine myself as a successful barrister's mistress. It always sounds fun to be the mistress. I imagine myself walking through town with my head held high. I will become impatient with people who waste my time. I will slap policemen. I will go up in lights: "FROM PRESCHOOL TEACHER TO COURTESAN." I will choose hats to wear at the horse show. I will overhear sharp remarks. I will be humming "Don't Cry for Me, Argentina."

We agree to meet again. But we have to be very careful, Pat Dolan says, and I have to remember that I'm back in Ireland again now, in the land of the squinting windows.

"But I'll show you how it's done within the rules," Pat Dolan says on his way out the door. I'm laughing. He's such a rascal or something, and he's such a relief from Mass cards and condolences, even though other people were only trying their best. Often when I'm out of Ireland I think to myself that there's still somewhere in the world to look forward to. I walk around the house thinking that there are still things to be happy about.

I MET PAT Dolan at my mother's funeral. I kept thinking about that when I got back to America. I was in a Detroit department store buying a dress one day, coming up to Christmas. "Panis Angelicus" came on over the recorded background music. I was standing there thinking that the last time I heard that song was at my mother's funeral. It was beautifully sung. I was standing in the store listening to it again. The shop assistant was on the phone ringing up to see if my check was all right. My dress was being wrapped up in white tissue paper. The store was warm. I was standing there seeing myself in the whole scene—the store now and me buying a dress and remembering Dublin—and I felt as if my life were a movie and not really my life at all.

But now my husband knows about me and Pat Dolan, and I'm in trouble with him. He wants to know all the details. I tell him that Pat Dolan is a deadly normal man in his fifties, with five grown sons who are probably clones. The way my husband is going on you'd swear I'd been carrying on with Mick Jagger. He notices a little mark on one of my breasts while I'm drying myself in the bathroom, and he wonders where it comes from since he hasn't been near me for a week. I can remember when it was longer between times, but I'm explaining away the place, saying that it could be a little stretch mark from pregnancy. I'm feeling very much the woman in demand. It's good for a woman to feel desired, so Pat Dolan says. He likes to invite people out to dinner and to know that he has slept with the other men's wives at the table. He wants to know what turns me on. I'm thinking that Pat Dolan sits opposite the Attorney General of Ireland in the law library of the Four

Courts, some days, and then I think of the Profumo affair and the downfall of governments or something on that line that I would like to happen. Not that I would do anything purposely mean to Pat Dolan. I would like something to happen, something big like the Profumo affair, and to see it in the headlines of the newspaper for some form of relief—from what, I am not quite sure. Show me what you're good at, says Pat Dolan when I tell him about the failures in my life. Yes, those men had sex with someone they're not supposed to, and, yes, it was me, I will say at my interview. I'm not a Russian spy, but I still consider my-self to be an important person to have sex with.

(1991)

ELKA AND MEIR

ISAAC BASHEVIS SINGER

On the nights that Meir Bontz could allow himself to sleep, his head would hit the pillow like a stone and, if undisturbed, he could pound away for twelve hours straight. But this night he awoke at dawn. His eyelids popped open and he could not close them again. His big, burly body heaved and jerked. He felt overcome with passion and worry. Meir Bontz was hardly a timid man. In his youth he had been a thief and a safecracker. In the thieves' den where the toughs congregated, he demonstrated his strength. None of them could bend his arm. Meir would often bet on his capacity for food and drink. He could put away half a goose and wash it down with a dozen mugs of beer. On the rare occasions that he was arrested, he would snap his handcuffs or smash the door of the patrol wagon.

After he married and was given a job at the Warsaw Benevolent Burial Society, which provided shrouds and burial plots for the indigent dead, Meir Bontz went straight. He received a salary of twenty rubles a week so long as the Russians ruled Poland, and later, when the Germans came in, a comparable sum in marks. He stopped associating with thieves, fences, and pimps. He had fallen in love with a beauty, Beilka Litvak, a cook in a wealthy house on Marszalkowska Street. But with time he perceived that he had made a mistake in his marriage. For one thing, Beilka didn't become pregnant. For another, she spat blood. For a third, he could never get used to her pronunciation—"Pig Litvak," he called it. She lost her looks as well. When she got angry, she cursed him with oaths the like of which he had never heard. She could read, and each day she read the serialized novels in the Yiddish newspaper about duped ladies, scheming counts, and seduced orphans. During meals, Meir Bontz liked to listen to the gramophone play theatre melodies, duets, and cantorial pieces, but Beilka complained that the gramophone gave her a headache. A quarrel would often break out on Friday evening just because Meir liked his gefilte fish prepared with sugar as his dead mother used to fix it, and Beilka prepared it with pepper. The few times that Meir hit her, Beilka fainted, and Zeitag the healer or Dr. Kniaster had to be called.

He would have run away from Warsaw if God hadn't sent along Red Elka. It was Red Elka's job in the Society to look after the female corpses, sew their shrouds, and wash them on the ablution board. Red Elka had no luck. She had trapped herself in a union with a sick husband who was surly and half crazy to boot. In addition, he turned out to be lazy. His name was Yontche. He was a bookbinder by trade. On Bloody Wednesday, in 1905, when the Cossacks killed dozens of revolutionaries who had converged on the town hall to demand a constitution from the czar, Yontche caught a bullet in the spine. Afterward, he had a kidney removed in the hospital on Czysta Street, and he never completely recovered. Elka had two children by him, both of whom died of scarlet fever. Although Elka had already passed forty—she was three years older than Meir—she still looked like a girl. Her red hair cut in a Dutch bob didn't have a gray strand in it. Elka was small and slim. Her eyes were green as a cat's, her nose beaklike, her cheeks red as apples. Elka's power lay in her mouth. When she laughed, you could hear her halfway down the street. When she abused somebody, words and phrases shot from her sharp tongue until you didn't know whether to laugh or cry. Elka had strong teeth, and in a fight she would bite like a bitch.

When Elka first came to the Society and Meir Bontz observed her antics, he was frightened of her. She bantered with the dead as if they were still alive. "Lie quiet there, hush!" she would admonish a corpse. "Don't play any of your tricks. We'll pack you in a shipping crate and send you off. You danced away your few years and now it's time to go nighty-night."

Once, Meir saw Elka take a cigarette from her mouth and stick it between a corpse's lips. Meir told her that one must not do such things. "Don't fret your head about it," she said. "I'll get so many whippings in Gehenna anyhow, it'll only mean one lash more." And she slapped her own buttock!

It wasn't long before Meir Bontz fell in love with Elka, with a passion he would not have thought possible. He yearned for her even when they were together. He could never get enough of her spicy talk.

As a boy, and even later, Meir Bontz had often boasted that he would never be tied to a woman's apron strings. When a wench started to play hard to get or to nag him, he would tell her to go to blazes. He used to say that in the dark all cats are gray. But he couldn't resist Elka. She made fun of his size and bulk, his enormous appetite, his huge feet, his rumbling voice—all in good nature. She called him "buffalo," "bear," "bull." Playfully, she tried to plait braids in his mop of bristly hair, as Delilah had done to Samson. It wasn't easy for Meir and Elka to have the time with each other they wanted. He couldn't come to her house or she to his. They tried to seek out rooms where you could spend the night without registering. Often they couldn't even do this; before they left their houses they would be summoned to the scene of a tragedy—someone had been run over, or had hanged himself, or jumped out of a window, or been burned to death. In such cases autopsies were demanded by the police, who had to be outwitted or bribed, since autopsies were against Jewish law. Red Elka always found a way. She spoke Russian and Polish, and after the Germans occupied Warsaw in 1915 she learned to converse with their policemen in German-Yiddish. She would flirt with the krauts and skillfully slip banknotes into their pockets.

Red Elka eventually managed it so that Meir Bontz became her assistant and her coachman, and later her chauffeur. The Society had acquired a car that was dispatched to bring in corpses from the outskirts and the resort towns on the Otwock line, and Meir learned to drive. Sometimes the couple had to ride at night through fields and forests, and this provided them the best opportunity to make love. Red Elka would sit beside Meir and with the eyes of a hawk search out a spot where they could lie down undisturbed. She would say, "The corpse will have to wait. What's his hurry? The grave won't go sour."

Elka smoked as she kissed Meir and at times even as she gave herself to him. Her time for childbearing had passed, but lust had grown within her over the years. When Meir Bontz was with her, he wanted to forget that he worked for a burial society, but Elka wouldn't let him forget. She would say, "Oy, Meir, when you kick the bucket what a heavy corpse you'll be! You'll need eight sets of pallbearers."

"Shut your yap!"

"You're trembling, eh? No one can avoid it."

Red Elka developed such power over Meir that things which had once seemed repellent now attracted him. He used her expressions, began smoking her brand of cigarettes, and ate only her favorite dishes. Elka never got drunk, but after a drink she became more flippant than ever. She blasphemed, made fun of the Angel of Death, the destroying angels, of Gehenna, and the saints in Heaven. One time Meir heard her say to a corpse, "Don't fret, corpse, rest in peace. You left your wife a pretty dowry and your successor will be in clover with her." And she gave the dead man a tickle under the armpit.

It wasn't Meir Bontz's way to think too much. As soon as he started to concentrate, his brain would cloud over and he'd get sleepy. He realized well enough that Elka's conduct toward the dead came from some idiotic urge stuck in her mind like a wedge, but he reminded himself that every woman he had known had had her peculiarities. Meir had even had one who ordered him to beat her with a strap and spit on her. During his few stays in prison, he heard stories from other convicts that made his hair stand on end.

Well, since he had commenced his affair with Elka, thoughts assailed Meir like locusts. Tonight, he slept at home—he in one bed and Beilka in the other. He had slept several hours when suddenly he awoke with the anxiety of one who has fallen into a dilemma. Beilka snored, whistled through her nose, sighed. Meir had proposed a divorce—he offered to go on supporting her—but Beilka refused. In the dark, he could see only Elka before his eyes. She joked with him and called him outlandish names. Elka was far from virtuous. For years she had worked in a brothel on Grzybowska Street. She had undoubtedly had more men in her life than Meir had hairs on his head. She had enjoyed a passionate affair with a panderer, Leibele Marvicher, who had been stabbed to death by Blind Feivel. Elka still cried when she talked about this pimp. Just the same, Meir was ready to marry her if she was free from Yontche. Someone had told him that in America there were private funeral parlors and one could get rich there from operating such an enterprise. Meir had a fantasy: he and Elka went to America and opened a funeral parlor. Yontche the consumptive died, and Meir got rid of Beilka. In the New Land no one knew of his criminal activities or of Elka's whoring. The whole day they would be busy with the corpses, and in the evenings they would go to the theatre. Meir would become a member of a rich synagogue. They had sons and daughters and lived in their own house. The wealthiest corpses in all New York were brought to their funeral parlor. A wild notion flashed through Meir's brain—they did not have to wait. He could make away with Beilka in half a minute; all he had to do was give her throat one squeeze. Elka could slip Yontche a pill. Since they were both sick anyhow, what difference did it make if they went a year sooner or a year later?

A fear fell over Meir from his own thoughts, and he began to grunt and scratch. He sat up with such force that the bed springs squealed.

Beilka awoke. "Why are you squirming around like a snake? Let me sleep!"

"Sleep, Litvak pig."

"You've got the itch, have you? So long as I breathe she'll never be your wife. A tart is what she'll stay, a slut, a tramp, a whore from 6 Krochmalna Street, may she burn like a fire, dear Father in Heaven!"

"Shut up, woman, or you're a dead one on the spot!"

"You want to kill me, eh? Take a knife and stab away. Compared to this life, death would be Paradise." Beilka began to cough, cry, spit.

Meir got out of bed. He knew that Elka had wallowed in a brothel on Grzybowska Street, but 6 Krochmalna Street was news to him. Ap-

parently Beilka knew more about Elka than he did. He was overcome
with rage and a need to shout, to drag Beilka around by her hair. He
knew the brothel at 6 Krochmalna—a windowless cellar, a living grave.
No, it couldn't be—she's making it up. He felt about to retch.

THE YEARS PASSED, and Meir Bontz didn't rightly know where. Beilka
suffered one hemorrhage after another, and he had to put her in a sanatorium in Otwock. The doctors said that she wasn't long for the world,
but somehow there in the fresh air they kept her soul flickering. Meir
had to pay her expenses. He now had the apartment to himself, and
Elka was free to come to him. Elka's husband Yontche ailed at home.
But the lovers didn't have the time to be together. After the war broke
out on that day of Ab in 1914, the shootings, stabbings, and suicides
multiplied. Refugees converged upon the city from half of Poland. The
black car was constantly in use collecting corpses. Meir and Elka
couldn't give up even an hour to pleasure. Their affair consisted of talk,
kisses, plans. When the Germans occupied Warsaw, hunger and typhus
emptied whole buildings. Still, Elka lost none of her light-mindedness.
Death remained a joke to her—an opportunity to revile God and man,
to repeat over and over that life hung on a hair, that hopes were spider-
webs, that all the promises about a world to come, the Messiah, and
Resurrection were lies, and that whatever wasn't seized now was lost forever. But to seize you needed time. Elka would complain, "You'll see,
Meir, we won't even have time to die."

Elka had almost stopped eating. She nibbled on a cookie, a sausage, a
bar of chocolate. She drank whiskey and smoked. Meir got along on un-
cooked food. In the middle of the night the telephone would ring and
they would be summoned to police headquarters, to the Jewish Hospital on Czysta Street, to the Hospital for Epidemic Diseases on Pokorna
Street, to the morgue. They no longer even took off Sabbaths and holidays. The other employees of the Society got summer vacations, but no
one could or would substitute for Elka or Meir. They were the only ones
who had established connections with the police, the civil authorities,
the military, the officials of the Gesia and the Praga Cemeteries.

Meir's apartment had grown dusty and neglected. Plaster fell from
the walls. Since tenants had stopped paying rent, landlords had ceased

making repairs. Pipes that burst from the frosts were not fixed. Toilets
became clogged. On the rare occasions Elka prepared to spend the
night at Meir's, she tried to straighten up, but the telephone always interrupted her. The couple was called in to attend victims of shootings,
of fires, of heart attacks in the street. As the telephone rang, Elka would
exclaim, "Congratulations. It's the Angel of Death!" And before Meir
could ask what had happened she would be throwing on her clothes.

IN RUSSIA, THE czar had abdicated. The Germans had begun to suffer
setbacks at the front. Somehow between a yes and a no, Poland had become independent, but this didn't slow the sicknesses and deaths. For a
short time peace prevailed; then the Bolsheviks invaded Poland, and
once again refugees from the provinces invaded Warsaw. In the towns
they captured, the Bolsheviks shot rabbis and wealthy men. The Poles
hanged Communists. Elka's husband, Yontche, died, but Elka didn't observe shivah. Meir couldn't read or write, and she was needed to read
documents, to sign papers, and mark down names and addresses. Because the two worked long hours, they earned a lot of money, but infla-
tion had made it worthless. The several hundred rubles Meir had saved
up for a rainy day were now worthless and lay in an open drawer—no
thief would bother to touch them. Elka had bought jewelry, but she had
no opportunity to wear it. When Meir asked one time why she didn't
put on her trinkets, she said, "When? You'll place them in the pockets of
my shrouds." She was referring to the proverb that shrouds have no
pockets.

Meir had long since gathered that Elka didn't only make fun of other
corpses—her own death too seemed to her a game, a jest, or the Devil
knew what. Meir disliked to talk of death, but Elka brought up at every
opportunity that what she was doing would undoubtedly be done to
her. She had already arranged for a plot at the Gesia Cemetery—the
Society had given her a bargain on it. She had made Meir vow that
when he died he would be put to rest not next to Beilka but next to her,
Elka. Meir would often lose his temper at her: she was just beginning
to live; what kind of talk was this?

But Elka would counter, "You're scared, eh, Meirl? No one knows
what his tomorrow will be. Death doesn't look at the calendar." Every-

one in her family had died young—her father, her mother, her sister Reitza, her brother Chaim Fishl. How was she any better than the others?

Meir received a phone call from Otwock telling him that Beilka had died. She had eaten breakfast that morning as on any other day. She had even tried reading the novel in the Yiddish newspaper, but at lunchtime when the nurse came to take her temperature she found Beilka dead. Meir wanted to go to Otwock by himself, but Elka insisted she come with him. As always, she got her way. Since Meir had arranged for a plot for himself next to Elka, Beilka was buried in Karczew, a village near Otwock. Although the women of the Karczew Burial Society considered this sacrilege, Elka fussed over Beilka's body, washed her with an egg yolk, and sewed her shrouds.

She shouted down into Beilka's grave, "We will come to you, not you to us. May you intercede for us on High!"

It seemed now that Meir and Elka would immediately marry. Why keep two apartments? Why maintain two households? But Elka kept putting it off. She refused to marry until a year had passed. She had read somewhere that until the first anniversary the soul still hovered among those close to it. After the year passed, Elka found new excuses. She wanted to change apartments, to buy new furniture, to get herself a wardrobe, to take a long leave of absence (she had years of vacation coming) and go to Paris. She talked this way and that—now seriously, now in jest. Meir Bontz hadn't forgotten his fantasies about America, but Elka argued, "What do you need with America? You don't live there forever either."

One night when Meir and Elka managed to get away and Meir was staying at her place, Elka took Meir's hand and guided it to her left breast. "Feel. Right there," she said.

Meir felt something hard. "What is it?"

"A growth. My mother died of the same thing. So did my Aunt Gittel."

"Go to the doctor first thing tomorrow."

"A doctor, eh? If my mother hadn't rushed to the doctors, she would have died an easy death. Those butchers hacked her to pieces. Meir, I'm not such a dunce."

"But it may turn out to be nothing."

"No, Meirl, it's a summons from up there."

These words served to arouse her, and the petting and kissing commenced. Elka liked to talk in bed, to question Meir about his former mistresses, his adventures with married women. She always demanded that he compare her with the others and describe in which ways she was better. At first, Meir hadn't liked this interrogation, but as always with Elka he got used to it. This time, she talked about the fact that neither the Society nor Meir would be able to get along without her. She would have to train a woman to replace her, teach her the trade. And while she was at it, the new woman could take Elka's place with Meir too.

Meir laid a heavy hand over Elka's mouth but she cried, "Take away your paw!" and she bit his palm.

From then on, by night and even by day as they drove around, Elka kept up her talk about dying. When Meir complained that he didn't want to hear such gabbing, Elka would say, "What's the big fuss? I'm no calf to be afraid of the slaughterer."

Elka didn't stop with words. Suddenly a cousin of hers materialized—a girl from a small town, who was black as a crow and slanty-eyed as a Tartar. She told Meir that she was twenty-seven, but she appeared to him to be past thirty. Like Elka, she drank whiskey and smoked cigarettes. Her name was Dishka. It was hard to believe that she and Elka were related. Where Elka was loquacious and playful, Dishka measured her words. No smile ever showed on her mouth or in her sulky dark eyes. Meir hated her on sight. Elka took her along to the funerals. She helped Elka wash down the corpses and sew shrouds. Dishka had been a seamstress in the sticks where she came from and she was even more skillful than Elka at tearing the linen—scissors were not allowed—and basting with broad stitches. One time when Elka had some business to attend to in the city, Dishka accompanied Meir in the hearse to a suburb where a slain Jew had been found. The entire way there Dishka didn't utter a word. Suddenly she laid her hand on Meir's knee and began to tickle him and arouse him. He took her hand and put it back in her lap. That night, Meir lay awake until dawn. His skull nearly burst from all the thinking he did. He both sweated and felt chills run up and down his spine. Should he force Elka to get rid of Dishka? Should he leave everything behind him and run off by himself to America? Should he wait till Elka passed on and then slit his throat over her grave? Should he leave the Burial Society and become a porter or teamster? Without Elka, the thought of everything seemed to be hollow. Meir had never drunk by himself, but now he uncorked a bottle in the dark and downed half of it. For the first time, he felt terror come over him. He knew that Dishka would bring misfortune upon him. No one could take Elka's place. Meir stationed himself by the window, gazed out into the night, and said to himself, "The whole damned thing isn't worth a penny anymore."

ELKA WAS CONFINED to bed. The growth in her breast had spread and the other breast had developed growths as if overnight. Elka suffered such pain the doctors kept her going with morphine. Professor Mintz tried to persuade Elka to enter the Jewish Hospital, where she could be treated with radium therapy. Maybe she could be operated on and saved from a quick death. But Elka told him, "To me, a quick death is better than a lingering illness. I'm ready for the journey."

Sick as she was, Elka remained employed by the Society. Meir had to report every corpse, every burial to her. Even though he despised Dishka—that country yokel—he had to admit she had her good points. When Elka became bedridden, Meir moved in with her, while Dishka moved into his place. She swept the rooms, took it upon herself to throw out all the old dishes and broken pots Beilka had left—she even persuaded the landlord to have the place painted, the ceiling patched, and new floors laid. In the mornings, when Meir met Dishka at the Society or at work, she always brought him food—not the cookies or chocolate on which Elka sustained herself but chicken, beefsteak, meatballs. Elka needed only one drink to commence babbling her nonsense, but Dishka could drink a lot and remain sober. Meir could never make her out. How was it that such a piece could emerge from some godforsaken village? From where did she draw her strength? His own experience had taught Meir that small-town creatures were all miserable cowards, foolish mollycoddles, always snivelling, complaining.

One day the woman who watched over Elka became sick herself, and the one who was supposed to substitute for her had gone to spend the night with a daughter in Pelcowizna. Elka had got an injection from Zeitag the healer, and Meir sat by her bed until it took hold. Just before she fell asleep, she demanded Meir's solemn vow that after her death he would marry Dishka, but Meir refused. Early in the morning he was wakened by the telephone. An actor who for many years had played the role of a lover on the Yiddish stage, first at the Muranow Theatre and later at other theatres and on the road, had died in the sanatorium in Otwock. On Smocza Street an alcohol cooker had caused a fire, killing five children. A young man on Nowolipki Street had hanged himself and the police wanted his body for dissection. Meir washed and shaved. Elka heard the news and wanted details. She had known the actor and admired his acting, singing, and jokes. All those deaths in one day revived her spirits, and for a while she conversed in a healthy voice. The woman who watched over her wasn't due till ten and Meir was loath to leave her alone, but Elka said, "What more can happen to me?" She smiled and winked.

The whole day, Meir and Dishka were so busy they didn't have time to eat. Meir tried to speak to her about the tragedy of the children. Dishka said nothing. Meir remembered that in similar circumstances Elka was always ready with an appropriate comment. He couldn't live with a grouch like Dishka for even two weeks.

The custom in the sanatorium was to keep a corpse all day in cold storage and release it late at night in order not to alarm the other patients. The whole day, Meir and Dishka were occupied in the city and it was late evening by the time they started out for Otwock. The night was dark and rainy, with no moon or stars. Meir tried again and again to strike up a conversation with Dishka but she replied so curtly that soon there was nothing left for him to say. What does she think about the whole time, Meir wondered. Surliness—it's nothing else. Doing you a favor by sitting beside you.

They drove past the Praga Cemetery. Against the big-city red sky the tombstones resembled a forest of wild toadstools. Meir began to speak in Elka's tone: "A city of the dead, eh? Wore themselves out and lay down. You believe in God?"

"I don't know," Dishka replied after a long pause.

"Who then created the world?"

Dishka didn't answer and Meir became enraged. He said, "What point is there in being born if this is how it ends? On Karmelicka Street there's a workers' house, that's what it's called, and a big shot was giving a speech there. I happened to be walking by and I went inside to listen. He said that there is no God. Everything had made itself. How can everything just come from itself? Stupid!"

Dishka still didn't respond, and Meir resolved not to say another word to her that night. He felt a deep longing for Elka. "She dare not die!" he mumbled. "She dare not! If it's fated that one of us must go, let it be me."

The car passed Wawer, a village full of Gentiles; then Miedzeszyn, which was being built; then Falenica, where rabbis, Chassidim, and plain pious Jews came out for the summers; and later Michalin, Jozefow, Swider, where the intelligentsia gathered—Zionists, Bundists, Communists, and those who no longer wanted to speak Yiddish but only Polish.

Elka's sickness had stirred Meir Bontz's brain and he began pondering things. What, for instance, had this Dishka done in that village she came from? No doubt in the war years she had been a smuggler or a whore. Suddenly he thought of Beilka. At first she hadn't wanted him, and he had knelt before her and sworn eternal love. He had found her Lithuanian accent especially endearing. Years later, when she got sick, every word she spoke irritated him. He had one request of her: that she be silent. Yet with Elka the more she talked the more he wanted to hear.

Meir drove up to the cold-storage room at the sanatorium. Everything went off quickly, quietly, like a conspiracy. A door opened and two individuals transferred a box into his hearse. He didn't even see their faces. Not a word was spoken. In the brief time the door to the cold-storage room stood open, Meir caught a glimpse of two more such boxes. Before a long table on which burning candles spluttered and dripped tallow sat an old man reciting Psalms. A blast of cold like that from an ice cellar issued from the room. Meir grabbed the bottle of vodka he carried in his pocket and in one gulp drained it. As he headed back toward Warsaw, his life flashed before him—the poverty-stricken home, the thefts, the fights, the brothels, the whores, the arrests. "How was I able to endure such a Gehenna?" he asked himself, and he recalled a saying of his mother's: "God preserve us from all the things one can get used to."

The car entered a forest. Meir drove fast and in zigzags. He wanted Dishka to plead with him to slow down but she sat obstinately silent, staring out into the darkness.

Meir said, "Don't be afraid. I won't kill the corpse."

A whim to be spiteful came over him, along with an impulse to test his luck, like the reckless desire of a gambler who grows tired of the game and risks all he possesses. The headlights cast a glare upon the pines, houses, gardens, pumps, balconies. From time to time Meir cast a sidelong glance at Dishka. "Life is apparently not worth a pinch of snuff to her," he said to himself.

The hearse came out onto a stretch of road running through a clearing. It skidded as if going downhill, carried along by its own impetus. At once Meir felt gay and lighthearted. Nothing to worry about, he thought. Things will take care of themselves. He almost forgot his sullen passenger. It's good to live. One day I may even go to America. There is no lack of females and corpses there. He drove and dreamed. Elka rode with him, disguised as someone else, joking and frolicking, challenging his prowess. Suddenly a tree materialized before his eyes. A tree in the middle of the road? No, he had gone off the highway. It's one of her tricks, Meir thought. He wanted to step on the brake, but his foot pressed the accelerator. "That's it!" something within him shouted. He heard a tremendous crash and everything went silent.

THE NEXT DAY, a peasant going to work early found a smashed car with three dead. The back door of the hearse had been torn off and the box containing the actor's body had fallen out. A crowd gathered; the police were called. From Warsaw the Benevolent Burial Society sent out two other hearses to pick up the bodies. The president and the warden decided not to let Elka know, but a female member who was watching over her learned the news on the radio and told Elka. When Elka heard it she began to laugh and couldn't stop. Soon the laughter turned into hiccups.

When they had stopped, she got out of bed and said, "Hand me my clothes."

In the two days it took to arrange the funerals Elka regained her strength. Everyone in the Society observed her liveliness with amazement. She cleansed Dishka and prepared shrouds for her and Meir. She ran from room to room, slammed doors, issued orders. She talked to the bodies with her usual teasing: "Ready for the journey? Packed away in the shipping crate?"

Warsaw had two big funerals. Actors, writers, and theatre lovers gathered around the actor's coffin. Around Meir's and Dishka's came the thieves, pimps, whores, fences from Krochmalna, Smocza, Pocezjow, and Tamki Streets. The war, the typhus epidemics, starvation had almost destroyed the city's underworld. The Communists had taken over their taverns, their dens, the square on Krochmalna Street, but enough of the old-timers remained to pay their final respects to Meir. Elka rode with them. She looked quite youthful and pretty in her black suit and black-veiled hat. Meir Bontz and Red Elka were still remembered. The droshkies stretched from Iron Street to Gnoyna Street. Meir Bontz had supported a Talmud Torah, and a teacher with dozens of students walked before the hearse crying, "Justice shall walk before him."

At the cemetery, two coachmen lifted Elka up onto a tombstone and she made a short eulogy: "My Meir, stay well. I'll come to you. Don't forget me, Meir. I've got a plot right next to yours. What we had together no one can ever take away from us, not even God!"

She addressed herself to Dishka: "Rest in peace, my sister. I wanted to give you everything, but it wasn't fated." With these words, Elka collapsed.

She was finally taken to a hospital, but the cancer had spread too far for there to be any hope of saving her. Elka sat up in bed propped against two pillows while the women from the Burial Society came to ask about her and to pass along word of what was going on. New people had been hired, but the Angel of Death remained the same. Linen had gone up, the community demanded more money for the plots, the headstone carvers had raised their prices. Jewish sculptors had begun to carve all kinds of designs on the tombstones of the rich—lions, deer, even faces of birds, almost like the practice of the Gentiles. Elka listened, asked questions. Her face had turned yellow, but her eyes remained as green as gooseberries. Now that Meir was in the beyond, Elka had nothing to regret. Everything was ready for her—a plot, shrouds, shards for her eyelids, and a branch of myrtle with which she, together with Meir, would dig their way through the caves and roll to the Land of Israel when the Messiah came.

(Translated, from the Yiddish, by Joseph Singer.)

(1977)

SCULPTURE 1

ANGELA PATRINOS

At the beginning of September, I went to the Artemis Academy of Figurative Art looking for work. There I was told a female model was needed for Sculpture 1. The pay wasn't as much as I had hoped, but I filled out the form with my name, Martha Gilmeister, my Social Security number, and the rest of it. This was a year ago; I was twenty-two. I'd been in New York City for nine months. The week before, I'd been working as a go-go dancer but not naked—not even partially. I felt I'd be O.K., though, as a nude model because I was used to standing on platforms and being looked at.

And so, on Monday morning, on the third floor of the Academy, I walked from the dressing room toward the sculpture studio wearing a new but cheap navy-blue robe, unprepared for the fear that was rising inside me. Garbage pails full of wet gray clay stood outside the studio door. Inside, bricks of fresh clay wrapped in plastic lay in opened cardboard boxes. The floor was chalky with dried clay. Metal and wood sculpture stands were being wheeled around by students, many of whom were my age, but the fact that they were in school made them seem younger to me. On top of the stands, nailed to boards, were wire armatures, three feet tall, ready to be bent into pose.

I sat on a stool and faced a wall of windows, which faced some windows of another building across the way, where a couple of people moved about in an office. Leaning against a windowsill next to his armature and stand was an Indian man in his middle forties. He had a container of coffee in one hand and a half-eaten Danish in the other. I'd seen him that very morning, walking from the subway, his head bent under a broken-jointed umbrella, the material flapping as he walked. He wore purple-and-black running shoes with shards of neon-green reflectors on the heels. It was the reflectors that reminded me I'd seen him earlier—it had surprised me how they shone even on this gray, wet day. He was wearing a maroon sweater over an oxford shirt, and had a high, compact belly.

The instructor came in and began yanking open the skinny locker doors that lined one wall. "It's not here," he said. "Nothing's ever where it's supposed to be, because the right hand of this school is the left's biggest mystery." Creases ran from his nose to the corners of his mouth; his brow was knotted but no laugh lines marked the skin around his eyes. He told me his name, Dewey Boxwell, and I laughed, mostly from nerves. No one else laughed: they knew his name and knew that he was an established sculptor.

Boxwell found what he was looking for in the last locker, a human skeleton, and hooked it onto a stand. The skeleton was so small that I thought it had been removed from a museum exhibit on evolution. Boxwell told me to get up on the platform, which was in the center of the room. The platform was two and a half feet high and had an outsized lazy Susan in the middle, so the model could be rotated periodically. I knew I would get a break every twenty minutes, but what did twenty minutes feel like? I didn't know.

As I untied my robe, the young students turned to their armatures and Boxwell blew his nose. But the Indian watched. The robe slipped out of my hands and I lowered myself to pick it up, bending at the knees so as not to stick out my behind. My nipples brushed my thighs, one knee made a clicking noise. I thought of home—Milwaukee! Lawn Avenue! My heart ticked rapidly. The robe was retrieved, and I stepped onto the platform. Single lines of sweat ran from my armpits down my thick torso.

AS A TEEN-AGER I'd worn a bracelet popular with the girls at Pershing High: a thin gold chain studded with diamond chips. The first morning after I got one, I put it on and felt dainty but by the last class of the day the smallness of it made me feel looming and slablike, and the recollection of the way my voice had sounded begging my parents to buy it pained me. I gave it away to a girl who thought I was doing it to be her friend.

I moved through the school hallways supporting my books on wide hips; my straight dark hair was pulled back in a ponytail, which I used hair spray on. I had a thin nose and a thin mouth set into a heavy, fleshy face. There were small scars under my eyebrows: during my second sophomore year (I'd flunked the first), I'd used a depilatory instead of tweezers and blistered the area so badly that it looked as though I'd whacked myself with a hot curling iron.

After I was finally permitted to graduate, I got a full-time job at the Milwaukee County Zoo, where I sat in a booth giving parking passes to hands sticking out of car windows. For four years, I worked at the zoo and lived at home. Sometimes, when I was in the primate house on my lunch break, the gorilla would lift a black hairy arm and pound with his fist on the thick Plexiglas in weighted slow-motion. Then he'd pause, rest his human fist on the concrete floor, and decide if the glass needed pounding once more. Do it again, I thought.

One summer evening, a party was held near the flamingo pond. I sold a parking pass to one of the guests. He had a New York license plate. On his way out, sitting behind the wheel of his car with his tie untied, he asked if he could call me. He said he'd be in town a few more days. Enough times I'd sat in the easy chair in front of the TV, saying to the girl on the screen, "Don't do it! Don't do it!"—knowing that she would and savoring the mistakes she was about to make.

This man, Ray, smiled both times he saw me in my ill-fitting bra, with the back riding up. Two weeks later, I moved to New York. Ray hadn't encouraged me—he didn't know I was there until after I had moved. My parents were surprised but probably relieved; there were houses in my neighborhood where thirty-five-year-old "kids" still lived with their mothers and fathers.

Ray and I went out a few times, but then he became too busy to see me. That was O.K. There wasn't room in the city for what had begun in another place. At first the speed of the subways scared me, and for a week I walked and walked, stopping to rest in the nearest park, drinking a soda or a can of beer from a paper bag. I found a two-room apartment in Alphabet City, which I shared with a girl who was a student at N.Y.U., and I looked for a job. I failed as a temp, was fired as a waitress, and then got the idea to try go-go dancing because Ray had once taken me to a place in Chelsea that had dancers. My roommate thought it would be a cool job.

For three months, at nine o'clock in the evening, I folded my net stockings, hot pants, and halter top neatly into a knapsack, put my lace-up boots in a shopping bag, and walked to the subway, token in hand so I wouldn't have to struggle to get it out of my tight jeans pocket. Each night the bouncer would look at me as though he'd never seen me before and then, without expression, say, "Marty."

My hips were agile but I was not a good dancer. Sometimes I would just stop moving and look around at all the activity in the place. I became aware that I was making less in tips than the other girls, so one night I stood in front of the clock on the microwave in my apartment until nine o'clock came and went, and again I was out of a job.

THAT FIRST DAY at the Academy it took only ten minutes for my curiosity to eclipse my fear. When that wore out, an interesting boredom took over, and when the boredom became ordinary I rested my eyes on the man from India. I felt it was lucky that there was such an ugly face to look at. Because of this, I liked him more than I had at first.

His cheeks were brown, with yellow highlights and an underlying blush. Near his eyes and nose, the skin was darker and ashy. His hairline receded almost to the top of his head; the hair in back was shiny and black and trimmed neatly down to his neck, where there was a roll of skin the width of a finger. His upper teeth pushed out too far over the lower, and this appeared to make it difficult for him to put his lips together.

He stood a couple of inches away from his armature while he worked, pinching off pieces of clay from the lump on his stand and pushing them into the wire. "Get into the habit right now of standing back so you can see what the hell you're doing," Boxwell told him. The Indian took three steps back and knocked into the skeleton, which clacked against its stand.

During the one-hour lunch break, I rested on a torn vinyl couch in the hall, near a pay phone and the elevator. I wished I had a magazine. The elevator was broken and from behind the closed doors I could hear the clanking of attempted repairs. Just before the afternoon session was to begin, the Indian man came up to me and held out a brown paper bag heavy with food smells.

"I could not eat it all," he said.

"No, thanks," I said.

"Take it," he said.

"No, thank you," I said.

He stood there looking at me with his sea-horsy face.

"I'm not hungry," I said.

He put the bag next to me on the couch and walked into the studio. I waited and then set the bag down inside a trash can and placed an old newspaper over it. I paused—I'd been taught not to waste. I reached back into the trash can for the bag. One of the other models, who'd been passing, stopped and looked at me.

"Did that Indian guy just try to give you his leftovers?" she asked.

"Uh, yeah," I said. "I mean, I guess."

"He tried to give me some the other day. I threw it out. Just wait— he'll ask you out for coffee next."

The sun came out in the afternoon and by four o'clock it was glaring off the windows of the building across the way. At four-thirty, class was over and I put my robe on and left the studio. The passage of the day felt miraculous—miraculous, I mean, in the true sense. In the bathroom, I changed into my jeans and shirt and noticed that my hands were shaking. I had the feeling that my childhood had suddenly and disproportionately grown farther away, yet this new distance between it and me made me more of a child instead of less. Hours of nakedness had done that.

When I got home, I found the bag of food in my knapsack. It turned out the food wasn't leftovers—it was a full and untouched container of rice, vegetables, and chicken. Heated up, it was good.

BY THE BEGINNING of my third week at the Academy, the job had become pedestrian: students needed to see the human figure and I was, for now, that figure. I urged the hours along by taking note of the forming sculptures around the room. The young students seemed to know what they were doing, but the Indian man—whom I had begun to refer to in my mind as Gandhi—clearly did not.

"Proportions," Boxwell told Gandhi one Monday, "aren't your only problem. Your forms look flat and dried out. Only cadavers are flat and dried out." He exhaled loudly, preparing for the chore of instruction. "Crouch down below the platform," he said, "so you can view the model from an oblique angle. So you can see how dynamic the form is."

Gandhi approached the platform. "Do not worry," he said to me, moving closer and then stooping below me.

I myself had observed from such an angle the dynamic forms passing to and from Lake Michigan as I lay on the beach back home: testicles like fetal pigs squeezed into nylon, and monumental female behinds. Now I looked down past the swells and knobs of my body at Gandhi. The smell of my sweat mixed with the scent of my anti-perspirant. I prayed that he could not make out the details of my genitalia, but if he could I hoped the sight would in some way hurt him, like a jellyfish dragging along someone's unlucky face.

The brown of his pupils seemed to bleed into the whites, which weren't really white but a yellow-pink. There was a tiny black mole on his right lower eyelid.

HE WAS STANDING on Eighth Avenue, near the steps of the Academy. "I'm sorry for saying to you 'Don't worry' in the class," he said. "I did not want to draw attention, but you seemed tense. You are brave. I don't think I could do it—stand there—and my point is, for this I admire you."

I rolled my eyes. "A lot of people do this," I said.

"Yes, but they are stupid people. I am Fazal Abdul Malik. Would you like to get a coffee?"

I was embarrassed for myself. I hadn't realized how much I longed for company.

"I AM NOT artist," he told me as we sat at the counter of Nick's Coffee Shop, "but ever since I went to Italy I want to try and make sculptures. I will try to make a good one of you, don't worry."

I said I didn't care if he made a good one or not. He dismissed this with a wave of his hand.

"The Academy must have been hard to get into," I said.

"The school takes anyone who does not need scholarship," he said. "They have money troubles. Everyone knows this."

I didn't know this. "It doesn't embarrass you?" I asked.

"I am there to make sculpture. The problem with school is not my problem. Are you married?"

I laughed. No one had asked me this before. "Yeah, right," I said, and to make sure he didn't misunderstand me, I shook my head.

"I have a wife in Pakistan," he said.

"Here I was thinking you were from India," I told him. "I was thinking of you as Gandhi."

"Gandhi! I am glad to not be!" He let out a high-pitched laugh, and I felt people turn to look at us.

"What's your wife like?" I asked.

"I don't know," he said.

"You don't know?"

"My point is, I know, but what to say? I'm afraid of her. I think she will shoot me when she sees me. I think she has already killed me five times." He laughed.

I didn't know what he meant so I just smiled. Then he asked, "You know the Michelangelo 'David'?"

"I've seen postcards," I said. And what else, I thought. "And those little plaster imitations or whatever."

"It is not the same. This is very beautiful sculpture. Are you student?"

"No."

"What university did you come from, then?"

"I didn't go to college."

I was too close to my failures to boast about my past, but I could not stop myself from adding, "I hardly made it through high school. I even flunked a grade. Tenth." In case he didn't know what "flunked" meant, I said, "They made me do it over again."

He frowned and sipped his coffee, one pinkie lifted. I looked around at the other people in the place, wondering how this conversation was going to end. Then he said, "I have fat belly, but my legs they are skinny. Also, I have short neck. Have you noticed these things?"

"I guess," I said.

"Do you like?"

I thought I was misunderstanding him. "Do I *like*?"

"Do you"—he made an emphatic sweeping gesture along his body— "*like*?"

He took a photograph out of his wallet. It was of him without a shirt. His belly was a milky ash-brown. He was standing next to a woman.

"My wife is pregnant here, but see—she does not look it. What I tell people when I show them this picture is, 'Guess which one is pregnant.' " He feigned seriousness and then laughed.

The woman in the photo had short black hair and chipped teeth. She had a hard, unforgiving face that didn't match her soft body. He put the photo away and looked at me. He pointed to the mole on his right lower eyelid.

"My mother had one also, but she used to draw over it with kohl. Now my daughter has one. Do you have children?"

I said I had none.

"Not anywhere?"

"Not anywhere that I know of."

"Ah, I was thinking"—he pressed his fingertips to his forehead—"I was thinking somewhere in my head that you were like a man—for just a small moment I was thinking that maybe you could have children you don't know about." He shook his head. "Sometimes I don't think right. But it's not because I see you as man. How could I? There you stand at the school."

By this point, I'd stopped listening to him. I was thinking how strange it was that he should show me a picture of himself without a shirt. Maybe he felt it was fair, because he'd seen me naked. But it wasn't as though I'd chosen what he had seen, and this made me want to make a selection, have a choice. It would have to be something personal—something I could tell him. I could tell him about Ray but that didn't seem very personal. I could tell him about the go-go bar and how I'd gotten less in tips than the other dancers, but that still kind of bothered me.

"Sometimes I don't remember if I dreamed something or if it really happened," I said. I'd heard a woman tell this to a man on the subway the other day.

"This never happens to me," he answered. "Sometimes they are very, very good and so it's impossible to take for real. Or they are very bad and so, same story. When you are awake, things are more . . . *even*."

Yes, I wanted to say, you're right, but I'd noticed that at the word "even" he had glanced at my chest, which is large and a bit lopsided. I told myself he already knew what I looked like, so what harm was a glance at my breasts, now that they were covered. I wanted to leave. I dug into my knapsack for money to pay for my coffee.

He reached over and pulled my hand out. A dollar bill drifted to the floor. "Do not offend me," he said, "by taking out this money."

On the train I could still feel the pressure on my wrist from his grasp.

BY OCTOBER, I was modelling at the Academy four days a week, not just for Sculpture 1 but also for painting, life drawing, and something called écorché. In sculpture class, I noticed that Boxwell continually had words for Fazal that were more nasty than constructive. Sometimes I was grateful for the meanness because it distracted me from the numbness and the pain in my legs, which was nearly unbearable at times. I saw the frustration and anger in Fazal's face when Boxwell spoke to him. Then I noticed the slight smiles some of the other students comforted themselves with, and I felt blood flow back into my fatigued, dense flesh.

Since the conversation we'd had over coffee, he and I had not spoken, but one Friday, at quarter to five, he was standing outside again. His posture was tight, and he shifted back and forth. When he saw me acknowledge him, he smiled as if we were dear friends, which annoyed me. But in his smile was eagerness, awe, and relief. The eagerness and awe were so real that they made me uncomfortable, and although the relief was somehow fake, this was what made me walk with him to a bar on Hudson Street.

Sitting at the bar, Fazal was quiet. I didn't want to talk about his failures at the Academy, so I came up with something I thought was safe. "Talk in your language," I said.

For a moment he was silent. Then words came and it seemed they could not stop. This isn't a real language, I thought, though I knew it was. What if my life depended on learning it? I could feel panic: I'd never be able to learn, even to save my life! As he continued, I started to pick up similar sounds and the pauses they were joined to, and thought maybe I would be able to save myself. I was so lost in this make-believe test that I didn't notice at first that tears were forming in his eyes. They spilled onto his cheeks and tracked along the sides of his nose and finally curved into his upper lip.

Since moving to New York, I had seen many things: a man defecating in the park, a woman with bright-red lipstick and no teeth, a crouching boy using the reflection in a hubcap to find a vein in his neck for a needle. But the sight of this man crying stung me. I stared at his shining face. I must have sensed that he was not asking for comfort and that to give it would be, in spite of his suffering, unnecessary. Or superfluous—I don't know. I didn't comfort him, though.

Fazal removed the damp napkin from under his glass of beer and blotted his eyes and wiped his mouth with it. He told me that he spent all his time at the Academy—sometimes he even stayed overnight—and no one there had asked about his language before. The only time he spoke Punjabi was with a shop owner from whom he bought special groceries a few times a month. This man was from India. But even if they had been from the same place Fazal would not have been friends with him. "You can tell if they are of the like mind," he said, "or if they are only taxi-driver."

He turned and looked me in the face. "And now you want to hear it but you do not know what I say. Martha, often I am thinking of you. Do you know why?"

With dread I thought, He's going to tell me he's in love with me. In my mind I heard myself telling somebody, "This old Pakistani guy, he thinks he's in love with me."

But he said, "You are the only naked woman in my life."

I said that the lives of students at the Academy were filled with naked women.

"Yes, but they are only picky nudes," he said, "and they act stuck up."

When I got home that night I said to my roommate, "This Indian guy, he thinks he's in love with me."

Of course I didn't believe it—that is, he hadn't said this, he hadn't even meant it. He had meant what he said.

THE NEXT MONDAY, Boxwell told Fazal that the head on his sculpture was too big and the hands and feet looked like stiff little flippers. "And those legs," he continued. "I don't know what they are, but they're not"—he jabbed at the clay—"*legs.*"

Boxwell walked away and Fazal pulled a large strip of clay off his sculpture and mashed it into the lump on the stand.

He was waiting for me outside at the end of the day. "I take 9 train," he said.

He lived at a hostel on Amsterdam Avenue. A printed fabric smelling of sausage covered the single bed, which served also as a couch. At a dresser, Fazal stood and unscrewed the lid of a tiny bottle and dabbed some scented oil on his neck. Above the dresser was a large poster of Michelangelo's "David."

To stall for time I asked how he met his wife.

"Why do you want to hear?" he said.

"Just because."

He sighed. "My sister said, when I was thirty-seven, 'I know someone for you to marry.' My sister had a friend who had a sister. One day, my sister, the woman, and I went walking. Sometimes my sister left me and this woman alone. And then, later, I went alone with my sister. 'Do you like each other?' she asked me. 'Yes,' I said, 'is O.K.' She was already thirty when we met and so it was past time for her to marry. But we both inside were thinking we could have done better. It is hard to get rid of that thought."

He looked at the poster for a moment and then continued. "Martha, it is bad to always expect pain, but pleasure it is good to be prepared for, right?" He removed a condom from the top drawer and turned to me. "It will be nice for you," he said. "First I will use my tongue."

He swooped down on me and pressed his lips on mine while reaching for the zipper on my jeans. My underwear was damp, which made no sense, because I wasn't attracted to him in that way. Maybe it was my body's way of telling me that it had stood around naked long enough without being touched. I grabbed Fazal's hands with my own and pressed his fingers together as hard as I could, squeezing them into clumps. When I let go, his knuckles were white. He sank into the couch as if I'd given him an injection.

"Forgive me for being too quick," he said. "It is just that I feel things must happen now if they are to happen at all."

That was the feeling I'd had in Milwaukee—the one that made me leave town. "I understand," I said.

"I understand," though, was the wrong thing to say. He tried to kiss me again and I had to put my hand over his face and push it away. I could feel his reaching tongue on my palm. "I'm going to leave," I threatened.

"Martha, don't leave. What else do you want to know? I will tell you anything."

I remembered that he had a daughter, so I asked about her.

"The last time I saw her was one year ago, at my mother's funeral. She kept running from me when I wanted to hold her. It is good for young girls to be afraid of strangers, so I should be happy for this, right?"

I said nothing.

"O.K., enough," he said. "Tell me what you think about the Michelangelo. For me, it is my favorite work of art."

I looked at the poster. "I don't like how its head doesn't match the body," I said. "It looks weird. Personally, I would have made the statue life-size. So people could relate to it more." I just added that—I hadn't considered it at all.

Abruptly, Fazal stood and turned his back to me. "If it were life-size," he said, "there would be no genius." He didn't even glance at me. It was hard to believe that minutes ago he'd wanted to have sex. Well, this is the end of this, I thought.

. . .

THE FOLLOWING AFTERNOON, Fazal tore the head off his sculpture and then removed a leg.

Boxwell, who was standing right there, said, "What are you doing?"

"I am starting again."

"It's too late for that. Put what you've taken off back on and do what you can with it."

Fazal did as he was told. It looked like a car accident. Then he left the studio.

After his exit, the dean of the Academy ushered in a group of men in dark, double-breasted suits and shiny shoes, and women with flat-link gold necklaces. There was to be a cocktail party for potential benefactors that evening at the school; the catering company had been setting up in the lobby that morning. I'd had no idea, though, that these people would be brought into the studio while I was on the platform.

When Boxwell noticed the group, he stepped in front of Fazal's sculpture and threw a large sheet of clay-splattered plastic over it. But the people were not really looking at Fazal's sculpture or at anyone's sculpture. They weren't looking at Boxwell or at the students. They were trying to look at these things until finally they gave in and looked at me.

Fazal returned and pushed past the group. He stood next to the skeleton and spoke. "It is inappropriate for these strangers to come in while the model is posing. There is nothing decent about this school. The instructor is hiding my sculpture while I am in toilet." He walked over to his sculpture, took the plastic off, and began to work, pinching and pushing the clay, his face inches away from it.

The dean ushered the group out with Boxwell following. "We have a few students who don't belong here," Boxwell was saying. It was not time for my break but I stepped off the platform and put my robe on.

"Go back up," Fazal told me. "The class is almost over for today and I have work."

"That's not her problem, man," one of the students said.

I took my robe off and went back up.

Again, he was waiting for me outside. Tiny flakes of snow, visible only against dark buildings, fell. "I have been awake since yesterday," he told me. "Will you come to my room?" His hands were pressed together.

MY ROOMMATE SUBSCRIBED to a number of thin, dull magazines, which I rarely looked at. But one evening I picked one up and turned to the ads in the back. "Teach English in Tashkent, Uzbekistan, No Experience Necessary," one said. I showed it to my roommate, laughing. She didn't know why I thought it was so funny. Neither did I—something about teaching a whole language and not needing to know how to do it. I sent for the information, and a couple of weeks later some pamphlets and an application form arrived. This was after Fazal had returned to Pakistan and I knew I was going to lose my job at the Academy. There were rumors that the school might close down.

Tashkent is the capital of Uzbekistan, a country in Central Asia in what used to be the Soviet Union. I had to come here to be able to say that. That is, know it by heart. It's a lethargic city made up of ugly modern buildings. But the buildings are not tall—there is plenty of open, dusty space for the sun to spill onto. A few mosques remain. I walked by one of them yesterday in the afternoon, and inside, where it was cool and dark, four mullahs were playing Ping-Pong.

You can't get a beer. The non-Americans I've met are infatuated with American English. Twice I've been told that I resemble Julia Roberts, and I have to remind myself that this comment isn't coming from stupid people. After all, every Pakistani I've met reminds me of Fazal, simply because of the accent.

Below Uzbekistan is Afghanistan and below that is Pakistan. I should say "south," but I do think of Pakistan as being under where I am, and I think of Fazal looking up at me from that oblique angle. I look down at his receding hairline.

I WENT WITH him on that day when he asked—it was the last time I saw him. We didn't sit down when we got to his room. He only wanted to change his clothes, he said, and then he'd take me out to dinner. It was early, only five-thirty. I knew we wouldn't make it to dinner.

"I am sorry," he said, "for reacting the way I did to your opinion about"—he flicked his hand over his shoulder toward the Michelangelo poster behind him. "I know you are only ignorant about the art. Last night I sat here looking at"—again, the gesture. "Maybe you were right, maybe it was cruel to make him so big. He is nothing but joke now. Oh, Martha, I have dread to go back home. I have failed. But I would like you to talk to me. Tell me something—I am begging you."

"Don't beg me," I said.

"I am not attractive when I beg? O.K., I will stop. Otherwise you will not lie down on the bed with me, right?"

He removed the cushions from the couch and we lay down. Almost immediately he began to snore; I remembered he hadn't slept in two days. I was hurt. I was relieved. I wasn't tired, though, and so I got up and quietly let myself out.

(1995)

DATING
YOUR MOM

IAN FRAZIER

In today's fast-moving, transient, rootless society, where people meet and make love and part without ever really touching, the relationship every guy already has with his own mother is too valuable to ignore. Here is a grown, experienced, loving woman—one you do not have to go to a party or a singles bar to meet, one you do not have to go to great lengths to get to know. There are hundreds of times when you and your mother are thrown together naturally, without the tension that usually accompanies courtship—just the two of you, alone. All you need is a little presence of mind to take advantage of these situations. Say your mom is driving you downtown in the car to buy you a new pair of slacks. First, find a nice station on the car radio, one that she likes. Get into the pleasant lull of freeway driving—tires humming along the pavement, air-conditioner on max. Then turn to look at her across the front seat and say something like, "You know, you've really kept your shape, Mom, and don't think I haven't noticed." Or suppose she comes into your room to bring you some clean socks. Take her by the wrist, pull her close, and say, "Mom, you're the most fascinating woman I've ever met." Probably she'll tell you to cut out the foolishness, but I can guarantee you one thing: she will never tell your dad. Possibly she would find it hard to say, "Dear, Piper just made a pass at me," or possibly she is secretly flattered, but, whatever the reason, she will keep it to herself until the day comes when she is no longer ashamed to tell the world of your love.

Dating your mother seriously might seem difficult at first, but once you try it I'll bet you'll be surprised at how easy it is. Facing up to your intention is the main thing: you have to want it bad enough. One problem is that lots of people get hung up on feelings of guilt about their dad. They think, Oh, here's this kindly old guy who taught me how to hunt and whittle and dynamite fish—I can't let him go on into his twilight years alone. Well, there are two reasons you can dismiss those thoughts from your mind. First, *every* woman, I don't care who she is, prefers her son to her husband. That is a simple fact; ask any woman who has a son, and she'll admit it. And why shouldn't she prefer someone who is so much like herself, who represents nine months of special concern and love and intense physical closeness—someone whom she actually created? As more women begin to express the need to have something all their own in the world, more women are going to start being honest about this preference. When you and your mom begin going together, you will simply become part of a natural and inevitable historical trend.

Second, you must remember this about your dad: you have your mother, he has his! Let him go put the moves on his own mother and stop messing with yours. If his mother is dead or too old to be much fun anymore, that's not your fault, is it? It's not your fault that he didn't realize his mom for the woman she was, before it was too late. Probably he's going to try a lot of emotional blackmail on you just because you had a good idea and he never did. Don't buy it. Comfort yourself with the thought that your dad belongs to the last generation of guys who will let their moms slip away from them like that.

Once your dad is out of the picture—once he has taken up fly-tying, joined the Single Again Club, moved to Russia, whatever—and your mom has been wooed and won, if you're anything like me you're going to start having so much fun that the good times you had with your mother when you were little will seem tame by comparison. For a while, Mom and I went along living a contented, quiet life, just happy to be with each other. But after several months we started getting into some different things, like the big motorized stroller. The thrill I felt the first time Mom steered me down the street! On the tray, in addition to my Big Jim doll and the wire with the colored wooden beads, I have my desk blotter, my typewriter, an in-out basket, and my name plate. I get a lot of work done, plus I get a great chance to people-watch. Then there's my big, adult-sized highchair, where I sit in the evening as Mom and I watch the news and discuss current events, while I paddle in my food and throw my dishes on the floor. When Mom reaches to wipe off my chin and I take her hand, and we fall to the floor in a heap—me, Mom, highchair, and all—well, those are the best times, those are the very best times.

It is true that occasionally I find myself longing for even more—for things I know I cannot have, like the feel of a firm, strong, gentle hand at the small of my back lifting me out of bed into the air, or someone who could walk me around and burp me after I've watched all the bowl games and had about nine beers. Ideally, I would like a mom about nineteen or twenty feet tall, and although I considered for a while asking my mom to start working out with weights and drinking Nutrament, I finally figured, Why put her through it? After all, she is not only my woman, she is my best friend. I have to take her as she is, and the way she is is plenty good enough for me.

(1978)

THE MAN
WITH THE DOG

R. PRAWER JHABVALA

I think of myself sometimes as I was in the early days, and I see myself moving around my husband's house the way I used to—freshly bathed, flowers in my hair, and going from room to room and looking in corners to see that everything is clean. I walk proudly; I know myself to be loved and respected as one who faithfully fulfills all her duties in life— toward God, parents, husband, children, servants, and the poor. When I pass the prayer room, I join my hands and bow my head, and sweet reverence flows through me from top to toe. I know my prayers to be pleasing and acceptable.

Perhaps it is because they remember me as I was in those days that my children get so angry with me every time they see me now. They are all grown up now and scattered in many parts of India. When they need me, or when my longing for them becomes too strong, I go and visit one or another of them. What happiness! They crowd round me, I kiss them and hug them and cry, I laugh with joy at everything my little grandchildren say and do, and we talk all night, because there is so much to tell. As the days pass, however, we touch on topics that are not so pleasant, or, even if we don't touch on them, they are there and we think of them, and our happiness becomes clouded. I feel guilty, and, worse, I begin to feel restless, and the more restless I am the more guilty I feel. I want to go home, though I dare not admit it to them. At the same time, I want to stay, I don't ever, ever want to leave them—my darling beloved children and grandchildren, for whom what happiness it would be to lay down my life! But I have to go, the restlessness is burning me up, and I begin to tell them lies. I say that some urgent matter has come up and I have to consult my lawyer. Of course, they know it is a lie, and they argue with me and quarrel and say things that children should not have to say to their mother, so that when at last I have my way and my bags are packed our grief is more than just that of parting. All the way home, tears stream down my cheeks and my feelings are in turmoil, as the train carries me farther and farther away from them, although it is carrying me toward that which I have been hungering and burning for all the time I was with them.

Yes, I—an old woman, a grandmother many times over—I hunger and burn! And for whom? For an old man. . . . And, having said that, I feel like throwing my hands before my face and laughing out loud, although of course it may happen, as it often does nowadays, that my laughter will change into sobs and then back again as I think of him, of that old man whom I love so much. And how he would hate it, to be called an old man! Again I laugh when I think of his face if he could hear me call him that. The furthest he has got is to think of himself as middle-aged. Only the other day, I heard him say to one of his lady friends, "Yes, now that we're all middle-aged, we have to take things a bit more slowly." And he stroked his hand over his hair, which he combs very carefully so that the bald patches don't show, and looked sad because he was middle-aged.

I think of the first time I ever saw him. I remember everything exactly. I had been to Spitzer's to buy some little Swiss cakes, and Ram Lal, who was already my chauffeur in those days, had started the car and was just taking it out of its parking space when he drove straight into the rear bumper of a car that was backing into the adjacent space. This car was not very grand, but the sahib who got out of it was. He wore a beautifully tailored suit with creases in the trousers, and a silk tie, and a hat on his head. Under his arm he carried a very hairy little dog, which was barking furiously. The sahib, too, was barking furiously; his face had gone red all over, and he shouted abuses at Ram Lal in English. He didn't see me for a while, but when he did he suddenly stopped shouting, almost in the middle of a word. He looked at me as I sat in the back of the Packard in my turquoise sari and a cape made out of an embroidered Kashmiri shawl; even the dog stopped barking. I knew that look well. It was one that men had given me from the time I was fifteen right until—yes, even till I was over forty. It was a look that always filled me with annoyance but also (now that I am so old I can admit it) pride and pleasure. Then, a few seconds later, still looking at me in the same way, but by this time with a little smile as well, he raised his hat to me. His hair was blond and thin. I inclined my head, settled my cape around my shoulders, and told Ram Lal to drive on.

In those days, I was very pleasure-loving. The children were all quite big; three of them were already in college and the two younger ones at their boarding schools. When they were small and my dear husband was still with us, we lived mostly in the hills or on our estate near X (which now belongs to my eldest son, Shammi); these were quiet, dull places where my dear husband could do all his reading, invite his friends, and listen to music. Our town house was let out in those years, and when we came to see his lawyer or consult some special doctor we had to stay in a hotel. But after I was left alone and the children were bigger, I kept the town house for myself, because I liked living in town best. I spent a lot of time shopping and bought many costly saris that I did not need; at least twice a week, I visited a cinema, and I even learned to play cards! I was invited to many tea parties, dinners, and other functions.

It was at one of these that I met him again. We recognized each other at once, and he looked at me in the same way as before, and soon we were making conversation. Now that we are what we are to each other and have been so for all these years, it is difficult for me to look back and see him as I did at the beginning—as a stranger, with a stranger's face and a stranger's name. What interested me in him the most at the beginning was, I think, that he was a foreigner; at that time, I hadn't met many foreigners, and I was fascinated by so many things about him that seemed strange and wonderful to me. I liked the elegant way he dressed, and the lively way in which he spoke, and his thin fair hair, and the way his face would go red. I was also fascinated by the way he talked to me and to the other ladies—so different from our Indian men, who are always a little shy with us and clumsy, and even if they like to talk with us they don't want anyone to see that they like it. But he didn't care who saw; he would sit on a little stool by the side of the lady with whom he was talking and he would look up at her and smile and make conversation in a very lively manner, and sometimes, in talking, he would lay his hand on her arm. He was also extra polite with us. He drew back the chair for us when we wanted to sit down or get up, and he would open the door for us, and he lit the cigarettes of those ladies who smoked, and offered all sorts of other little services that our Indian men would be ashamed of and think beneath their dignity. But, the way he did it, it was full of dignity. And one other thing—when he greeted a lady and wanted her to know that he thought highly of her, he would kiss her hand, and this, too, was beautiful, although the first time he did it to me I felt a shock like electricity going down my spine and I wanted to snatch away my hand from him and wipe it clean on my sari. But afterward I got used to it and I liked it.

His name is Boekelman—he is a Dutchman—and when I first met him he had already been in India for many years. He had come out to do business here, in ivory, and was caught by the war and couldn't get back, and when the war was over he no longer wanted to go back. He did not earn a big fortune, but it was enough for him. He lived in a hotel suite, which he had furnished with his own carpets and pictures. He ate well, he drank well, he had his circle of friends, and a little hairy dog called Susi. At home, in Holland, all he had left were two aunts and a wife, from whom he was divorced and whom he did not even like to think about. (Her name was Annemarie, but he always spoke of her as "Once bitten, twice shy.") So India was home for him, although he had not learned any Hindustani except "*achchha*," which means "all right," and "*pani*," which means "water," and he did not know any Indians. All his friends were foreigners; his lady friends also.

. . .

MANY THINGS HAVE changed from what they were when I first knew him. He no longer opens the door for me to go in or out, nor does he kiss my hand; he still does it for other ladies, but no longer for me. That's all right—I don't want it, it is not needed. We live in the same house now, for he has given up his hotel room and has moved into a suite of rooms in my house. He pays rent for this, which I don't want but can't refuse, because he insists. And, anyway, perhaps it doesn't matter, because it isn't very much money (he has calculated the rent not on the basis of what would have to be paid today but on what it was worth when the house was first built, almost forty years ago). In return, he wishes that the rooms be kept quite separate and that everyone should knock before going in. He also sometimes gives parties in there for his European friends, to which he may or may not invite me. If he invites me, he will do it like this: "One or two people are dropping in this evening. I wonder if you would care to join us?" Of course, I have known long before this about the party, because he has told the cook to get something ready, and the cook has come to me to ask what should be made, and I have given full instructions; if something very special is needed, I make it myself. After he has invited me and I have accepted, he asks me, "What will you wear?" and looks at me very critically. He always says women must be elegant, and that was why he first liked me, because in those days I was very careful about my appearance; I bought many new saris, and had blouses made to match them, and I went to a beauty parlor and had facial massage and other things. But now all that has vanished. I no longer care what I look like.

It is strange how often in one lifetime one changes and changes again, even an ordinary person like myself. When I look back, I see myself first as the young girl in my father's house, impatient, waiting for things to happen; then as the calm wife and mother, fulfilling all my many duties; and then again, when the children are bigger and my dear husband, many years older than myself, has moved far away from me and I am more his daughter than his wife—then again I am different. In those years, we lived mostly in the hills, and I would go for long walks by myself, for hours and hours, sometimes with great happiness to be there among those great green mountains in sun and mist. But sometimes also I was full of misery and longed for something as great and beautiful as those mountains to fill my own life, which seemed, in those years, very empty. But when my dear husband left us forever, I came down from the mountains and then began that fashionable town life of which I have already spoken. But that, too, has finished. Now I get up in the mornings, I drink my tea, I walk round the garden with a peaceful heart; I pick a handful of blossoms, and these I lay at the feet of Vishnu in my prayer room. Without taking my bath or changing out of the old cotton sari in which I have spent the night, I sit for many hours on the veranda, doing nothing—only looking out at the trees and flowers and the birds. My thoughts come and go.

At about twelve o'clock, Boekelman is ready and comes out of his room. He always likes to sleep late, and after that it always takes him at least one or two hours to get ready. His face is pink and shaved, his clothes are freshly pressed, and he smells of shaving lotion and eau de cologne and all the other things he applies out of the rows of bottles on his bathroom shelf. In one hand he has his rolled English umbrella, with the other he holds Susi on a red leather lead. He is ready to go out. He looks at me, and I can see he is annoyed at the way I am sitting there, rumpled and unbathed. If he is not in a hurry to go, he may stop and talk with me for a while, usually to complain about something; he is never in a very good mood at this time of day. Sometimes he will say the washerman did not press his shirts well, another time that his coffee that morning was stone cold, or that he could not sleep all night because of noise coming from the servant quarters, or that a telephone message was not delivered to him promptly enough, or that it looked as if someone had tampered with his mail. I answer him shortly or sometimes not at all, but only go on looking out into the garden, and this always makes him angry. His face becomes very red and his voice begins to shake a little, though he tries to control it. "Surely it is not too much to ask," he says, "to have such messages delivered to me clearly and at the right time?" As he speaks, he stabs tiny holes into the ground with his umbrella to emphasize what he is saying. I watch him doing this and then I say, "Don't ruin my garden." He stares at me in surprise for a moment, after which he deliberately makes another hole with his umbrella and goes on talking. "It so happened it was an extremely urgent message—" I don't let him get far. I'm out of my chair and I shout at him, "You are ruining my garden!," and then I go on shouting about other things and I advance toward him, and he begins to retreat. "This is ridiculous," he says, and some other things as well, but he can't be heard because I am shouting so loud and the dog, too, has begun to bark. He walks faster now in order to get out of the gate more quickly, pulling the dog along with him. I follow them. I'm very excited by this time and no longer know what I'm saying. The gardener, who is cutting the hedge, pretends not to hear or see anything but concentrates on his work. At last, Boekelman is out in the street with the dog, and they walk down it very fast, with the dog turning round to bark and he pulling it along, while I stand at the gate and pursue them with my angry shouts until they have disappeared from sight.

That is the end of my peace and contemplation. Now I am very upset. I walk up and down the garden and through the house, talking to myself and sometimes striking my two fists together. I think bad thoughts about him and talk to him in my thoughts, and, also in my thoughts, he is answering me, and these answers make me even more angry. If some servant comes and speaks to me at this time, I get angry with him, too, and shout so loud that he runs away, and the whole house is very quiet and everyone keeps out of my way. But slowly my feelings begin to change. My anger burns itself out, and I am left with the ashes of remorse. I remember all my promises to myself, all my resolutions never to give way to my bad temper again. I remember my beautiful morning hours, when I felt so full of peace, so close to the birds and trees and sunlight and other innocent things. And with that memory tears spring into my eyes, and I lie down sorrowfully on my bed. Lakshmi, my old woman servant who has been with me nearly forty years, comes in with a cup of tea for me. I sit up and drink it, the tears still on my face and more tears rolling down into my cup. Lakshmi begins to smooth my hair, which has come undone in the excitement, and while she is doing this I talk to her in broken words about my folly and bad character. She clicks her tongue, contradicts me, praises me, and that makes me suddenly angry again, so that I snatch the comb out of her hand and throw it against the wall and drive her out of the room.

So the day passes, now in sorrow, now in anger, and all the time I am waiting only for him to come home again. As the hour draws near, I begin to get ready. I have my bath, comb my hair, wear a new sari. I even apply a little scent. I begin to be very busy around the house, because I don't want it to be seen how much I am waiting for him. When I hear his footsteps, I am busier than ever and pretend not to hear them. He stands inside the door and raps his umbrella against it and calls out in a loud voice, "Is it safe to come in? Has the fury abated?" I try not to smile, but in spite of myself my mouth corners twitch.

AFTER WE HAVE had a quarrel and have forgiven each other, we are always very gay together. These are our best times. We walk round the garden, my arm in his, he smoking a cigar and I chewing a betel leaf. He tells me some funny stories, and makes me laugh so much that sometimes I have to stand still and hold my sides and gasp for air while begging him to stop. Nobody ever sees us like this, in this mood; if they did, they would not wonder, as they all do, why we are living together. Yes, everyone asks this question, I know it very well, not only my people but his, too—all his foreign friends who think he is miserable with me and that we do nothing but quarrel and that I am too stupid to be good company for him. Let them see us like this only once, then they would know; or afterward, when he allows me to come into his rooms and stay there with him the whole night.

It is quite different in his rooms from the rest of the house. The rest of the house doesn't have very much furniture in it, only some of our old things—some carved Kashmiri screens and little carved tables with mother-of-pearl tops. There are chairs and a few sofas, but I always feel most comfortable on the large mattress on the floor, which is covered with an embroidered cloth and many bolsters and cushions; here I recline for hours, very comfortably, playing patience or cutting betel nuts with my little silver shears. But in his rooms there is a lot of furniture, and a radio-gramophone and a cabinet for his records and another for his bottles of liquor. There are carpets and many pictures—some paintings of European countryside and one old oil painting of a pink-and-white lady with a fan and in old-fashioned dress. There is also a framed pencil sketch of Boekelman himself, which was made by a friend of his—a chemist from Vienna who was said to have been a very good artist but who died from heatstroke one very bad Delhi summer. Hanging on the walls or standing on the mantelpiece or on little tables all over the rooms are a number of photographs, and these I like to look at even better than the paintings, because they are all of him as a boy or as oh such a handsome young man, and of his parents and the hotel they owned and all lived in, in a place called Zandvoort. There are other photographs in a big album, which he sometimes allows me to look at. In this album there are also a few pictures of his wife ("Once bitten, twice shy"), which I'm very interested in, but he never lets me look at the album for long, because he is afraid I might spoil it, and he takes it away from me and puts it back in the drawer where it belongs. He is neat and careful with all his things, and gets very angry when they are disarranged by the servants during dusting; yet he also insists on very thorough dusting, and woe to the whole household if he finds some corner has been forgotten! So, although there are so many things in his rooms, it is always tidy there, and it would be a pleasure to go in there if it were not for Susi.

He has always had a dog, and it has always been the same very small, very hairy kind, and it has always been called Susi. This is the second Susi I have known. The first died of very old age. This Susi, too, is getting quite old now. Unfortunately, dogs have a nasty smell when they get old, and since Susi lives in Boekelman's rooms all the time, the rooms also have this smell, although they are so thoroughly cleaned every day. When you enter, the first thing you notice is this smell, and it always fills me with a moment's disgust, because I don't like dogs and certainly would never allow one inside a room. But for B., dogs are like children. How he fondles this smelly Susi with her long hair! He bathes her with his own hands and brushes her, and at night she sleeps in his bed. It is horrible. So when he lets me stay in his room in the night, Susi is always there with us, and she is the only thing that prevents me from being perfectly happy then. I think Susi also doesn't like it that I'm there. She looks at me from the end of the bed with her running eyes, and I can see that she doesn't like it. I feel like kicking her off the bed and out of the room and out of the house, but because that isn't possible I try to pretend she is not there. In any case, I don't have any time for her, because I am so busy looking at B. He is usually asleep before me, and then I sit up in bed beside him and look and look my eyes out at him. I can't describe how I feel. I have been a married woman, but I have never known such joy as I have in being there alone with him in bed and looking at him—at this old man who has taken his front teeth out, so that his upper lip sags over his gums. His skin is gray and loose; he makes ugly sounds from his mouth and nose as he sleeps. It is rapture for me to be there with him.

No one else ever sees him like this. All those friends he has, all his European lady friends—they only see him dressed up and with his front teeth in. And although they have known him all these years, longer than I have, they don't really know anything about him. Only the outer part is theirs, the shell, but what is within, the essence—that is known only to me. But they wouldn't understand that, for what do they know of outer part and inner, of the shell and of the essence? It is all one to them. For them it is only a good time and food and drink that matter in this life, even though they are old women like me and should not have their thoughts on these things.

I have tried hard to like these friends of his, but it is not possible for me. They are very different from anyone else I know. They have all of them been in India for many, many years—at least twenty-five or thirty—but I know they would much rather be somewhere else. They only stay here because they feel too old to go anywhere else and start a new life. They came here for different reasons—some because they were married to Indians, some to do business, and others as refugees or because they couldn't get a visa for anywhere else. None of them has ever tried to learn any Hindustani, or to get to know anything about our India. They have some Indian "friends," but these are all very rich and important people like maharanis and cabinet ministers. They don't trouble with ordinary people at all. But really they are friends only with one another, and they always like each other's company best. That doesn't mean they don't quarrel together; they do it all the time, and sometimes some of them are not on speaking terms for months or even years. Whenever two of them are together, they are sure to be saying something bad about a third. Perhaps they are really more like family than friends, the way they both love and hate each other and are closely tied together whether they like it or not. None of them has any other family, so they are really dependent on each other. That's why they are always celebrating one another's birthday, the way a family does, and why they are always together on their big days, like Christmas or New Year. If one of them is sick, the others are there at once with grapes and flowers, and sit all day and half the night round the sickbed, even if they have not been on speaking terms.

I know that Boekelman has been very close with some of the women, and there are a few of them who are still fond of him and would like to start all over again with him. But he has had enough of them—at least in that way, although of course he is still on very friendly terms with them and meets them almost every day. When he and I are alone together, he speaks of them very disrespectfully and makes fun of them and tells me things about them that no woman would like anyone to know. He makes me laugh, and I feel proud, triumphant, that he should be saying all this to me. But he never likes me to say anything about them. He gets very angry if I do and starts shouting that I have no right to talk, I don't know them, and don't know all they have suffered. So I keep quiet, although often I feel very annoyed with them and would like to speak my mind.

The time I feel most annoyed is when there is a party in Boekelman's rooms and I'm invited there with them. They all have a good time. They eat and drink, tell jokes, and sometimes they quarrel; they laugh a lot and kiss each other more than is necessary. No one takes much notice of me, but I don't mind that; I'm used to it with them. Anyway, I'm busy most of the time running in and out of the kitchen to see to the preparations. I am glad I have something to do, because otherwise I would be very bored just sitting there. What they say doesn't interest me, and their jokes don't make me laugh. Often, I don't understand what they are talking about, even when they are speaking in English—which is not always, for sometimes they speak in other languages, such as French or German. But I always know, whatever the language they are speaking, when they start saying things about India. Sooner or later, they always come to this subject, and then their faces change and they look mean and bitter, like people who feel they have been cheated by some shopkeeper and it is too late to return the goods. Now it becomes very difficult for me to keep calm. How I hate to hear them talking in this way, saying that India is dirty and everyone is dishonest! But because they are my guests, because they are in my house, I have to keep hold of myself and sit there with my arms folded. I must keep my eyes lowered, so that no one can see how they are blazing with fire. Once they have started on this subject, it always takes them a long time to stop, and the more they talk the more bitter they become. The expression on their faces becomes more and more unpleasant. I suffer, and yet I begin to see that they, too, are suffering. All the terrible things they are saying are not only against India but against themselves, too—because they are here and have nowhere else to go—and against the fate that has brought them here and left them here, so far from where they belong and everything they hold dear.

Boekelman often talks about India in this way, but I have got used to it with him. I know very well that whenever something is not quite right—for instance, when a button is missing from his shirt, or it is a very hot day in summer—at once he will start saying how bad everything is in India. Well, with him I just laugh and take no notice. But once my eldest son, Shammi, overheard him and was so angry with him—as angry as I get with B.'s friends when I hear them talking in this way. It happened some years ago. It is painful for me to recall this occasion. . . .

Shammi was staying with me for a few days. He was alone that time, though often he used to come with his whole family—his wife, Monica, and my three darling grandchildren. Shammi is in the Army—he was still a major then, though now he is a lieutenant colonel—which is a career he has wanted since he was a small boy and which he loves passionately. At the cadet school, he was chosen as the best cadet of the year, for there was no one whose buttons shone so bright or who saluted so smartly as my Shammi. He is a very serious boy. He loves talking to me about his regiment and about tank warfare and 11.1-bore rifles and other such things, and I love listening to him. I don't really understand what he is saying, but I love his eager voice and the way he looks when he talks—just as he looked when he was a small boy and told me about his cricket. Anyway, this is what we were doing that morning, Shammi and I—sitting on the veranda, he talking and I looking sometimes at him and sometimes out into the garden, where everything was green and cool and birds bathed themselves in a pool of water that had oozed out of the hose pipe and sunk into the lawn. This peace was broken by Boekelman. It started off with his shouting at a servant, very loudly and rudely, as he always does. Nobody minds this. I don't mind it, the servant doesn't mind it; we are so used to it and we know it never lasts very long. In any case, the servant doesn't understand what is said, for it is in English, or even in some other language that none of us understands, and afterward, if he has shouted very loudly, Boekelman always gives the servant a little tip or one of his old shirts or a pair of old shoes. But Shammi was very surprised, for he had never heard him shout and abuse someone in this way (B. was always very careful how he behaved when any of the children were there). Shammi tried to continue talking to me about his regiment, but B. was shouting so loud that it was difficult to pretend not to hear him.

But it might still have been all right and nothing would have been said if Boekelman had not suddenly come rushing out onto the veranda. He held his shaving brush in one hand, and half his face was covered in shaving lather and on the other half there was a spot of blood where he had cut himself. He was in his undervest and trousers, and the trousers had braces dangling behind like two tails. He had completely lost control of himself, I could see at once, and he didn't care what he said, or before whom. He was so excited that he could hardly talk and he shook his shaving brush in the direction of the servant, who followed him and stood helplessly watching him from the doorway. "These people!" he screamed. "Monkeys! Animals!" I didn't know what had happened but could guess that it was something quite trivial, such as the servant's removing a razor blade before it was worn out. "Hundreds, thousands of times I tell them!" B. screamed, shaking his brush. "The whole country is like that! Idiots! Fools! Not fit to govern themselves!"

Shammi jumped up. His fists were clenched, his eyes blazed. Quickly I put my hand on his arm. I could feel him holding himself back, his whole body shaking with the effort. Boekelman did not notice anything but went on shouting, "Damn rotten backward country!" I kept my hand on Shammi's arm, though I could see he had himself under control now and was standing very straight and at attention, as if on parade, with his eyes fixed above Boekelman's head. "Go in now," I told B., trying to sound as if nothing very bad was happening. "At least finish your shaving." Boekelman opened his mouth to shout some more abuses, this time probably at me, but then he caught sight of Shammi's face and he remained with his mouth open. "Go in," I said to him again, but it was Shammi who went in and left us, turning suddenly on his heel and marching away with his strong footsteps. The screen door banged hard behind him on its spring hinges. Boekelman stood and looked after him, his mouth still open and the soap caking on his cheek. I went up close to him and shook my fist under his nose. "*Fool!*" I said to him, in Hindustani and with such violence that he took a step backward in fear. I didn't glance at him again, but turned away and swiftly followed Shammi into the house.

Shammi was packing his bag. He wouldn't talk to me and kept his head averted from me while he took neat piles of clothes out of the drawer and packed them neatly into his bag. He has always been a very orderly boy. I sat on his bed and watched him. If he had said something, if he had been angry, it would have been easier, but he was quite silent, and I knew that under his shirt his heart was beating fast. When he was small and something had happened to him, he would never cry, but when I held him close to me and put my hand under his shirt I used to feel his heart beating wildly inside his child's body, like a bird in a frail cage. And now, too, I longed to do this, to lay my hand on his chest and soothe his suffering. Only now he was grown up, a big major with a wife and children, who had no need of his foolish mother anymore. And worse, much worse—now it was not something from outside that was the cause of his suffering but I, I myself! When I thought of that, I could not restrain myself. A sob broke from me, and I cried out, "Son!," and the next moment, before I knew what I was doing, I was down on the ground holding his feet and bathing them with my tears to beg his forgiveness.

He tried to raise me, but I am a strong, heavy woman and I clung obstinately to his feet, so he, too, got down on the floor and in his effort to raise me took me in his arms. Then I broke into a storm of tears and hid my face against his chest, overcome with shame and remorse and yet also with happiness that he was so near me and holding me so tenderly. We stayed like this for some time. At last, I raised my head, and I saw tears on his lashes, like silver drops of dew. And these tender drops on his long lashes like a girl's, which always seem so strange in his soldier's face—these drops were such a burning reproach to me that at this moment I decided I must do what he wanted desperately, he and all my other children, and what I knew he had been silently asking of me since the day he came. I took the end of my sari and with it wiped the tears from his eyes, and as I did this I said, "It's all right, Son. I will tell him to go." And to reassure him, because he was silent and perhaps didn't believe me, I said, "Don't worry at all, I will tell him myself," in a firm, promising voice.

SHAMMI WENT HOME the next day. We did not mention the subject anymore, but when he left he knew that I would not break my promise. And, indeed, that very day I went to Boekelman's room and told him that he must leave. It was a very quiet scene. I spoke calmly, looking not at B. but over his head, and he answered calmly, saying very well, he would go. He asked only that I should give him time to find alternative accommodation, and of course I agreed readily to this, and we even had a quiet little discussion about what type of place he should look for. We spoke like two acquaintances, and everything seemed very nice till I noticed that although his voice was quite firm and he was talking so reasonably, his hands were slightly trembling. Then my feelings changed, and I had to leave the room quickly in order not to give way to them.

From now on, he got up earlier than usual in the mornings and went out to look for a place to rent. He would raise his hat to me as he passed me sitting on the veranda, and sometimes we would have a little talk together, mainly about the weather, before he passed on, raising his hat again and with Susi on a lead walking behind him, her tail in the air. The first few days, he seemed very cheerful, but after about a week I could see he was tired of going out so early and never finding anything, and Susi, too, seemed tired and her tail was no longer so high. I hardened my heart against them. I could guess what was happening—how he went from place to place and found everywhere that rents were very high and the accommodations very small compared with the large rooms he had had in my house all these years for almost nothing. Let him learn, I thought, and said nothing except "Good morning" and "The weather is changing fast. Soon it will be winter" as I watched him going with slower and slower footsteps day after day out of the gate.

At last, one day, he confessed to me that in spite of all his efforts he had not yet succeeded in finding anything suitable. He had some hard things to say about rapacious landlords. I listened patiently but did not offer to extend his stay. My silence prompted him to stand on his pride and say that I need not worry, that very shortly he would definitely be vacating the rooms. And, indeed, only two days later he informed me that although he had not yet found any suitable place, he did not want to inconvenience me any further and had therefore made an alternative arrangement, which would enable him to leave in a day or two. Of course, I should have answered only "Very well" and inclined my head in a stately manner, but like a fool I asked, "What alternative arrangement?" This gave him the opportunity to be stately with me; he looked at me in silence for a moment and then gave a little bow and, raising his hat, proceeded toward the gate with Susi. I bit my lip in anger. I would have liked to run after him and shout, as in the old days, but instead I had to sit there by myself and brood. All day I brooded about what alternative arrangement he could have made. Perhaps he was going to a hotel, but I didn't think so, because hotels nowadays are very costly, and although he is not poor, the older he gets the less he likes to spend.

In the evening, his friend Lina came to see him. There was a lot of noise from his rooms and also some thumping, as of suitcases being taken down; Lina shouted and laughed at the top of her voice, as she always does. I crept halfway down the stairs and tried to hear what they were saying. I was very agitated. As soon as she had gone, I walked into his room—without knocking, which was against his strict orders—and said at once, standing facing him with my hands at my waist, "You are not moving in with *Lina*?" Some of his pictures had already been removed from the walls and his rugs rolled up; his suitcases stood open and ready.

Although I was very heated, he remained calm. "Why not Lina?" he asked, and looked at me in a mocking way.

I made a sound of contempt. Words failed me. To think of him living with Lina, in her two furnished rooms that were already overcrowded with her own things and always untidy! And Lina herself, also always untidy—her hair blond when she remembered to dye it, her swollen ankles, and her loud voice and laugh! She had first come to India in the nineteen-thirties to marry an Indian, a boy from a very good family, but he left her quite soon. Of course—how could a boy like that put up with her ways? She is very free with men—even now, though she is old and ugly—and I know she has liked B. for a long time. I was quite determined on one thing—never would I allow him to move to her place, even if it meant keeping him here in the house with me for some time longer.

But when I said what was the hurry, and told him he could wait till he found a good place of his own, he said thank you, he had made his arrangements, and—as I could see with my own eyes—he had already begun to pack up his things. He turned away and began to open and shut various drawers and take out clothes, just to show me how busy he was with packing. He had his back to me, and I stood looking at it and longed to thump it.

The next day, too, Lina came to the house and again I heard her talking and laughing very loudly, and there was some banging about, as if they were moving the suitcases. She left very late at night, but even after she had gone I could not sleep and tossed this side and that on my bed. I no longer thought of Shammi but only of B. Hours passed—one o'clock, two o'clock, three. Still I could not sleep. I walked up and down my bedroom, then I opened the door and walked up and down the landing. After a while, it seemed to me I could hear sounds from downstairs, so I crept halfway down the stairs to listen. There was some movement in his room, and then he coughed—a very weak cough— and he cleared his throat as if it were hurting him. I put my ear to the door of his room. I held my breath, but I could not hear anything further. Very slowly I opened the door. He was sitting in a chair with his head down and his arms hanging loose between his legs, like a sick person. The room was in disorder, with the rugs rolled up and the suitcases half packed, and there were glasses and an empty bottle, as if he and Lina had been having a party. There was also the stale smoke of her cigarettes; she never stops smoking and she throws the stubs, red with lipstick, anywhere she likes.

He looked up for a moment at the sound of the door opening, but when he saw it was I he looked down again without saying anything. I tiptoed over to his armchair and sat at his feet on the floor. My hand slowly and soothingly stroked his leg, and he allowed me to do this and did not stir. He stared in front of him with dull eyes; he had his teeth out and looked an old, old man. There was no need for us to say anything, to ask questions and give answers. I knew what he was thinking as he stared in front of him this way, and I, too, thought of the same thing. I thought of him gone away from here and living with Lina, or alone with his dog in some rented room—no contact with India or Indians, no words to communicate with except "*achchha*" and "*pani.*" No one to care for him as he grew older and older, and perhaps sick, and his only companions people just like himself—as old, as lonely, as disappointed, and as far from home.

He sighed, and I said, "Is your indigestion troubling you?," although I knew it was something worse than indigestion. But he said yes and added, "It was the spinach you made them cook for my supper. How often do I have to tell you I can't digest spinach at night?" After a while, he allowed me to help him into bed. When I had covered him and settled his pillows the way he liked them, I threw myself on the bed and begged, "Please don't leave me."

"I've made my arrangements," he said in a firm voice. Susi, at the end of the bed, looked at me with her running eyes and wagged her tail as if she were asking for something.

"Stay," I pleaded with him. "Please stay."

There was a pause. At last, he said, as if he were doing me a big favor, "Well, we'll see," and added, "Get off my bed now. You're crushing my legs. Don't you know what a big heavy lump you are?"

None of my children ever comes to stay with me now. I know they are sad and disappointed with me. They want me to be what an old widowed mother should be, to devote myself entirely to prayer and self-sacrifice. I, too, know it is the only state fitting to this last stage of life which I have now reached. But that great all-devouring love that I should have for God I have for B. Sometimes I think, Perhaps this is the path for weak women like me. Perhaps B. is a substitute for God, whom I should be loving, just as the little brass image of Vishnu in my prayer room is a substitute for that great god himself. These are stupid thoughts that sometimes come to me when I am lying next to B. on his bed and looking at him and feeling so full of peace and joy. I wonder how I came to be so, when I am living against all right rules and the wishes of my children. How do I deserve the great happiness that I find in that old man? It is a riddle.

(1966)

THE PLAN

EDNA O'BRIEN

It is morning. What is more, it is a beautiful morning. There is a sparkle on everything and even the dullest things are shot with radiance. From my back window, the bedroom window, I see that the cats—those wise barometers—are already stretched out on the tiled roofs, taking the sun through their thick fur. From the front window, if I were to walk to the next room, I would no doubt see girls and women going off to work in their sleeveless dresses, the women carrying their cardigans just in case. And I would probably note that the pensioners are out that bit early in search of a shady seat in Dove-house Green. It is amazing what a steady sunshine does for these blanched English souls.

Just now I put powder on, and the translucency that the shop assistant guaranteed showed up for the first time. It is like seeing specks of mica on a road. I am reminded suddenly of those travelling actresses who came to our little village in Ireland long ago and made such an impression on me. They were quite bedraggled and unhappy when in the daytime they pushed prams down the seedy street that was called Main Street, but at night they were creatures endowed with glitter—glitter on their faces, glitter on their bodices, glitter in their eyes, possibly owing to nerves or maybe fever. They were transformed beings. I loved watching them. I luxuriated in their pain as they strode about the stage, or halted, or flung themselves onto some velvet-covered sofa. Their characters were invariably ones that had to endure pain. There was the young flighty mother who abandoned her little son in order to elope with a rake, and, of course, when she repented her wild impulse and tried to come back to her own home her upright husband had married her rival, who was naturally a woman of steel. The mother was forced to return disguised as a maid, and nurse her little son but behave with distance, as if they were not of the same blood—as if she had not once intrepidly carried him within her. There was another, in direct contrast, who chose the vows of chastity, and was kneeling on a little dais, haloed in white, taking those final and irreversible vows when her errant scoundrel came to claim her and found that he was too late!

Yes, those ladies come to mind when I pat the powder on and look in my long wardrobe mirror and see that the effect is indeed cheering. Why am I putting the powder on so early, when in fact I have household chores to do and when I know that it is best to leave my skin untampered with through the day, to let it breathe, while no one is seeing me? Ah, to be seen is the big nourishment, the sop of content. If only we could go to each other's houses and show ourselves to other women's husbands, or valets, or sons, or employers, then we could display ourselves, come home, and feel justified. We could feel that the effort we put into sereneness, into smiling, into pursing, into deportment, was not completely in vain. I think of all the women in all the houses in London at this moment for whom a visit would change everything, even fleetingly, and I think that if I had organizing abilities I would do something about it. For some reason, I see a young woman, an Eastern woman of sallow complexion, with her baby, and they are placed in an English garden. There are poppies sprouting red in the high yellow unmown grass, and I realize that her baby tugging at her breast defers the emptiness that she might otherwise feel, and yet she is being emptied and one day her breasts will be like discarded shells. But there is no need for pessimism. This is a special day. It is marked in my diary with a little asterisk and it says "*pour dîner.*" I have already laid my outfit on the bed. It is a lace blouse that would not go amiss as an altar cloth. The discs of thick cream lace are stitched loosely together, so that the skin can be seen through the webbing. The skirt is also cream, with spatters of red and violet, just as if one took a marking pen and childishly indented these colored points.

It is probable that we will eat out-of-doors. There will be several tables covered in white cloth, and the crystal goblets will be like sentinels at each place setting. There will be roses in special glass bowls. The bowls are high, like cake stands, and the roses will be cut close to their petals and laid in there like confectionery; if they are pink, as indeed they may be, they will be like those iced sweets that I loved in childhood, and it will not be hard to recapture that beautiful synthetic almond taste. The lights will be concealed in the foliage, and the smell will be a blend of roses, honeysuckle, and various expensive perfumes. There will perhaps be a summerhouse or a little gazebo where a couple will wander, apparently to study some facet of its design but really to make an assignation. That will not be him and me. If he gives me five minutes of his time without taking a tweezers to my nervous system, I shall consider myself lucky. To be fair to myself, I did not plan this meeting. The opposite. Two days ago, when I heard of it from my hostess, I flinched. She had come here to discuss her dilemma with her lover and her impatience with her paunchy husband. Just as she was leaving, I asked who were the other guests. As soon as she told me, I tried to get out of going. She said my name sharply. She said, "Anna," and I could feel the inevitable rebuke. She said, "Finding a woman at the last minute is almost as difficult as finding a man." Her nails, her eyes, and the heels of her lizard shoes were all very pointed, and I was afraid to cross her. But my heart did start to gallop.

I am envisioning each group, with the new arrivals like extras waiting for their moment to be received, to be introduced, to find excitement or shock in some unexpected face. The men will all be wearing black tie, and I pray that at least two of them will be personable. I will need all the discipline that I have got. My lover is going to be there. My lover's wife is going to be there. I have never met her. That is not quite true; I once saw her, and so I will recognize her. My eyes will land on her, and rest on her, so that she will know that I am not flinching, and not turning away. She is dark. She is dark, like the raven. At least that is how I remember her. It may have been the lighting, in which green was impregnated with blackness. It was in a marquee at a wedding and there was a great storm outside, so that the event was marked by a kind of menace that I took to be talismanic. Among the guests I saw a dark woman in a cape, but I did not know then to whom she was attached. He and I had just met and we were eating canapés on which there was a single sprig of limp tinned asparagus. I refused a second one, to which he said, "You don't look as if you need to diet," and then announced that he was not as thin as he looked, that the hollows in his face made him seem thinner than he actually was. His face reminds me of those stone effigies that decorate the ceilings or columns of a monastery or a chapel. It is a graven face. In contrast, our conversation was merry and stirring.

"And you don't know how lovely you are," he said, half joking. The marquee was freezing, as there was only one gas heater at the far end, around which the older people had converged. It being spring, the bride and groom naturally had anticipated a warmer day. After all, the daffodils were out; but the wind was blowing their wrinkled flutes. Seeing in the distance the blue coronet of the gas fire, I thought of baby chicks curled up next to each other under a lamp, and I had a sudden unaccountable longing to nestle nearer to him, when I saw that already he had come a few steps closer. Between us was only a fraction of space, in which I could feel a shudder. It was getting to be the moment when the bride's father was to make his speech, and I realized who the dark woman was. She came toward us and said to the man, "Having a good time?" And at once I moved away.

Of course, it could have been that she trusted him so utterly, that they lived in such an understanding, that they even liked to share people such as me, so as to talk about us afterward. At any rate, on that first occasion I could not find words, or the words I could find would have sounded caustic or maybe even brazen. My future lover saw me move, and came and touched my elbow so lightly and so gracefully that I felt as if a ghost had taken charge of his body and brushed against mine, and I thought, Oh, Christ, I am falling in love with a ghost, just as always, and I saw in him shades of others—saw his disappearing tricks, his appearing tricks, his inability to give love, along with his restless pursuit of it. When he touched me, it was as if we had met before, as if we knew each other in some hidden way and the time had now come for us to cross that barrier and to savor each other, to cease to be strangers. Though of course we would always be strangers. Is that not the essence, the requisite, of love?

So I can say—because now I am better acquainted with him—that my instinct was flawless and that I could have predicted almost everything that would happen, that has happened, and that is yet to happen. Even as he is asking to see me, he is asking not to see me; when I am distant, he loves me like a clinging schoolboy, and when I reveal my feelings he looks at his watch and says he has a meeting at four. Only my near-absence guarantees his near-presence, and it is an exhausting game to play. Yet I feel that if I could reach him things would be different. I believe that he does not know himself, and that if I could lead him to himself he would dispense with all artifice, he would welcome this rapture, he would not shirk it. When he is trying to shrug me off, he eats hurriedly. He throws the cherries into his mouth and gulps them down. He did that the last time he was here to lunch, and in his haste one fell onto his white shirt, which was still open. "Damn," he said, as he looked for it. It had slipped into his belly button, and fitted there like the stone of a ring, a ruby. It had burst. He picked it out. It left a red stain on his shirt. He began to suck the white fabric. He sucked it with such determination. I hated him then. I thought, He is sucking it clean, so that when he goes home he will not be asked, "How did that get there?" I saw his ruthlessness and I saw his fear. In myself I saw stirrings of pain, a dip into that fount of sorrow, a reintroduction to a loss that I thought I had finished with. Perhaps it was then I hatched my revenge.

Sensing a coolness, he reached out for me and drew me onto his knee, and he said, "Do you fantasize about me?" and I said, "Yes," but I was too shy to say how. I asked if he fantasized about me, and he said yes, in the car, when on his way to see me, and then he said that I fantasized too much and that it was unhealthy. I was about to say that so did he, when I realized with staggering clarity that he was right and that I was misled. He only fantasizes when he is on his way to see me, when he is assured of the sight of me and all that I can give, whereas I spin fantasies as the hours go by, as the sprinkler in the garden makes a damp circle around the base of every rosebush, as the shadow on the sundial moves lower, and as the floor that I have polished gleams and has the magic of a ballroom waiting for its waltzers—him and me.

TONIGHT, I FEAR that he will snub me. In fact, I know that he is in danger of snubbing me unless I am cunning, unless I preëmpt him by giving him a glacial look. That will unnerve him, make him doubt the certainty of next week's luncheon date. I will look past him at the moment of being introduced to him, and then I will hurry to some other man, and I know that unwisely but impulsively he will follow me and mutter, "You're very aloof tonight and very beautiful." His flattery is always undisguised, and for that reason it never fails to thrill me. Perhaps I see the transparency of it, and flagrant reason for it, the truth and the untruth of it. Tonight, I shall guard myself, so that I can carry out my little scheme. I shall join the group that his wife is in. I know that she will want to talk to me. I know that she will detach herself from the others and veer toward me, that she will talk about everything under the sun— her twins, summer holidays, their garden, her busyness—deferring what she most wants to know, and presently I will unnerve her. She will not be sure whether her little jabs of inner dread are validated or not. What I have decided to do is to listen to her, to admire her dress or her blouse or her jewelry, to admire anything that can be admired without my being obsequious. I am going to be as soft and as patient as a wet nurse. When she needs a drink, I will be the one to signal the waiter, and I will down mine more quickly so that our glasses can be filled, then clinked together. Even if she thinks that I am overfriendly, she will not think it by the time I am finished, because of my trump card. Naturally, others will come over and interrupt this tête-à-tête; others will delay my strategy. Her husband, fearing the worst, may come over and say, "What are you two nattering about?" or our hostess may not allow two lovely women to slink into a corner and while away that half hour when they should be mixing with and delighting the men.

I have no doubt but that we will be alone, because we both want it. I shall whisper. I may even touch her elbow or her wrist. I shall ask if by any chance she has smelling salts or a tranquillizer in her bag, and once she has appraised the question, and felt my shiver, she will ask me why. I shall tell her in all truth that I doubt if I can get through the dinner. Again she will ask me why. She will look at me, and when I say, "The usual," she will know that my trouble is man trouble. I can already see her eyes—dark eyes becoming potent with curiosity—and her blood will quicken, and it will not be long before she asks me who he is, what he does, and I will tell her so much and yet so little. I will describe to her her own husband and any other woman's husband, because do they, do they, differ so radically, those men in dark suits, white shirts, and tasteful silk ties, who want peace in their nests and excitement on their forays? I will say that he gives me pleasure, that he gives me pain, that I never know when to expect him and when not, and that I mean to give him up but I lack the necessary strength, the determination. Then comes my coup. I will ask her to have lunch with me in my favorite restaurant. I will tell her that I long to talk to someone whom I don't know—someone who can help—and with every word I say suspicion will redound in her womb. She may hesitate, but she will not refuse me. I will pin her to a day, and the sooner the better. Nor will he be able to force her to cancel, since that would show him to be implicated, show his culpability. I can hardly wait for tonight to be over, so that I can get on with the proceedings. Their unknown world will gradually unfold to me. I may even meet their twins. She and I may become friends, or getting to know him through her I may be cured of this passion, or together we may overthrow him, and send him out into the world stripped of his duplicity. I scarcely know what will happen. All I know is that I cannot endure it alone, and as they have become part of my life I shall become part of theirs; our lives, you see, are intertwined, and if they destroy me they cannot hope to be spared.

(1980)

Spring Fugue

Harold Brodkey

The first orchestral realization that something is up: Playing Vivaldi's "The Four Seasons" on a spavined CD player. It was a gray day in early February and the sun came out; and I was thinking, "The Dry Cleaners, The Dry Cleaners, The Dry Cleaners, The Dry Cleaners."

The first crocus: The Sunflower Market, Thai Vegetables and Seeds, 2809 Broadway, February 14th. Spindly and snow-flecked.

First cold, March 19th–April 2nd. My wife and I are on our way to our accountant's. On the way I see two drunks fighting in front of the OTB on Broadway at Ninety-first; April is the duellists' month. Tacitly flirting with my wife, I carry two small packets of Kleenex in my pockets—one for her, because of her allergies: she makes a small nifty nasal piccolo announcement of the annual change in her life. I make the second really bad pun of the season: We sound like Bruce Springsteen and accompanist doing Bach's "The Cold Bug Variations."

First episode of spring nosiness not having to do with allergies or noseblowing: I don't know why the soul's primary mechanics should consider spying or snooping a natural attribute of renewed life, but in the office icebox I see a small gold-colored can, shaped like a shoe-polish can, of caviar, and I wonder, jealously, who is so happy and so bent on celebration (or self-indulgence), but when I open it, it is empty, and written on the bottom of the can, in pencil, is the phrase "Hard Cheese."

First philosophical guess: My guess is that spring is a natural way of suggesting adolescence as something one should start to go through again: genetic duty and genetic activity *are* romance. Hmm. . . . Nature is as tricky as any politician.

The thought of George Bush leads to The First Depression of the Season.

First emotional detail: More light on the windowsill.
First piece of strange advice to one's self: *Lighten up.*

First symptom of intellectual confusion (on waking after dreams of fair women and of various unspeakable acts with them; memory, those astonishing chambers of lost realities, becomes overactive, leaving a broad sensation of gambling. . . . Roué-lette): The enumeration of the bedroom furnishings—a nightstand, one-night stand, two-night stands, three-night stands. . . .

No, no.

In the bathroom, first session practicing smile.

First impulse of active love: A sloppy kiss while my wife is putting on her shoes.

She gazes at me. "Oh, it's spring," she says.

Shopping list for first three-day weekend in the country to rent a house for the summer: Contac, Kleenex, Beatles tape, citronella candles (to leave in the rented house if we find it), jump rope (for losing weight), walking shoes, jeans one size too small (to force oneself to diet), a handful of short-lived cut lilac to carry in the car as an *aide-mémoire*. . . .

FIRST EQUINOCTIAL DEATH shudder and racial memory of human sacrifice for the sake of warmth and the return of summer: A roadkill on 32A outside of Saugerties—a no longer hibernating but probably still torpid, thin woodchuck.

Second such event after returning home: Cutting my thumb while using a new, Belgian, serrated-edge slicing knife that slipped on a small Israeli tomato, while I was thinking about Super Tuesday two years ago and whistling Dixie.

Am I unconsciously Angry?

First hysterical delusion: Advertised medicines that come to mind when seeing in a moment of stress spring flowers in the mind—Nuprin-yellow jonquils, tetracycline-colored tulips (red-and-yellow ones). Tylenol-colored clouds (Tylenol is Lonely T spelled backward). Advil-colored dirt. Theragran-M-colored drying blood.

With my hand betowelled and my soul a little mad with pessimism about the current ways we live, and with gaiety, heroism, and the spring wound, I phone my wife at her office. She makes more money than I do.

Advice, sympathy, *information* from my wife's assistant while I am waiting for my wife to end a meeting. It is possible that even the assistant makes more money than I do. (I am a schoolteacher.) She says that in the stores is a helping-the-blood-clot-and-disinfectant-and-anesthetic spray; and there are clutch bandages. But: "Beware," she says, "the spray depletes the ozone layer, and the clutch bandage harms circulation." The finger may turn Nuprin-yellow, crocus-yellow, coward's yellow.

The conversation with my wife is out of a melodramatic domestic novel, except that at work she is Nietzschean. I refer to her being possessed by the will-to-power.

My wife says, "How deep is the cut?"

"I think I see the bone."

She says, "Do you see any white?"

"Yes."

"That's the tendon. Bones aren't white while you're still alive. They're not white until you clean them after you rob them from a grave. You may have cut the tendon. Can you move it?"

"No. Yes. It looks like a bone."

"It isn't the bone. But there are nerves in there—"

"Is that true? That's not just hypochondria?"

"You should be able to see only one nerve, unless it's a really big cut—do you see it?"

"See the nerve?"

"It's a thing, it's visible."

"What does it look like?"

"A thread. Does it make you sick to look at the wound?"

"No. What makes you think that?"

"Well, take a look and tell me what you see."

There is a silence and then she calls out, "Hey, hey, hey."

"I fainted a little. I'm sort of on my knees here. Hold on, let me get up. Whoo, that was stupid. What I saw was gray-white; there's quite a lot of gray-white. I suppose I saw blood but it looked gray-white and blood isn't gray-white, it's bluish, I remember, I—"

"You're in shock. Is there anyone with you?"

"I was cutting a tomato."

"Yes?"

"Someone is coming over—someone will be here soon. You. But you can't come home. You're at work. Should I go get a clotting spray?"

"Go to the emergency room at the hospital. You did this call?"

"I don't remember," I say miserably.

"You cut your thumb?"

"Yes. I guess so. Unless this is all a dream," I say hopefully.

"Did you dial with your left hand?"

"I wrapped my hand in a towel and I squeezed the towel with the other hand. I dialled with my little finger. It's touch-tone, the phone is. . . . I think."

"I forget if there are large numbers on the touch-tone phone or small ones."

"Tiny, really."

"Are they stubborn or easy?"

"Stubborn."

"Then if you dialled and didn't bleed all over the phone you're probably O.K."

"Would you say you were showing sympathy?"

"You may quiver with madness and shock at my saying this, but I promise that if you stay overnight at the hospital I will bring you volumes of Kundera, Solzhenitsyn, Havel, so you can see what horror and suffering truly are."

"Shit."

"On the other hand, our Maltese doorman's sister-in-law died of sepsis after a knife cut in her hand which she got chopping beets when she was visiting her mother-in-law in Valletta. Wait for me. I'm coming home."

MY WIFE IS a Spring Goddess. A Nietzschean Nightingale (Florence). "Here," she says. "Let me look. . . . A kiss won't make that well. Let's go." A kiss or two later, as we pass a homeless guy who at first I think is me in the third person hailing a taxi, and as my shock begins to lift, I say to her, sadly, "When I was a child, I had a Swiss barometer with a wooden house on it. The house had two doors. Out of one came a boy in shorts and with a Tyrolean hat on, and I think a girl in a dirndl came out of the other. They went inside if it was going to rain." Nowadays I suppose you might have a homeless person carved in wood and sleeping on a subway grating to indicate good weather and going into an arcade or a subway to indicate rain.

Some prose written after the third kiss from her (and after the doctor took three stitches in my thumb). I sit at her desk in her office looking out her large window: Give me the huge actual clouds of the Republic and not the meagre udders of water vapor painted on the old backdrops the Republic Studio used in John Wayne's day. We like the actual big baggy clouds of a New York spring. One doesn't want to flog a transiting cloud to death, but if we are to have sentimental light, let us have it at least in its obvious local form—dry, white, sere, and, I guess, provincial. The spiritual splendor of our drizzly and slaphappy spring weather, our streets jammed with sneezing pedestrians, our skies loony with bluster are our local equivalents of lilac hedges and meadows.

Blustery, raw, and rare—and more wind-of-the-sea-scoured than half-melted St. Petersburg. Yuck to cities that have an immersed-in-swamp-and-lagoon moist-air light. They are for watercolorists. Where water laps at the edges of the stones and bricks of somewhat wavery real estate is not home. Home is New York, stony and tall: its real estate is real.

So is its spring.

(1990)

In the Gloaming

Alice Elliott Dark

Her son wanted to talk again, suddenly. During the days, he still brooded, scowling at the swimming pool from the vantage point of his wheelchair, where he sat covered with blankets despite the summer heat. In the evenings, though, Laird became more like his old self—his *old* old self, really. He became sweeter, the way he'd been as a child, before he began to cloak himself with layers of irony and clever remarks. He spoke with an openness that astonished her. No one she knew talked that way—no man, at least. After he was asleep, Janet would run through the conversations in her mind, and realize what it was she wished she had said. She knew she was generally considered sincere, but that had more to do with her being a good listener than with how she expressed herself. She found it hard work to keep up with him, but it was the work she had pined for all her life.

A month earlier, after a particularly long and gruelling visit with a friend who'd come up on the train from New York, Laird had declared a new policy: no visitors, no telephone calls. She didn't blame him. People who hadn't seen him for a while were often shocked to tears by his appearance, and, rather than having them cheer him up, he felt obliged to comfort them. She'd overheard bits of some of those conversations. The final one was no worse than the others, but he was fed up. He had said more than once that he wasn't cut out to be the brave one, the one who would inspire everybody to walk away from a visit with him feeling uplifted, shaking their heads in wonder. He had liked being the most handsome and missed it very much; he was not a good victim. When he had had enough he went into a self-imposed retreat, complete with a wall of silence and other ascetic practices that kept him busy for several weeks.

Then he softened. Not only did he want to talk again; he wanted to talk to *her*.

It began the night they ate outside on the terrace for the first time all summer. Afterward, Martin—Laird's father—got up to make a telephone call, but Janet stayed in her wicker chair, resting before clearing the table. It was one of those moments when she felt nostalgic for cigarettes. On nights like this, when the air was completely still, she used to blow her famous smoke rings for the children, dutifully obeying their commands to blow one through another or three in a row, or to make big, ropy circles that expanded as they floated up to the heavens. She did exactly what they wanted, for as long as they wanted, sometimes going through a quarter of a pack before they allowed her to stop. Incredibly, neither Anne nor Laird became smokers. Just the opposite; they nagged at her to quit, and were pleased when she finally did. She wished they had been just a little bit sorry; it was a part of their childhood coming to an end, after all.

Out of habit, she took note of the first lightning bug, the first star. The lawn darkened, and the flowers that had sulked in the heat all day suddenly released their perfumes. She laid her head back on the rim of the chair and closed her eyes. Soon she was following Laird's breathing, and found herself picking up the vital rhythms, breathing along. It was so peaceful, being near him like this. How many mothers spend so much time with their thirty-three-year-old sons? she thought. She had as much of him now as she had had when he was an infant; more, in a way, because she had the memory of the intervening years as well, to round out her thoughts about him. When they sat quietly together she felt as close to him as she ever had. It was still him in there, inside the failing shell. *She still enjoyed him.*

"The gloaming," he said, suddenly.

She nodded dreamily, automatically, then sat up. She turned to him. "What?" Although she had heard.

"I remember when I was little you took me over to the picture window and told me that in Scotland this time of day was called the 'gloaming.' "

Her skin tingled. She cleared her throat, quietly, taking care not to make too much of an event of his talking again. "You thought I said 'gloomy.' "

He gave a smile, then looked at her searchingly. "I always thought it hurt you somehow that the day was over, but you said it was a beautiful time because for a few moments the purple light made the whole world look like the Scottish Highlands on a summer night."

"Yes. As if all the earth were covered with heather."

"I'm sorry I never saw Scotland," he said.

"You're a Scottish lad nonetheless," she said. "At least on my side." She remembered offering to take him to Scotland once, but Laird hadn't been interested. By then, he was in college and already sure of his own destinations, which had diverged so thoroughly from hers. "I'm amazed you remember that conversation. You couldn't have been more than seven."

"I've been remembering a lot, lately."

"Have you?"

"Mostly about when I was very small. I suppose it comes from having you take care of me again. Sometimes, when I wake up and see your face, I feel I can remember you looking in on me when I was in my crib. I remember your dresses."

"Oh, no!" She laughed lightly.

"You always had the loveliest expression," he said.

She was astonished, caught off guard. Then, she had a memory, too—of her leaning over Laird's crib and suddenly having a picture of looking up at her own mother. "I know what you mean," she said.

"You do, don't you?"

He looked at her in a close, intimate way that made her self-conscious. She caught herself swinging her leg nervously, like a pendulum, and stopped.

"Mom," he said. "There are still a few things I need to do. I have to write a will, for one thing."

Her heart went flat. In his presence she had always maintained that he would get well. She wasn't sure she could discuss the other possibility.

"Thank you," he said.

"For what?"

"For not saying that there's plenty of time for that, or some similar sentiment."

"The only reason I didn't say it was to avoid the cliché, not because I don't believe it."

"You believe there is plenty of time?"

She hesitated; he noticed, and leaned forward slightly. "I believe there is time," she said.

"Even if I were healthy, it would be a good idea."

"I suppose."

"I don't want to leave it until it's too late. You wouldn't want me to suddenly leave everything to the nurses, would you?"

She laughed, pleased to hear him joking again. "All right, all right, I'll call the lawyer."

"That would be great." There was a pause. "Is this still your favorite time of day, Mom?"

"Yes, I suppose it is," she said, "although I don't think in terms of favorites anymore."

"Never mind favorites, then. What else do you like?"

"What do you mean?" she asked.

"I mean exactly that."

"I don't know. I care about all the ordinary things. You know what I like."

"Name one thing."

"I feel silly."

"Please?"

"All right. I like my patch of lilies of the valley under the trees over there. Now can we change the subject?"

"Name one more thing."

"Why?"

"I want to get to know you."

"Oh, Laird, there's nothing to know."

"I don't believe that for a minute."

"But it's true. I'm average. The only extraordinary thing about me is my children."

"All right," he said. "Then let's talk about how you feel about me."

"Do you flirt with your nurses like this when I'm not around?"

"I don't dare. They've got me where they want me." He looked at her. "You're changing the subject."

She smoothed her skirt. "I know how you feel about church, but if you need to talk I'm sure the minister would be glad to come over. Or if you would rather have a doctor . . ."

He laughed.

"What?"

"That you still call psychiatrists 'doctors.' "

She shrugged.

"I don't need a professional, Ma." He laced his hands and pulled at them as he struggled for words.

"What can I do?" she asked.

He met her gaze. "You're where I come from. I need to know about you."

That night she lay awake, trying to think of how she could help, of what, aside from her time, she had to offer. She couldn't imagine.

SHE WAS ANXIOUS the next day when he was sullen again, but the next night, and on each succeeding night, the dusk worked its spell. She set dinner on the table outside, and afterward, when Martin had vanished into the maw of his study, she and Laird began to speak. The air around them seemed to crackle with the energy they were creating in their effort to know and be known. Were other people so close, she wondered.

She never had been, not to anybody. Certainly she and Martin had never really connected, not soul to soul, and with her friends, no matter how loyal and reliable, she always had a sense of what she could do that would alienate them. Of course, her friends had the option of cutting her off, and Martin could always ask for a divorce, whereas Laird was a captive audience. Parents and children were all captive audiences to each other; in view of this, it was amazing how little comprehension there was of one another's stories. Everyone stopped paying attention so early on, thinking they had figured it all out. She recognized that she was as guilty of this as anyone. She was still surprised whenever she went over to her daughter's house and saw how neat she was; in her mind, Anne was still a sloppy teen-ager who threw sweaters into the corner of her closet and candy wrappers under her bed. It still surprised her that Laird wasn't interested in girls. He had been, hadn't he? She remembered lying awake listening for him to come home, hoping that he was smart enough to apply what he knew about the facts of life, to take precautions.

Now she had the chance to let go of these old notions. It wasn't that she liked everything about Laird—there was much that remained foreign to her—but she wanted to know about all of it. As she came to her senses every morning in the moment or two after she awoke, she found herself aching with love and gratitude, as if he were a small, perfect creature again and she could look forward to a day of watching him grow. Quickly, she became greedy for their evenings. She replaced her half-facetious, half-hopeful reading of the horoscope in the daily newspaper with a new habit of tracking the time the sun would set, and drew satisfaction from seeing it come earlier as the summer waned; it meant she didn't have to wait as long. She took to sleeping late, shortening the day even more. It was ridiculous, she knew. She was behaving like a girl with a crush, behaving absurdly. It was a feeling she had thought she'd never have again, and now here it was. She immersed herself in it, living her life for the twilight moment when his eyes would begin to glow, the signal that he was stirring into consciousness. Then her real day would begin.

"Dad ran off quickly," he said one night. She had been wondering when he would mention it.

"He had a phone call to make," she said automatically.

Laird looked directly into her eyes, his expression one of gentle reproach. He was letting her know he had caught her in the central lie of
her life, which was that she understood Martin's obsession with his
work. She averted her gaze. The truth was that she had never understood. Why couldn't he sit with her for half an hour after dinner, or, if
not with her, why not with his dying son?

She turned sharply to look at Laird. The word "dying" had sounded
so loudly in her mind that she wondered if she had spoken it, but he
showed no reaction. She wished she hadn't even thought it. She tried to
stick to good thoughts in his presence. When she couldn't, and he had
a bad night afterward, she blamed herself, as her efficient memory
dredged up all the books and magazine articles she had read emphasiz-
ing the effect of psychological factors on the course of the disease. She
didn't entirely believe it, but she felt compelled to give the benefit of the
doubt to every theory that might help. It couldn't do any harm to think
positively. And if it gave him a few more months . . .

"I don't think Dad can stand to be around me."

"That's not true." It was true.

"Poor Dad. He's always been a hypochondriac—we have that in
common. He must hate this."

"He just wants you to get well."

"If that's what he wants, I'm afraid I'm going to disappoint him
again. At least this will be the last time I let him down."

He said this merrily, with the old, familiar light darting from his
eyes. She allowed herself to be amused. He had always been fond of
teasing, and held no subject sacred. As the de-facto authority figure in
the house—Martin hadn't been home enough to be the real discipli-
narian—she had often been forced to reprimand Laird, but, in truth,
she shared his sense of humor. She responded to it now by leaning over
to cuff him on the arm. It was an automatic response, prompted by a
burst of high spirits that took no notice of the circumstances. It was a
mistake. Even through the thickness of his terry-cloth robe, her knuckles knocked on bone. There was nothing left of him.

"It's his loss," she said, the shock of Laird's thinness making her serious again. It was the furthest she would go in criticizing Martin. She
had always felt it her duty to maintain a benign image of him for the

children. He had become a character of her invention, with a whole range of postulated emotions whereby he missed them when he was away on a business trip and thought of them every few minutes when he had to work late. Some years earlier, when she was secretly seeing a doctor—a psychiatrist—she had finally admitted to herself that Martin was never going to be the lover she had dreamed of. He was an ambitious, competitive, self-absorbed man who probably should never have got married. It was such a relief to be able to face it that she had wanted to share the news with her children, only to discover that they were dependent on the myth. They could hate his work, but they could not bring themselves to believe he had any choice in the matter. She had dropped the subject.

"Thank you, Ma. It's his loss in your case, too."

A throbbing began behind her eyes, angering her. The last thing she wanted to do was cry. There would be plenty of time for that. "It's not all his fault," she said when she had regained some measure of control. "I'm not very good at talking about myself. I was brought up not to."

"So was I," he said.

"Yes, I suppose you were."

"Luckily, I didn't pay any attention." He grinned.

"I hope not," she said, and meant it. "Can I get you anything?"

"A new immune system?"

She rolled her eyes, trying to disguise the way his joke had touched on her prayers. "Very funny. I was thinking more along the lines of an iced tea or an extra blanket."

"I'm fine. I'm getting tired, actually."

Her entire body went on the alert, and she searched his face anxiously for signs of deterioration. Her nerves darted and pricked whenever he wanted anything; her adrenaline rushed. The fight-or-flight response, she supposed. She had often wanted to flee, but had forced herself to stay, to fight with what few weapons she had. She responded to his needs, making sure there was a fresh, clean set of sheets ready when he was tired, food when he was hungry. It was what she could do.

"Shall I get the nurse?" She pushed her chair back from the table.

"O.K.," Laird said weakly. He stretched out his hand to her, and the incipient moonlight illuminated his skin, so it shone like alabaster. His face had turned ashy. It was a sight that made her stomach drop. She ran for Maggie, and by the time they returned Laird's eyes were closed, his head lolling to one side. Automatically, Janet looked for a stirring in his chest. There it was: his shoulders expanded; he still breathed. Always, in the second before she saw movement, she became cold and clinical as she braced herself for the possibility of discovering that he was dead.

Maggie had her fingers on his wrist and was counting his pulse against the second hand on her watch, her lips moving. She laid his limp hand back on his lap. "Fast," she pronounced.

"I'm not surprised," Janet said, masking her fear with authority. "We had a long talk."

Maggie frowned. "Now I'll have to wake him up again for his meds."

"Yes, I suppose that's true. I forgot about that."

Janet wheeled him into his makeshift room downstairs and helped Maggie lift him into the rented hospital bed. Although he weighed almost nothing, it was really a job for two; his weight was dead weight. In front of Maggie, she was all brusque efficiency, except for the moment when her fingers strayed to touch Laird's pale cheek and she prayed she hadn't done any harm.

WHO'S YOUR FAVORITE author?" he asked one night.

"Oh, there are so many," she said.

"Your real favorite."

She thought. "The truth is there are certain subjects I find attractive more than certain authors. I seem to read in cycles, to fulfill an emotional yearning."

"Such as?"

"Books about people who go off to live in Africa or Australia or the South Seas."

He laughed. "That's fairly self-explanatory. What else?"

"When I really hate life I enjoy books about real murders. 'True crime,' I think they're called now. They're very punishing."

"Is that what's so compelling about them? I could never figure it out. I just know that at certain times I loved the gore, even though I felt absolutely disgusted with myself for being interested in it."

"You need to think about when those times were. That will tell you a lot." She paused. "I don't like reading about sex."

"Big surprise!"

"No, no," she said. "It's not for the reason you think, or not only for that reason. You see me as a prude, I know, but remember, it's part of a mother's job to come across that way. Although perhaps I went a bit far . . ."

He shrugged amiably. "Water under the bridge. But go on about sex."

"I think it should be private. I always feel as though these writers are showing off when they describe a sex scene. They're not really trying to describe sex, but to demonstrate that they're not afraid to write about it. As if they're thumbing their noses at their mothers."

He made a moue.

Janet went on. "You don't think there's an element of that? I *do* question their motives, because I don't think sex can ever actually be portrayed—the sensations and the emotions are . . . beyond language. If you only describe the mechanics, the effect is either clinical or pornographic, and if you try to describe intimacy instead, you wind up with abstractions. The only sex you could describe fairly well is bad sex—and who wants to read about that, for God's sake, when everyone is having bad sex of their own?"

"Mother!" He was laughing helplessly, his arms hanging limply over the sides of his chair.

"I mean it. To me it's like reading about someone using the bathroom."

"Good grief!"

"Now who's the prude?"

"I never said I wasn't," he said. "Maybe we should change the subject."

She looked out across the land. The lights were on in other people's houses, giving the evening the look of early fall. The leaves were different, too, becoming droopy. The grass was dry, even with all the watering and tending from the gardener. The summer was nearly over.

"Maybe we shouldn't," she said. "I've been wondering. Was that side of life satisfying for you?"

"Ma, tell me you're not asking me about my sex life."

She took her napkin and folded it carefully, lining up the edges and running her fingers along the hems. She felt very calm, very pulled together and all of a piece, as if she'd finally got the knack of being a dignified woman. She threaded her fingers and laid her hands in her lap. "I'm asking about your love life," she said. "Did you love, and were you loved in return?"

"Yes."

"I'm glad."

"That was easy," he said.

"Oh, I've gotten very easy, in my old age."

"Does Dad know about this?" His eyes were twinkling wickedly.

"Don't be fresh," she said.

"You started it."

"Then I'm stopping it. Now."

He made a funny face, and then another, until she could no longer keep from smiling. His routine carried her back to memories of his childhood efforts to charm her: watercolors of her favorite vistas (unrecognizable without the captions), bouquets of violets self-consciously flung into her lap, chores performed without prompting. He had always gone too far, then backtracked to regain even footing. She had always allowed herself to be wooed.

Suddenly she realized: Laird had been the love of her life.

ONE NIGHT IT rained hard. Janet decided to serve the meal in the kitchen, since Martin was out. They ate in silence; she was freed from the compulsion to keep up the steady stream of chatter that she used to affect when Laird hadn't talked at all; now she knew she could save her words for afterward. He ate nothing but comfort foods lately: mashed potatoes, vanilla ice cream, rice pudding. The days of his strict macrobiotic regime, and all the cooking classes she had taken in order to help him along with it, were past. His body was essentially a thing of the past, too; when he ate, he was feeding what was left of his mind. He seemed to want to recapture the cosseted feeling he'd had when he'd been sick as a child and she would serve him flat ginger ale, and toast soaked in cream, and play endless card games with him, using his blanket-covered legs as a table. In those days, too, there'd been a general sense of giving way to illness: then, he let himself go completely because he knew he would soon be better and active and have a million things expected of him again. Now he let himself go because he had fought long enough.

Finally, he pushed his bowl toward the middle of the table, signalling that he was finished. (His table manners had gone to pieces. Who cared?) She felt a light, jittery excitement, the same jazzy feeling she got when she was in a plane that was just picking up speed on the runway. She arranged her fork and knife on the rim of her plate and pulled her chair in closer. "I had an odd dream last night," she said.

His eyes remained dull.

She waited uncertainly, thinking that perhaps she had started to talk too soon. "Would you like something else to eat?"

He shook his head. There was no will in his expression; his refusal was purely physical, a gesture coming from the satiation in his stomach. An animal walking away from its bowl, she thought.

To pass the time, she carried the dishes to the sink, gave them a good hot rinse, and put them in the dishwasher. She carried the ice cream to the counter, pulled a spoon from the drawer and scraped off a mouthful of the thick, creamy residue that stuck to the inside of the lid. She ate it without thinking, so the sudden sweetness caught her by surprise. All the while she kept track of Laird, but every time she thought she noticed signs of his readiness to talk and hurried back to the table she found his face still blank.

She went to the window. The lawn had become a floodplain and was filled with broad pools; the branches of the evergreens sagged, and the sky was the same uniform grayish yellow it had been since morning. She saw him focus his gaze on the line where the treetops touched the heavens, and she understood. There was no lovely interlude on this rainy night, no heathered dusk. The gray landscape had taken the light out of him.

"I'm sorry," she said aloud, as if it were her fault.

He gave a tiny, helpless shrug.

She hovered for a few moments, hoping, but his face was slack, and she gave up. She felt utterly forsaken, too disappointed and agitated to sit with him and watch the rain. "It's all right," she said. "It's a good night to watch television."

She wheeled him to the den and left him with Maggie, then did not know what to do with herself. She had no contingency plan for this time. It was usually the one period of the day when she did not need the anesthesia of tennis games, bridge lessons, volunteer work, errands. She had not considered the present possibility. For some time, she hadn't given any thought to what Martin would call "the big picture." Her conversations with Laird had lulled her into inventing a parallel big picture of her own. She realized that a part of her had worked out a whole scenario: the summer evenings would blend into fall; then, gradually, the winter would arrive, heralding chats by the fire, Laird resting his feet on the pigskin ottoman in the den while she dutifully knitted her yearly Christmas sweaters for Anne's children.

She had allowed herself to imagine a future. That had been her mistake. This silent, endless evening was her punishment, a reminder of how things really were.

She did not know where to go in her own house, and ended up wandering through the rooms, propelled by a vague, hunted feeling. Several times, she turned around, expecting someone to be there, but, of course, no one ever was. She was quite alone. Eventually, she realized that she was imagining a person in order to give material properties to the source of her wounds. She was inventing a villain. There should be a villain, shouldn't there? There should be an enemy, a devil, an evil force that could be driven out. Her imagination had provided it with aspects of a corporeal presence so she could pretend, for a moment, that there was a real enemy hovering around her, someone she could have the police come and take away. But the enemy was part of Laird, and neither he nor she nor any of the doctors or experts or ministers could separate the two.

She went upstairs and took a shower. She barely paid attention to her own body anymore, and only noticed abstractly that the water was too hot, her skin turning pink. Afterward, she sat on the chaise longue in her bedroom and tried to read. She heard something; she leaned forward and cocked her head toward the sound. Was that Laird's voice? Suddenly she believed that he had begun to talk after all—she believed he was talking to Maggie. She dressed and went downstairs. He was alone in the den, alone with the television. He didn't hear or see her. She watched him take a drink from a cup, his hand shaking badly. It was a plastic cup with a straw poking through the lid, the kind used by small children while they are learning to drink. It was supposed to prevent accidents, but it couldn't stop his hands from trembling. He managed to spill the juice anyway.

LAIRD HAD ALWAYS coveted the decadent pile of cashmere lap blankets she had collected over the years in the duty-free shops of the various British airports. Now he wore one around his shoulders, one over his knees. She remembered similar balmy nights when he would arrive home from soccer practice after dark, a towel slung around his neck.

"I suppose it has to be in the church," he said.

"I think it should," she said, "but it's up to you."

"I guess it's not the most timely moment to make a statement about my personal disbeliefs. But I'd like you to keep it from being too lugubrious. No lilies, for instance."

"God forbid."

"And have some decent music."

"Such as?"

"I had an idea, but now I can't remember."

He pressed his hands to his eyes. His fingers were so transparent that they looked as if he were holding them over a flashlight.

"Please buy a smashing dress, something mournful yet elegant."

"All right."

"And don't wait until the last minute."

She didn't reply.

JANET GAVE UP on the idea of a rapprochement between Martin and Laird; she felt freer when she stopped hoping for it. Martin rarely came home for dinner anymore. Perhaps he was having an affair? It was a thought she'd never allowed herself to have before, but it didn't threaten her now. Good for him, she even decided, in her strongest, most magnanimous moments. Good for him if he's actually feeling bad and trying to do something to make himself feel better.

Anne was brave and chipper during her visits, yet when she walked back out to her car, she would wrap her arms around her ribs and shudder. "I don't know how you do it, Mom. Are you really all right?" she always asked, with genuine concern.

"Anne's become such a hopeless matron," Laird always said, with fond exasperation, when he and his mother were alone again later. Once, Janet began to tease him for finally coming to friendly terms with his sister, but she cut it short when she saw that he was blinking furiously.

They were exactly the children she had hoped to have: a companionable girl, a mischievous boy. It gave her great pleasure to see them together. She did not try to listen to their conversations but watched from a distance, usually from the kitchen as she prepared them a snack reminiscent of their childhood, like watermelon boats or lemonade. Then she would walk Anne to the car, their similar good shoes clacking across the gravel. They hugged, pressing each other's arms, and their brief embraces buoyed them up—forbearance and grace passing back and forth between them like a piece of shared clothing, designated for use by whoever needed it most. It was the kind of parting toward which she had aimed her whole life, a graceful, secure parting at the close of a peaceful afternoon. After Anne left, Janet always had a tranquil moment or two as she walked back to the house through the humid September air. Everything was so still. Occasionally there were the hums and clicks of a lawnmower or the shrieks of a band of children heading home from school. There were the insects and the birds. It was a straightforward, simple life she had chosen. She had tried never to ask for too much, and to be of use. Simplicity had been her hedge against bad luck. It had worked for so long. For a brief moment, as she stepped lightly up the single slate stair and through the door, her legs still harboring all their former vitality, she could pretend her luck was still holding.

Then she would glance out the window and there would be the heart-catching sight of Laird, who would never again drop by for a casual visit. Her chest would ache and flutter, a cave full of bats.

Perhaps she had asked for too much, after all.

"WHAT DID YOU want to be when you grew up?" Laird asked.

"I was expected to be a wife and mother. I accepted that. I wasn't a rebel."

"There must have been something else."

"No," she said. "Oh, I guess I had all the usual fantasies of the day, of being the next Amelia Earhart or Margaret Mead, but that was all they were—fantasies. I wasn't even close to being brave enough. Can you imagine me flying across the ocean on my own?" She laughed and looked over for his laughter, but he had fallen asleep.

A FRIEND OF Laird's had somehow got the mistaken information that Laird had died, so she and Martin received a condolence letter. There was a story about a time a few years back when the friend was with Laird on a bus in New York. They had been sitting behind two older women, waitresses who began to discuss their income taxes, trying to decide how much of their tip income to declare to sound realistic so they wouldn't attract an audit. Each woman offered up bits of folk wisdom on the subject, describing in detail her particular situation. During a lull in the conversation, Laird stood up.

"Excuse me, I couldn't help overhearing," he said, leaning over them. "May I have your names and addresses, please? I work for the I.R.S."

The entire bus fell silent as everyone watched to see what would happen next. Laird took a small notebook and pen from the inside pocket of his jacket. He faced his captive audience. "I'm part of a new I.R.S. outreach program," he told the group. "For the next ten minutes I'll be taking confessions. Does anyone have anything he or she wants to tell me?"

Smiles. Soon the whole bus was talking, comparing notes—when they'd first realized he was kidding, and how scared they had been before they caught on. It was difficult to believe these were the same New Yorkers who were supposed to be so gruff and isolated.

"Laird was the most vital, funniest person I ever met," his friend wrote.

Now, in his wheelchair, he faced off against slow-moving flies, waving them away.

"THE GLOAMING," LAIRD said.

Janet looked up from her knitting, startled. It was midafternoon, and the living room was filled with bright October sun. "Soon," she said.

He furrowed his brow. A little flash of confusion passed through his eyes, and she realized that for him it was already dark.

He tried to straighten his shawl, his hands shaking. She jumped up to help; then, when he pointed to the fireplace, she quickly laid the logs as she wondered what was wrong. Was he dehydrated? She thought she recalled that a dimming of vision was a sign of dehydration. She tried to remember what else she had read or heard, but even as she grasped for information, facts, her instincts kept interrupting with a deeper, more dreadful thought that vibrated through her, rattling her and making her gasp as she often did when remembering her mistakes, things she wished she hadn't said or done, wished she had the chance to do over. She knew what was wrong, and yet she kept turning away from the truth, her mind spinning in every other possible direction as she worked on the fire, only vaguely noticing how wildly she made the sparks fly as she pumped the old bellows.

Her work was mechanical—she had made hundreds of fires—and soon there was nothing left to do. She put the screen up and pushed him close, then leaned over to pull his flannel pajamas down to meet his socks, protecting his bare shins. The sun streamed in around him, making him appear trapped between bars of light. She resumed her knitting, with mechanical hands.

"The gloaming," he said again. It did sound somewhat like "gloomy," because his speech was slurred.

"When all the world is purple," she said, hearing herself sound falsely bright. She wasn't sure whether he wanted her to talk. It was some time since he had talked—not long, really, in other people's lives, perhaps two weeks—but she had gone on with their conversations, gradually expanding into the silence until she was telling him stories and he was listening. Sometimes, when his eyes closed, she trailed off and began to drift. There would be a pause that she didn't always realize she was making, but if it went on too long he would call out "Mom?" with an edge of panic in his voice, as if he were waking from a nightmare. Then she would resume, trying to create a seamless bridge between what she had been thinking and where she had left off.

"It was really your grandfather who gave me my love for the gloaming," she said. "Do you remember him talking about it?" She looked up politely, expectantly, as if Laird might offer her a conversational reply.

He seemed to like hearing the sound of her voice, so she went on, her needles clicking. Afterward, she could never remember for sure at what point she had stopped talking and had floated off into a jumble of her own thoughts, afraid to move, afraid to look up, afraid to know at which exact moment she became alone. All she knew was that at a certain point the fire was in danger of dying out entirely, and when she got up to stir the embers she glanced at him in spite of herself and saw that his fingers were making knitting motions over his chest, the way people did as they were dying. She knew that if she went to get the nurse, Laird would be gone by the time she returned, so she went and stood behind him, leaning over to press her face against his, sliding her hands down his busy arms, helping him along with his fretful stitches until he finished this last piece of work.

LATER, AFTER THE most pressing calls had been made and Laird's body had been taken away, Janet went up to his old room and lay down on one of the twin beds. She had changed the room into a guest room when he went off to college, replacing his things with guest-room décor, thoughtful touches such as luggage racks at the foot of each bed, a writing desk stocked with paper and pens, heavy wooden hangers and shoe trees. She made an effort to remember the room as it had been when he was a little boy; she had chosen a train motif, then had to redecorate when Laird decided trains were silly. He had wanted it to look like a jungle, so she had hired an art student to paint a jungle mural on the walls. When he decided *that* was silly, he hadn't bothered her to do anything about it, but had simply marked time until he could move on.

Anne came over, offered to stay, but was relieved to be sent home to her children.

Presently, Martin came in. Janet was watching the trees turn to mere silhouettes against the darkening sky, fighting the urge to pick up a true-crime book, a debased urge. He lay down on the other bed.

"I'm sorry," he said.

"It's so wrong," she said angrily. She hadn't felt angry until that moment; she had saved it up for him. "A child shouldn't die before his parents. A young man shouldn't spend his early thirties wasting away talking to his mother. He should be out in the world. He shouldn't be thinking about me, or what I care about, or my opinions. He shouldn't have had to return my love to me—it was his to squander. Now I have it all back and I don't know what I'm supposed to do with it," she said.

She could hear Martin weeping in the darkness. He sobbed, and her anger veered away.

They were quiet for some time.

"Is there going to be a funeral?" Martin asked finally.

"Yes. We should start making the arrangements."

"I suppose he told you what he wanted."

"In general. He couldn't decide about the music."

She heard Martin roll onto his side, so that he was facing her across the narrow chasm between the beds. He was still in his office clothes. "I remember being very moved by the bagpipes at your father's funeral."

It was an awkward offering, to be sure, awkward and late, and seemed to come from someone on the periphery of her life who knew her only slightly. It didn't matter; it was perfectly right. Her heart rushed toward it.

"I think Laird would have liked that idea very much," she said.

It was the last moment of the gloaming, the last moment of the day her son died. In a breath, it would be night; the moon hovered behind the trees, already rising to claim the sky, and she told herself she might as well get on with it. She sat up and was running her toes across the bare floor, searching for her shoes, when Martin spoke again, in a tone she used to hear on those long-ago nights when he rarely got home until after the children were in bed and he relied on her to fill him in on what they'd done that day. It was the same curious, shy, deferential tone that had always made her feel as though all the frustrations and boredom and mistakes and rushes of feeling in her days as a mother did indeed add up to something of importance, and she decided that the next round of telephone calls could wait while she answered the question he asked her: "Please tell me—what else did my boy like?"

(1993)

ATTRACTION

DAVID LONG

She was fifteen that summer of 1963, living with her mother in a rented house by a stretch of dead water called McCafferty's Slough. It was only a short walk through a stand of aspen to the back door of the skating rink, a huge, watery-green Quonset. She lugged her own roller skates, in a blue tin case with her name, "Marly Wilcox," stencilled on it in nail polish. In love with nothing else just then, she loved the sensations of skating, the swift cuts, the sweat like a cool metal comb delving into her hair. She didn't paw stupidly at the air, didn't grab her arms behind her back like a showoff—they pumped at her sides, thin, efficient, her fingertips tucked together like rosettes. The music crackled from tiny loudspeakers, out-of-date show tunes and slurpy waltzes, the occasional 45 by Duane Eddy or Chubby Checker or Little Eva. None of the boys pulled at her clothes or whipped her into the rails. She gave off a signal, an aura: Hands off, you'll get no satisfaction from me. More likely, they just weren't interested.

Charlie Bitterman was there. Willowy, pale-skinned, with his gauzy shirts, his flop of sandy hair. His eyes were the color of cinnamon toast, his smile abrupt, astonished, maybe a little toothy. It was the summer he was going by "Chas." He'd graduated from high school in Sperry that June, and was going out East to study engineering. He was the son of Ike Bitterman, the architect. The Bittermans had sent an older boy to West Point, a daughter to veterinary school in California, and now this last one to Rensselaer. Afterward, he would come and join Ike's firm—the way Jamie Shirtliff and Evan St. Clair had come home and breezed into their fathers' law practices. "It's the pattern," Marly's mother, Jeanette, said. "Time-honored. Old as the world." Marly had been watching him, keeping tabs. He was the most interesting thing going, she'd decided. And she wasn't the only one. She'd caught Mlle. Picard, her French teacher, languidly staring after Charles one winter afternoon—a flush rose to Mlle. Picard's temples, but she had shrugged, smiled, shamelessly dragged Marly into the moment with her, so that it was Marly who turned away, embarrassed, found out.

All that year, until spring, Charles had gone out with Cynthia Lumquist. They'd made a famous couple, no question about it. Cynthia was a loopy, smart-alecky girl, flagrantly blond, with a tantalizing gap between her front teeth. It was a romance oblivious of social standing. Cynthia had no parents, as far as anyone knew—she floated, skirted catastrophe, lived with an aunt or an older sister, emerged at school from an amazing array of vehicles. Her hair was platinum, silver-white like a movie star's.

Invisible amid the horseplay, the clattering trays, Marly had watched the two of them dance to the record-player in the cafeteria. Charles danced like no local boy. No flailing, no sappy grin. He kept his eyes shut, his moves cool and minimal. Cynthia stuck her arms straight out over his shoulders, let her fingers dangle (*languorously*, Marly thought, like wind chimes in a sultry movie), while Charles aimed a stream of incantation into her ear. They might have been dancing on the deck of a ship, they might have been the last two people on earth. Eventually, the vice-principal would come and bust up this display—Cynthia would bristle, ready for battle, but Charles always steered her away, unfazed. He might show up in the library later with one of Cynthia's crimson kisses enamelled to his forehead.

He had plenty of friends, Marly had observed, but no best friend, and didn't travel in any pack. It was as if he'd siphoned people out of different cliques, one by one. He was smart in an amused, leapfrogging way. Marly had had one class with him—civics (Charles had gotten mono as a sophomore, and was still picking off requirements in his last semester). He couldn't have cared less about politics (he obviously read only what he wanted to read), but every few days Marly would watch fat, tonsured Mr. Nardi cave in to boredom and address Charles with something like "Mr. Bitterman, how'd you like to give us the succession to the Presidency?" Charles always looked genuinely happy to have been called on. No, he didn't know about that, but what did Mr. Nardi think about "Silent Spring," and what about this news report he'd seen that the world's population would hit nine billion by the year 2025? He consulted some ink marks on the back of his hand. Roughly five hundred and sixty-two million tons of human being, he said.

Cynthia had broken up with him, finally. After Charles, she had an affair with an older man, Casper Gault, who ran the news agency. The news agency, up on First near the Opera House, was one of Marly's haunts—she drank sludgy chocolate Cokes, killed late-afternoon hours flipping through paperbacks on the swivel stands. Gault had once played ball for Montana State; he was beefy, with a prickly, brick-red face. Marly always pictured him down on one knee, snipping the wire that bound the newspapers and magazines—it made an indecent thump as it released. The thought of lying spread-eagled under Gault, that heaving weight on her—it was appalling, engrossing. Above the news agency was a string of cheap rooms where a couple of the waitresses lived. People claimed that the man who'd had the building before Gault had run girls out of those rooms. That's how it was said, "running girls."

Gault had a daughter in Marly's class, but Marly had never paid her much attention. A pallid, homely girl in wrinkled corduroy jumpers: Ruth Ann Gault. But one night, that night at the rink, Marly noticed her trudging across the dusty hardwood in her oxford shoes, a strange, earthbound creature among the streaking shapes. Marly ducked into the girls' locker room. Cynthia Lumquist sat worming her feet into her skates, laughing about something. She'd just taken a drag on her Winston and parked it on the edge of the bench, where it began to sear the varnish. She wore a blue leotard and hair ribbons and a batch of loud bracelets. As Marly watched, Ruth Ann rounded the doorway, came silently at Cynthia with a locker key in her fist, and put Cynthia's eye out.

It happened in an instant, a tiny glint. Cynthia toppled over backward, and Marly, without a thought, threw her arms out and caught her. Someone shrieked. The owner of the rink and his son and some other men shoved their way in through the commotion. Cynthia was peeled out of Marly's arms and carried off, her face in wet paper towels. Ruth Ann was wrestled into custody. Songs kept scratching through the loudspeakers, but the skaters were all packed against the railings. Even the light seemed wrong—thin and gold. Marly scanned the place for Charles, couldn't locate him. (She'd seen him earlier, watched him taking in Cynthia's arrival, tracking her through the crowd, his face expressionless for once.) Now she went out the front door, still in her skates, and crunched into the edge of the parking lot. It was a breathless night—a fog of clay dust eddied in the air, blurring the tail-lights, leaving a film on everything. She looked for his car, his father's pale-gold Thunderbird, but it wasn't there. In a few minutes, they closed the rink. The floodlights were doused, the last knots of people dissolved.

This was the year of the tent worms. They fell from the aspens as Marly made her way home that night, splattering down like the first heavy drops of a storm. She smelled them—awful things, vile, hormonal. She found a few still plastered to her scarf when she peeled it off under the vestibule light at home. Gagging, she ran to the bathroom and flushed the scarf away—it clogged the line and had to be retrieved the next day with a metal snake.

CYNTHIA'S EYES HAD been honey-colored, but the glass eye was a jazzy emerald. Who could deny her? "Now what are *you* staring at?" she'd say to men, flicking at her bangs. It was as if she'd caught them gawking at her chest. They did that, too. She was shorter and rounder than Marly; she had a good figure, a dreamy, slangy way of rolling her shoulders. She wore puffy angora tops and stretch pants and cowboy boots, or red lace-less sneakers. Like her mother, Jeanette, Marly was all torso—Slats, she'd been called in junior high (mercifully, no one remembered).

Charges were filed against Ruth Ann—Marly had to go down to the courthouse and give her deposition—but somehow there was no trial. Casper Gault put the news agency up for sale, and the family left Sperry for good. Charlie Bitterman was gone, too. Every morning, downshifting raucously, threatening not to make the hill, Marly's school bus cornered by the Bittermans' house. It occupied a spit of ground above the park, a faint salmon color, all flat roofs and eccentric jutting angles, with a few dwarf trees deposited around the lawn. At Christmas, it would float in a bath of blue floodlights. Marly squashed her books against her chest and burrowed down in the seat.

Her own house was an embarrassment: squat and shingled, peeling turquoise, with a glaring tin roof. One winter, an accumulation of cot-tonwood leaves and fallen-in chimney bricks plugged the heater vent, so that Marly and Jeanette both got dangerous, woozy headaches from the fumes. The landlord was ancient—he appeared every August in the fair parade, a spindly old farmer piloting a goat cart. Jeanette couldn't stand the sight of him. "We're absolutely not spending another month in this hellhole," she told Marly periodically. Yet they never moved.

Out the back door was McCafferty's Slough, one of the countless oxbows the river had cut, then abandoned. It gave off clouds of mos-quitoes in the spring; it smelled of cattails and rotting bark. Later in the summer, algae clumped in the shallows like green tapioca. When the cottonwoods shed, the air was blinding—the screens clogged, great berms of cotton collected in the weeds. But there were turtles in the slough, too, and once in a while a pileated woodpecker. And no traffic, and no yapping dogs, and no neighbors—she and Jeanette could do as they wished down there and never feel spied on.

Jeanette had managed to hold on to some of her father's furniture. There was a heavy sideboard, a gumwood mirror (it hung at the eye level of an ordinary person—Jeanette bent and aimed a wincing pout into it every time she left the house). The headboard of Marly's bed went clear to the ceiling, scrolled black walnut, with a frieze of dusty cherub faces. Marly's grandfather had been a doctor in Sperry—saw to diphtheria patients, drilled out horrible infected mastoids, amputated fingers. "This wasn't like now," Jeanette told Marly. "They'd sometimes pay in potatoes or cordwood, or send him these pathetic notes." He was a charmer in a black fedora, and the source of all their lanky height. He was also a drunk, Jeanette said, and not averse to injecting himself with morphine. He'd died at fifty-one, his finances in a shambles. She talked openly about all this. "Why be full of secrets?" she said. Jeanette could be like that, blithe, modern. "You don't know how it used to be, Marly. People suffocated. They couldn't be their true selves."

Still, Jeanette's true self had its own shadowy spots. The subject of Marly's father, for one. He was an indiscretion, that's all she'd say. Poor judgment on her part.

"Yes, but what did—"

"You can save your wind, honey," Jeanette said, fending her off. "It's unfair, I know it is, but I'm not parading that around again. It's just a fact you're going to have to live with."

Well, she'll slip up sometime, Marly thought. Not as to his name and whereabouts, maybe, but how it was, before he got to be a mistake. Something regarding the nature of the attraction. But no, she didn't.

MARLY HAD GROWN up believing there was a cache of money tucked away for her college. When the time finally came, Jeanette admitted it had dwindled. It had been invested rashly, nibbled at. "Try not to hate me," she said. Jeanette could be that way, too. A vein of melodrama could surface; her voice would turn lavish and sentimental.

"Oh, I'm *sure*," Marly said. She and Jeanette might rub each other wrong for days, but their quarrelling had no depth. They were companionable, mainly. And, anyway, this news didn't crush her—somehow she'd suspected it. It had more to do with Jeanette not being ready to give her up. Nor did it cancel her vision of herself as one of the ones, like Charles, who wasn't trapped, who had a rightful life to go to. She could wait awhile, it wouldn't kill her.

The September after her graduation, Marly started work at a supper club called Daugherty's. It was out on the highway, the place people went for prime rib or Sunday brunch, a maze of dark, muffled rooms. It was at Daugherty's she ran into Cynthia again. Marly waited tables, Cynthia worked the bar and card room. She'd gotten married, had a ring to flash, but she was the same: flirty and wisecracking, hard to pin down. The winter was long and heavy; on weekends, Daugherty's was crazy with skiers, the lot overflowing with tour buses. Cynthia acted as if she and Marly were fast friends from another life. They went on break together, laughed and complained, drank champagne Cynthia lifted from the banquet rooms. Many nights, Marly stayed late and gave Cynthia a ride home.

The husband's name was Rory Blanchard. He was older by a little, twenty-seven or so, wiry, pale as coconut milk. He'd been in and out of the military. "What's he do?" Marly asked. Cynthia made one of her faces. Apparently, Rory bought and sold for somebody—vanloads of this and that. Sometimes deals went wrong and he was required to re-possess things. He was often gone. He could be funny in a rough way, and when he was like that—easy with his money, eyes flashing—Marly caught a glimpse of what Cynthia had seen in him. But he could be sullen for no obvious reason; mean. He was always teasing them, plying Cynthia and Marly with jokes. Often as not they blipped right past Marly—there'd be some nasty angle that escaped her at first. Such as the night he said, "You hear them North Dakotans figured out a new use for sheep?"

"What's that?" Cynthia asked.

"Wool," Rory said. He had that grin. His teeth were as big and white as Chiclets.

One evening, the Bittermans stomped into Daugherty's from the cold, and sat in Marly's section. Mr. Bitterman had an imposing head—square, heavy browed, his hair slicked back in silver furrows as if engraved. Mrs. Bitterman was in fawn-colored suede. She had an air-brushed quality, a touch of a smile, as if she'd spent her life looking out through a train window.

Marly brought their dinners, loitered within earshot, heard nothing exceptional. "And how's that son of yours doing?" she finally got up the nerve to ask, pouring coffee. "Chas? Charlie?"

Mr. Bitterman blinked and glanced up over his half-lenses. Did he know this waitress? His wife tapped her lips with her napkin, looked away. "He's doing fine work," Mr. Bitterman said. "Couldn't be better."

Marly flushed. "Really, well—that's great," she said, ducking, backing from the table. How easily she could be lied to.

SOMETIME THAT WINTER, Cynthia got pregnant. Marly couldn't believe she'd been so careless. No, she could, she could see it perfectly. Why not? Cynthia worked a few more months, then got herself fired. Now it was summer, and Cynthia was enormous. She and Rory lived in an apartment over a three-car garage up on Ash. It had two miserly dormers, an accumulation of spindly furnishings, a miniature stove and refrigerator. The bathroom was an afterthought, a tiny, oblong plywood partition sticking out into the room. Rory hated the place—he vowed to move them onto "his land." It consisted of a one-acre lot out in the west valley, which he'd taken in trade for a Volkswagen bus. Flat, exposed, with nothing growing on it but knapweed and clumps of Russian thistle. He'd talked his cousin into digging the cellar hole and setting the forms for the concrete, but Cynthia had a vision of them living down there indefinitely. "In the crypt," she called it. Tarpaper roof, splintery planks laid across the mud, the electrical service on a little pole. No way.

The apartment had a sweet, cloistered feel in the mornings, but after lunch it got sticky hot. Marly made a point of never coming by when Rory was likely to be home. She didn't even like to imagine Rory being alone there with Cynthia, slouching at the dinette, recounting some pointless transaction. But this particular afternoon Cynthia had called her, begged her to come over. Marly found her on the edge of the bed with her feet splayed. She was staring. "This has gotten too weird," she said finally.

"Don't you have a fan?"

"Just blows it around," Cynthia said.

She lay back on her elbows and stuck her belly out. "Well, I et the watermelon this time," she said.

"You did," Marly said.

"Swallowed the big fruit."

She hoisted herself and made a stab at clearing the mess from the table. "Rory thinks I'm kind of disgusting." She stuck her tongue out. "Hey, how'd you like to get me out of here?"

"Don't they want you to just kind of take it easy?"

"Oh, *pul-ease*," Cynthia said.

Marly owned a little black Ford Falcon. She got Cynthia down the stairs and loaded into it.

"Any place in particular?"

"Just go fast," Cynthia said.

So Marly got them two cans of pop and took the back roads into the lower valley. There hadn't been a storm or any semblance of clouds for twenty straight days. The first cut of hay had been made, and the wheat was starting to lean over and show the tracks of the wind. Cynthia rode with her eyes closed.

"Any better?" Marly asked.

Cynthia rolled her head back and tried to shake some air down into her scalp.

They swung onto Dutchman's Grade, and Cynthia looked up. "What's that smell?"

"Mint," Marly said. "That's all mint out there, that dark green?"

"How do you know stuff like that?"

"I just do. Anyway, can't you smell it?"

Cynthia laughed. "Stinks," she said. "Smells worse than Rory."

"You're terrible," Marly said.

Cynthia flipped a cigarette from her little plaid case and strained forward to poke in the lighter.

"You want to go back yet?"

"Oh, Jesus, no," Cynthia said. Then, in a minute, she said she wanted to be driven up by the new part of the golf course.

Why not? Marly thought.

A contractor had bought the clover field alongside the new golf holes, and a string of houses was going up. This was the back way to Stillwater. Paper birches had stood in this field, Marly remembered, huge, shivering clumps of them. Up by the road, there'd been stacks of bee boxes, almost too white to look at on a sunny day.

"Slow down!" Cynthia shouted. "Here, turn."

Marly bumped onto the dirt. The gumbo had hardened into deep ruts, the width of truck axles. She tried to balance on top of the ridges, but slid off. Both their heads banged up against the roof.

"Jesus, watch it," Cynthia said. She pointed, told Marly to pull up behind a mound of topsoil, within view of the last house. It was two stories, bare plywood with staging and planks skirting the upstairs.

Cynthia scooched down in her seat.

"What are we looking at?" Marly said.

"Just hold on."

Marly wiped her eyes. In a moment, she saw Charlie Bitterman creep out onto the staging, wearing a nail pouch and no shirt. It was the strangest place to see him. His upper body had gotten some color—a washboard of glistening muscle.

"How'd you know?" Marly said.

"Spies. Now go get him to come over here, will you?"

"I can't do that," Marly said.

Cynthia squeezed her arm, almost roughly.

Marly got out and did it—bounced up the gangplank into the half-built house and brought him down off the scaffolding. "Somebody wants to see you," she said. "Over in that car."

He squinted past her. His face was leaner, his teeth shone. He tapped her shoulder in thanks, studied her a second. "Marly Wilcox," he said.

Marly hugged her elbows. "Go *on*," she said.

She watched him make his way toward Cynthia, his gait long and springy, the hammer banging against his leg. The sky was white. A few bees plied the air around her.

IT AMAZED MARLY, thinking of it later, that Cynthia would want to be seen looking like that: sweaty, her hair snarled by the wind, her lap full of that bulky weight. But no, Cynthia always knew her powers. It was a picture Marly couldn't shake. Charles had leaned against the car roof and looked in at Cynthia and let himself be asked question after question in that voice of hers while she sat rubbing her belly with both hands, the shirt pulled way up.

The baby came two weeks early. Rory was out of state. Marly had expected to be called on to drive Cynthia to the hospital when the time came, but she learned the news from Jeanette, who was rattling the newspaper under her nose. "Isn't this that friend of yours?"

Marly stared: "Discharged, Mrs. R. Blanchard and baby girl."

Cynthia met her on the landing, in a baggy gown. She looked awful, Marly thought—shocking, as if her face had deflated.

"How come you didn't tell me?" Marly said. "Who'd you get to drive?"

"Don't start in on me, all right?" Cynthia said in the apartment. The baby was sleeping heavily in a bassinet. Her eyelashes were long and fine, as transparent as fishing line. Cynthia had named her Cher. "And don't tell me it's a dumb name, O.K.?"

"I wouldn't," Marly said. "It's beautiful. And she's beautiful."

Cynthia shook her head tiredly. Then, in one rough motion, she slipped the gown off her shoulders and turned to face Marly. "You believe this?" she said.

Her breasts stuck straight out, hard as marble, crosshatched with bright-blue veins. The nipples were almost maroon, raw and distressed, leaking milk.

Marly was speechless.

Flowers drooped in the center of the dinette, baby roses in a spray of greens.

"So what's Rory think about all this?" Marly asked. "He must be pretty excited?"

Cynthia looked up from the bassinet. "Who knows?" she said. "He's stranded down in Sheridan."

God, Marly thought. Charles.

JEANETTE WORKED IN the Clerk and Recorder's office. She demanded peace and quiet when she got home—her eyes hurt, she was sick of pacifying people, didn't want a lot of chitchat. That was fine by Marly. But, as evenings wore on, the peace and quiet seemed to eat at Jeanette. Everything got louder—the TV blared, the blower in the furnace wheezed on and off. Jeanette sat on the love seat with a goblet of red wine and flung her voice back over her shoulder. "What's that?" Marly was always having to say from the tiny kitchen.

One such night in early fall, the phone rang, and it was Charles.

"Who's that bothering you so late?" Jeanette yelled.

"It's not *late*," Marly hissed at her. She dragged the cord down into the bathroom and shut the door.

"God, I'm at loose ends," he started in. No "How are you?" Nothing.

She pictured him the way he'd been, shirt off, toughened up. Now he sounded winded, his voice choppy, whiny.

"I think about going back to that school and my heart freezes. I'm not cut out for this."

Why spill this to *her?* What had become of all his tony friends? She listened, stunned, watching a ladybug traverse the window sash.

"None of this was my idea," he said. "I'd rather just stay and work."

"You can't do that," Marly said.

"The point is, why can't I? What exactly would be the trouble with that?"

"I don't know," Marly said. "It's not you."

There was a stubborn silence on his end. "I tried getting hold of Cynthia," he said finally. "But he answered. The husband. I tried three times."

"Well, he lives there," Marly said. "What do you want with her, anyway?" She wished he'd just say it out loud.

"Marly, listen, you suppose you could get out?" he asked her.

"What, me?" Marly said. "I don't think so. It's awful late, and anyway—"

But of course she did meet him. Once the news agency had closed, at ten, the only thing open besides the bars was the Park Inn, a bright, square box up on Montana. Charles was waiting in the window, cupping his face against the glass. He wore a snap-studded workshirt and had a blue bandanna tied across his forehead.

Trying to blend in, Marly thought—he never would. She came straight to him but saw at once that it was the wrong place for this talk. The booths were right on top of each other, the lights merciless.

They ended up riding in his car, splitting cans of malt liquor. It had a dark taste Marly liked, and she drank most of it, her back against her door, while she watched him battle himself.

"You know, if I stayed here he'd make sure I got laid off," he said. "He'd engineer it. He'd twist arms."

"Who? Your father?"

"Is that too paranoid?"

"I think if you got the chance you should get out of here," she said. "It's a gift."

"No, it's not," he said. "It's a debt. It's a big, convoluted initiation rite. It's ordained. It's . . ."

He barely looked at her as he drove. They crossed back and forth over the same streets—now it *was* late. Marly cranked her window down, letting the wind hit her face, and felt the faint buoyancy of the alcohol. He'd worked himself into an impasse, pushed himself right up against it. But he still hadn't gotten at what it really was, what he was afraid of. Was it competing? she wondered. Being found, of all things, ordinary?

She turned back to him. "You can't moon around," she heard herself say, full of spiky energy. It was all she could do not to add, "I expected a lot more from you."

WHATEVER SHE SAID that night, it worked: Charles disappeared back to school. She got a postcard from him, two old-time, pasty-white boxers facing off in the Federal Street Gym in Albany. "Knuckling down," it said.

The hunter's moon came and went. It snowed on Halloween, there was a week of slop and gray, then a blast of pure arctic air. Sometimes, on her nights off, Marly babysat for Rory and Cynthia. She brought Cher a mobile of stuffed animals made of calico, and also a couple of crocheted comforters Jeanette had been saving. Cold leaked into the apartment as badly as heat did in the summer. Two space heaters ran constantly. The lights dimmed and flickered, fuses blew. Cynthia never had anything more to read than *TV Guide,* so Marly brought a bag of plastic-covered library books. She pulled a chair beside the crib, laid a hand on the railing, and read "East of Eden" or "Exodus" as the baby slept. "Up to the 'E's, huh?" Jeanette had teased her.

One night, Cynthia and Rory didn't get home—it was one o'clock, then two. Marly heated a bottle and fed Cher and laid her back to sleep. Finally, she went to the window and saw Rory's truck in the driveway. Snow lay on the hood and windshield, as if the truck had been parked for some time. Marly ran down and found Cynthia passed out on the seat, with one arm snaked around the shift knob. She was wearing an unlined windbreaker. "Hey, you've got to *wake up*," Marly said. Cynthia was dopey. She sent her hand up into Marly's face; her nails hooked

Marly's little neck chain and snapped it off. Now Marly could see that Cynthia's face was cut—her hair was actually sticky with blood.

Rory had hit something with the truck, Cynthia said. Something concrete, some kind of a post.

And where was he now? She had no idea.

"You've got to come upstairs," Marly said. "I can't carry you, you've got to get up." Eventually, Cynthia roused herself. Marly steered her to the bed, covered her. She didn't dare leave. She slept sitting up on the couch, under a heap of blankets. Near dawn, she heard Cynthia throwing up on the other side of the plywood wall.

In the morning, she got Cynthia some aspirin, and made her bouillon, which she wouldn't drink. Marly bundled the baby and took her out. The day was pearly, with a fine snow sifting down. They walked uptown, under the awnings, and Marly wished she'd run into someone she knew, so she could peel back the flap of blanket and show off the sleeping face. On the way back home, she stopped to have a look at Rory's truck. It hardly seemed dented at all, she thought.

"I don't see you anymore," Jeanette said. Marly got ready to whip back some smart answer. But it was true. "Sorry," she offered, but let it go at that. She started typing a letter to Charles, read over the half-dozen pathetic sentences. She'd stooped to complaining about the gloomy skies. "It's like living under a trailer," she'd written, which wasn't even original—it was an old line of Jeanette's. Nothing about Cynthia or Rory or the baby. She crumpled the paper, feeling stunted, boxed in. She sensed Jeanette studying her, on the verge of further assessment.

Then one night, mid-March, Charles called.

"Where are you?" she said. "Still in school, aren't you?"

"Still here," he said. "Out in the greater world."

"Glad to hear it," Marly said. It had to be after midnight where he was. "Tell me how Cynthia is."

"Exactly the same."

"What's she think about us—her and me, I mean. She tell you anything?"

No, she wasn't going to get into that with him. "You any happier?" she said. "You don't sound like it. You sound like you're going to fly apart."

"Me? No, I'm fine," he said. "Getting it all straightened out."

Somehow she didn't tell Cynthia about the call.

A few weeks later, she went to Cynthia's and found her wearing huge mirrored sunglasses. She had tripped going down the stairs, she said. There were tricky shadows, and, after all, her depth perception was weird.

"What if you'd been carrying the baby?" Marly said. "You've got to watch yourself."

Cynthia floated her that wicked, pitying smile. "Oh, I'll be sure to do that," she said. "I'll be sure to watch where I'm going."

EASTER CAME AT last, but spring was still sluggish. The cold was gone, but nothing took its place: no color, no hard dry ground. Jeanette had talked Marly into going to church with her, the sunrise service. It was held every year—despite damp, or ponderous banks of clouds—at a farm belonging to one of the members, up on a knoll. There was a card table with doughnuts and cider, paper napkins anchored with a rock. A friend of Jeanette's came and squeezed her and dabbed a kiss on her cheek. "Aren't we honored," the woman said.

Marly made no effort to smile. She stood hugging her arms—why hadn't she worn more clothes? An edgy, unmoored feeling had been creeping over her for days. In the center of this gathering a pump organ rested, not quite levelly, on an old rug; a girl in a pink dress and bulky overcoat operated it. There were maybe twenty other people, holding mimeographed sheets of lyrics for the two songs. Not hymns, exactly. One was "Working at the Real Work." More of a folk song, Marly thought—it was that kind of church. No one sang very loud. How could you with the mountains leaning over you? After that, people began to speak up, thoughts on spring, on feeling hopeful—even Jeanette offered a few words. Oh, God, Marly thought, don't make me have to do this. Jeanette's hand slid down and felt for hers, and, as it turned out, she was not required to say anything after all.

But the feeling hung on, the sense of being called on. That night, as if in answer, she saw Charles. He was alone, wearing an old flapping trenchcoat, striding under the elms on Jackson Street. A block from Cynthia and Rory's. There was still red in the sky, a fading band showing between the houses.

"What are you *doing*?" she said out the car window as she stopped. "Don't tell me. I know what you're doing."

"It's not what you think," he said.

But it was. It was exactly that—actually, it was worse. He'd left school without telling a soul. He was living in an old panel truck, which he'd taken to parking in a shallow gravel pit down by the river.

In the weeks following, Marly fell into a new routine—not babysitting for Rory and Cynthia on her free evenings but taking the baby out in the afternoon, so that Charles could go upstairs and be with Cynthia. Why did she do such a thing? "Can't you at least go somewhere?" she wanted to say, but she kept her mouth shut. Cynthia had a way of forcing you to look into her glass eye when she didn't want to be challenged—it was mesmerizing, disorienting. Marly took the baby and rushed outside, lightheaded, in a daze; she refused to be there when Charles arrived. She didn't want to see that flushed, ready-to-burst look on him. But how could they count on where Rory was going to be at any particular hour? Couldn't he just materialize in the doorway, lugging home some grievance? It was stupid, dangerous. Next time, she thought, she'd flat refuse.

But she didn't. She climbed back up to the landing, carrying Cher, whispering into her ear, "Sweet girl, sweet girl." She waited in the hot shade listening for that shrieky, gulping laughter of Cynthia's, praying they wouldn't still be going at it. If she was lucky, when she nudged open the door again Charles might be sitting on the kitchen table in just his cut-off jeans, with his bony knees pointing out. Sometimes Cynthia's legs would still be twisted in the bedsheets, her breasts flopped out on display.

"You're an angel," Cynthia would say to Marly distantly.

Marly sometimes changed Cher and put her down and left without making eye contact with either of them. She dug at herself later: What do I *want* with these people—who are they to me? But other times it was all friendly and conspiratorial. One afternoon, Charles even looped his sweaty, satisfied arm around Marly's neck, and she let herself fall into his hug and relax there while Cynthia rattled around in the bathroom, ran the water, and threw on clothes, as if this were all a reasonable way to live.

"I'm starving," Charles said. "Cynthia doesn't believe in food. Her icebox is a wasteland." He rubbed his bare stomach and stretched, looking about—where had his shirt gotten to? His other sneaker?

Cynthia came out flat-footed, yawning. "You two better beat it," she said. She looked bored to death with both of them.

On his way out, Charles detoured over by the crib and gave Cher's foot a soft tug. He bounded down the stairs, waiting by the flimsy door at the bottom so he and Marly could step out together. She walked up the alley with him to where he'd left the van, under a tumble of lilacs.

"Excuse the debris," he said, leaning in, clearing the seat of paperbacks, stacking them up his arm. "The Phenomenon of Man," a couple of books by Buckminster Fuller, a thick, comically austere-looking batch of mimeographing called "Means of Adhesion."

"This stuff looks deadly," Marly said, wedging herself in. There was another sprawl on the floor—catalogues, floppy pamphlets, a bunch of steno pads rubber-banded together.

"Absolutely," Charles said. "Mind-numbing." She caught a whiff of Cynthia as he threw his arm over the seat and backed around.

Days like this—not true summer yet, a break before the June rains— the valley floated in a polleny haze. The sun bore down on her bare, freckled legs. Charles drove them to a diner called Stell's, out beyond the viaduct. The way he looked, she could never imagine him *eating*. But he ate and ate—hot sandwiches and fries, another order of fries, lemon pie, and cup after cup of coffee. Away from Cynthia, the rest of him surfaced again, shook off the drowsiness.

"O.K., so what's a yurt? What's so great about domes?" she teased him, steering him into what he knew. It wasn't so hard.

"Got a pen?" he said. She had a blue felt-tip in her shirt pocket. He filled a pile of napkins with his sketches. Marly sat across from him with her iced tea, paying attention more or less, eerily happy. His father hadn't read him so wrong, she realized.

She interrupted him finally, touching his wrist. "You know you could sleep with me," she said.

Charles laughed, his long fingers spread across his lips. Not a cruel laugh—as if the idea were absurd, beyond imagining. No, he had thought about it; he already knew. He looked away, out into the shadow of the awning, with the laugh settling into a soft, distracted smile.

· · ·

DID SHE LOVE him, was that possible?

Now she was provoked, propelled into thinking. She kicked her-self—her idea of the future had been unforgivably lazy, worse even than his. She'd thought only as far as Rory catching them in bed. Being caught, and then what? Some shocking scene out of a movie? Rory had been hitting Cynthia from the beginning, why hadn't that been obvious before? The truck, the tumble on the stairs. Cynthia had a dinged-up quality—always sore, scuffed, dotted with bruises. She'd just lacquered over it, worked it into her act. And she'd lied to Marly anytime she felt like it—that was clear, too. What talk did they ever have that amounted to anything? Wasn't it all just mocking or bitching or Cynthia wanting favors done?

Marly never came straight home from work anymore. She changed out of her skirt and drove, aimlessly, playing the radio; the local station was dismal, but in the late twilight you could pull in CFUN from Van-couver, or WLS in Chicago. Album cuts came in, one after another, in-spiring her to an alert, restless mood. She drove, thumping on the wheel, managing to forget Cynthia for minutes on end.

One evening, she crossed the Old Steel Bridge and bumped off the crumbling blacktop onto a sandy lane that wound through the scrub trees. This is stupid, she thought. I won't find him, and, anyway, what if I do? But right away she spotted the truck. There was a wet, smoky fire going beside it. The double doors in the back had been flung open and Charles was sitting inside, with his legs out on the ground. She walked up close enough to touch him. He didn't look surprised to see her in the slightest. "You smell good," he said.

But how could she—fried meat, ammonia rags? "Tell me what you do out here," she said. "No, don't." She slipped onto his lap and kissed him. She hated her lips. They were chapped and thin as a pencil line, she thought. They would never have the deep, fleshy feel of Cynthia's. She tried, instead, to make them busy.

Charles put his hands on her back, under her shirt. "You sure you want to do this?" he asked.

"Shut up," Marly said. She pushed him down on his back and wrapped her legs around one of his. He made the long muscle in his thigh hard, so she could press against it. The backs of his fingers roamed up and down her cheek, gently, or patiently—or was he only bored?

"Get my clothes off," she said. *"Hurry."*

He had a limp air mattress in there, and a couple of backpacks and a mishmash of picky wool blankets and sleeping bags with exposed zippers—and probably, if she could see, dirty shirts and underwear and food wrappers.

But then they were naked, more or less. Marly scrambled on top. From up there, she could see out through the windshield—a smudge of light still showed at the mouth of the valley. Across the river, the birches glowed and shook. Beneath her, Charles was doing his part, trying to act interested.

"I'm too stringy, aren't I?" Marly said.

"No, no," Charles said. "You're—"

It wasn't the same for him, she knew that—she had none of Cynthia's slummy danger. But so be it. "Are you having any fun?" she said. "Tell me."

He gave a pleasant sound. It might have been *uh-huh.*

"*I* am," Marly said. She was. It wasn't sublime, nothing like that. It didn't make her crazy and greedy. Even so, it was sweet. Sweet work. She wanted to do it forever. She felt like laughing, and then went ahead and let the laugh come out.

Charles raised his hips suddenly, one huge poke, and Marly's head cracked on the dome light—they could both hear it splinter in the dark.

"Oh, Jesus," Charles said. "Jesus, I'm sorry."

He rolled her over. She felt his fingers gingerly inspecting her scalp, felt them slide on blood.

"Wait," he said. He rummaged under the front seat, located a flashlight, and smacked it until it gave a coppery light. He shot it first at the ceiling—a jagged, diamond-shaped piece of plastic dangled from the fixture. He made Marly sit up, facing away from him.

There was a surprising amount of blood, it turned out. He dug a bandanna from his pack, folded it, and pressed it down on the cut.

"God, you must be freezing," he said in a minute. He tried to maneuver one of the loose sleeping bags around her without taking his fingers from her head.

He kept her that way a while longer. "I don't know," he said finally. "Doesn't seem like it wants to stop. You know, your head's all full of little capillaries."

Marly's chest was goose-bumped, her limbs tingling, numb-feeling.

"You're going to have to get this stitched up," Charles said.

God, just imagine, Marly thought.

Charles switched around to where he could see her. "We can think up some story," he said, perfectly calm. He took her hand and guided her fingertips onto the cloth pad, then wriggled into his pants.

"You didn't even—" she said.

"What?"

"You know."

Charles slid out the back. "Keep the pressure on that," he said. "O.K.?"

Then she was under the excruciating glare of the examining room, her arm stuck with a tetanus shot, a patch of hair shaved, and eight stitches laced into her scalp. The doctor was short and gruff, and unimpressed with the fumbling lie she'd offered. Charles waited in the hallway, in a turquoise chair. His head was resting on his fists—she stole looks at him through the open door of the examining room. She tried to say something, but the doctor shushed her. "Don't get this wet," he said. "And no bending over. Bend with the knees." He demonstrated, had difficulty hauling himself up, and seemed to blame Marly.

She looked for Charles again. His chair was empty.

Released, she hurried out under the canopy. The three red lights of the radio tower blinked in the distance. There was the momentary, sickening smell of the hospital incinerator. Charles slid up behind her in the shadows. "I couldn't stand it, watching you in there," he said.

"I have to get my car," Marly said, but the thought of that almost brought her to tears, all that extra horsing around.

"You shouldn't drive," he said.

"I'm *O.K.*"

"Then I'll follow you."

He was quiet all the way back to the river. She kept to her side of the seat, her hands flat on the vinyl. She was full of apology—what for, though? The sky was clear and starry, but a wind had kicked up. Thistles were knocking about in a borrow pit; streamers of torn plastic whipped from the wire fences.

Jeanette called out when Marly let herself in at last, but her voice was startled and sleepy.

"It's only me," Marly said, and went into the bathroom. She shook out a handful of Anacin, tucked all but three back. She sat on the edge of the tub and swallowed them down. There was a little blood on her arm, already flaky, where Charles had held her. She went to her bedroom, let the shirt fall to the floor. She was positive that the moment she lay down her exhaustion would disappear and leave her prickling with thoughts.

She woke later, still in her camisole and jeans. Her heart was hammering. It wasn't yet morning, but the sky was a faint charcoal. The wind was louder, thrashing the trees, sending branches scraping down the tin roof. A loose wire slapped against the clapboards. The house strained and rattled, let in air.

She had to go talk to him again. Too much was floating, undeclared.

She got up and listened outside Jeanette's room, certain that the wind had disturbed her, too. She edged the door open. Jeanette was curled in a sliver of the king-size bed, wound up in the covers, with the rest of the bed a chaos of books and papers. The curtains swayed and jiggled out away from the sash, but Jeanette didn't budge. Her breathing came in deep, abrupt sighs. After a moment, Marly backed out.

A truck from the Electric Co-op was the only thing on the road. Its yellow light beat in her mirror, receding finally. She swerved down onto the dirt, banged up to the opening of the gravel pit, and flipped off her lights before they showed. The van was there, parked in a puddle of leaves. The fire was out—doused, kicked apart. She stepped past it and walked straight to the back doors and yanked them open. It took her a second, speaking sharply into the dim interior and then feeling about with her hand, to realize nobody was there.

He was down at the edge of the water, his legs over the embankment. The river poured by, churned up with runoff. He'd wrapped himself in a flannel shirt and canvas jacket. Been up all night, she guessed. He had a huddled look—cold, not elegant for a change, in no way enigmatic. She wanted to run and squeeze herself against his back. At the same time, she felt an extraordinary patience—it flooded into her limbs, giving them a graceful and weighted feeling. Hours before, hurrying out of the truck—exhausted, mortified—she'd been hit by the absurd intuition that all their lives depended on her now, even Cher's. By daylight, the momentousness of the night before had washed off, the nervous glitter. It was just true, as Jeanette would say—a fact she'd have to live with.

She held her hair down against the wind and walked ahead, calling out. She had to get right up next to him before his head shot around.

She started to bend over, caught herself, and then squatted as the doctor had instructed. "This is one ridiculous life," she said.

She rubbed her hand on his pants leg and waited until he was looking straight at her.

"Don't go up there anymore," she said finally.

He wouldn't want to talk about this, she knew. He'd prefer to stare at the edge of the sky where a rosy light was appearing.

"Look, I mean it. Don't go up there. That's over. Promise me."

"I can't promise you."

"No, but you *can*," she said.

She let that sink in, as she sat back, warming her fingers under her arms. Out on the river, a boat swept out of the shadow of the cutbank— a lacquered canvas hull with two figures, one at the motor, the other up front keeping the prow down. A red setter stood between them, barking noiselessly at the current. Marly watched until they could no longer be seen. On the far shore, the aspens bent and tossed. Even in this first light, the new leaves had that shocking, liquid green. Like parrot feathers, Marly thought. She gave his hand a quick kiss. In a moment, it would occur to him what she was asking. They were joined, they were allies—it was awkward to have to say it like that, she had to admit, but in this she wasn't wrong.

(1991)

OCEAN AVENUE

MICHAEL CHABON

If you can still see how you could once have loved a person, you are still in love; an extinct love is always wholly incredible. One day not too long ago, in Laguna Beach, California, an architect named Bobby Lazar went downtown to have a cup of coffee at the Café Zinc with his friend Albert Wong and Albert's new wife, Dawn (who had, very sensibly, retained her maiden name). Albert and Dawn were still in that period of total astonishment that follows a wedding, grinning at each other like two people who have survived an air crash without a scratch, touching one another frequently, lucky to be alive. Lazar was not a cynical man and he wished them well, but he had also been lonely for a long time, and their happiness was making him a little sick. Albert had brought along a copy of *Science,* in which he had recently published some work on the String Theory, and it was as Lazar looked up from Al's name and abbreviations in the journal's table of contents that he saw Suzette, in her exercise clothes, coming toward the café from across the street, looking like she weighed about seventy-five pounds.

She was always too thin, though at the time of their closest acquaintance he had thought he liked a woman with bony shoulders. She had a bony back, too, he suddenly remembered, like a marimba, as well as a pointed, bony nose and chin, and she was always—but *always*—on a diet, even though she had a naturally small appetite and danced aerobically or ran five miles every day. Her face looked hollowed and somehow mutated, as do the faces of most women who get too much exercise, but there was a sheen on her brow and a mad, aerobic glimmer in her eye. She'd permed her hair since he last saw her, and it flew out around her head in two square feet of golden Pre-Raphaelite rotini— the lily maid of Astolat on an endorphin high. A friend had once said she was the kind of woman who causes automobile accidents when she walks down the street, and, as a matter of fact, as she stepped up onto the patio of the café a man passing on his bicycle made the mistake of following her with his eyes for a moment and nearly rode into the open door of a parked car.

"Isn't that Suzette?" Al said. Albert was, as it happened, the only one of his friends after the judgment who refused to behave as though Suzette had never existed, and he was always asking after her in his pointed, physicistic manner, one skeptical eyebrow raised. Needless to say, Lazar did not like to be reminded. In the course of their affair, he knew, he had been terribly erratic, by turns tightfisted and profligate, glum and overeager, unsociable and socially aflutter, full of both flattery and glib invective—a shithead, in short—and, to his credit, he was afraid that he had treated Suzette very badly. It may have been this repressed consciousness, more than anything else, that led him to tell himself, when he first saw her again, that he did not love her anymore.

"Uh-oh," said Dawn, after she remembered who Suzette was.

"I have nothing to be afraid of," Lazar said. As she passed, he called out, "Suzette?" He felt curiously invulnerable to her still evident charms, and uttered her name with the lightness and faint derision of someone on a crowded airplane signalling to an attractive but slightly elderly stewardess. "Hey, Suze!"

She was wearing a Walkman, however, with the earphones turned up very loud, and she floated past on a swell of Chaka Kahn and Rufus.

"Didn't she hear you?" said Albert, looking surprised.

"No, Dr. Five Useful Non-Implications of the String Theory, she did not," Lazar said. "She was wearing *ear*phones."

"I think she was ignoring you." Albert turned to his bride and duly consulted her. "Didn't she look like she heard him? Didn't her face kind of blink?"

"There she is, Bobby," said Dawn, pointing toward the entrance of the café. As it was a beautiful December morning, they were sitting out on the patio, and Lazar had his back to the Zinc. "Waiting on line."

He felt that he did not actually desire to speak to her but that Albert and Dawn's presence forced him into it somehow. A certain tyranny of in-touchness holds sway in that part of the world—a compulsion to behave always as though one is still in therapy but making real progress, and the rules of enlightened behavior seemed to dictate that he not sneak away from the table with his head under a newspaper—as he might have done if alone—and go home to watch the Weather Channel or Home Shopping Network for three hours with a twelve-pack of Mexican beer and the phone off the hook. He turned around in his chair and looked at Suzette more closely. She had on one of those glittering, opalescent Intergalactic Amazon leotard-and-tights combinations that seem to be made of cavorite or adamantium and do not so much cling to a woman's body as seal her off from gamma rays and lethal stardust. Lazar pronounced her name again, more loudly, calling out across the sunny patio. She looked even thinner from behind.

"Oh. Bobby," she said, removing the headphones but keeping her place in the coffee line.

"Hello, Suze," he said. They nodded pleasantly to one another, and that might have been it right there. After a second or two she dipped her head semi-apologetically, smiled an irritated smile, and put the earphones—"earbuds," he recalled, was the nauseous term—back into her ears.

"She looks great," Lazar said magnanimously to Albert and Dawn, keeping his eyes on Suzette.

"She looks so thin, so drawn," said Dawn, who, frankly, could have stood to drop about fifteen pounds.

"She looks fine to me," said Al. "I'd say she looks better than ever."

"I know you would," Lazar snapped. "You'd say it just to bug me."

He was a little irritated himself now. The memory of their last few days together had returned to him, despite all his heroic efforts over the past months to repress it utterly. He thought of the weekend following that bad review of their restaurant in the *Times* (they'd had a Balearic restaurant called Ibiza, in San Clemente)—a review in which the critic had singled out his distressed-stucco interior and Suzette's Majorcan paella, in particular, for censure. Since these were precisely the two points around which, in the course of opening the restaurant, they had constructed their most idiotic and horrible arguments, the unfavorable notice hit their already shaky relationship like a dumdum bullet, and Suzette went a little nuts. She didn't show up at home or at Ibiza all the next day—so that poor hypersensitive little José had to do all the cooking—but instead disappeared into the haunts of physical culture. She worked out at the gym, went to Zahava's class, had her body waxed, and then, to top it all off, rode her bicycle all the way to El Toro and back. When she finally came home she was in a mighty hormonal rage and suffered under the delusion that she could lift a thousand pounds and chew her way through vanadium steel. She claimed that Lazar had bankrupted her, among other outrageous and untrue assertions, and he went out for a beer to escape from her. By the time he returned, several hours later, she had moved out, taking with her *only his belongings,* as though she had come to see some fundamental inequity in their relationship—such as their having been switched at birth—and were attempting in this way to rectify it.

This loss, though painful, he would have been willing to suffer if it hadn't included his collection of William Powelliana, which was then at its peak and contained everything from the checkered wingtips Powell wore in "The Kennel Club Murder Case" to Powell's personal copy of the shooting script for "Life with Father" to a 1934 letter from Dashiell Hammett congratulating Powell on his interpretation of Nick Charles, which Lazar had managed to obtain from a Powell grandnephew only minutes before the epistolary buzzards from the University of Texas tried to snap it up. Suzette sold the entire collection, at far less than its value, to that awful Kelso McNair, up in Lawndale, who only annexed it to his vast empire of Myrna Loy memorabilia and locked it away in his vault. In retaliation Lazar went down the next morning to their safe-deposit box at Dana Point, removed all six of Suzette's 1958 and '59 Barbie Dolls, and sold them to a collectibles store up in Orange for not quite four thousand dollars, at which point she brought the first suit against him.

"Why is your face turning so red, Bobby?" said Dawn, who must have been all of twenty-two.

"Oh!" he said, not bothering even to sound sincere. "I just remembered. I have an appointment."

"See you, Bobby," said Al.

"See you," he said, but he did not stand up.

"You don't have to keep looking at her, anyway," Al continued reasonably. "You can just look out at Ocean Avenue here, or at my lovely new wife—hi, sweetie—and act as though Suzette's not there."

"I know," Lazar said, smiling at Dawn, then returning his eyes immediately to Suzette. "But I'd like to talk to her. No, really."

So saying, he rose from his chair and walked, as nonchalantly as he could, toward her. He had always been awkward about crossing public space, and could not do it without feeling somehow cheesy and hucksterish, as though he were crossing a makeshift dais in a Legion Hall to accept a diploma from a bogus school of real estate; he worried that his pants were too tight across the seat, that his gait was hitched and dorky, that his hands swung chimpishly at his sides. Suzette was next in line now and studying the menu, even though he could have predicted, still, exactly what she would order: a decaf au lait and a wedge of frittata with two little cups of cucumber salsa. He came up behind her and tapped her on the shoulder; the taps were intended to be devil-may-care and friendly, but of course he overdid them and they came off as the brusque importunities of a man with a bone to pick. Suzette turned around looking more irritated than ever, and when she saw who it was her dazzling green eyes grew tight little furrows at their corners.

"How are you?" said Lazar, daring to leave his hand on her shoulder, where, as though it were approaching c_2 very quickly it seemed to acquire a great deal of mass. He was so conscious of his hand on her damp, solid shoulder that he missed her first few words, and finally had to withdraw it, blushing.

". . . great. Everything's really swell," Suzette was saying, looking down at the place on her shoulder where his hand had just been. Had he laid a freshly boned breast of raw chicken there and then taken it away her expression could not have been more bemused. She turned away. "Hi, Norris," she said to the lesbian woman behind the counter. "Just an espresso."

"On a diet?" Lazar said, feeling his smile tighten.

"Not hungry," she said. "You've gained a few pounds."

"You could be right," he said, and patted his stomach. Since he had thrown Suzette's Borg bathroom scale onto the scrap heap along with her other belongings (thus leaving the apartment all but empty), he had no idea of how much he weighed, and, frankly, as he put it to himself, smiling all the while at his ex-lover, he did not give a rat's ass. "I probably did. You look thinner than ever, really, Suze."

"Here's your espresso," said Norris, smiling oddly at Lazar, as though they were old friends, and he was confused, until he remembered that right after Suzette left him he'd run into this Norris at a party in Bluebird Canyon, and they had a short, bitter, drunken conversation about what it felt like when a woman left you, and Lazar impressed her by declaring, sagely, that it felt as though you'd arrived home to find that your dearest and most precious belongings in the world had been sold to a man from Lawndale.

"What about that money you owe me?" he said. The question was halfway out of his mouth before he realized it, and although he appended a hasty ha-ha at the finish, his jaw was clenched and he must have looked as if he was about to slug her.

"Whoa!" said Suzette, stepping neatly around him. "I'm getting out of here, Bobby. Goodbye." She tucked her chin against her chest, dipped her head, and slipped out the door, as though ducking into a rainstorm.

"Wait!" he said. "Suzette!"

She turned toward him as he came out onto the patio, her shoulders squared, and held him at bay with her cup of espresso coffee.

"I don't have to reckon with you anymore, Bobby Lazar," she said. "Colleen says I've already reckoned with you enough." Colleen was Suzette's therapist. They had seen her together for a while, and Lazar was both scornful and afraid of her and her linguistic advice.

"I'm sorry," he said. "I'll try to be, um, yielding. I'll yield. I promise. I just—I don't know. How about let's sit down?"

He turned to the table where he'd left Albert, Dawn, and his cup of coffee, and discovered that his friends had stood up and were collecting their shopping bags, putting on their sweaters.

"Are you going?" he said.

"If you two are getting back together," said Albert, "this whole place is going. It's all over. It's the Big One."

"Albert!" said Dawn.

"You're a sick man, Bob," said Albert. He shook Lazar's hand and grinned. "You're sick, and you like sick women."

Lazar cursed him, kissed Dawn on both cheeks, and laughed a reckless laugh.

"Is he drunk or something?" he heard Dawn say before they were out of earshot, and, indeed, as he returned to Suzette's table the world seemed suddenly more stressful and gay, the sky more tinged at its edges with violet.

"Is that Al's new wife?" said Suzette. She waved to them as they headed down the street. "She's pretty, but she needs to work on her thighs."

"I think Al's been working on them," he said.

"Shush," said Suzette.

They sat back and looked at each other warily and with pleasure. The circumstances under which they parted had been so strained and unfriendly and terminal that to find themselves sitting, just like that, at a bright café over two cups of black coffee seemed as thrilling as if they were violating some powerful taboo. They had been warned, begged, and even ordered to stay away from each other by everyone, from their shrinks to their parents to the bench of Orange County itself; yet here they were, in plain view, smiling and smiling. A lot of things had been lacking in their relationship, but unfortunately mutual physical attraction was not one of them, and Lazar could feel that hoary old devouring serpent uncoiling deep in its Darwinian cave.

"It's nice to see you," said Suzette.

"You look pretty," he said. "I like what you've done with your hair. You look like a Millais."

"Thank you," she said, a little tonelessly; she was not quite ready to listen to all his prattle again. She pursed her lips and looked at him in a manner almost surgical, as though about to administer a precise blow with a very small axe. She said, " 'Song of the Thin Man' was on last week."

"I know," he said. He was impressed, and oddly touched. "That's pretty daring of you to mention that. Considering."

She set down her coffee cup, firmly, and he caught the flicker of her right biceps. "You got more than I got," she said. "You got six thousand dollars! I got five thousand four hundred and ninety-five. I don't owe you anything."

"I only got four thousand, remember?" he said. He felt himself blushing. "That came out, well, in court—don't you remember? I— well. I lied."

"That's right," she said slowly. She rolled her eyes and bit her lip, re-membering. "You lied. Four thousand. They were worth twice that."

"A lot of them were missing hair or limbs," he said.

"You pig!" She gave her head a monosyllabic shake, and the golden curls rustled like a dress. Since she had at one time been known to call him a pig with delicacy and tenderness, this did not immediately alarm Lazar. "You sold my dolls," she said, dreamily, though of course she knew this perfectly well, and had known it for quite some time. Only now, he could see, it was all coming back to her, the memory of the cruel things they had said, of the tired, leering faces of the lawyers, of the acer-bic envoi of the county judge dismissing all their suits and countersuits, of the day they had met for the last time in the empty building that had been their restaurant, amid the bare fixtures, the exposed wires, the crumbs of plaster on the floor; of the rancor that from the first had been the constant flower of their love. "You sold their things, too," she re-membered. "All of their gowns and pumps and little swimwear."

"I was just trying to get back at you."

"For what? For making sure I at least got something out of all the time I wasted on you?"

"Take it easy, Suze."

"And then to lie about how much you got for them? Four thousand dollars!"

"At first my lawyers instructed me to lie about it," he lied.

"Kravitz! Di Martino! Those sleazy, lizardy, shystery old fat guys! Oh, you pigs!"

Now she was on her feet, and everyone out on the patio had turned with great interest to regard them. He realized, or, rather, remembered, that he had strayed into dangerous territory here, that Suzette had a passion for making scenes in restaurants. This is how it was, said a voice within Lazar—a gloomy, condemnatory voice—this is what you've been missing. He saw the odd angle at which she was holding her cup of coffee, and he hoped against hope that she did not intend to splash his face with espresso. She was one of those women who like to hurl beverages.

"Don't tell me," he said, despite himself, his voice coated with the most unctuous sarcasm, "you're *reckoning* with me again."

You could see her consulting with herself about trajectories and wind shear and beverage velocity and other such technical considerations— collecting all the necessary data, and courage—and then she let fly. The cup sailed past Lazar's head, and he just had time to begin a tolerant, superior smile, and to uncurl partially the middle finger of his right hand, before the cup bounced off the low wall beside him and ricocheted into his face.

Suzette looked startled for a moment, registering this as one registers an ace in tennis or golf, and then laughed the happy laugh of a lucky shot. As the unmerciful people on the patio applauded—oh, but that made Lazar angry—Suzette turned on her heel and, wearing a maddening smile, strode balletically off the patio of the café, out into the middle of Ocean Avenue. Lazar scrambled up from his chair and went after her, cold coffee running in thin fingers down his cheeks. Neither of them bothered to look where they were going; they trusted, in those last couple of seconds before he caught her and kissed her hollow cheek, that they would not be met by some hurtling bus or other accident.

(1989)

LOVE LIFE

BOBBIE ANN MASON

Opal lolls in her recliner, wearing the Coors cap her niece Jenny brought her from Colorado. She fumbles for the remote-control paddle and fires a button. Her swollen knuckles hurt. On TV, a boy is dancing in the street. Some other boys dressed in black are banging guitars and drums. This is her favorite program. It is always on, night or day. The show is songs, with accompanying stories. It's the music channel. Opal never cared for stories—she detests those soap operas her friends watch—but these fascinate her. The colors and the costumes change and flow with the music, erratically, the way her mind does these days. Now the TV is playing a song in which all the boys are long-haired cops chasing a dangerous woman in a tweed cap and a checked shirt. The woman's picture is in all their billfolds.

They chase her through a cold-storage room filled with sides of beef. She hops on a motorcycle, and they set up a roadblock, but she jumps it with her motorcycle. Finally, she slips onto a train and glides away from them, waving a smiling goodbye.

On the table beside Opal is a Kleenex box, her glasses case, a glass of Coke with ice, and a cut-glass decanter of clear liquid that could be just water for the plants. Opal pours some of the liquid into the Coke and sips slowly. It tastes like peppermint candy, and it feels soothing. Her fingers tingle. She feels happy. Now that she is retired, she doesn't have to sneak into the teachers' lounge for a little swig from the jar in her pocketbook. She still dreams algebra problems, complicated quadratic equations with shifting values and no solutions. Now kids are using algebra to program computers. The kids in the TV stories remind her of her students at Hopewell High. Old age could have a grandeur about it, she thinks now as the music surges through her, if only it weren't so scary.

But she doesn't feel lonely, especially now that her sister Alice's girl, Jenny, has moved back here, to Kentucky. Jenny seems so confident, the way she sprawls on the couch, with that backpack she carries everywhere. Alice was always so delicate and feminine, but Jenny is enough like Opal to be her own daughter. She has Opal's light, thin hair, her large shoulders and big bones and long legs. Jenny even has a way of laughing that reminds Opal of her own laughter, the boisterous scoff she always saved for certain company but never allowed herself in school. Now and then Jenny lets loose one of those laughs and Opal is pleased. It occurs to her that Jenny, who is already past thirty, has left behind a trail of men, like that girl in the song. Jenny has lived with a couple of men, here and there. Opal can't keep track of all of the men Jenny has mentioned. They have names like John and Skip and Michael. She's not in a hurry to get married, she says. She says she is going to buy a house trailer and live in the woods like a hermit. She's full of ideas, and she exaggerates. She uses the words "gorgeous," "adorable," and "wonderful" interchangeably and persistently.

Last night, Jenny was here, with her latest boyfriend, Randy Newcomb. Opal remembers when he sat in the back row in her geometry class. He was an ordinary kid, not especially smart, and often late with his lessons. Now he has a real-estate agency and drives a Cadillac. Jenny kissed him in front of Opal and told him he was gorgeous. She said the placemats were gorgeous, too.

Jenny was asking to see those old quilts again. "Why do you hide away your nice things, Aunt Opal?" she said. Opal doesn't think they're that nice, and she doesn't want to have to look at them all the time. Opal showed Jenny and Randy Newcomb the double-wedding-ring quilt, the star quilt, and some of the crazy quilts, but she wouldn't show them the craziest one—the burial quilt, the one Jenny kept asking about. Did Jenny come back home just to hunt up that old rag? The thought makes Opal shudder.

The doorbell rings. Opal has to rearrange her comforter and magazines in order to get up. Her joints are stiff. She leaves the TV blaring a song she knows, with balloons and bombs in it.

At the door is Velma Shaw, who lives in the duplex next to Opal. She has just come home from her job at Shop World. "Have you gone out of your mind, Opal?" cries Velma. She has on a plum-colored print blouse and a plum skirt and a little green scarf with a gold pin holding it down. Velma shouts, "You can hear that racket clear across the street!"

"Rock and roll is never too loud," says Opal. This is a line from a song she has heard.

Opal releases one of her saved-up laughs, and Velma backs away. Velma is still trying to be sexy, in those little color-coordinated outfits she wears, but it is hopeless, Opal thinks with a smile. She closes the door and scoots back to her chaise longue.

OPAL IS JENNY's favorite aunt. Jenny likes the way Opal ties her hair in a pony-tail with a ribbon. She wears muumuus and socks. She is tall and only a little thick in the middle. She told Jenny that middle-age spread was caused by the ribs expanding and that it doesn't matter what you eat. Opal kids around about "old Arthur"—her arthritis, visiting her on damp days.

Jenny has been in town six months. She works at the courthouse, typing records—marriages, divorces, deaths, drunk-driving convictions. Frequently, the same names are on more than one list. Before she returned to Kentucky, Jenny was waitressing in Denver, but she was growing restless again, and the idea of going home seized her. Her old rebellion against small-town conventions gave way to curiosity.

In the South, the shimmer of the heat seems to distort everything, like old glass with impurities in it. During her first two days there, she saw two people with artificial legs, a blind man, a man with hooks for hands, and a man without an arm. It seemed unreal. In a parking lot, a pit bull terrier in a Camaro attacked her at the closed window. He barked viciously, his nose stabbing the window. She stood in the parking lot, letting the pit bull attack, imagining herself in an arena, with a crowd watching. The South makes her nervous. Randy Newcomb told her she had just been away too long. "We're not as countrified down here now as people think," he said.

Jenny has been going with Randy for three months. The first night she went out with him, he took her to a fancy place that served shrimp flown in from New Orleans, and then to a little bar over in Hopkinsville. They went with Kathy Steers, a friend from work, and Kathy's husband, Bob. Kathy and Bob weren't getting along and they carped at each other all evening. In the bar, an attractive, cheerful woman sang requests for tips, and her companion, a blind man, played the guitar. When she sang, she looked straight at him, singing to him, smiling at him reassuringly. In the background, men played pool with their girlfriends, and Jenny noticed the sharp creases in the men's jeans and imagined the women ironing them. When she mentioned it, Kathy said she took Bob's jeans to the laundromat to use the machine there that puts knifelike creases in them. The men in the bar had two kinds of women with them: innocent-looking women with pastel skirts and careful hairdos, and hard-looking women without makeup in T-shirts and jeans. Jenny imagined that each type could be either a girlfriend or a wife. She felt odd. She was neither type. The singer sang "Happy Birthday" to a popular regular named Will Ed, and after the set she danced with him, while the jukebox took over. She had a limp, as though one leg were shorter than the other. The leg was stiff under her jeans, and when the woman danced Jenny could see that the leg was not real.

"There, but for the grace of God, go I," Randy whispered to Jenny. He squeezed her hand, and his heavy turquoise ring dug into her knuckle.

. . .

"THOSE QUILTS WOULD bring a good price at an estate auction," Randy says to Jenny as they leave her aunt's one evening and head for his real-estate office. They are in his burgundy Cadillac. "One of those star quilts used to bring twenty-five dollars. Now it might run three hundred."

"My aunt doesn't think they're worth anything. She hides all her nice stuff, like she's ashamed of it. She's got beautiful dresser scarves and starched doilies she made years ago. But she's getting a little weird. All she does is watch MTV."

"I think she misses the kids," Randy says. Then he bursts out laughing. "She used to put the fear of God in all her students! I never will forget the time she told me to stop watching so much television and read some books. It was like an order from God Almighty. I didn't dare not do what she said. I read 'Crime and Punishment.' I never would have read it if she hadn't shamed me into it. But I appreciated that. I don't even remember what 'Crime and Punishment' was about, except there was an axe murderer in it."

"That was basically it," Jenny says. "He got caught. Crime and punishment—just like any old TV show."

Randy touches some controls on the dashboard and Waylon Jennings starts singing. The sound system is remarkable. Everything Randy owns is quality. He has been looking for some land for Jenny to buy—a couple of acres of woods—but so far nothing on his listings has met with his approval. He is concerned about zoning and power lines and frontage. All Jenny wants is a remote place where she can have a dog and grow some tomatoes. She knows that what she really needs is a better car, but she doesn't want to go anywhere.

Later, at Randy's office, Jenny studies the photos of houses on display, while he talks on the telephone to someone about dividing up a sixty-acre farm into farmettes. His photograph is on several certificates on the wall. He has a full, well-fed face in the pictures, but he is thinner now and looks better. He has a boyish, endearing smile, like Dennis Quaid, Jenny's favorite actor. She likes his smile. It seems so innocent, as though he would do anything in the world for someone he cared about. He doesn't really want to sell her any land. He says he is afraid she will get raped if she lives alone in the woods.

"I'm impressed," she says when he slams down the telephone. She points to his new regional award for the fastest-growing agency of the year.

"Isn't that something? Three branch offices in a territory this size—I can't complain. There's a lot of turnover in real estate now. People are never satisfied. You know that? That's the truth about human nature." He laughs. "That's the secret of my success."

"It's been two years since Barbara divorced me," he says later, on the way to Jenny's apartment. "I can't say it hasn't been fun being free, but my kids are in college, and it's like starting over. I'm ready for a new life. The business has been so great, I couldn't really ask for more, but I've been thinking—Don't laugh, please, but what I was thinking was if you want to share it with me, I'll treat you good. I swear."

At a stoplight, he paws at her hand. On one corner is the Pepsi bottling plant, and across from it is the Broad Street House, a restaurant with an old-fashioned statue of a jockey out front. People are painting the black faces on those little statues white now, but this one has been painted bright green all over. Jenny can't keep from laughing at it.

"I wasn't laughing at you—honest!" she says apologetically. "That statue always cracks me up."

"You don't have to give me an answer now."

"I don't know what to say."

"I can get us a real good deal on a house," he says. "I can get any house I've got listed. I can even get us a farmette, if you want trees so bad. You won't have to spend your money on a piece of land."

"I'll have to think about it." Randy scares her. She likes him, but there is something strange about his energy and optimism. Everyone around her seems to be bursting at the seams, like that pit bull terrier.

"I'll let you think on it," he says, pulling up to her apartment. "Life has been good to me. Business is good, and my kids didn't turn out to be dope fiends. That's about all you can hope for in this day and time."

JENNY IS HAVING lunch with Kathy Steers at the Broad Street House. The iced tea is mixed with white grape juice. It took Jenny a long time to identify the flavor, and the Broad Street House won't admit it's grape juice. Their iced tea is supposed to have a mystique about it, probably because they can't sell drinks in this dry county. In the daylight, the statue out front is the color of the Jolly Green Giant.

People confide in Jenny, but Jenny doesn't always tell things back. It's an unfair exchange, though it often goes unnoticed. She is curious, eager to hear other people's stories, and she asks more questions than is appropriate. Kathy's life is a tangle of deceptions. Kathy stayed with her husband, Bob, because he had opened his own body shop and she didn't want him to start out a new business with a rocky marriage, but she acknowledges now it was a mistake.

"What about Jimmy and Willette?" Jenny asks. Jimmy and Willette are the other characters in Kathy's story.

"That mess went on for months. When you started work at the office, remember how nervous I was? I thought I was getting an ulcer." Kathy lights a cigarette and blows at the wall. "You see, I didn't know what Bob and Willette were up to, and they didn't know about me and Jimmy. That went on for two years before you came. And when it started to come apart—I mean, we had *hell!* I'd say things to Jimmy and then it would get back to Bob because Jimmy would tell Willette. It was an unreal circle. I was pregnant with Jason and you get real sensitive then. I thought Bob was screwing around on me, but it never dawned on me it was with Willette."

The fat waitress says, "Is everything all right?"

Kathy says, "No, but it's not your fault. Do you know what I'm going to do?" she asks Jenny.

"No, what?"

"I'm taking Jason and moving in with my sister. She has a sort of apartment upstairs. Bob can do what he wants to with the house. I've waited too long to do this, but it's time. My sister keeps the baby anyway, so why shouldn't I just live there?"

She puffs the cigarette again and levels her eyes at Jenny. "You know what I admire about you? You're so independent. You say what you think. When you started work at the office, I said to myself, 'I wish I could be like that.' I could tell you had been around. You've inspired me. That's how come I decided to move out."

Jenny plays with the lemon slice in the saucer holding her iced-tea glass. She picks a seed out of it. She can't bring herself to confide in

Kathy about Randy Newcomb's offer. For some reason, she is embarrassed by it.

"I haven't spoken to Willette since September 3rd," says Kathy.

Kathy keeps talking, and Jenny listens, suspicious of her interest in Kathy's problems. She notices how Kathy is enjoying herself. Kathy is looking forward to leaving her husband the same way she must have enjoyed her fling with Jimmy, the way she is enjoying not speaking to Willette.

"Let's go out and get drunk tonight," Kathy says cheerfully. "Let's celebrate my decision."

"I can't. I'm going to see my aunt this evening. I have to take her some booze. She gives me money to buy her vodka and peppermint schnapps, and she tells me not to stop at the same liquor store. She says she doesn't want me to get a reputation for drinking! I have to go all the way to Hopkinsville to get it."

"Your aunt tickles me. She's a pistol."

The waitress clears away the dishes and slaps down dessert menus. They order chocolate pecan pie, the day's special.

"You know the worst part of this whole deal?" Kathy says. "It's the years it takes to get smart. But I'm going to make up for lost time. You can bet on that. And there's not a thing Bob can do about it."

OPAL'S HOUSE HAS a veranda. Jenny thinks that verandas seem to imply a history of some sort—people in rocking chairs telling stories. But Opal doesn't tell any stories. It is exasperating, because Jenny wants to know about her aunt's past love life, but Opal won't reveal her secrets. They sit on the veranda and observe each other. They smile, and now and then roar with laughter over something ridiculous. In the bedroom, where she snoops after using the bathroom, Jenny notices the layers of old wallpaper in the closet, peeling back and spilling crumbs of gaudy ancient flower prints onto Opal's muumuus.

Downstairs, Opal asks, "Do you want some cake, Jenny?"

"Of course. I'm crazy about your cake, Aunt Opal."

"I didn't beat the egg whites long enough. Old Arthur's visiting again." Opal flexes her fingers and smiles. "That sounds like the curse. Girls used to say they had the curse. Or they had a visitor." She looks down at her knuckles shyly. "Nowadays, of course, they just say what they mean."

The cake is delicious—an old-fashioned lemon chiffon made from scratch. Jenny's cooking ranges from English-muffin mini-pizzas to brownie mixes. After gorging on the cake, Jenny blurts out, "Aunt Opal, aren't you sorry you never got married? Tell the truth, now."

Opal laughs. "I was talking to Ella Mae Smith the other day—she's a retired geography teacher?—and she said, 'I've got twelve great-great-grandchildren, and when we get together I say, "Law me, look what I started!" ' " Opal mimics Ella Mae Smith, giving her a mindless, chirpy tone of voice. "Why, I'd have to use quadratic equations to count up all the people that woman has caused," she goes on. "All with a streak of her petty narrow-mindedness in them. I don't call that a contribution to the world." Opal laughs and sips from her glass of schnapps. "What about you, Jenny? Are you ever going to get married?"

"Marriage is outdated. I don't know anybody who's married and happy."

Opal names three schoolteachers she has known who have been married for decades.

"But are they really happy?"

"Oh, foot, Jenny! What you're saying is why are *you* not married and why are *you* not happy. What's wrong with little Randy Newcomb? Isn't that funny? I always think of him as little Randy."

"Show me those quilts again, Aunt Opal."

"I'll show you the crazies but not the one you keep after me about."

"O.K., show me the crazies."

Upstairs, her aunt lays crazy quilts on the bed. They are bright-colored patches of soft velvet and plaids and prints stitched together with silky embroidery. Several pieces have initials embroidered on them. The haphazard shapes make Jenny imagine odd, twisted lives represented in these quilts.

She says, "Mom gave me a quilt once, but I didn't appreciate the value of it and I washed it until it fell apart."

"I'll give you one of these crazies when you stop moving around," Opal says. "You couldn't fit it in that backpack of yours." She polishes her glasses thoughtfully. "Do you know what those quilts mean to me?"

"No, what?"

"A lot of desperate old women ruining their eyes. Do you know what I think I'll do?"

"No, what?"

"I think I'll take up aerobic dancing. Or maybe I'll learn to ride a motorcycle. I try to be modern."

"You're funny, Aunt Opal. You're hilarious."

"Am I gorgeous, too?"

"Adorable," says Jenny.

AFTER HER NIECE leaves, Opal hums a tune and dances a stiff little jig. She nestles among her books and punches her remote-control paddle. Years ago, she was allowed to paddle students who misbehaved. She used a wooden paddle from a butter churn, with holes drilled in it. The holes made a satisfying sting. On TV, a nineteen-fifties convertible is out of gas. This is one of her favorites. It has an adorable couple in it. The girl is wearing bobby socks and saddle oxfords, and the boy has on a basketball jacket. They look the way children looked before the hippie element took over. But the boy begins growing cat whiskers and big cat ears, and then his face gets furry and leathery, while the girl screams bloody murder. Opal sips some peppermint and watches his face change. The red and gold of his basketball jacket are the Hopewell school colors. He chases the girl. Now he has grown long claws.

The boy is dancing energetically with a bunch of ghouls who have escaped from their coffins. "Grisly ghouls are closing in to seal your doom," Vincent Price says in the background. The girl is very frightened. The ghouls are so old and ugly. That's how kids see us, Opal thinks. She loves this story. She even loves the credits: "Scary Music by Elmer Bernstein." This is a story with a meaning. It suggests all the feelings of terror and horror that must be hidden inside young people. And inside, deep down, there really are monsters. An old person waits, a nearly dead body that can still dance.

Opal pours another drink. She feels relaxed, her joints loose like a dancer's now.

Jenny is so nosy. Her questions are so blunt. Did Opal ever have a crush on a student? Only once or twice. She was in her twenties then, and it seemed scandalous. Nothing happened—just daydreams. When she was thirty, she had another attachment to a boy, and it seemed all right then, but it was worse again at thirty-five, when another pretty boy stayed after class to talk. After that, she kept her distance.

But Opal is not wholly without experience. There have been men, over the years, though nothing like the casual affairs Jenny has had. Opal remembers a certain motel room in Nashville. She was only forty. The man drove a gray Chrysler Imperial. When she was telling about him to a friend, who was sworn to secrecy, she called him "Imperial," in a joking way. She went with him because she knew he would take her somewhere, in such a fine car, and they would sleep together. She always remembered how clean and empty the room was, how devoid of history and association. In the mirror, she saw a scared woman with a pasty face and a shrimpy little man who needed a shave. In the morning he went out somewhere and brought back coffee and orange juice. They had bought some doughnuts at the new doughnut shop in town before they left. While he was out, she made up the bed and put her things in her bag, to make it as neat as if she had never been there. She was fully dressed when he returned, with her garter belt and stockings on, and when they finished the doughnuts she cleaned up all the paper and the cups and wiped the crumbs from the table by the bed. He said, "Come with me and I'll take you to Idaho." "Why Idaho?" she wanted to know, but his answer was vague. Idaho sounded cold, and she didn't want to tell him how she disliked his scratchy whiskers and the hard, powdery doughnuts. It seemed unkind of her, but if he had been nicer-looking, without such a demanding dark beard, she might have gone with him to Idaho in that shining Imperial. She hadn't even given him a chance, she thought later. She had been so scared. If anyone from school had seen her at that motel, she could have lost her job. "I need a woman," he had said. "A woman like you."

ON A HOT Saturday afternoon, with rain threatening, Jenny sits under a tent on a folding chair while Randy auctions off four hundred acres of woods on Lake Barkley. He had a road bulldozed into the property, and he divided it up into lots. The lakefront lots are going for as much as two thousand an acre, and the others are bringing up to a thousand. Randy has several assistants with him, and there is even a concession stand, offering hot dogs and cold drinks.

In the middle of the auction, they wait for a thundershower to pass. Sitting in her folding chair under a canopy reminds Jenny of graveside services. As soon as the rain slacks up, the auction continues. In his cowboy hat and blue blazer, Randy struts around with a microphone as proudly as a banty rooster. With his folksy chatter, he knows exactly how to work the crowd. "Y'all get yourselves a cold drink and relax now and just imagine the fishing you'll do in this dreamland. This land is good for vacation, second home, investment—heck, you can just park here in your camper and live. It's going to be paradise when that marina gets built on the lake there and we get some lots cleared."

The four-hundred-acre tract looks like a wilderness. Jenny loves the way the sun splashes on the water after the rain, and the way it comes through the trees, hitting the flickering leaves like lights on a disco ball. A marina here seems farfetched. She could pitch a tent here until she could afford to buy a used trailer. She could swim at dawn, the way she did on a camping trip out West, long ago. All of a sudden, she finds herself bidding on a lot. The bidding passes four hundred, and she sails on, bidding against a man from Missouri who tells the people around him that he's looking for a place to retire.

"Sold to the young lady with the backpack," Randy says when she bids six hundred. He gives her a crestfallen look, and she feels embarrassed.

As she waits for Randy to wind up his business after the auction, Jenny locates her acre from the map of the plots of land. It is along a gravel road and marked off with stakes tied with hot-pink survey tape. It is a small section of the woods—her block on the quilt, she thinks. These are her trees. The vines and underbrush are thick and spotted with raindrops. She notices a windfall leaning on a maple, like a lover dying in its arms. Maples are strong, she thinks, but she feels like getting an axe and chopping that windfall down, to save the maple. In the distance, the whining of a speedboat cuts into the day.

They meet afterward at Randy's van, his mobile real-estate office, with a little shingled roof raised in the center to look rustic. It looks like an outhouse on wheels. A painted message on the side says, "REALITY IS REAL ESTATE." As Randy plows through the mud on the new road,

Jenny apologizes. Buying the lot was like laughing at the statue at the wrong moment—something he would take the wrong way, an insult to his attentions.

"I can't reach you," he says. "You say you want to live out in the wilderness and grow your own vegetables, but you act like you're somewhere in outer space. You can't grow vegetables in outer space. You can't even grow them in the woods unless you clear some ground."

"I'm looking for a place to land."

"What do I have to do to get through to you?"

"I don't know. I need more time."

He turns onto the highway, patterned with muddy tire tracks from the cars at the auction. "I said I'd wait, so I guess I'll have to," he says, flashing his Dennis Quaid smile. "You take as long as you want to, then. I learned my lesson with Barbara. You've got to be understanding with the women. That's the key to a successful relationship." Frowning, he slams his hand on the steering wheel. "That's what they tell me, anyhow."

JENNY IS HAVING coffee with Opal. She arrived unexpectedly. It's very early. She looks as though she has been up all night.

"Please show me your quilts," Jenny says. "I don't mean your crazy quilts. I want to see that special quilt. Mom said it had the family tree."

Opal spills coffee in her saucer. "What is wrong with young people today?" she asks.

"I want to know why it's called a burial quilt," Jenny says. "Are you planning to be buried in it?"

Opal wishes she had a shot of peppermint in her coffee. It sounds like a delicious idea. She starts toward the den with the coffee cup rattling in its saucer, and she splatters drops on the rug. Never mind it now, she thinks, turning back.

"It's just a family history," she says.

"Why's it called a burial quilt?" Jenny asks.

Jenny's face is pale. She has blue pouches under her eyes and blue eyeshadow on her eyelids. Her eyes are ringed like a raccoon's.

"See that closet in the hall?" Opal says. "Get a chair and we'll get the quilt down."

Jenny stands on a kitchen chair and removes the quilt from beneath several others. It's wrapped in blue plastic and Jenny hugs it closely as she steps down with it.

They spread it out on the couch, and the blue plastic floats off somewhere. Jenny looks like someone in love as she gazes at the quilt. "It's gorgeous," she murmurs. "How beautiful."

"Shoot!" says Opal. "It's ugly as homemade sin."

Jenny runs her fingers over the rough textures of the quilt. The quilt is dark and sombre. The backing is a heavy gray gabardine, and the nine-inch-square blocks are pieced of smaller blocks of varying shades of gray and brown and black. They are wools, apparently made from men's winter suits. On each block is an appliquéd off-white tombstone—a comical shape, like Casper the ghost. Each tombstone has a name and date on it.

Jenny recognizes some of the names. Myrtle Williams. Voris Williams. Thelma Lee Freeman. The oldest gravestone is "Eulalee Freeman 1857–1900." The shape is irregular, a rectangle with a clumsy foot sticking out from one corner. The quilt is knotted with yarn, and the edging is open, for more blocks to be added.

"Eulalee's daughter started it," says Opal. "But that thing has been carried through this family like a plague. Did you ever see such horrible old dark colors? I pieced on it some when I was younger, but it was too depressing. I think some of the kinfolks must have died without a square, so there may be several to catch up on."

"I'll do it," says Jenny. "I could learn to quilt."

"Traditionally, the quilt stops when the family name stops," Opal says. "And since my parents didn't have a boy, that was the end of the Freeman line on this particular branch of the tree. So the last old maids finish the quilt." She lets out a wild cackle. "Theoretically, a quilt like this could keep going till doomsday."

"Do you care if I have this quilt?" asks Jenny.

"What would you do with it? It's too ugly to put on a bed and too morbid to work on."

"I think it's kind of neat," says Jenny. She strokes the rough tweed. Already it is starting to decay, and it has moth holes. Jenny feels tears start to drip down her face.

"Don't you go putting my name on that thing," her aunt says.

. . .

JENNY HAS TAKEN the quilt to her apartment. She explained that she is
going to study the family tree, or that she is going to finish the quilt. If
she's smart, Opal thinks, she will let Randy Newcomb auction it off. The
way Jenny took it, cramming it into the blue plastic, was like snatching
something that was free. Opal feels relieved, as though she has pushed
the burden of that ratty old quilt onto her niece. All those miserable,
cranky women, straining their eyes, stitching on those dark scraps of
material.

For a long time, Jenny wouldn't tell why she was crying, and when
she started to tell, Opal was uncomfortable, afraid she'd be required to
tell something comparable of her own, but as she listened she found
herself caught up in Jenny's story. Jenny said it was a man. That was always the case, Opal thought. It was five years ago. A man Jenny knew
in a place by the sea. Opal imagined seagulls, pretty sand. There were
no palm trees. It was up North. The young man worked with Jenny in
a restaurant with glass walls facing the ocean. They waited on tables
and collected enough tips to take a trip together near the end of the
summer. Jenny made it sound like an idyllic time, waiting on tables by
the sea. She started crying again when she told about the trip, but the
trip sounded nice. Opal listened hungrily, imagining the young man,
thinking that he would have had handsome, smooth cheeks, and hair
that fell attractively over his forehead. He would have had good manners, being a waiter. Jenny and the man, whose name was Jim, flew to
Denver, Colorado, and they rented a car and drove around out West.
They visited the Grand Canyon and Yellowstone and other places Opal
had heard about. They grilled salmon on the beach, on another ocean.
They camped out in the redwoods, trees so big they hid the sky. Jenny
described all these scenes, and the man sounded like a good man. His
brother had died in Vietnam and he felt guilty that he had been the one
spared, because his brother was a swimmer and could have gone to the
Olympics. Jim wasn't athletic. He had a bad knee and hammertoes. He
slept fitfully in the tent, and Jenny said soothing things to him, and she
cared about him, but by the time they had curved northward and over
to Yellowstone the trip was becoming unpleasant. The romance wore
off. She loved him, but she couldn't deal with his needs. One of the last

nights they spent together, it rained all night long. He told her not to touch the tent material, because somehow the pressure of a finger on the nylon would make it start to leak at that spot. Lying there in the rain, Jenny couldn't resist touching a spot where water was collecting in a little sag in the top of the tent. The drip started then, and it grew worse, until they got so wet they had to get in the car. Not long afterward, when they ran short of money, they parted. Jenny got a job in Denver. She never saw him again.

Opal listened eagerly to the details about grilling the fish together, about the zip-together sleeping bags and setting up the tent and washing themselves in the cold stream. But when Jenny brought the story up to the present, Opal was not prepared. She felt she had been dunked in the cold water and left gasping. Jenny said she had heard a couple of times through a mutual friend that Jim had spent some time in Mexico. And then, she said, this week she had begun thinking about him, because of all the trees at the lake, and she had an overwhelming desire to see him again. She had been unfair, she knew now. She telephoned the friend, who had worked with them in the restaurant by the sea. He hadn't known where to locate her, he said, and so he couldn't tell her that Jim had been killed in Colorado over a year ago. His four-wheel drive had plunged off a mountain curve.

"I feel some trick has been played on me. It seems so unreal." Jenny tugged at the old quilt, and her eyes darkened. "I was in Colorado, and I didn't even know he was there. If I still knew him, I would know how to mourn, but now I don't know how. And it was over a year ago. So I don't know what to feel."

"Don't look back, hon," Opal said, hugging her niece closely. But she was shaking, and Jenny shook with her.

OPAL MAKES HERSELF a snack, thinking it will pick up her strength. She is very tired. On the tray, she places an apple and a paring knife and some milk and cookies. She touches the remote-control button, and the picture blossoms. She was wise to buy a large TV, the one listed as the best in the consumer magazine. The color needs a little adjustment, though. She eases up the volume and starts peeling the apple. She has a little bump on one knuckle. In the old days, people would take the family Bible and bust a cyst like that with it. Just slam it hard.

On the screen, a Scoutmaster is telling a story to some Boy Scouts around a campfire. The campfire is only a fireplace, with electric logs. Opal loses track of time, and the songs flow together. A woman is lying on her stomach on a car hood in a desert full of gas pumps. TV sets crash. Smoke emerges from an eyeball. A page of sky turns like a page in a book. Then, at a desk in a classroom, a cocky blond kid with a pack of cigarettes rolled in the sleeve of his T-shirt is singing about a sexy girl with a tattoo on her back who is sitting on a commode and smoking a cigarette. In the classroom, all the kids are gyrating and snapping their fingers to wild music. The teacher at the blackboard with her white hair in a bun looks disapproving, but the kids in the class don't know what's on her mind. The teacher is thinking about how, when the bell rings, she will hit the road to Nashville.

(1984)

AFTER RAIN

WILLIAM TREVOR

In the dining room of the Pensione Cesarina solitary diners are fitted in around the walls, where space does not permit a table large enough for two. These tables for one are in three of the room's four corners—by the door of the pantry where the jugs of water keep cool, between one family table and another, on either side of the tall casement windows that rattle when they're closed or opened. The dining room is large, its ceiling high, its plain cream-colored walls undecorated. It is noisy when the pensione's guests are there, the tables for two that take up all the central space packed close together, edges touching. The solitary diners are well separated from this mass by the passage left for the waitresses, and have a better view of the dining room's activity and of the food before it's placed in front of them—whether tonight it is *brodo* or pasta, beef or chicken, and what the *dolce* is.

"*Dieci*," Harriet says, giving the number of her room when she is asked. The table she has occupied for the last eleven evenings has been joined to one that is too small for a party of five: she doesn't know where to go. She stands a few more moments by the door, with the serving dishes busily going by her and wine bottles being grabbed from the marble-topped sideboard by the rust-haired waitress, or the one with a wild look, or the one who is plump and pretty. It is the rust-haired waitress who eventually leads Harriet to the table by the door of the pantry where the water jugs keep cool. "*Da bere?*" she asks, and Harriet, still feeling shy, although no one glanced in her direction when she stood alone by the door, orders the wine she has ordered on other nights, Santa Cristina.

Wearing a blue dress unadorned except for the shiny blue buckle of its belt, she has earrings that hardly show and a necklace of opaque white beads that isn't valuable. Angular and thin, her dark hair cut short, her long face strikingly like the sharply chiselled faces of Modigliani, she passed out of her twenties a month ago. She is alone in the Pensione Cesarina because a love affair is over.

A holiday was cancelled, there was an empty fortnight. She wanted to be somewhere else then, not in England with time on her hands. "*Io sola,*" she said on the telephone, hoping she had got that right, choosing the Cesarina because she'd known it in childhood, because she thought that being alone would be easier in familiar surroundings.

"*Va bene?*" the rust-haired waitress inquires, proffering the Santa Cristina.

"*Sì, sì.*"

The couples who mostly fill the dining room are German, the guttural sound of their language drifting to Harriet from the tables that are closest to her. Middle-aged, the women more stylishly dressed than the men, they are enjoying the heat of August and the low-season tariff: demi-pensione at a hundred and ten thousand lire. The heat may be too much of a good thing for some, although it's cooler by dinnertime, when the windows of the dining room are all open, and the Cesarina is cooler anyway, being in the hills. "If there's a breeze about," Harriet's mother used to say, "it finds the Cesarina."

Twenty years ago Harriet first came here with her parents, when she was ten and her brother twelve. Before that she had heard about the pensione, how the terra-cotta floors were oiled every morning before the guests were up, and how the clean smell of oil lingered all day, how breakfast was a roll or two, with tea or coffee on the terrace, how dogs sometimes barked at night, from a farm across the hills. There were photographs of the parched garden and of the stately, ochre-washed exterior, and of the pensione's vineyard, steeply sloping down to two enormous wells. And then she saw for herself, summer after summer in the low season: the vast dining room at the bottom of a flight of stone steps from the hall, and the three salons where there is Stock or grappa after dinner, with tiny cups of harsh black coffee. In the one with the bookcases there are Giotto reproductions in a volume on the table lectern, and "My Brother Jonathan" and "Rebecca" among the detective novels by George Goodchild on the shelves. The guests spoke in murmurs when Harriet first knew these rooms, English mostly, for it was mostly English who came then. To this day, the Pensione Cesarina does not accept credit cards, but instead will take a Eurocheque for more than the guaranteed amount.

"*Ecco, signora.*" A waitress with glasses, whom Harriet has seen only once or twice before, places a plate of tagliatelle in front of her.

"*Grazie.*"

"*Prego, signora. Buon appetito.*"

If the love affair hadn't ended—and Harriet has always believed that love affairs are going to last—she would now be on the island of Skíros. If the love affair hadn't ended, she might one day have come to the Cesarina as her parents had before their children were born, and later might have occupied a family table in the dining room. There is an American family tonight, and an Italian one, and other couples besides the Germans. A couple, just arrived, spoke what sounded like Dutch upstairs. Another Harriet knows to be Swiss, another she also guesses to be Dutch. A nervous English pair are too far away to allow eavesdropping.

"*Va bene?*" the rust-haired waitress inquires again, lifting away her empty plate.

"*Molto bene. Grazie.*"

Among the other solitary diners is a gray-haired dumpy woman who has several times spoken to Harriet upstairs, an American. A man is noticeable every evening because of his garish shirts, and there's a man who keeps looking about him in a jerky, nervous way, and a woman—stylish in black—who could be French. The man who looks about—small, with delicate, well-tended good features—often glances in this woman's direction, and sometimes in Harriet's. An elderly man whose white linen suit observes the formalities of the past wears a differently striped silk tie each dinnertime.

On the first night of her stay Harriet had "The Small House at Allington" in her handbag, intending to prop it up in front of her in the dining room, but when the moment came that seemed all wrong. Already, then, she regretted her impulse to come here on her own and wondered why she had. On the journey out the rawness of her pain had in no way softened, if anything had intensified, for the journey on that day should have been different, and not made alone: she had forgotten there would be that.

With the chicken pieces she's offered, there are roast potatoes, tomatoes and zucchini, and salad. Then Harriet chooses cheese: pecorino, a little Gorgonzola. Half of the Santa Cristina is left for tomorrow, her room number scribbled on the label. On the envelope provided for her napkin this is more elegantly inscribed, in a sloping hand: *Camera Dieci*. She folds her napkin and tucks it away, and for a moment as she does so the man she has come here to forget pushes through another crowded room, coming toward her in the King of Poland, her name on his lips. "I love you, Harriet," he whispers beneath the noise around them. Her eyes close when their caress is shared. "My darling Harriet," he says.

Upstairs, in the room where the bookcases are, Harriet wonders if this solitude is how her life will be. Has she returned to this childhood place to seek whatever comfort a happy past can offer? Is that a truer reason than what she told herself at the time? Her thoughts are always a muddle when a love affair ends, the truth befogged; the truth not there at all, it often seems. Love failed her was what she felt when another relationship crumbled into nothing; love has a way of doing that. And since wondering is company for the companionless, she wonders why it should be so. This is the first time that a holiday has been cancelled, that she has come away alone.

"*Mi dispiace,*" a boy in a white jacket apologizes, having spilled some of a liqueur on a German woman's arm. The woman laughs and says in

English that it doesn't matter. "*Non importa*," her husband adds when the boy looks vacant, and the German woman laughs again.

"*Mais oui*, I study the law," a long-legged girl is saying. "And Eloise is a stylist."

These girls are Belgian: the questions of two Englishmen are answered. The Englishmen are young, both of them heavily built, casually turned out, one of them mustached.

"Is 'stylist' right? Is that what you say?"

"Oh, yes." And both young men nod. When one suggests a liqueur on the terrace Eloise and her friend ask for cherry brandy. The boy in the white jacket goes to a cupboard off the hall to pour it, where the espresso machine is.

"And you?" Eloise inquires as the four pass through the room, through the French windows to the terrace.

"Nev's in business. I go down after wrecks." The voice that drifts back is slack, accented, confident. English or German or Dutch, these are the people who have made the Pensione Cesarina move with the times, different from the people of Harriet's childhood.

A bearded man is surreptitiously sketching a couple on one of the sofas. The couple, both reading, are unaware. In the hall the American family is much in evidence, the mother with a baby in her arms pacing up and down, the father quieting two other children, a girl and a boy.

"Good evening," someone interrupts Harriet's observations, and the man in the linen suit asks if the chair next to hers is taken by anyone else. His tie tonight is brown and green, and Harriet notices that his craggy features are freckled with an old man's blotches, that his hair is so scanty that whether it's gray or white doesn't register. What is subtle in his face is the washed-out blue of his eyes.

"You travel alone, too," he remarks, openly seeking the companionship of the moment, when Harriet has indicated that the chair beside her is not taken.

"Yes, I do."

"I can always pick out the English."

He offers the theory that this is perhaps something the traveller acquires with age and with the experience of many journeys. "You'll probably see," he adds.

The companion of the bearded man who is sketching the couple on the sofa leans forward and smiles over what she sees. In the hall the American father has persuaded his older children to go to bed. The mother still soothes her baby, still pacing up and down. The small man who so agitatedly glanced about the dining room passes rapidly through the hall, carrying two cups of coffee.

"They certainly feed you," Harriet's companion remarks, "these days at the Cesarina."

"Yes."

"Quite scanty, the food was once."

"Yes, I remember."

"I mean, a longish time ago."

"The first summer I came here I was ten."

He calculates, glancing at her face to guess her age. Before his own first time, he says, which was the spring of 1987. He has been coming since, he says, and asks if she has.

"My parents separated."

"I'm sorry."

"They'd been coming here all their married lives. They were fond of this place."

"Some people fall for it. Others not at all."

"My brother found it boring."

"A child might easily."

"I never did."

"Interesting, those two chaps picking up the girls. I wonder if they'll ever cope with coach tours at the Cesarina."

He talks. Harriet doesn't listen. This love affair had once, like the other affairs before it, felt like the exorcism of the disappointment that so drearily colored her life when her parents went their separate ways. There were no quarrels when her parents separated, no bitterness, no drama. They told their children gently, neither blamed the other. Both—for years, apparently—had been involved with other people. Both said the separation was a happier outcome than staying together for the sake of the family would be. They used those words, and Harriet has never forgotten them. Her brother shrugged the disappointment off, but for Harriet it did not begin to go away until the first of her love affairs. And always, when a love affair ended, there had been no exorcism after all.

"I'm off tomorrow," the old man says.

She nods. In the hall the baby in the American mother's arms is sleeping at last. The mother smiles at someone Harriet can't see and then moves toward the wide stone staircase. The couple on the sofa, still unaware that they've been sketched, stand up and go away. The agitated little man bustles through the hall again.

"Sorry to go." Harriet's companion finishes something he has been saying, then tells her about his journey: by train because he doesn't care for flying. Lunch in Milan, dinner in Zurich, on neither occasion leaving the railway station. The eleven-o'clock sleeper from Zurich.

"We used to drive out when I came with my parents."

"I haven't ever done that. And of course won't ever now."

"I liked it."

At the time, it didn't seem unreal or artificial. Their smiling faces didn't, nor the pleasure they seemed to take in poky French hotels where only the food was good, nor their chattering to one another in the front of the car, their badinage and arguments. Yet retrospect insisted that reality was elsewhere; that reality was surreptitious lunches with two other people, and afternoon rooms, and guile; that reality was a web of lies until one of them found out, it didn't matter which; that reality was when there had to be something better than what the family offered.

"So this time you have come alone?"

He may have said it twice, she isn't sure. Something about his expression suggests he has.

"Yes."

He speaks of solitude. It offers a quality that is hard to define; much more than the cliché of getting to know yourself. He himself has been on his own for many years and has discovered consolation in that very circumstance, which is an irony of a kind, he supposes.

"I was to go somewhere else." She doesn't know why she makes this revelation. Politeness, perhaps. On other evenings, after dinner, she has seen this man in conversation with whomever he has chosen to sit beside. He is polite himself. He sounds more interested than inquisitive.

"You changed your mind?"

"A friendship fell apart."

"Ah."

"I should be on an island in the sun."

"And where is that, if I may ask?"

"Skíros, it's called. Renowned for its therapies."

"Therapies?"

"They're a fashion."

"For the ill, is this? If I may say so, you don't look ill."

"No, I'm not ill." Unable to keep the men she loves in love with her. But of course not ill.

"In fact, you look supremely healthy." He smiles. His teeth are still his own. "If I may say so."

"I'm not so sure that I like islands in the sun. But even so, I wanted to go there."

"For the therapies?"

"No, I would have avoided that. Sand therapy, water therapy, sex therapy, image therapy, holistic counselling. I would have steered clear, I think."

"Being on your own's a therapy, too, of course. Although it's nice to have a chat."

She doesn't listen; he goes on talking. On the island of Skíros tourists beat drums at sunset and welcome the dawn with song. Or they may simply swim and play, or discover the undiscovered self. The Pensione Cesarina—even the pensione transformed by the Germans and the Dutch—offers nothing like it. Nor would it offer enough to her parents anymore. Her divided parents travel grandly now.

"I see 'The Spanish Farm' is still on the shelves." The old man has risen and hovers for a moment. "I doubt that anyone's read it since I did in 1987."

"No, probably not."

He says good night and changes it to goodbye because he has to make an early start. For a moment, it seems to Harriet, he hesitates, something about his stance suggesting that he'd like to be invited to stay, to be offered a cup of coffee or a drink. Then he goes, without saying anything else. Lonely in old age, she suddenly realizes, wondering why she didn't notice that when he was talking to her. Lonely in spite of all he claims for solitude.

"Goodbye," she calls after him, but he doesn't hear. They were to come back here the summer of the separation; instead, there were cancellations then, too, and an empty fortnight.

"Buona notte." The boy in the white jacket smiles tentatively from his cupboard as she passes through the hall. He's new tonight; it was another boy before. She hasn't realized that either.

SHE WALKS THROUGH the heat of the morning on the narrow road to the town, by the graveyard and the abandoned petrol pumps. A few cars pass her, coming from the pensione, for the road leads hardly anywhere else, petering out eventually. It would have been hotter on the island of Skíros.

Clouds have gathered in one part of the sky, behind her as she walks. The shade of clouds might make it cooler, she tells herself, but so far they are not close enough to the sun for that. The road widens and gradually the incline becomes less steep as she approaches the town. There's a park with concrete seats and the first of the churches, dedicated to Santa Agnese, of this town.

There's no one in the park until Harriet sits there beneath the chestnut trees in a corner. Far below her, as the town tails off again, a main road begins to wind through clumps of needle pines and umbrella pines to join, far out of sight, a motorway. "But weren't we happy?" she hears herself exclaim, a little shrill because she couldn't help it. Yes, they were happy, he agreed at once, anxious to make that clear. Not happy enough was what he meant, and you could tell; something not quite right. She asked him and he didn't know, genuine in his bewilderment.

When she feels cooler she walks on, down shaded, narrow streets to the central piazza of the town, where she rests again, with a cappuccino at a pavement table.

Italians and tourists move slowly in the unevenly paved square, women with shopping bags and dogs, men leaving the barber's, the tourists in their summery clothes. The church of Santa Fabiola dominates the square, gray steps in front, a brick-and-stone façade. There is another café, across from the one Harriet has chosen, and a line of market stalls beside it. The town's banks are in the square but not its shops.

There's a trattoria and a gelateria, their similar decoration connecting them, side by side. "Yes, they're all one," her father said.

In this square her father lifted her high above his head and she looked down and saw his laughing, upturned face and she laughed, too, because he joked so. Her mother stuttered out her schoolgirl French in the little hotels where they stayed on the journey out, and blushed with shame when no one understood. "Oh, this is pleasant!" her mother murmured, a table away from where Harriet is now.

A priest comes down the steps of the church, looks about him, does not see whom he thought he might. A skinny dog goes limping by. The bell of Santa Fabiola chimes twelve o'clock and when it ceases another bell, farther away, begins. Clouds have covered the sun, but the air is as hot as ever. There's still no breeze.

It was in the foyer of the Rembrandt Cinema that he said he didn't think their love affair was working. It was then that she exclaimed, "But weren't we happy?" They didn't quarrel. Not even afterward, when she asked him why he had told her in a cinema foyer. He didn't know, he said; it just seemed right in that moment, some fragment of a mood they shared. If it hadn't been for their holiday's being quite soon, their relationship might have dragged on for a while. Much better that it shouldn't, he said.

"The fourteenth of February in London was quite as black, and cold, and as wintersome as it was at Allington, and was, perhaps, somewhat more melancholy in its coldness." She has read that bit before and couldn't settle to it, and cannot now. She takes her dark glasses off: the clouds are not the pretty bundles she noticed before, white cotton wool as decoration is by Raphael or Perugino. The clouds that have come up so quickly are gray as lead, a sombre panoply pegged out against a blue that's almost lost. The first drops fall when Harriet tries the doors of Santa Fabiola and finds them locked. They will remain so, a notice tersely states, until half past two.

"It had been finally arranged that the marriage should take place in London," she reads in the trattoria. "There were certainly many reasons which would have made a marriage from Courcy Castle more convenient. The De Courcy family were all assembled at their country family residence, and could therefore have been present at the ceremony without cost or trouble." She isn't hungry; she has ordered risotto, hoping it will be small, and mineral water without gas.

"*C'è del pane o della farina nel piatto? Non devo mangiare della farina*," a woman is saying, and the gaunt-faced waiter carefully listens, not understanding at first and then excitedly nodding. "*Non c'è farina*," he replies, pointing at items on the menu. The woman is from the pensione. She's with a lanky young man who might be her son, and Harriet can't identify the language they speak to each other.

"Is fine?" the same waiter asks Harriet as he passes, noticing that she has begun to eat her risotto. She nods and smiles and reads again. The rain outside is heavy now.

THE ANNUNCIATION IN the church of Santa Fabiola is by an unknown artist, perhaps of the school of Filippo Lippi, no one is certain. The angel kneels, gray wings protruding, his lily half hidden by a pillar. The floor is marble, white and green and ochre. The Virgin looks alarmed, right hand arresting her visitor's advance. Beyond—background to the encounter—there are gracious arches, a balustrade and then the sky and hills. There is a soundlessness about the picture, the silence of a mystery: no words are spoken in this captured moment, what's said between the two has been said already.

Harriet's eye records the details: the green folds of the angel's dress, the red beneath it, the mark in the sky that is a dove, the Virgin's book, the stately pillars and the empty vase, the Virgin's slipper, the bare feet of the angel. The distant landscape is soft, as if no heat had ever touched it. It isn't alarm in the Virgin's eyes, it's wonderment. In another moment there'll be serenity. A few tourists glide about the church, whispering now and again. A man in a black overall is mopping the floor of the central aisle and has roped it off at either end. An elderly woman prays before a statue of the Virgin, each bead of her rosary fingered, lips silently murmuring. Incense is cloying on the air.

Harriet walks slowly past flaring candles and the tomb of a local family, past the relics of the altar, and the story of Santa Fabiola, which is flaking in a side chapel. She has not been in this church before, neither during her present visit nor in the past. Her parents didn't bother much with churches; she might have come here on her own yesterday or on any day of her stay but she didn't bother either. Her parents liked the sun in the garden of the pensione, the walk down to the cafés, and drives into the hills or to other little towns, to the swimming pool at Ponte Nicolo.

The woman who has been praying hobbles to light another candle, then prays again, and hobbles off. Returning to the Annunciation, Harriet sits down in the pew that's nearest it. There is blue as well as gray in the wings of the angel, little flecks of blue you don't notice when you look at first. The Virgin's slipper is a shade of brown, the empty vase is bulb-shaped with a slender stem, the Virgin's book had gold on it but only traces remain.

The rain has stopped when Harriet leaves the church, the air is fresher. Too slick and glib, to use her love affairs to restore her faith in love: that thought is there mysteriously. She has cheated in her love affairs: that comes from nowhere, too.

Harriet stands a moment longer, alone on the steps of the church, bewildered by this personal revelation, aware instinctively of its truth. The dust of the piazza paving has been washed into the crevices that separate the stones. At the café where she had her cappuccino the waiter is wiping dry the plastic of the chairs.

THE SUN IS still reluctant in the watery sky. On her walk back to the Pensione Cesarina it seems to Harriet that in this respite from the brash smother of heat a different life has crept out of the foliage and stone. A coolness emanates from the road she walks on. Unseen, among the wild geraniums, one bird sings.

Tomorrow, when the sun is again in charge at its time of year, a few midday minutes will wipe away what lingers of this softness. New dust will settle, marble will be warm to touch. It may be weeks, months perhaps, before rain coaxes out these fragrances that are tender now.

The sun is always pitiless when it returns, harsh in its punishment. In the dried-out garden of the Pensione Cesarina they made her wear a hat she didn't like but they could take the sun themselves, both of them skulking behind dark glasses and high-factor cream. Skíros's sun is its attraction. "What I need is sun," he said, and Harriet wonders if he went there after all, if he's there today, not left behind in London, if he even found someone to go with. She sees him in Skíros, windsurfing in Atsitsa Bay, which he has talked about. She sees him with a companion who is uncomplicated and happy in Atsitsa Bay, who tries out a therapy just to see what it's like.

The deck chairs are sodden at the Pensione Cesarina, rose petals glisten. A glass left on a terrace table has gathered an inch of water. The umbrellas in the outer hall have all been used. Windows, closed for a while, are opened; on the vineyard slopes the sprinklers are turned on again.

Not wanting to be inside, Harriet walks in the garden and among the vines, her shoes drenched. From the town comes the chiming of bells: six o'clock at Santa Fabiola, six o'clock a minute later somewhere else. While she stands alone among the dripping vines she cannot make a connection that she knows is there. There is a blankness in her thoughts, a density that feels like muddle, until she realizes: the Annunciation was painted after rain. Its distant landscape, glimpsed through arches, has the temporary look that she is seeing now. It was after rain that the angel came: those first cool moments were a chosen time.

IN THE DINING room, the table where the man with the garish shirts sat has been joined to a family table to allow for a party of seven. There is a different woman where the smart Frenchwoman sat, and no one at the table of the old man. The woman who was explaining in the trattoria that she must not eat food containing flour is given consommé instead of ravioli. New faces are dotted everywhere.

"*Buona sera*," the rust-haired waitress greets Harriet, and the waitress with glasses brings her salad.

"*Grazie*," Harriet murmurs.

"*Prego, signora.*"

She pours her wine, breaks off a crust of bread. It's noisy in the dining room now, dishes clattering, the babble of voices. It felt like noise in the foyer of the Rembrandt Cinema when he told her: the uproar of shock, although in fact it was quite silent there. Bright, harsh colors flashed through her consciousness, as if some rush of blood exploded in a kaleidoscope of distress. For a moment in the foyer of the cinema she closed her eyes, as she had when they told her they weren't to be a family anymore.

She might have sent them postcards, but she hasn't. She might have reported that breakfast at the pensione is more than coffee and rolls since the Germans and the Dutch and the Swiss have begun to come: cheese and cold meats, fruit and cereals, fresh sponge cake, a buffet on the terrace. Each morning she has sat there reading "The Small House at Allington," wondering if they would like to know of the breakfast-time improvement. She wondered today if it would interest them to learn that the abandoned petrol pumps are still there on the road to the town, or that she sat in the deserted park beneath the chestnut trees. She thought of sending him a postcard, too, but in the end she didn't. His predecessor it was who encouraged her to bring long novels on holiday: "The Tenant of Wildfell Hall," "The Mill on the Floss."

It's beef tonight, with spinach. And afterward Harriet has *dolce*, remembering this sodden yellow raisin cake from the past. She won't taste that again; as mysteriously as she knows she has cheated without meaning to in her love affairs, she knows she won't come back, alone or with someone else. Coming back has been done, a private journey that chance suggested. Tomorrow she'll be gone.

In the room with the bookcases and the Giotto reproductions she watches while people drink their grappa or their Stock, or ask the white-jacketed boy for more coffee, or pick up conversations with one another. The Belgian girls have got to know the young Englishman who goes down after wrecks and Nev who's in the business world. All four pass through the room on their way to the terrace, the girls with white cardigans draped on their shoulders because it isn't as warm as it was last night. "That man drew us!" a voice cries, and the couple who were sketched last night gaze down at their hardly recognizable selves in the pensione's comment book.

He backed away, as others had, when she asked too much of love, when she tried to change the circumstances that are the past by imposing a brighter present, and constancy in the future above all else. She has been the victim of herself: with vivid clarity she knows that now and wonders why she does and why she didn't before. Nothing tells her when she ponders the solitude of her stay in the Pensione Cesarina, and she senses that nothing ever will. She sees again the brown-and-green-striped tie of the old man who talked about being on your own, and the freckles that are blotches on his forehead. She sees herself walking in the morning heat past the graveyard and the rusted petrol pumps. She sees herself seeking the shade of the chestnut trees in the park, and crossing the piazza to the trattoria when the first raindrops fell. She hears the swish of the cleaner's mop in the church of Santa Fabiola, she hears the tourists' whisper. The fingers of the praying woman flutter on her beads, the candles flare. The story of Santa Fabiola is lost in the shadows that were once the people of her life, the family tomb reeks odorlessly of death. Rain has sweetened the breathless air, the angel comes mysteriously also.

(1995)

OVERNIGHT TO MANY DISTANT CITIES

DONALD BARTHELME

A *GROUP of Chinese in brown jackets preceded us through the halls of Versailles.* They were middle-aged men, weighty, obviously important, perhaps thirty of them. At the entrance to each room a guard stopped us, held us back until the Chinese had finished inspecting it. A fleet of black government Citroëns had brought them, they were much at ease with Versailles and with each other, it was clear that they were being rewarded for many years of good behavior.

Asked her opinion of Versailles, my daughter Katie said she thought it was overdecorated.

Well, yes.

Again in Paris, years earlier, without Katie, we had a hotel room opening on a courtyard, and late at night through an open window heard a woman expressing intense and rising pleasure. We blushed and fell upon each other.

Right now sunny skies in mid-Manhattan, the temperature is forty-two degrees.

In Stockholm we ate reindeer steak and I told the Prime Minister . . . That the price of booze was too high. Twenty dollars for a bottle of J & B! He (Olaf Palme) agreed, most politely, and said that they financed the Army that way. The conference we were attending was held at a workers' vacation center somewhat outside the city. Shamelessly, I asked for a double bed, there were none, we pushed two single beds together. An Israeli journalist sat on the two single beds drinking our costly whiskey and explaining the devilish policies of the Likud. Then it was time to go play with the Africans. A poet who had been for a time a Minister of Culture explained why he had burned a grand piano on the lawn in front of the Ministry. "The piano," he said, "is not the national instrument of Ghana."

A boat ride through the scattered islands. A Warsaw Pact novelist asked me to carry a package of paper to New York for him.

Woman is silent for two days in San Francisco. And walked through the streets with her arms raised high touching the leaves of the trees.

"But you're *married!*" she said.

"But that's not my fault!"

Tearing into cold crab at Scoma's we saw Chill Wills at another table, doing the same thing. We waved to him.

In Taegu the air was full of the noise of helicopters. The helicopter landed on a pad, General A jumped out and walked with a firm, manly stride to the spot where General B waited—generals visiting each other. They shook hands, the honor guard with its blue scarves and chromed rifles popped to, the band played, pictures were taken. General A followed by General B walked smartly around the rigid honor guard and then the two generals marched off to the generals' mess, to have a drink.

There are eight hundred and twenty-seven generals now in U.S. armed services. There are four hundred and seventeen brigadier generals, two hundred and ninety-nine major generals, eighty-seven lieutenant generals, and twenty-four full generals. The funniest thing in the world is a general trying on a nickname. Sometimes they don't stick. "Howlin' Mad," "Old Hickory," "Old Blood and Guts," and "Buck" have already been taken. "Old Lacy" is not a good choice.

If you are a general in the field you will live in a general's van, which is a kind of motor home for generals. I once saw a drunk two-star general, in a general's van, seize hold of a visiting actress—it was Marilyn Monroe—and seat her on his lap, shrieking all the while "R.H.I.P.!," or Rank Has Its Privileges.

Enough of generals.

Thirty per cent chance of rain this afternoon, high in the mid-fifties.

In London I met a man who was not in love. Beautiful shoes, black as black marble, and a fine suit. We went to the theatre together, matter of a few pounds, he knew which plays were the best plays, on several occasions he brought his mother. "An American," he said to his mother, "an American I met." "Met an American during the war," she said to me. "Didn't like him." This was reasonably standard, next she would tell me that we had no culture. Her son was hungry, starving, mad in fact, sucking the cuff buttons of his fine suit, choking on the cuff buttons of his fine suit, left and right sleeves jammed into his mouth—he was not in love, he said, "again not in love, not in love again." I put him out of his misery with a good book, Rilke, as I remember, and resolved never to find myself in a situation as dire as his.

In San Antonio we walked by the little river. And ended up in Helen's Bar, where John found a pool player who was, like John, an ex-Marine. How these ex-Marines love each other! It is a flat scandal. The Congress should do something about it. The I.R.S. should do something about it. You and I talked to each other while John talked to his Parris Island friend, and that wasn't too bad, wasn't too bad. We discussed twenty-four novels of normative adultery. "Can't *have* no adultery without adults," I said, and you agreed that this was true. We thought about it, our hands on each other's knees, under the table.

In the car on the way back from San Antonio the ladies talked about the rump of a noted poet. "Too big," they said, "too big too big too big." "Can you imagine going to bed with him?" they said, and then all said, "No no no no no," and laughed and laughed and laughed and laughed and laughed.

I offered to get out and run alongside the car, if that would allow them to converse more freely.

In Copenhagen I went shopping with two Hungarians. I had thought they merely wanted to buy presents for their wives. They bought leather gloves, chess sets, frozen fish, baby food, lawnmowers, air-conditioners, kayaks . . . We were six hours in the department store.

"This will teach you," they said, "never to go shopping with Hungarians."

Again in Paris, the hotel was the Montalembert . . . Katie jumped on the bed and sliced her hand open on an open watercolor tin, blood everywhere, the concierge assuring us, "In the war, I saw much worse things."

Well, yes.

But we couldn't stop the bleeding, in the cab to the American Hospital the driver kept looking over his shoulder to make sure that we weren't bleeding on his seat covers, handfuls of bloody paper towels in my right and left hands . . .

On another evening, as we were on our way to dinner, I kicked the kid with carefully calibrated force as we were crossing the Pont Mirabeau, she had been pissy all day, driving us crazy. Her character improved instantly, wonderfully. This is a tactic that can be used exactly once.

In Mexico City we lay with the gorgeous daughter of the American ambassador by a clear, cold mountain stream. Well, that was the plan, it didn't work out that way. We were around sixteen and had run away from home, in the great tradition, hitched various long rides with various sinister folk, and there we were in the great city with about two T-shirts to our names. My friend Herman found us both jobs in a jukebox factory. Our assignment was to file the slots in American jukeboxes so that they would accept the big, thick Mexican coins. All day long. No gloves.

After about a week of this we were walking one day on the street on which the Hotel Reforma is to be found and there were my father and grandfather, smiling. "The boys have run away," my father had told my grandfather, and my grandfather had said, "Hot damn, let's go get 'em." I have rarely seen two grown men enjoying themselves so much.

Ninety-two this afternoon, the stock market up in heavy trading.

In Berlin everyone stared, and I could not blame them. You were spectacular, your long skirts, your long dark hair. I was upset by the staring, people gazing at happiness and wondering whether to credit it or not, wondering whether it was to be trusted and for how long, and what it meant to them, whether they were in some way hurt by it, in some way diminished by it, in some way criticized by it, good God get it out of my sight—

I correctly identified a Matisse as a Matisse even though it was an uncharacteristic Matisse, you thought I was knowledgeable whereas I was only lucky, we stared at the Schwitters show for one hour and twenty minutes, and then lunched. Vitello tonnato, as I recall.

When Herman was divorced in Boston . . . Carol got the good bar-beque pit. I put it in the Blazer for her. In the back of the Blazer were cartons of books, tableware, sheets and towels, plants, and, oddly, two dozen white carnations fresh in their box. I pointed to the flowers. "Herman," she said, "he never gives up."

In Barcelona the lights went out. At dinner. Candles were produced and the shiny langoustines placed before us. Why do I love Barcelona above most other cities? Because Barcelona and I share a passion for walking? I was happy there? You were with me? We were celebrating my hundredth marriage? I'll stand on that. Show me a man who has not married a hundred times and I'll show you a wretch who does not deserve God's good world.

Lunching with the Holy Ghost I praised the world, and the Holy Ghost was pleased. "We have that little problem in Barcelona," He said. "The lights go out in the middle of dinner." "I've noticed," I said. "We're working on it," He said. "What a wonderful city, one of our best." "A great town," I agreed. In an ecstasy of admiration for what is we ate our simple soup.

Tomorrow, fair and warmer, warmer and fair, most fair. . . .

(1982)

ABOUT THE EDITOR

ROGER ANGELL has been a fiction editor with *The New Yorker* since 1956, and a frequent contributor since 1943. He has published collections of fiction and humor, and five books about baseball, including *The Summer Game* and *Late Innings*. He lives with his wife, Carol, in New York City and Brooklin, Maine.

ABOUT THE TYPE

This book was set in Caslon, a typeface first designed in 1722 by William Caslon. Its widespread use by most English printers in the early eighteenth century soon supplanted the Dutch typefaces that had formerly prevailed. The roman is considered a "workhorse" typeface owing to its pleasant, open appearance, while the italic is exceedingly decorative.